REMEMBER ME

Sheila Walsh was born in Birmingham, but has lived in Southport for many years. She has been a writer for some sixteen years, during which time she has written eighteen historical novels of which the seventh, *A Highly Respectable Marriage*, won the 1983 RNA Romantic Novel of the Year Award.

She is a past chairman of the RNA, Life President of her local Writer's Circle and is happily married to a retired jeweller. She has two daughters, one married – and a Burmese cat. Her previous novel, *Until Tomorrow* is also published by Arrow.

REMEMBER ME

Sheila Walsh

ARROW

First published 1994

1 3 5 7 9 10 8 6 4 2

The right of Sheila Walsh to be identified as the author
of this work has been asserted by her in accordance
with the Copyright, Designs and Patents Act, 1988

First published in the United Kingdom in 1994 by Century,
Random House UK Limited

This edition is published by Arrow in 1994,
Random House, 20 Vauxhall Bridge Road, London SW1V 2SA

Random House Australia (Pty) Limited
20 Alfred Street, Milsons Point, Sydney,
New South Wales 2061, Australia

Random House New Zealand Limited
18 Poland Road, Glenfield
Auckland 10, New Zealand

Random House South Africa (Pty) Limited
PO Box 337, Bergvlei, South Africa

Random House UK Limited Reg. No. 954009

ISBN 0 09 933441 0

Printed and bound in Great Britain by
Cox & Wyman Ltd, Reading, Berkshire

Dedication

To my husband, Des, for putting up with my absentmindedness and providing meals at regular intervals when necessary. Also to Tom and Marie Murray for their many kindnesses.

Acknowledgements

My thanks to all who have helped me in researching this book, especially Janet Smith at Liverpool Central Library and Carol Bidston at Birkenhead Central Library who went to so much trouble to find and send the relevant newspaper cutting relating to the ceremony honouring the Royal Iris and Royal Daffodil, which took place on St George's Day in 1919.

Remember me when I am gone away,
Gone far away into the silent land;
When you can no more hold me by the hand,
Nor I half turn to go yet turning stay . . .

(Christina Rossetti – 1830–1894)

PART ONE

I

THE FEBRUARY MORNING was pitch dark and ice frosted the windows as Matilda Shaw crept down the stairs, being careful to avoid the ones that creaked. Irene, Kevin and Moira would sleep through anything, but little Daisy was teething again, and the least sound might set her off whingeing, and with Mam not getting in till after midnight, and Dad spending half the night coughing his heart up, they both needed every bit of sleep they could get. Quiet as she was, however, as she reached the lobby, the thin thread of voice came from beyond the half-open door of the front parlour.

'Are you off out then, Matty, love?'

She pushed the door wider and put her head round. The fire had been built up with slack overnight, but now it burned low in the grate and the atmosphere was what Kevin, with the bluntness of a thirteen-year-old, always called 'pongy'. Her stomach had grown accustomed to stuffy sickroom smells, and anyway, when you loved someone it didn't matter. The oil lamp turned low cast deep shadows over the man slumped on the edge of the truckle bed behind the door, making his face seem full of hollows. His striped nightshirt hung in crumpled folds from protruding shoulder bones, but Patrick Shaw's eyes burned in their sockets with a special radiance at the sight of his favourite daughter, not far off eighteen and as pretty as her mammy at the same age, with the dark curls brushing her cheeks beneath her woolly hat and fierce accusation in her eyes. His voice was a breathless wheeze.

'I was trimming the lamp before the smoke got on me chest.'

'You should be asleep,' she said severely.

'And miss the sight of you? Not a bit of it. Sure, I'll have all the time in the world to sleep, soon enough.'

'Don't say that!' Fear sharpened her voice. 'You're doing just fine, if only you'd behave yourself. Hasn't Dr Hutton said as much, time and again?'

'Bossy, you are, just like your mam.' His chuckle turned to a rasping, choking cough that shook his whole frame and brought Matty flying to his side to hold the hunched quivering shoulders as he pressed the towel, already stained from previous coughing bouts, to his mouth.

And as she hushed him, fighting down her own panic, she was filled with an unreasoning rage. How could a good and merciful God allow such things to happen? And to Dad, of all people, who was one of the grandest men in the whole world, an' wouldn't hurt a fly.

His breath still rasped, but the coughing bout was over.

'There, you see?' she reproached him, the thickness of tears in her voice as she laid him back on the pillows. 'If you'd been doin' as you should, that wouldn't have happened.' She whisked away swiftly to hide her distress. 'I might as well mend the fire now I'm here.'

Matty lifted the fireguard to one side and, seizing the poker, vented all her pent-up fury on the sluggish embers until the sparks flew upwards. She was just shovelling on some precious coal when her mam came in.

'What's all this, then?'

Dad had always teased Mam, saying there wasn't two penn'eth of her, and indeed the long thick plait of her chestnut hair hanging over the shoulder of the faded blue dressing-gown, did give her the look of a thin wiry child. Matty was already half a head taller. But what Mam lacked in inches, she more than made up for in force of personality.

Even so, she looked tired, and in the lamplight, Matty saw that the chestnut plait was becoming increasingly laced with silver, which was small wonder after the worry of the past few months.

Their eyes met, and just for a moment the anguish of the older woman showed. But when she spoke, Agnes Shaw's voice was rock firm.

'I was wide awake, so I thought I'd come down and make a brew.' She glanced at the mantelpiece where the little oak clock with the twisted sugarstick legs ticked away merrily. 'Here, give me that shovel, our Matty. It's gone seven, an' it's little enough

4

that skinflint pays you without havin' any of it docked for being late.'

'Better do as you're bid, me darlin' girl, before your mam belts you one, hard woman that she is.'

Dad's voice still held an echo of the good days – not so long ago – when he would tease Mam rotten, calling her the mighty midget and making a great show of fending her off with one big capable hand when she berated him for some chore left undone. Remembering brought the threat of tears close again, and Matty kissed the top of his head and, pausing only to wash her hands in the bowl by the door, ran out of the room.

As she turned the corner into Falkner Street, a veil of freezing fog swirled about her, driven by the piercing wind that came up from the Mersey and nearly took the feet from under her. Relieved that she didn't have to face into it, Matty gave her scarf an extra turn about her neck and stuffed her hands with their woolly mitts deep in the pockets of the grey flannel coat. It was quality cloth, and had needed only a stitch here and there to make it look almost as good as new. Even so, by the time she reached Lodge Lane, her fingers were numb.

It didn't seem right that Mam should have to do so much, taking in more and more washing for a niggardly return so that she didn't have to leave Dad alone of a daytime, and then cleaning offices at night to earn the money for little extras. But Mam had a fierce streak of independence that made her refuse to accept anything that smacked of charity.

'You don't get nothin' for nothin' in this world,' was her motto, and no amount of argument would shift her.

Eager as Matty had been to learn all she could back in 1914, she had felt guilty about being apprenticed to Mrs Crawley, a much patronized dressmaker. War was declared soon after, and a part of her glowed with patriotism and a longing to do her bit like Phil and Irene. Mam insisted that it would be daft, wasting her talents when she was so obviously gifted with a needle, and that sometimes it paid to take the long view.

'Everyone knows the war won't last. And we aren't short,' she'd said proudly. 'Your dad's the best riveter this side of the river, an' everyone knows it. There aren't many as can pick and choose their jobs like he can. If our Phil hadn't been daft enough to volunteer for the Pals right off, he'd be well on the way to matching him by now. Still, Phil's a good lad – he'll send me something regular, and if our Holy and Blessed Mother watches over him and brings him home safe, your dad'll get him taken on in the yard soon enough.'

'But Irene's goin' on the munitions – '

'Irene's older than you. And she doesn't have your skills. Just think on – at the end of your apprenticeship, you'll be set up with a trade for life – one you'll be able to carry on from home, even after you're married.'

But at fourteen, marriage had been the last thing on Matty's mind, just as her sights had always been set far beyond being a tuppeny-ha'penny dressmaker working from home – beyond even the likes of Mrs Crawley. One day she was going to have her own elegant establishment in Bold Street, no matter how long it took.

But not a stitch had she been allowed to sew for the first twelve months. As a junior apprentice, it was all fetch and carry.

'Bring me those pins and don't drop any or you'll be working an extra half-hour to make up for it.' Or: 'I need two dozen buttons the same as this one. And I do mean exactly the same.'

And buttons was about all she'd been paid, with never so much as a thank you. Even when she did finally get to use a needle, her situation had been little better, her wage a mere pittance.

Matty shrugged and quickened her step. Now, after four frustrating years with Mrs Crawley – who was well named, the way she sucked up to her clients – her dream still seemed as far away as ever.

But from the first day she had listened as Mrs Crawley talked to her posher clients about *haute couture*, which, so far as Matty could make out, was French for the elegant clothes sketched in the fashion magazines scattered about Mrs Crawley's reception room. And when she could sneak a minute, she would pore over some out-of-date ones piled up in a back room.

They were mostly from Paris, and written in French, which made them seem even more glamorous. As for the women whose pictures filled the glossy pages – graceful women they were, but so thin you'd think they'd never eaten a square meal in their lives, and striking exaggerated poses that must have given them terrible backache. They were wearing narrow skirts and flimsy blouses with V necks that she'd heard nicknamed 'pneumonia blouses' by

Mam's friends, who thought them indecent. There were daring oriental tunics fashioned from beautiful flowing fabrics, with never a hint of a corset – hardly even room for a stitch underneath, except maybe a few wispy bits of silk and lace. These styles, so one rare English caption stated, had been inspired by the Russian Ballet's costumes for *Schéhérazade*, and made popular by a designer called Paul Poiret around the time the hobble skirt became popular in England. They were beautiful, exciting and they set all kinds of ideas milling round in Matty's head.

The more time went on, the more she felt a great well of creativity inside her, bursting to find expression, but she did not as yet possess the skill or the opportunity to give it life. The war had cut down the demand for high fashion; utility clothes and plainer, fuller gowns had replaced the hobble skirt, and these, though more comfortable, were very uninspiring. Mrs C's customers, like most folk, seemed to feel that extravagant dresses were out of place in wartime, so a lot of the apprentices' present work involved alterations and making over. This still called for a certain amount of ingenuity, but sometimes Matty sketched her ideas in a notebook and dreamed of the day when she would be famous in Liverpool and beyond, as Matilda Shaw, the queen of *haute couture*.

And then, just before last Easter, Dad had been taken bad with what Dr Hutton said was a bad dose of bronchial pneumonia. 'Thirty years out in all weathers and never a day off work till now,' he'd fretted. But the cough didn't go away, even when Dad gave up his beloved pipe. The pneumonia had left a weak patch on the lung, the doctor said. Finally, he'd coughed up blood and the dread word 'Tuberculosis' had been mentioned.

After he'd had a spell in hospital, Mam had brought him home. The hospitals were full up with wounded soldiers, she said, and Pat might well pick up something worse than he already had. Anyway, he would get better sooner at home where he belonged. But he had to be kept away from the children, so the front parlour had become his room – almost his prison.

Even then Mam wouldn't hear of Matty giving up her training. There had been a big argument about it at the time. It had started, as most arguments did, with their Irene, who was two years older than Matty and liked to throw her weight about.

Irene was as fair as Matty was dark, with a flawless complexion and fluffy blonde hair, which, unlike most of the girls in the factory, she had refused to have cut short. 'Mr Brighouse said it would be a pity to spoil such pretty hair, and that as long as I keep it well covered up with a cap, it'll be okay.'

Irene had lost that earlier argument over Matty's work, but it had come up again last night.

The curtains had been closed in the back room and the range glowed red as Mam put the iron to heat on the hob. Matty finished siding the pots and helped her mother to lay the thick folds of the ironing blanket across the table.

'It's all scrimp and scrape in this house,' Irene was complaining, her pretty features twisted with discontent. 'The shortages are bad enough without havin' to make every penny stretch six ways. I'm just about sick of it.'

Mam took a shirt from a basket full of washing and wearily began to smooth it out. 'There's a lot of folk in the same boat, girl. We manage well enough with your dad's panel money, and what the rest of us bring home between us . . .'

'I earn the most, and little enough I see of it.'

Matty was incensed. 'That's not fair.'

'Yes it is,' Irene retorted. 'I work bloomin' long shifts for that money.'

'We all work long hours. But I haven't noticed you staying in much of an evening to help round the house.'

'I do what I can. And I'm older than you. I'm entitled to a bit of fun occasionally, except I'm getting ashamed to go out looking such a frump. This frock's the only one I've got that's halfway decent, an' it's been washed that often, the pattern's all but worn off.'

Matty saw the tight-lipped strain on Mam's face and bit back her indignation. 'If you get some material, I'll make you one.'

'Thanks, but I don't want home-made,' Irene said ungraciously. 'I've seen the one I want, and if you got a proper job, I might stand some chance of buying it.'

'There's plenty worse off than you, my girl, and don't you forget it,' Mam snapped. 'And keep your voices down, the both of you. I won't have your dad upset.' She drew a deep breath. 'But you've got a point, for all that. I've been thinking that there's no reason why our Kevin can't leave school a few months early and find himself a job.'

'Hey, Mam, can I really?' Kevin's head appeared over the top of his comic. 'That's be great. Just wait till I tell Albert. He'll be furious, me gerrin' one up on him.'

Agnes Shaw eyed her tow-haired thirteen-year-old. 'Never you mind about Albert Finch. And don't get yourself excited,' she said dryly. 'I haven't cleared it with the school yet, though I doubt there'll be any problem. You're not so bright as they'll miss you. It's possible your dad might be able to get you taken on down the docks as an apprentice. That's how Phil started, and look how he got on. It won't pay much to begin with, but if you shape, you might end up as good as your dad one day. Meanwhile every little helps and together we'll get by . . .'

'Will we, though? If you keep on the way you're going, Mam, you'll wear yourself out.' Exasperation made Matty sharp. 'Here, sit down, before you fall down. I'll do that.'

She snatched up the iron holder she'd knitted last Christmas and reached for the iron, spat on it to test the heat and set about the waiting shirt with a speed and deftness born of practice.

For once, her mother didn't argue. She sat in the creaking armchair, rubbing her legs to ease her throbbing veins.

'Moira's a big help when she gets home from school of an afternoon, aren't you, chuck? Got a lot of sense for her ten years.'

Moira was stretched full length on the rag rug in front of the fire with her colouring book and chalks, tongue caught between her teeth in fierce concentration. She lifted her head and flipped back a neat fair pigtail.

'Little Daisy minds me more than she does you, our Irene,' she said virtuously.

'There's no call to be smug,' Irene retorted. 'Anyhow, I still think Matty should leave that Mrs Crawley and come on the munitions with me while they're still takin' folk.'

But she'd pushed her luck too far. Mam went mad.

'Indeed, our Matty'll do no such thing. She's worked like a Trojan for years, for very little reward, and I'll not have her throwin' away all that training now for the sake of a few bob extra, especially not to go in that factory. To tell the truth, I'll be glad when you're out of it, Irene, for all that you bring good money

9

home. Mrs Bennett's friend's daughter nearly got blown up last week, an' what's more, she says the girls skin's already turnin' as yellow as a canary.'

'People say a lot of daft things,' Irene said dismissively. 'It depends how you go about things. You won't catch me turnin' yellow, an' there's no risk of gettin' blown up unless you're put on filling shells.'

Matty remembered how Irene, in a rare moment of frankness, had confided to her in bed one night that the factory foreman had put her on special jobs where she wouldn't encounter any of the usual hazards. She had sworn Matty to secrecy in case Eddie got into trouble.

But it worried Matty. You didn't have to be worldly wise to suspect that men who did favours usually wanted something in return. 'I just hope you know what you're doing, that's all. He's miles older than you.'

But Irene had just thumped her pillow into shape and turned over. 'Don't you fret. I can handle Eddie Brighouse any day.'

She probably could, too, Matty thought with a twinge of envy, setting about the pile of ironing with renewed vigour. Her sister took the curling tongs from the fire, tested them on a sheet of newspaper, and with an air of injured innocence set about curling her hair. Mam would be hopping mad if she knew that the friend Irene was meeting later that evening wasn't Ellie Briggs, but Eddie Brighouse. She folded a shirt with deft hands and reached for another. 'I could maybe get an evening job somewhere.'

'And fall asleep over your work in the day? Where's the sense in that, Matty? You're doing ever so well. And Mrs Crawley's bound to increase your money now she's made you a bodice hand. Mind, I had wondered if we might get hold of a second-hand sewing machine cheap, then you could do a bit of dressmaking for folk round here in your spare time. Marge Flynn was askin' only the other day if you could make her a frock for her sister's wedding. It's be good practice.'

Matty thought of their neighbour, big-hearted and with a figure to match. She'd want something cheap and garish. Her fingers curled convulsively round the handle of the iron. 'Mrs Crawley'd go mad if she found out I was doing work on the side,' she said evasively. 'I could get dismissed.'

'There'd be no reason for her to know.'

'She'd find out. She's got ears everywhere, that one.'

'Don't be disrespectful about your betters, my girl.'

'I'm not . . . but,' she sighed, 'it's just . . . well, Mrs Flynn . . .'

'So what's wrong with Marge Flynn? Heart as big as a bucket, she has. I'd be hard pressed many a time without Marge to call on. A knock on the wall is all it takes an' she's here, so don't you go upsetting her.'

'As if I would. I really like Mrs Flynn, but – '

'But you'd rather be making fancy clothes for them as has more money than sense,' Irene murmured, goading her to fresh fury. 'Pigs might fly, our Matty, but they're unlikely birds.'

'Just because you've got no ambition – '

'That's enough from the both of you.' Agnes watched the light blaze and then fade in Matty's eyes, and her voice softened. 'Ah, listen now, if we could all do what we wanted to, I wouldn't be taking in other folks' washing. Like I've told the lot of you many a time – strawberries and cream are very tasty, but they don't fill an empty belly half as well as bread.'

'I know that,' Matty said grudgingly. 'And I don't mind making a frock for Mrs Flynn, truly I don't. It's just . . .' The smell of scorching brought her up short. 'Oh glory!' she snatched up the iron, and stared in dismay at the neat brown stain slap in the middle of the shirt front. 'Oh, Mam, I'm sorry!'

'Heaven help us, that's all we need.' Agnes's veins screamed in silent protest as she eased herself out of the chair. 'Move over, girl, an' let's have a look. Maybe we can do something with it.'

'No, we can't. It's ruined! I'll have to buy a new one, an' it'll take every penny I've saved. And it's all Irene's fault!'

'How dare you blame me for your own clumsiness!'

'Be quiet, the both of you.'

'What's going on in there?' Dad's voice rose above the din.

'Now see what you've done!' Mam shouted. 'I told you not to upset your dad!' And Matty was horrified to see the tears rolling down her face.

'I'm sorry, Dad,' she confided later, kneeling beside his bed, her own tears spent. She ought not to bother him with their troubles, and Mam'd kill her if she knew. 'It was awful. The room was awash with tears. An' it was all my fault. Well, nearly all,' she amended. 'Irene seems to take a delight in riling me.'

Pat ruffled her hair, his voice gentle. 'Do you not think that might be because she's a wee bit jealous? You have a rare talent, Matty, and talented folk are often inclined to be single-minded. That's not always easy for others to live with.'

'But there's so much I want to do!'

'I know, child. And your mother knows too, deep down. But real success – success worth having – seldom happens overnight. You have to work at it for years. Just be thankful you have a trade at your fingertips. That's no bad thing, believe me. It was the saving of me and your mother many a time when you lot were babbies.' His eyes had clouded over, remembering, and Matty wanted to cry for reminding him and making him sad.

But now, as Matty ran down Wandsworth Street and mounted the steps to the dressmaker's house, she wondered how much longer things could go on as they were.

'Matilda.' The sharp voice banished all thoughts of home. 'It is twenty minutes to eight, and that trousseau for Miss Fortesqueue must be finished today.' The rigidly corseted black figure bristled. 'You will have to make up the time during your dinner break, and if necessary, stay late this evening.'

It was no use telling her about Dad. In fact, Matty had been at great pains not to mention his illness, knowing that the mere mention of tuberculosis would earn her instant dismissal for fear that she might contaminate the clientele.

2

VICTORIA STATION WAS noisy, full of steam and bustle, and packed with people: weary-looking soldiers coming home on leave, some with uniforms still caked with mud, being welcomed into loving arms, some standing apart looking dazed and rather lost. And there were others with clean uniforms and strained faces, being wept over by loving relations as they departed for the Front. Aimée Buchanan was determined not to be one of the latter.

Passers-by occasionally gave the young couple more than a brief glance, for they were very much alike; the girl in her smart brown coat with its fur collar, a neat little hat perched on her abundant hair, linking arms with the handsome young officer in the distinctive uniform of the King's Own Royal Rifles, the famous Green Jackets. Close, yet not lovers. Both were tall and slim, both possessed of velvety brown eyes and the pale translucent skin that so often goes with auburn hair.

Aimée and Gerald were indeed close as only twins can be. He had always supported the suffragist cause, for which Aimée had campaigned with enthusiasm during her days at medical school, and it seemed particularly apt that the last night of his leave had coincided with the day that the woman suffrage bill giving votes to married women over thirty, was passed in the House of Lords, having received the Royal Assent. After all the agony and spectacle of the fight that had gone before, this triumphant first step had crept in without pomp, overshadowed as it was by greater exigences that had led Mrs Pankhurst to throw her support behind the government for the duration of the war. The irony of the moment did not escape the twins.

'It's only the beginning, of course,' Gerald said, adding pro-vocatively, 'I imagine women will have to register in order to qualify, and I doubt many will wish to admit to being over thirty.'

'Chauvinist,' she retorted. 'How dare you think so poorly of women.'

But they had celebrated nevertheless with a grand dinner, sharing the satisfaction of this vital first step towards the wider freedom as they had shared so many triumphs and disasters. For Gerald was more than Aimée's twin – he was also her dearest friend and confidant.

'We both hate goodbyes,' she said now, reaching up to cup his face with a gloved hand, 'so I shan't stay. But do take care of yourself, dearest boy.'

He covered her hand with his own, and a tide of colour, the curse of people with their delicate complexion, flooded his face.

'Take care yourself, Aimée, and for heaven's sake give up that mad scheme of yours. It is madness, I promise you.' His voice was suddenly harsh. 'You can have no idea how dreadful conditions are in France. It's a certainty they won't take you as a doctor, and anything less would be such a waste. I love you for wanting to be in the thick of it, but I had far rather you were here, safe and sound.'

But he knew from the light in her eyes that he was wasting his breath.

'And I had far rather be in France where the action is, and where I can be as much a part of it as you are. One way or another, I mean to find a proper use for my skills.'

'You can do that here. And we have to think of Mother,' he said. 'She tries to be brave, poor dear, but she was terribly cut up when I said goodbye this time. If you put yourself in danger, too – '

But Aimée would not be moved from her resolution. 'I'm not a child. And Mother's tougher than you think. She'll get used to the idea.'

When Gerald's train had left, she turned her back on Victoria Station, intending to go straight to the British Red Cross Society's enrolment centre. But on the way to Grosvenor Crescent she passed a smart little hairdressing salon she had not noticed before and, to give herself Dutch courage, she succumbed to the luxury of a shampoo and set. Two hours later she emerged into the weak February sunshine, light-headed in more ways than one, and impetuously, gloriously reborn. Her long auburn hair was no more; in its place, a stylish bob curved sleek and shining into the nape of her neck and framed her face. Mother would die when she saw it, but Aimée had no regrets. It was a sign.

She came down to earth, however, when faced with officialdom. Her services as a doctor would be received with open arms almost anywhere but in France, said the prim lady with the steely grey eyes who interviewed her, and who clearly thought she was mad even to contemplate such a brush with danger.

'You will have considered the Women's Service Hospital, I suppose? They have quite a strong contingent working with the refugees in Serbia. I can give you their address in Edinburgh . . .'

Aimée said that, much as she admired the excellent work the Scottish women's medical units were doing, she wished to aid British troops wounded in battle. The woman lifted a faintly uncredulous eyebrow.

'I can perhaps arrange for you to go to Malta, where some of the less seriously wounded and convalescent patients are sent to recuperate. The War Office have begun to employ women doctors there in order to relieve pressures elsewhere.'

'Thank you,' Aimée said politely, 'but convalescent work is not what I had in mind. I can find more fulfilling duties here. What alternatives do you have? I can drive, if that is any help.'

And, as easily as that, her immediate future was decided.

Her mother, when told, turned pale and groped for her smelling salts.

'But, darling, you can't! An ambulance driver indeed. Your father won't hear of you exposing yourself to so much danger.'

'I'm twenty-four, Mother,' Aimée said dryly. 'I don't really see how he can stop me.'

'But you're a doctor. Heavens knows, even *that* isn't what I had hoped for, but . . .' Minna Buchanan's lip trembled. 'Oh dear, everything is so horrid. Do you know, Mrs Evans had to queue for two hours yesterday for a pound of sugar – and we haven't had a decent piece of cheese in weeks. But I don't expect you to care for that.'

'Mother – '

'You young people can be so thoughtless. It is almost more than I can bear, knowing that poor Gerald has gone back to face terrible danger, and the army is so bad at delivering letters, for I'm sure he doesn't get half the ones I send.'

As if the postman popped across to France especially to deliver her weekly missives. This example of her mother's simplistic, almost childlike attitude to life filled Aimée with a sudden rush of love. And guilt.

'Now, here you are, talking of leaving me and going off to this dreadful war.' Minna's voice faltered on a sob. 'And as for your beautiful hair . . .' She averted her tear-filled blue eyes from the hated bob, instinctively lifting a hand to her own pretty fair hair, untouched by even a hint of grey, as if to reassure herself that the whole world hadn't gone mad.

'Darling, I'm sorry.' Aimée felt close to tears herself as she came to perch on the arm of her mother's chair, hugging her close. 'I'm a terrible disappointment to you, aren't I?'

'Oh, no, never that!'

'But, you see, this is something I just have to do.'

Aimée looked round her mother's pretty pink and green drawing room with its apple-green velvet sofas and elegant bow-fronted mahogany chiffoniers. The long windows embraced the garden where herbaceous borders, riotous with bloom in summer, were now undressed for winter, the huge beech tree in the centre of the lawn bare of leaf.

Beyond the garden bounded by a stout yew hedge, lay the sheltered little Lancashire valley that she loved. Through it, guarded by a belt of elms, ran a stream, deep and clear between steep banks, which in summer overflowed with wild garlic and meadowsweet. In the nearby little town of Coram, her father's mills worked overtime to meet the needs of a country at war. As children, she and Gerald had ridden their ponies through fragrant meadows towards the outcrop of rock that gave the vale its name, and dared each other to jump the chuckling water. Now the elms were bare-branched above meadows dug over by an army of sturdy young women, ready for the production of vegetables, and smoke from the mill chimneys two miles away drifted above a lone clump of Scots pines, their tops etched against the sky like a cluster of umbrellas tilted drunkenly against the biting wind.

Aimée's father had invested heavily in new machinery to cope with ever-growing demands for miles of cotton sheeting and ticking for hospitals at home and abroad. Crisp white aprons and uniforms were needed for the nurses, and khaki drill and webbing, poplin shirts, even canvas for tents, and unlimited supplies of bandages.

Many folk in Crag Vale had assumed that hard-headed Seth Buchanan had married pretty little butterfly Minna Howard, from nearby Liverpool, to further his ambitions. For wasn't her father Sir Amos Howard of the Howard and Mellish shipping line, and didn't his ships carry Seth's cotton goods halfway round the world, bringing back from America and India the raw cotton on which his prosperity depended?

But no such inducement was necessary, for Minna had captured big Seth's heart from the first. He had denied her nothing, and she adored him. He had built for her Fernlea, this charming manor house nestling in the lee of the valley.

Poor Mother, Aimée thought, with her arm about the trembling silk-clad shoulders. She must have entertained such dreams for her only daughter – a genteel education, followed by a London Season and marriage to someone who would keep her in style. Instead, Aimée had insisted on following a very decided path of her own, eschewing every eligible young man presented for her approval – and, at twenty-four going on twenty-five, was still single and talking about going to war – as an ambulance driver.

'I suppose you do know what you're doing?' her father, a man of few words, had said in his blunt way when she told him. 'I'd hate to think I'd wasted good money putting you through medical school, only to have to throw it away for a whim.'

'Not a whim, Dad. A compulsion, if you like. Oh, I can't explain properly. Of course I'd rather go out there as a doctor, but the petty bureaucrats haven't taken their heads out of the sand yet, so I must go any way I can. It's as if something is drawing me – '

'Oh, spare me all y'r airy-fairy notions of equality. Just remember, I won't have y'r mother upset.'

Aimée was about to tell him that her mother's air of gentle helplessness concealed a resilience that would see her through most eventualities. But even as she framed the words, the look in his eyes brought a lump to her throat, and she held her tongue. There was a greyish tinge to his skin these days. The cause was easy enough to pinpoint. Like so many people he was working too hard, and keeping his troubles to himself. But it was no secret that supplies of raw cotton were dwindling. Thanks to Grandpa

Howard's long-standing Indian connections, he had not so far suffered the shortages that were afflicting many of his competitors, but the worry must always be there.

Now Aimée was adding a new worry. Yet she could not forsake her principles, even for him. Nor, in his heart, would he wish her to do so, for all that he disapproved.

Aimée's mentor, Dr Lomax, was equally disapproving, though not surprised. He knew Aimée's stubborn streak better than most; without it, she would not have fulfilled her burning ambition this far. Frank Lomax had been her unfailing champion when her father had at first dismissed any mention of her becoming a doctor. And when she had worn down all resistance, he had continued as her ally throughout the years of her training. Now, he recognized that stubborn set of her mouth and jaw.

'And I've no doubt you'll be expecting my blessing?'

She looked into the grizzled, weatherbeaten face and there was a hint of pleading in her wry smile. 'Your understanding at least, Doctor dear.'

'Oh, I gave over expecting you to take the easy path years ago, though as for understanding – I don't know what you hope to achieve driving ambulances. Waste of a damned good doctor, if you ask me. There are several excellent hospitals in this country run by women, and enough wounded coming home to enable you to put your surgical skills to good use and study for your fellowship at the same time.'

'I know. And I *have* given it a lot of thought. But, crazy as it sounds, I must know for myself what it's really like out there – the kind of things Gerald won't talk about even to me. Back here one only sees the end result: the poor blind soldiers shuffling in lines, each man clinging to the one in front like lost souls; men without limbs; with shattered minds like poor Cousin Toby. And I feel inadequate to deal with them.'

'My dear girl,' he said heavily, 'we all feel inadequate. We simply do what we can.'

'Yes, I know, but for me that's not enough. I keep thinking that one day it might happen to Gerald.' There was passion in her voice as she reiterated. 'If I can be a part of it, for a while at least, in whatever capacity, I may better understand and be better able to help. Don't you see?'

He saw, right enough. And he knew there'd be no stopping her.

Of all her relations, the one who best understood was the one whom most of the family held in awe, and the whole of Liverpool revered and respected. Grandpa Howard was a big man in every sense of the word, though at seventy-eight, he suffered increasingly with rheumatism.

'Damned nuisance,' he'd barked at her when, before leaving, she visited Hightowers, the large house in Aigburth, where he lived alone except for the servants. The rest of the family found the house too gloomy, though it still held a powerful attraction for Aimée. It had not always been so: when her grandmother was alive, there had been grand parties and balls. The house was set on rising ground, with gardens running down almost to the river, and from the twin towers that gave it its name, you could see right the way downriver to the estuary.

Aimée found her grandfather with his chair drawn up close to the fire in the oak-lined library, a blanket across his knees. 'Can't move anywhere these days without this wretched stick.'

She pushed back the shock of white hair and dropped a kiss lightly on his forehead. 'Which doesn't stop you going to the office every day.'

'Someone has to keep a hand on the tiller. We lost another ship to those damned U-boats last week, cargo and crew all gone. It has to be dealt with, and that brother of mine's no use – never takes his nose out of the accounts book, except to go home to that soulless house in Woolton to play with his butterfly collection. He's a good accountant, I'll give him that, but he's got no imagination – no flair for the cut and thrust of business – and y'r Uncle George has his heart set on change.'

A fit of coughing doubled Sir Amos up, but he waved away the glass of water Aimée offered him, and when he resumed, there was an added tetchiness in his voice.

'He's too busy hobnobbing in government circles at present to give me chapter and verse, but I do know that when this damned war ends he wants to build a fleet of new passenger liners – reckons cruising's going to take off in a big way. He could be right, but I told him, commerce has always been the backbone of Howard and Mellish, and has made us respected throughout the world.'

Aimée shook her head at him. 'No use telling you that you should rest more, I suppose?'

'Rest? Bah! I've watched folk die, resting.'

Amos Howard's keen eyes, so like her own, dared her to contradict him, but she only laughed. His autocratic ways had never held any terrors for her, and perhaps because everyone said she was the image of her late grandmother whom she could hardly remember, she was his favourite, the only one of the family who could persuade him to see reason when all else failed.

'Perhaps if you took the medicine Andrew Graham prescribed instead of pouring it away, you might see some improvement. Poor Judd is in despair.'

'The old fool should know better after fifty years. Coloured water isn't the answer to what ails me, as you of all people must know. The machinery's wearing out.'

Her heart lurched, knowing it to be true. 'Even so,' she coaxed, 'the medicine can help. Take it to please me. I'm going away, you see, and I'm counting on you to be here when I get back.' She explained the gist of her intentions and waited, for once unsure how he would react.

There was a long silence. Then, to her distress, his eyes filled with tears, his mouth quivered.

'Grandpa . . .'

'Damned fire – always smokes when the wind's in the east.' He fumbled for a handkerchief and blew his nose. 'Should have known y'd want to be in the thick of it, independent baggage!' he muttered fiercely. 'Just see you do come back, that's all, or y'r mother'll give us all hell to pay.'

Two weeks later, with her mother's tearful appeals for her to change her mind still ringing in her ears, Aimée, still sore from the compulsory inoculations, and feeling rather queasy after a rough crossing, thankfully unmolested by U-boats, arrived in France, and was directed to a stuffy hotel in Boulogne to join a number of other 'new girls', mostly VADs, who were filling out drafts. And almost at once the German Spring Offensive began.

She was sent down the line to one of the many Advance Casualty Clearing Stations, and from the moment she arrived, all hell seemed to be let loose. Nothing in her medical training or anywhere else could have prepared her for what followed, as, one after another, the towns fell to the oncoming horde and the thunder of the guns became an unending roar. Defeat, once unthinkable, became a frightening possibility. Terrible sights, injuries obscene beyond belief, and the sickly sweet stench of gas gangrene, filled every waking moment, so that it seemed impossible that men could sustain such horrific injuries and still live. And occasionally, her frustration at being unable to use her skills to treat them as she would wish, boiled to the surface.

Always at the back of her mind was the dread that one day she might find Gerald among the casualties. Somehow they had managed to keep up a regular if spasmodic correspondence, and had even managed to meet once or twice during a brief lull when his battalion was engaged in the defence of Amiens, though she hadn't heard from him since.

Gradually a kind of unreality took over; it became possible to push the gnawing worry about Gerald to the back of her mind, to sustain a high level of urgency and still function. There was a wonderful spirit of camaraderie between the ambulance crews, who were required to drive anything that had wheels and could be adapted to carry stretchers, from taxis to cattle trucks. Back and forth to the battlefront they went, bounced by intermittent explosions, dodging exploding shells and potholes, and strafed by the occasional enemy plane, in spite of the red crosses clearly visible. They rattled over churned up mounds of mud with bruising intensity as they raced out, and tried desperately to avoid the same hazards on the way back.

It was exhilarating, exhausting and at times quite terrifying, and Aimée occasionally wondered how long she could keep going.

'A Tommy in my last lot said the Germans were pulling back from Amiens,' muttered one of her co-drivers, a morose Welshman. 'Sounded remarkably cheerful for a man with one leg blown clean off, he did.'

Aimée managed a tired grin as she loaded up her stretchers for one last run before the light went completely. 'I don't know how they manage it. It's the gassed cases I hate most. I sometimes think I'll never get the smell out of my system.'

At least the rain has stopped, she thought as she bumped and splashed through rubble and mud. Much more, and we'd be in danger of getting bogged down.

She pulled up beside a small waiting group, including an officer, five in all, the most she could manage in her converted taxi. As a young corporal appeared from nowhere to help her load the stretchers, she made a quick assessment. A man with half his leg blown away, two more with terrible abdominal injuries, and a critical head injury.

'Is this the lot?'

'Yes, ma'am.' He glanced back. 'The rest got blown away.'

The officer hadn't moved or spoken throughout, not even when an explosion shook the ground beneath their feet. His face was white, with a tight-drawn mouth. Looking closer she saw that his right arm hung limply at his side, and a tear in his breeches had exposed a large gash in one thigh, dark with blood.

'Will you ride in the back, Major, or up front with me?'

A shell exploded close by, and she clutched at her helmet. He scarcely flinched.

'Neither,' he said. 'I must get back to my men.'

His clipped expressionless voice, sounding so out of touch with reality, was strangely affecting.

'You can't possibly do that,' she said gently. 'At a pinch you might manage with a broken arm, but your leg – '

'Corporal Banks can put a field dressing on it for now.'

'A dressing won't do. A wound like that needs urgent attention.'

'Don't tell me what I can and can't do. When I want a diagnosis, I'll consult an expert, not an impertinent jumped-up slip of a girl.'

'Well, I intend to spell it out for you, just the same,' she retorted, stung. 'And you'd better listen.'

He said through gritted teeth, 'No, you listen. It's time someone reminded you that you're paid to ferry the wounded, not to play at doctors.'

Frustrated, and impatient to be away as another shell exploded, she threw caution to the wind. 'I am a doctor, dammit! And you'd better listen to me. If you want to live the rest of your life with a useless arm, that's your business. But if that leg isn't properly treated – and quickly, you'll develop septicaemia and most certainly gangrene, either of which will kill you within a matter of days. You won't be much use to your men then.'

The major's eyes narrowed to mere slits. Nearby, the young soldier shuffled his feet, and waited for the sky to fall in.

'Listen,' she entreated, already regretting her outburst, 'if your presence here is that important, come with me now and I'll see you're treated at once. I'll even bring you back afterwards.'

Inside the ambulance, one of the men began to scream. It was as if the sound galvanized the major into action. He turned without a word and gave brisk orders to the young soldier, who trotted off. Then, still without speaking, he limped forward and slid awkwardly into the passenger seat. Aimée sighed with relief and switched on the engine. It had grown dark as they argued, and she peered ahead, trying to see the lie of the land, but it was impossible to avoid every hazard, and the screams and groans from the back became pitiful.

As they drew up outside the Advance Casualty Clearing Station, two orderlies ran out to unload the stretchers.

'Come with me,' Aimée said, helping the major out, but not looking at him.

'One moment,' he said, and limped round to the back as the last stretcher was being brought out. The boy, for that was all he was, was writhing and screaming for his mother. The major took his hand and bent to speak quietly to him. Aimée longed to know what he said, for as the soldier was carried away his screams were reduced to sobs. But the major's profile, etched in stark rigidity against the night sky, precluded questions.

The inside of the tent resembled nothing so much as Dante's Inferno. Even she, who was used to it, felt a sense of hopeless inadequacy as she took in the chaotic scene – stretchers everywhere, muddy khaki torn back to expose smashed limbs, and gangrene and other unspeakable vilenesses betrayed by their smell, lying hidden beneath hastily applied field dressings; men obscenely disfigured and choking from mustard gas burns, and men screaming. And doctors, nurses and VADs desperately trying to cope.

'Oh God!' The horror and disgust in the major's voice brought her swiftly back to her duty.

'I'll find you somewhere to sit, and get you attended to . . .' Aimée found a corner away from the main area, but as for a seat . . .

'It doesn't matter. I'll stand,' he said.

It was some time before she returned to find him, still standing where she had left him, his head thrown back, his eyes closed. Thick dark eyelashes fanned out across high cheekbones. For a moment she studied him. A damp tangle of black hair had fallen across his forehead, and against it his dirt-streaked face glowed alabaster pale, those cheekbones and a strongly aquiline nose giving him more than a hint of hauteur. I bet they jump to attention when he barks, she thought, and touched his good arm. He started violently and stifled a groan.

'I'm sorry,' she said, putting down the bag she was carrying, and beginning her preparations. 'It's impossible to find a free doctor. You'll have to make do with me.'

'Will I now?' An expression that might have been pain or humour flickered in his eyes. 'As a matter of interest, are you really a doctor?'

'Yes, of course I am.' She had the grace to blush. 'But I'd be grateful if you kept the fact to yourself.'

'At this present moment, I couldn't give a damn what you are, so long as you're up to the job.'

Aimée knew he must be in considerable pain, and excused his ungraciousness. She cut away his jacket sleeve and the shirt beneath. 'How did this happen?'

'A shell exploded in the middle of us – flung me to the ground and shrapnel tore into my leg. Most of my men were less fortunate.'

There was bitterness and a hint of self-blame in his voice. Aimée's heart went out to him, but her own voice remained deliberately matter-of-fact.

'I'm sorry.' She made a quick assessment of the misshapen forearm. It was already bruised and swollen, but the skin wasn't broken. 'Well, at least this seems to be a relatively straightforward fracture.'

'You needn't sound so damned cheerful,' he said through his teeth.

She gently manipulated the two edges of bone together and splinted the arm, not looking at him, but talking all the while to distract his attention. She told him about Gerald. 'He's with the Thirteenth Battalion of the KRRC. I suppose you wouldn't happen to know him? No, silly of me. There is no reason why you should. I'll bind the arm to your chest. It's the best in the circumstances, and it should heal reasonably well if you're careful . . .'

She was surprised to hear what sounded like a choked laugh, and a smile briefly curved her own mouth. 'Yes, I suppose that was a stupid thing to say. But if you could favour it, just for a day or two? Now for the leg.' She flushed, grabbed a stool someone had just vacated and made him sit down. 'This is going to hurt rather more, I'm afraid.'

It did, and he was very white around the mouth by the time she had dug out the shrapnel, cleaned the wound with scrupulous care and dressed it.

'I'm sorry. It's a pretty deep gash, and it's going to need a few stitches, but the bone isn't chipped, thank goodness. I'll see if I can find you something for the pain – '

'Don't bother,' he said abruptly. 'Pain is the least of my problems right now.'

'Well, if you're sure?' She worked as swiftly as she could, not daring to look at his face. 'There. I've bandaged it as thoroughly as possible, so the dressings should hold, but please, whatever you do, don't disturb them. If the pain becomes really bad, a good shot of brandy might take the edge off it. You really should be admitted, you know – '

'Not possible.'

'Well, at least try to have the leg properly looked at again in a day or two, if you can. Should any dirt get in – '

'For God's sake, woman, do you never stop talking? I've got the message.' He ground the words out, his teeth gritted against the pain as he came to his feet. 'Can we go, now?'

Well, really! she thought. 'Here, take this.' She seized an abandoned crutch. 'It might come in useful.'

The man at the ambulance pool gave her a funny look as they left. 'A bit late to be going out, isn't it?'

'Emergency,' she said.

This seemed to satisfy him. 'Rather you than me.'

The return journey to the Front was uneventful – and he was silent as before, which was hardly surprising in the circumstances, except that every bump in the ground must have been pure agony to him.

Aimée stopped where he told her to, but he made no immediate attempt to leave, and she was by now too weary to care.

'I – thank you,' he said at last, surprising her. He opened the door and eased himself painfully from the seat with the aid of the crutch. Grasping the door for support with his free hand, he peered in at her. 'If that lot back there had any sense, they'd make proper use of you.'

Surprise robbed her of speech. He saluted awkwardly and hobbled away. Only then did she realize that she didn't even know his name.

3

THE ROLLS-ROYCE purred to a halt outside Mrs Crawley's house, and as usual the curtains all along Wandsworth Street twitched. Edna, the new apprentice, thought it the most beautiful motor car she had ever seen. She watched, her nose pressed to the upper window, as the chauffeur in dark green livery came round to open the door for his mistress.

'Hey, Doris, Matilda, come an' look at what's just stopped outside. It's big and silver, an' I think there's a lady getting out.'

'That'll be Mrs Mellish. She's a bit early.'

'Will I go and tell Mrs Crawley?'

Doris Booth, at the sewing machine, didn't lift her eyes from the skirt she was seaming. 'Well, someone'd better,' she said sharply above the click of the treadle and the whirr of the machine. 'She'll likely have nodded off after 'er dinner, but she won't want an important client kept waiting. And don't look at me. I can't leave this seam half done.'

Edna continued to watch, her eyes big as saucers, as a silk-clad leg came into view, followed unhurriedly by its partner, and a figure in a soft powdery blue stepped gracefully to the pavement. 'She's ever so elegant, in't she? Just like them pictures of Queen Mary in the newspaper.'

'I'm sure she'd be flattered to know that,' Matty teased, though not unkindly. After all, Mrs Mellish was quite their most important customer. Not only was her father one of Liverpool's most important ship-owners, and a much revered alderman, her husband was a partner in the same firm, as well as being a Member of Parliament. 'Come on, young Edna, you'd best get your nose away from that window and finish padding up that new stand before Miss Helen comes back and catches you mooning.'

The young girl relinquished her position with a sigh and turned back to tedious duty. Matty sympathized, remembering her own early apprentice days, at everyone's bidding. At that time the war hadn't seemed quite real and many of Mrs Crawley's clients still wanted the kind of clothes that entailed quality hand sewing and a lot of decorative work. Now the sewing machine was used more and more. Which was a pity, because Matty relished the challenge of creating something new by hand out of beautiful materials like the bodice she was working on at present.

Doris thought she was daft. To her and most of the other girls, except for Miss Helen, who was a skilled cutter and supervised their work, it was just a case of learning enough to get by and keep them employed. Quite sharp-tongued, Doris could be. She had accused Matty more than once of getting above herself, which wasn't true. Everyone else liked her, and she liked them.

Just as well, really. When everyone was here, it was a hive of industry. Just now May and Evie were down in the kitchen, eating the meagre dinner provided by their employer, and Miss Helen had gone out to fit a lady too frail to come to the house. Even so, the big central work table and a number of stands with gowns in varying stages of completion seemed to crowd the room.

The knocker sounded below and they heard the housekeeper's steady tread. Matty laid aside the bodice she had been pain-stakingly beading.

'It's okay. I'll go and tell Mrs Crawley. I need a break, or I'll start seeing double.'

She made her way hurriedly down the passage to Mrs Crawley's back sitting room and knocked on the door. In answer to a muffled grunt, she stepped inside. The curtains were partly drawn, but there was light enough to allow Matty a gloriously revealing glimpse of her stiff-necked employer, shoes kicked off, sprawled on the sofa near the fire, showing inches of petticoat.

'I'm sorry, Mrs Crawley. I thought you said "come in".'

'Well you thought wrong,' came the sharp retort.

The dressmaker struggled to extricate herself from a pile of cushions, and sat up abruptly. Her joints protested and she stifled a groan as stiff fingers attempted to straighten the rustling black skirts and smooth her dishevelled hair at one and the same time. She was mortified at being caught out in such an undignified posture, and by Matilda Shaw, of all people.

'Only I was sure you'd want to know that Mrs Mellish is here, madam,' Matty said innocently.

'Well, keep her entertained, Matilda. Surely I don't have to tell you what to do. Get along at once. I shall not be above five minutes.'

'Yes, Mrs Crawley.'

Matty bobbed a curtsy, and whisked out of the room, leaving her employer seething with annoyance. The girl might look as po-faced as she pleased, but the story would be round the workroom fast enough, and grow in the telling, no doubt. Matilda Shaw was clever, and quick to learn – too quick for Mrs Crawley's liking. She would need watching. Already she was displaying a talent beyond her years when it came to knowing what suited the various clients, and was not above telling them so. Of course, she was too young to be a threat, but the clients were already beginning to take notice of her.

Felicity Mellish had been patronizing Mrs Crawley on and off for almost as long as she could remember. These days her visits were few, amounting to the occasional alteration of one of her own gowns, a dress for Celia, the only one of her children still at home, or new uniforms for the servants. But as a child she and her sister had come regularly with their mama.

She had always loved beautiful clothes, and George liked her to dress well. He had never begrudged paying the bills, or taking her on twice yearly visits to Paris where she had patronized the House of Worth, and Doucet, and that strange, rather exciting young man Paul Poiret. The war had put an end to all that, of course, as it had to so many of the pleasures one had taken for granted.

Needless extravagance was out of keeping with the present mood of the country. Even so, as the wife of a man who somehow managed to combine his position as junior partner of Howard and Mellish with the prestigious role of chief advisor on shipping to Lloyd George, her own position at the forefront of various charitable committees entailed a great deal of entertaining, to say nothing of attending public functions, in London as well as Liverpool. And, war or no war, a varied wardrobe was a necessity. A talented, volatile French modiste who had recently opened premises in Bold Street now catered more than adequately for her needs, but Mrs Crawley's skill at remodelling last season's gowns and suits could occasionally come in useful.

Very little had changed over the years, she mused, looking round the fitting room. Except for the sewing girls. They were certainly less timid than in the days when Mama had brought Minna and herself here for their first party frocks. But that was a general trend – one of the many changes brought about by this terrible war. Much as one longed for the war to end, the fact must be faced that things would never be quite the same again.

'If you would like to take a seat, madam, Mrs Crawley won't be a moment. And perhaps you would care for a glass of sherry while you wait?'

Felicity smiled at the pretty dark-haired girl in her neat grey dress that showed the sweet curves of her figure. Matilda was a case in point; bright, intelligent, polite. But there was nothing in the least subservient in her manner.

'Thank you, that would be very pleasant. I am in no hurry.'

Felicity sat gracefully, easing the skirt of her softly tailored foulard two piece. The elbow chair was Chippendale in style – a copy, of course, but in excellent taste, as was everything Mrs Crawley owned. There had never been any evidence of a Mr Crawley. She suspected that he had been invented to lend an aura of respectability. The woman was certainly a snob, but she had her uses.

'How old are you, Matilda?' she asked, watching with some amusement the confidence with which the girl poured the wine from the decanter into the fluted glass, placed it on a silver salver and set it down on the little mahogany table beside her chair.

'Eighteen, madam.'

'And nearing the end of your apprenticeship, I suppose. Have you thought what you will do, then?'

'Not really. I still have best part of another year to go.'

'Might you perhaps stay on with Mrs Crawley?'

'Oh no, madam!'

Felicity was surprised at the vehemence of the girl's reply.

Matty blushed, and rushed to explain. 'I didn't mean . . . it's just that I need to widen my experience if I'm to do what I really want.'

'And may I know what that is?'

Matty looked towards the closed door and lowered her voice.

'Well, I don't mind telling you, madam, but I don't want anyone else knowing, 'cos they'd think I was daft and most likely laugh at me. One day I mean to specialize in high fashion.'

The words, so serious, but uttered with such confidence, sounded strange coming from a gamine apprentice seamstress. However, she was so obviously in earnest that Felicity kept a straight face.

Matty warmed to her theme. 'Oh, it won't happen for a long time yet. I know I've still got a lot to learn, but I've watched Miss Helen cutting, and she's let me try my hand a few times cutting out a toile when things are quiet. She says I've got the knack, and she should know. Besides, it sort of felt right. Do you know what I mean?'

Felicity murmured assent, though the girl was clearly too absorbed to notice.

'What I'd really like, of course, would be to get a job in one of the fashion shops. That way, I could learn about the business side as well as earn a proper wage at the same time. And maybe I'd be able to do a bit of dressmaking at home, so I can help Mam more. It hasn't been easy for her, with my brother Phil away and Dad – ' She stopped abruptly, and blushed.

Trouble at home, Felicity guessed. Well, who among us hasn't got problems these days? Her thoughts flew to Toby, her poor sensitive Toby, who should never have volunteered for the army, and who was now locked away in some terrible world of his own. His father didn't understand, of course. Like so many people, George dismissed the distressing consequences of shell shock and nervous breakdowns as mere funk. But then, imagination did not figure strongly among George's many excellent qualities. He was a very down-to-earth, very physical man, as was her elder son, Giles. She sighed.

Matty heard the sigh, and wondered. She liked Mrs Mellish very much. She wasn't a bit stuck up like a lot of the ladies that patronized Mrs Crawley. And she had true elegance – the kind you couldn't learn, the kind that sat as easily upon her as the stylish feathered toque, dyed to exactly match her blue foulard suit, sat upon her fair hair.

The Mellish house, too, was like a palace. Matty had been sent there several times to deliver dress boxes – up a long drive it was, set on high ground with long sloping lawns that made you think it was right out in the country. From the back windows you'd most likely be able to get a great view of the river. Not that she had ever been inside, except once on a hot day when the cook had asked her into the kitchen for a glass of lemonade and a piece of ginger cake. And, Lord, wasn't that kitchen as big as a house itself, with great copper pans hanging from hooks above her head, and servants scurrying back and forth?

You wouldn't think anyone who lived in a house like that could possibly be unhappy, but that's how Mrs Mellish seemed right now. Her eyes had the same look as Mam's did when she was talking about Dad.

'Your brother is in the army?'

The abruptness of the question aroused Matty's curiosity even further. Something was eating at her, that was for sure. But if Mrs Mellish had lost someone close to her, Mrs Crawley would be sure to know, and anyway, she'd be wearing black.

Lacking the nerve to ask outright, Matty struck to answering the question: 'Yes, madam. Our Phil's done ever so well. He was home the other week, and though he was a bit tired, he looked ever so smart. He's been promoted to sergeant. Mam and Dad are that made up.'

'I'm sure they must be.' Felicity Mellish smiled and sipped her sherry, but again Matty noticed that the smile didn't quite meet her eyes, and as she continued, it seemed as though she was talking to herself. 'My younger son, Toby, is now . . . back from the war, but Giles is still out in France. And Gerald and Aimée, my nephew and niece, are there, too.' She gave a little shake of her head and said more positively, 'Ah well, please God it will be over soon, and we shall have them all safely home.'

Matty didn't know what to make of it all, but in order to cheer Mrs Mellish up, and because she wanted the opinion of somebody who would know about such things, she pulled from her pocket a folded sheet of paper and opened it. 'I wonder – would you take a look at this, madam, an' tell me what you think?'

Felicity smoothed out the sketch, and was surprised and impressed by the degree of sophistication that even the rather crude drawing couldn't disguise. The evening gown had long dolman sleeves, close-fitting at the wrist, a high neck, and a skirt suggestive of Turkish harems, crossing over just above the ankles to show a tantalizing glimpse of leg, and gathered up into fine pleating at the waist. Over this was a plain sleeveless hip-length tunic edged with heavy braid or lace. The design had clearly been influenced by Poiret, and yet it had about it a touch of originality. All in all, it was an extraordinarily sophisticated design. She was curious to know how Matilda had come by it, and when she learned that it was the girl's own work, her surprise was unfeigned.

'My dear, I am impressed.'

'Thank you, madam.' Matty blushed, for this surely could be taken as a compliment. 'It's very rough, of course. I only got the idea this morning, and I hadn't got my proper sketchbook with me.' She hurried to explain. 'I thought it would be nice to have the gown itself in a fine patterned silk that would drape nicely, preferably in shades of gold. Then the over-tunic could be in plain white or cream with a rich brocade trimming.' She paused for breath. 'You don't think it's too daring?'

'A little, perhaps.' Felicity's eyes twinkled. 'But there are times when it is fun to be daring.' As Mrs Crawley bustled into the room accompanied by Miss Helen, she handed the sketch back to Matty, who quickly folded it and pushed it back into her pocket. 'We will talk about this again,' she murmured. 'And I would like to see any other ideas you might have.'

The exchange did not go unnoticed. Mrs Crawley said nothing, but when Mrs Mellish had left, she summoned Matty to her room.

'You know, of course, why I have sent for you?'

Matty's heart lurched. 'No, Mrs Crawley.'

'I don't like deceit, and I won't tolerate even a hint of disloyalty in my girls.'

'I have never been disloyal, Mrs Crawley!'

'What would you call it then, I'd like to know? Going behind my back, making up to the likes of Mrs Mellish?' The dressmaker's hand shot out imperiously. 'I will have that sheet of paper, if you please.'

Matty felt sick and dizzy. 'It's nothing, honestly, Mrs Crawley. Just a bit of a drawing I thought Mrs Mellish might be interested to see. I was only doing like you said, keeping her entertained until you came . . .'

'The sheet of paper, Matilda.' The cold, inexorable voice repeated.

Matty pulled it from her pocket and handed it over. Mrs Crawley unfolded it, and stared at the drawing, her thin nose pinched, her pale-lipped mouth almost vanishing into a tight little wad. It seemed a long time before she spoke, and when she did, her voice was enough to freeze you to the marrow.

'You had the temerity to show this – this crude rubbish to Mrs Mellish?'

'It isn't crude!' Matty was stung. 'An' it isn't rubbish. The actual drawing maybe isn't that good, but she liked it!'

'Don't talk nonsense, girl. A lady of taste could not possibly like it. And do not call Mrs Mellish "she". It is vulgar and ill-mannered. Now tell me, where did you get this – this scrawl?'

'I've already said. It's my own idea.'

'Don't lie to me. As if a girl like you could think up such ideas.'

'It isn't a lie! I did design it myself.' Matty, sure by now that she would be dismissed, drew a deep breath and held out her hand. 'An' I'd like it back, please.'

For answer, Mrs Crawley tore it across again and again, and threw it in her waste basket. 'You ungrateful little madam. After all I have taught you, this is how I am rewarded – going behind my back and ingratiating yourself with the clients.'

'I didn't . . . I haven't . . .' Matty thought of Mam, and all her hopes – all her sacrifices. She'd be that upset – more, she'd be flaming mad, and who could blame her, letting her down – letting them all down? 'It was just a drawing,' she insisted. 'I was only doing like you said, keeping Mrs Mellish entertained . . .'

But looking into those unrelenting eyes that had always reminded her of a cod's head on the fishmonger's slab, she knew there was no point in arguing. She waited for the blow to fall.

'I have dismissed girls for less. However, in this instance I am prepared to overlook your behaviour. But, make no mistake, Matilda Shaw, if I have the slightest cause to reprimand you again, you will be instantly dismissed. Now, get out.'

Matty stood transfixed, hardly daring to believe she was not to be sacked. Then, as the words sank in, she whisked out of the room before Mrs C could change her mind. There was a salty taste in her mouth, and she discovered that she had been biting so hard on her tongue, she'd drawn blood.

In the room behind her, Mrs Crawley shuddered as though coming out of a trance. Then she lifted the waste basket and carefully retrieved the torn slips of paper. She smoothed them out and began carefully to piece them together.

The girls all knew something was wrong, though Matty made light of it. It was nice, the way they all rallied round her as she explained. Even Miss Helen, in her quiet way, tempered her reproaches with kindness. Only Doris Booth was silent, her mouth drawn into a thin self-righteous line.

When Matty left for home that night, she clutched her coat tightly round her middle, not for warmth, but to keep hold of the two outdated fashion magazines tucked into the waistband of her frock. Nobody except her ever looked at them, and anyway it wasn't stealing, she told herself – just tit for tat. After all, Mrs Crawley had taken her sketch and torn it up. She was nothing but a mean, dried up old woman, too set in her ways to appreciate new ideas.

4

AIMÉE WENT THROUGH the mechanics of preparing for a
double amputation, the stench of gangrene by now familiar.
The steady rumble of the guns from the fighting around Arras
intensified suddenly, shaking the hospital's foundations. But at
least the Germans had not attempted to bomb the hospital for over
a week. We were slowly but steadily winning the war, she had been
told, but at what cost? This was her fifth operation tonight, and
she had lost count of how many she and others had performed
over recent weeks, some of them hopeless before the first incision
had been made. Experience had taught her that it was better not to
dwell on such things.

But tonight was different.

As she picked up the scalpel, her hand began to shake and she
could not stop it. She watched it with a kind of mute fascination
until Sister Munster removed the blade from her grasp and quietly
led her away. There were whispered consultations, a dose of
precious sedative was measured out and meekly swallowed, and
then she was put to bed and knew no more.

By the time Aimée awoke to the dull headache that had by now
become commonplace, Hannah Parsons, the sister with whom she
shared the cramped hut, had already gone on duty. As memory
returned, a black cloud of depression added to Aimée's misery. She
swung her feet to the ground, shivering as she poured cold water
from the jug into the bowl, and splashed her face. Then she dressed
quickly, pulling on a clean white blouse, and her skirt and coat.

Thank God I had my hair cut, she thought, brushing it
vigorously. She peered at her reflection in the cracked mirror
between the beds. Her half-hearted attempts to sustain the stylist's
art had long since reduced it to a clubbed bob, which served only
to emphasize the hollows in a face that was all eyes and dark

shadows. She abandoned the brush, and turned to tug her blankets into some kind of order before throwing the counterpane over them.

Of late Aimée caught herself fantasizing about her bedroom back home, so lovingly decorated by her mother during Aimée's final year at medical school. How little she had appreciated it at the time, thinking the pastel-pink cabbage roses strewn across a creamy white background much too fussy. But: 'I knew you would find it so restful, Aimée dear, after those horrid cramped rooms in Liverpool,' her mother had exclaimed. And she would not for the world have spoiled her pleasure.

She wasn't on duty for another hour, but the thought of facing her colleagues killed all appetite for breakfast. Instead she stood at the open door, shivering with cold, and watching the rain sheeting down. The ground beyond the hut was a quagmire still littered with the abandoned detritus of last night's incoming wounded from one of the many casualty clearing stations that straggled back from the hospital towards the Front Line. She lit a cigarette with fingers that still trembled, and inhaled deeply.

That was better. If nothing else, it helped to mask the noxious smells. Strange how one never quite got used to the smells. Sometimes she yearned quite passionately for the scent of freshly mown lawns, her mother's lovingly tended flowers, a cornfield, ripe for cutting ... Her thoughts jerked to a painful halt. Cornfields brought memories of summer – and David. Now, of all times, she must not think of David.

A lone train rattled past on its way to Boulogne, almost certainly filled with more wounded bound for Blighty. The service was becoming increasingly erratic with the added hazard of bombs, and might soon cease altogether with their refusal to heed the ultimatum from the Germans to move the hospitals or stop using the railway.

Aimée tossed her cigarette stub into the mud and shut the door. Time she stopped shirking and went to check on the acute surgical ward to see how her latest patients were faring.

Two had died. The stomach wound had never had a chance, nor had the poor boy with the shrapnel embedded in his skull. The rest were holding on, including the double amputee that she had reneged on. He was conscious, but feverish.

'He's very poorly,' Sister Munster said quietly beside her. 'Colonel Grant operated, but he doesn't hold out any great hope, which may be for the best, poor boy. He's lost his right eye, too.'

Aimée knew that the soldier had been in the best possible hands, yet, looking into the white tortured face, feeling that remaining eye burning into her, she was conscious of an over-whelming weight of guilt. Sister was still speaking, her tone impersonally kind.

'The Colonel would like a few words with you, Doctor, before you go on duty.'

It was the summons she had expected, and there was no point in fudging it.

'Ah, Dr Buchanan.' The gruff Scottish voice gave nothing away. 'Come in and sit down. I'll be with you in a moment.'

The MO, who was also the senior surgeon with a string of letters after his name, was a large, untidy red-haired man, known for his occasional choleric rages, more often directed at the Hun or the bungling incompetence of 'those damned fools at the War Office' than at members of staff. It was an image totally at odds with his consummate skill as a surgeon, for which Aimée had the greatest admiration.

She watched, her own hands tightly clasped, as he shuffled through the papers on the table before him with those long spatulate fingers that were capable of performing the most delicate operations. At last he looked up. His eyes, bloodshot from too much work and too little sleep, were still unnervingly keen.

'You'll have guessed why you're here, of course.'

'Yes,' she said jerkily. 'About last night. I'm sorry. It was good of you to ... to take over for me. I don't quite know what happened, but it won't happen again.'

'Ah, but it will, you see. We both know that.' Colonel Grant pulled a file of papers towards him. 'I've been looking up your record. I remember, of course, how you first came to us, but do you know how long ago that was?'

Aimée blushed, as if she could forget the night she had been observed treating the major, and had been obliged to confess her true status. Briefly she had been on the receiving end of the Colonel's awesome temper. But because she had a particular aptitude for surgery, and he was desperately short in that department, he had growled that as long as she was there, she might as well remain and make herself useful.

'It was the end of February, to be exact. And we are now at the beginning of October. That's a long stretch without a proper break.'

'I had several days during the summer,' she said swiftly. And then wished she had remained silent, as, for an instant, David's face was before her, so vividly alive.

'True, but it's still too long,' Colonel Grant said. There was no hint in his voice to denote that he knew about her brief tragic affair, though in such a tight community, it would be wonderful if he did not. 'Fortunately we are at last in a position to do something about it. Two relief doctors are due any time, and when they arrive, I'm sending you home for well-earned rest. In the meantime you can work on the light medical ward.'

Aimée had expected some kind of reprimand – a transfer to nonsurgical duties for a while. But this arbitrary decision, brusquely delivered, had a finality about it that carried the stigma of dismissal. She was shocked into passionate protest.

'But I can't go – not now. We're already short-handed. Even with the extra doctors – '

He leaned forward abruptly. 'Dr Buchanan – hold out your hands.'

Aimée did so, reluctantly, and was ashamed to see how they shook, however hard she tried to prevent them. I will not break down, she told herself. Crying is weak and stupid, and I despise weakness.

'A few days' break and I will be fine.'

'That isn't true, and you know it.'

'You've been here much longer,' she declared passionately, desperation overriding prudence. 'Sister Munster told me.'

'That is different. I have years of experience behind me.'

'And you are a man.'

The bitter accusation spilled out before Aimée could stop it. He had never expressed his views about women doctors, as had some of her male colleagues, and until this moment she had deliberately suppressed her own strong opinions so as to give no cause for criticism. She waited for that well-known wrath to descend.

Instead: 'And I am a man,' he agreed quietly. 'And if you are honest with yourself, as every good doctor should be, you will admit that, physically, at least, there is a difference.'

She struggled to deny it, and could not. But she wasn't giving up without a fight. 'All right,' she said, 'I'll do as you say – stop operating and go over to light medical for a while, until I am fully rested. That way I could continue to be of use. There are rumours of an Armistice any day now.'

'Perhaps. But rumours are notoriously fickle, and in any case, a declaration of Armistice won't stop the wounded coming.' Quite suddenly he dropped the formality. 'Och, lassie, you're a sensible young woman. You know in your heart that I'm right. If it's any consolation, you've done splendid work here – one of the best young surgeons I've had working with me. You might consider pursuing surgery when all this is over – if you've a mind to, that is. I don't mind admitting I'll find you damned hard to replace.'

'Well then?' Her voice sounded pathetically eager.

'But my first duty is to my patients, and I would be failing in that duty if I allowed you to continue in your present state.' He paused. 'I would also be failing you if I allowed you to crack up completely.'

Aimée left Boulogne two weeks later, in a ship crowded with wounded bound for Blighty, with herself, an orderly and two VADs to care for them, together with a handful of soldiers going home on leave. Hannah had come to see her off, and as they waited, an incoming ship was disembarking fresh troops. They looked remarkably sprightly, marching with an easy swinging gait.

'Americans,' she heard one of the crew mutter. 'They maybe won't be so cocky after a taste of what this lot's had.'

'I'm really going to miss you,' Hannah said glumly. 'We've shared a lot. I may be forced to fraternize more with Sister Munster now.'

'You could do worse. She's not so bad underneath that schoolmarm manner. In fact, she's been quite kind to me this last couple of weeks.'

Aimée had written to tell Gerald she was going home. They had never had any secrets from one another until now, when she had allowed him to believe this was a normal leave. She could not bear him to know the truth – the more so as, in his last letter, he had told her almost off-handedly that he was being recommended for a DSO, for leading the remnants of his battalion to safety under heavy fire, and escaping, praise be to God, with no more than minor injuries.

Aimée was proud of the honour being accorded him. It was long overdue, but the knowledge of it merely added to her own feelings of guilt and failure. And she could not rid herself of the notion, however absurd, that she was deserting him.

She was also cutting her last link with David. For months now she had managed to survive by blotting him, and that whole brief spell of summer madness, out of her conscious mind, but he was still there, hovering on the edge of her subconscious.

Beyond the harbour, the weather worsened and she guessed they were in for a rough crossing. Daylight had paled to a distant line on the horizon, and she went down to check on the men in her charge. For some, seasickness on top of their injuries could prove dangerous as well as distressing. But most of them were remarkably cheerful – even if there was a strong hint of bravado in their repartee.

'As long as the Hun don't let us 'ave one of them torpedoes, Doc, the weather can do its worst.'

'Yeah. I can't wait to get back to good old Blighty, if only for a decent pint of old and mild and some proper grub. My missus does an 'ot pot you'd kill for.'

'There are severe shortages back home, too,' she reminded them.

'Maybe so, but home's home, innit?'

It was still the passive helplessness of the blind that disturbed Aimée most. Some were also horribly disfigured by the mustard gas that had choked them as well as robbing them of their sight. Yet, in spite of the pain, they were for the most part quiet, withdrawn, as though there was nothing left of their poor bodies but a shell.

Her duty done, she went back on deck, needing fresh air and peace rather than sleep, only to find her head throbbing in time with the ship's engines. Even here she was not to be granted solitude. One of the officers who had come aboard at the last minute was standing aft, watching the land recede. She moved a reasonable distance from him and stood hunched over the rail, mesmerized by the frothing waves churned up by the ship.

'Are you all right, Doctor?'

The voice was clipped, vaguely familiar, but there had been so many voices – like ghosts, the images crowded her mind.

'Thank you, yes. Just a little tired.'

'Going home for a well-earned leave, I suppose?'

'Something like that.' Aimée straightened up and turned, hoping he wasn't going to become a nuisance. She saw his face outlined against the darkening sky – a profile dominated by a most distinctive nose. Oh, surely, it couldn't be . . .

'I saw you come aboard earlier. I'm sorry. I don't know your name.' He moved towards her and extended a hand. 'I'm Oliver Langley.'

'Aimée Buchanan.' She took the hand, feeling its firm grip through her woollen glove, and for the sake of politeness, asked, 'I hope your injuries healed well, Major?'

'Splendidly. A little stiffness in the arm from time to time,' there was an enigmatic note in his voice, 'but all in all you did an excellent job on me.'

'Not bad for an impertinent slip of a girl.' The words slipped out before she could stop them.

'Touché,' he said dryly. 'I doubt I expressed my gratitude adequately at the time.'

'There was no need. The circumstances were hardly conducive to polite conversation.'

'I suppose not.'

'Are you a soldier by profession, Major?'

'No. A barrister.'

Which probably accounts for his not tolerating fools gladly, Aimée thought.

In the silence that followed, she turned to the rail again. The last of the light was going fast, and the water glinted with a gunmetal sheen. Somewhere beneath those waves, a U-boat might be lurking; the possibility failed to raise so much as a shudder. Her throat was dry, and there was a dull throbbing ache at her temples.

'I heard about you more than once as time went on. I'm glad you finally achieved recognition.'

'Oh, I did that, all right.' There was a caustic edge to her voice and Aimée saw one eyebrow shoot up. 'Forgive me. I'm not very good company tonight. I have the father and mother of a headache.'

'Do you want some aspirin? I'm sure I have some.' He reached towards an inner pocket.

'Thanks, but I took some earlier when I went below.'

'Of course. I was forgetting.'

She inclined her head, and the horizon tilted giddily. This was no time to succumb to seasickness. A moment or two earlier she had wished the major far away. Now, suddenly, she didn't want to be alone. 'Will you be home for long?'

'That rather depends.' He hesitated before adding, 'The fact is, I'm on compassionate leave. Several days ago I received a wire, telling me that my wife had given birth to a baby – a boy. And today I received a second wire, recommending that if possible I should return home at once.'

'Oh, I'm so sorry,' she exclaimed, sympathy ousting her own problems. 'Is it your first child?'

'No. I have a three-year-old daughter.'

'I see. Do you know what is wrong?'

'The telegram wasn't specific.' His voice was expressionless, but in what little light remained, she could see the tautness round his mouth. 'Would you care to hazard a guess?'

Without stopping to think, she said, 'I suppose it could be puerperal fever.'

'Can such a fever be fatal?'

He shot the question back at her, and she wished with all her heart that she had not allowed herself to be drawn. 'How can I possibly answer that? Any conclusion arrived at on the basis of supposition would be both irrelevant and misleading. For all I know, your wife could be suffering from any one of several minor postnatal complications.'

'Don't quibble, Dr Buchanan. Not with me. We both know that such telegrams are not sent lightly.'

His soft-voiced vehemence hardly surprised her; even so, she felt driven to defend herself. 'I am not quibbling. Nor am I in any position to make a diagnosis. It was very wrong of me to attempt to do so.'

The fire went out of him. 'You are right. The fault was mine. I'm sorry.'

'There is no need to apologize.' Aimée felt the ridiculous threat of tears, and knew she had to get away. 'I must go below in case I am needed.'

'Then I won't detain you,' he said formally.

In turning, she felt the deck tilt again, and almost fell. His hand came suddenly to steady her. Aimée made some feeble comment about needing to find her sea legs, but her pulse was beating with feverish intensity. I cannot – must not – be unwell, she thought. Not now. She glanced up into his eyes and found she could not look away.

'Are you *sure* you're all right?'

The major's voice sounded very loud, very autocratic.

'Yes, of course.' With a superhuman effort, Aimée released herself, and reached for the companion rail as he half-turned away. 'Major Langley?' She ran her tongue round parched lips. 'Try not to worry. I'm sure your wife is in good hands.'

By the time the ship reached Folkestone, Aimée's throat was feeling enlarged, and in spite of the cold, she felt uncomfortably warm. But old disciplines die hard. She gritted her teeth, and supervised the disembarkation of the wounded, touched by their gratitude as she handed them over to the waiting doctors and nurses who would take them on to their appointed destinations.

The London train was freezing, and by the time she reached Victoria her feet were numb, and she was feeling like death, shivering and burning up at one and the same time. For several moments she leaned against a wall, surrounded by her luggage, unable to think coherently, bombarded by noise, and with people rushing past unheeding.

'Dr Buchanan?'

She straighened up, weak with relief at hearing a familiar voice. Any voice. She moistened her mouth, which kept drying up. 'Major. We seem destined to meet. Do you suppose there's any chance of my getting a taxi to Euston? I really don't feel like attempting the tube.'

'Wait here. I'll find one.'

She could have told him that it was unnecessary to bark orders at her as she had no intention of going anywhere. But it was all too much trouble. In the taxi he discovered that she, too, was bound for Liverpool, en route to her home. From that moment he took charge, dismissing her half-hearted attempts to pay her share of the taxi, and supervising the luggage. And Aimée abandoned all her high-flown feminist ideals and let him.

On Euston Station Oliver Langley stood looking down at her. Her face had an unhealthy sheen of pallor, but that could simply be tiredness combined with the sea journey. The vivid splashes of colour on each cheek were more ominous.

'I'm not sure you're going to make it to Liverpool,' he said abruptly, 'let alone reach your home.'

'Of course I will,' she croaked. 'I haven't come this far to be incarcerated in a London hospital.'

'What nonsense.' He was angry with himself for getting involved when he had more than enough to worry about, and the anger rasped in his voice. 'You know what's wrong with you?'

'At a guess, I'd say trench fever. We had some new cases in recently.'

'Almost certainly trench fever,' he agreed grimly.

'But I've got plenty of aspirin to keep me going. If you could just lend me your assistance as far as the train, I'll be fine.'

'Dr Buchanan, you are, without doubt, the most obstinate woman of my acquaintance.'

'If you say so.' Aimée inclined her head, and immediately wished she hadn't. 'But I know what I'm doing.'

'I hope you do.'

She made her way to the Ladies' Retiring Room to freshen up, and returned feeling slightly better. From somewhere Major Langley had procured a hot drink, which he assured her was tea, though it might have been dish water for all she could taste of it. But it soothed her raw throat and gave her the strength to walk straight-backed down the platform behind the porter. The sibilant hiss of steam, the shouts and the echoing feet of passengers hurrying past gave everything a surreal quality, and she was glad of the major's supporting hand beneath her arm.

The train was fairly full, but she saw Major Langley slip the porter a tip, and halfway along the corridor he found them an empty first-class carriage. As the man left, the major pulled down the blinds and closed the door firmly behind him.

'Thank you,' Aimée said politely. 'You have been very kind. But you don't have to remain with me, you know.'

'I may as well be here as anywhere else. And you certainly aren't fit to be left alone.'

Too exhausted to argue, she sank into the window seat and closed her eyes. Outside, doors were banging, people were running, and there was a fresh surge of steam. Soon she would be home in the peace of Crag Vale – in her own bed – and dear Dr Lomax would make her better as he always did. A whistle shrilled and the train jerked forward. As it gathered speed and rhythm, her thoughts became more confused.

Oliver Langley sat watching her, but his own thoughts soon drifted away to his lovely Catherine. He had tried to find a telephone at Folkestone, and again at Euston, but a great many other people had the same idea, and time had run out.

Until now he had been able to keep reality at bay, to refrain from contemplating the possibility that Catherine might already be gone from him forever. He ought to be inured to death, for he had seen it in all its most violent and obscene forms. But that was war, something of which Catherine knew nothing.

Unlike Aimée Buchanan, who knew too much. Her present vulnerability had touched a raw nerve in him; and in some totally illogical way that his lawyer's mind would normally reject, it seemed as if by helping the one, he might save the other.

Catherine had not been strong since the birth of their daughter, Alice, three years ago. The specialist had warned them then that it would be unwise for her to have another child, but on his last leave, she had been insistent, almost to the point of obsession, that she wished to give him a son. And because in his heart he craved an heir, he had allowed himself to be persuaded. If the worst had indeed happened, he would never forgive himself for that moment of weakness.

Dr Buchanan was muttering in her sleep. Something about angels and ghosts. She had slipped sideways. He shifted her into a more comfortable position and felt her forehead, which was burning. Her upper lip was beaded with perspiration.

'Damn,' he said aloud, and she half-opened her eyes.

'Have you seen them, Major? I have ... men I knew were dead ...' Her voice was little more than a croak. 'And I've heard patients talk of strange happenings, dead comrades coming to help them ...'

She was clearly rambling.

'We are running into a station, Dr Buchanan. I'll see if I can get us a hot drink.'

Oliver explained the situation to the guard.

'Poor lady. I'll see what I can do,' the man said and hurried away, returning with remarkable speed carrying two large cups, slopping over. 'Not our usual standard, I'm afraid, sir. It's a bit wet and watery, but it's all I could get.'

Oliver thanked him, took the cups from him and handed over a shilling, telling him to keep the change.

Aimée was sitting much as he had left her. He took out some of his own aspirin, pressing them into her hand. 'Take those, and then the tea,' he ordered.

She did as she was told without question, wrapping her hands round the cup and greedily gulping the liquid down.

'Now then, Dr Buchanan – ' He pushed up the arm rests, and reaching for the smaller of his two bags, took out a thick hand-knitted jumper, which he folded to make a pillow. 'Come. You'll rest better lying down.'

She laid her head on the soft wool as meekly as a child, curling up as he lifted her legs into a comfortable position and covered her with his greatcoat. But still the muttering continued.

'Sometimes the dead take a wrong turning ... or aren't ready ...' Her voice tailed off, then came back more strongly: 'David has lost his way. I wish he would find rest ...'

'Time you gave your throat a rest, Doctor. Go to sleep.'

Oliver wondered briefly if David was the brother she had spoken about. She flung her arm out. He tucked it firmly back under cover, cursing himself for getting involved. It was becoming clearer by the minute that she would be in no condition to switch to the local train in order to complete her journey home. And his own priorities were equally clear – he must go immediately to Catherine.

As the train approached Lime Street, he shook Aimée awake.

47

'Dr Buchanan? Is there anyone in Liverpool to whom I can take you?' She stared at him, blank-eyed, and he shook her again. 'Listen to me. If you have no friends in Liverpool, I shall have to take you to the nearest hospital.'

Aimée heard the words through a stifling cloying heat.

'Aunt . . . dear Aunt Fliss . . .' she croaked, trying to pull herself together as some of his urgency communicated itself to her. She cleared her throat. 'Sorry. Mrs Mellish . . . Sefton Park.'

'Wife of George Mellish, the MP?'

She nodded – and winced.

Thank God for that, he thought.

'It's all right,' he said. 'I know them well.'

5

IT HAD NOT been a good morning for Agnes Shaw. She had
arrived home from her office cleaning in the early hours to find
that Matty had been up half the night with little Daisy, who had
been sick several times all over her cot. The general disturbance
had set Pat off on one of his attacks and he had almost coughed his
heart up. By morning, every available bucket stood in a haphazard
line leading from the back scullery, overflowing with bedding
waiting to be washed, in addition to her normal pile.

'I've lit the boiler, Mam, and put the first load in,' Matty had
said, stifling a yawn as she left for work. Small wonder she'd
looked half-asleep, poor kid. Irene was useless when it came to
anything to do with sickness. By mid-morning the first lot of sheets
was working up a fine head of steam on the rack in front of the
range, the day not being fit for putting anything in the yard
without it freezing solid, and the second batch was well on the way
to being finished when Dr Hutton, the panel doctor, called.

By then, Agnes had a throbbing head and her varicose veins
were giving her gyp. She was in no mood for his cheerful dismissal
of Daisy's sickness as teething problems.

'And you know how to deal with that, Mrs Shaw,' he said
heartily. 'Just boiled sugar water for now, until she settles. The
gum's quite red, so that molar should be through any time now.'

Hutton was a good enough doctor, though – probably better
than most – and he certainly gave Pat a thorough going over,
pursing his lips a few times before straightening up and putting his
stethoscope away.

'Well, you've had a rough time of it, by all accounts, but you're
over the worst, please God. A pity we can't get you into a
sanitorium for a while – give you and everyone else a bit of a rest
and a change.'

Agnes felt her heart lurch, but before she could protest, the doctor was already shaking his head.

'It wouldn't be easy, mind. Every spare bed is being filled by these poor lads coming back from the war. Shocking state, some of them are in.' And recollecting that the Shaws had a boy out in France, added heartily, 'Still, the armistice is expected any day now.'

Agnes sniffed. 'They keep saying that, but I'll believe in their armistice when it happens. As for Pat, you needn't trouble yourself, Doctor. He'll do well enough here among his own.'

Pat heard the forced cheerfulness in her voice, so at odds with the weariness in her face when she thought no one was looking. He exchanged a meaningful glance with Dr Hutton. 'And do I get to have a say, woman? Sure, a change might be just the thing to set me up, if the good doctor could get me in somewhere.'

Agnes pursed her lips, the sharpness in her voice betraying her hurt. 'I'd no idea you was that mad keen to get away.'

'Aggie love, you know I didn't mean – '

'Oh, give over your blather. I know well enough what you mean,' but her voice had softened.

'Your husband does have a point, Mrs Shaw. Sometimes a change can be beneficial.'

'If you say so, Doctor.' Agnes was grudging. 'I suppose anything's worth a try.'

'It might mean him going some distance away, of course, but,' Dr Hutton shrugged on his coat and picked up his hat, 'I'll have a word in a few quarters, and we'll see what happens.'

It hadn't been a good morning for Matty, either. She was used to disturbed nights, but this one had been worse than most, and from then on everything she did seemed to go wrong.

'Yer dad poorly again, is he? The time of year's bad fer 'is chest, I dare say.'

'Keep your voice down, Edna, for pity's sake,' whispered Evie.

'Sorry, I'm sure. But anyone with 'alf an eye can see as Matty in't 'erself. I was only being friendly, like, askin'.'

Edna knew someone who knew someone who knew the Shaws, and had let slip what was wrong with Matty's dad, and that he was 'proper bad'. By common consent, the girls had agreed not to mention it when Mrs Crawley was around. She was so finicky about illness of any kind, and they knew the dressmaker already had her knife into Matty, especially since the incident of the sketch.

Doris had been tight-lipped about the whole thing. She knew in her heart that Matty had a natural talent that she would never acquire, no matter how hard she worked. And that didn't seem fair. What's more, she was popular with everyone – except Mrs Crawley – so she couldn't take it out on her. Now, jealousy brought all that festering enmity to the surface once more.

'That's the second time you've unpicked that bodice,' she said spitefully, as Matty swore and flung down the offending work. 'You'll get the rough end of Mrs C's tongue if she catches you. And then she'll want to know why you're being so ham-fisted.'

'And you'd just love the chance to tell on me, wouldn't you?' Matty retorted, her temper snapping suddenly.

'I don't know what you mean. Anyhow, my mam doesn't think it's right, me workin' with someone whose dad's gorra nasty disease like that, an' the old bat might just think the same if she was to know.'

'Don't talk daft,' Evie said.

'That's enough, girls,' said Miss Helen quietly. 'Get on with your work.'

'And what exactly is it that the *old bat* should know?'

They had been too busy arguing to notice the door opening. Mrs Crawley stood there, stiffly erect, her tight-lipped face masked in fury.

It was all over very quickly, as Matty had known it would be, though not before she had given vent to all her pent-up grievances against the narrow-minded bigot who had so often made her life a misery. The girls had been in tears when she left, all except Doris, and even she wouldn't meet Matty's eyes.

'That Doris is a spiteful cow,' Evie had whispered. 'Her and Mrs C, both. But you'll soon gerra job, see if you don't. You're cleverer than the lot of us put together.'

Matty didn't feel clever as she made her way down Wandsworth Road and turned towards the river, into the teeth of a sleet-laden wind. She didn't feel or think anything very much except that she couldn't face Mam – not yet. She paused by a rail to watch the arrival of the Isle of Man steamer; gulls appeared from nowhere, screeching and swooping in the hope of easy pickings from the water as it slapped grey and cold against the wall beneath her, flecked with a frothy scum.

'I wouldn't jump if I was you, gairl,' said a voice behind her. 'No matter what yer trouble, there's wairse things happen at sea.'

She turned to find a wizened old man with rheumy eyes, grinning at her. His coat was threadbare, the soles of his shoes flapping in the wind, and he looked frozen stiff. But his grin held no trace of self-pity.

'Yes,' she said, suddenly ashamed of her own maudlin thoughts. 'Here . . .' She fumbled in her pocket, bringing out a threepenny bit, which she thrust into his hand. 'Get yourself somewhere warm and have a hot drink and something to eat. You look as if you could do with it.'

'God luv yer, gairl. An' He does, you'll see.' He scurried away.

It was time to go home and face the music.

Agnes was still brooding on what Dr Hutton had said, and was in no mood to sympathize. Instead, all her tiredness and misery vented itself upon her hapless daughter, who had decided to cloak her apprehension in bravado.

'I knew this would happen. Didn't I tell you? Fillin' your head with all that fashion rubbish . . . an' where's it got you?' Agnes could feel the blood beating in her head, burning her skin as the words spilled out in a torrent of vicious accusation.

Matty had expected her to be angry. Mam could wipe the floor with you better than most. But not like this. This wasn't like Mam at all. Something terrible must have happened.

'Oh dear God, is it Dad?' she whispered. 'Has something happened to him?'

Agnes Shaw stopped, horrified by her own loss of control. Matty was already halfway to the door when she caught at her arm.

'No, wait, love. Your dad's no worse. Honest. But, what with everything, I'm a bit on edge. The doctor gave him a right going over this morning and, God forgive me for forgetting, he gave him a sleeping draught before he left. And here's me screaming like a banshee! If he wakes now, he'll never get off again.'

Matty felt the trembling in her mother's hand, and her own

troubles were forgotten. 'It's all right, Mam. You sit down. I'll go and see if he's all right.'

'Are you sure, love? Perhaps I should – '

'Mam!'

Agnes sat down abruptly.

Matty's heart was beating right up in her throat as she pushed the parlour door open. Her dad was lying on his side, his face relaxed, his breath rattling slightly in his throat.

'Sleeping like a baby,' she said, coming back. Her mother drew a shuddering breath. 'Speaking of which, where's our Daisy?'

'Marge Flynn's taken her for a bit, so's I could get on. It's her teeth, the doctor said. She's a treasure, is Marge.'

'She is, that. Still, she's got plenty of her own, so I suppose one more doesn't make any difference. Now I'm going to make us a nice cup of tea. We could both do with one.'

'You're a good girl, our Matty,' Agnes said as her daughter came back from the scullery with the kettle and set it on the fire. 'I ought not to have gone on at you like I did. Dr Hutton was talking again about sending Dad to a sanitorium – and your dad eggin' him on like he was eager to go.'

'Oh, Mam!' Matty heard the heartbreak in her mother's voice, and forgot her own troubles. She leaned over the back of the chair and put her arms round Agnes. 'He'd only be thinking of you.'

'I know that. D'you think I don't? But it doesn't make it any easier. And what with Daisy – '

'And then I crowned everything by coming home with bad news. I never did pick me moments that well.' Matty withdrew her arms. 'I'm sorry, Mam.'

'Ah well, sorry never mended anything. What's done is done.' Agnes got up, suddenly brisk once more. 'It's a pity, though. Less than a year – that's all you had to go. Couldn't you keep your fancy ideas to yourself for just a bit longer?'

'It wasn't that.' The words tumbled out unthinking as she sought to justify herself. 'Mrs Crawley found out about Dad, and as good as said I'd contaminate her customers with TB.' She bit her lip. It sounded awful, put like that. 'I didn't half let fly at her! Said some terrible things – all the things I'd been wanting to say for years.'

'There's not much hope of her changing her mind then,' Agnes said dryly. 'Seems it's the Shaws' day for losing their tempers. Still, you'll just have to find another job. Irene said they aren't taking anyone else on at her place, what with all the talk of an armistice.' She got up and busied herself turning the cot sheets on the rack. 'You could try some of the clothing manufacturers. Lewton's factory on Brownlow Hill were wanting someone a couple of weeks back. And there's others you can try.'

With every word her mother was trampling on Matty's most cherished hopes, and she could only stand there, numb with misery, and let her.

'If all else fails – well, it's still maybe not the end of the world. In fact, perhaps it was meant. Mr Levi down the pawn shop had quite a decent sewing machine in his window yesterday. It was more than I'd reckoned on paying, but maybe he'd knock a bit off for ready cash. If we put the word round a bit, I dare say you could work up a nice little clientele.'

The disappointment Agnes was trying so hard to hide came through the false enthusiasm in her voice. It cut Matty to the heart, for it was an echo of her own broken dreams. The lid of the blackened kettle began to rattle, and to hide her feelings, she swiftly bent to make the tea. Then she straightened up, shoulders back.

'You're quite right. That's what we'll do,' she said with cheerful determination. 'While this tea brews, I'm going upstairs to take this frock off. And if I never see it again, it'll be too soon.'

6

THE DREAM, SO long held at bay, was back again, so real this time that she could actually smell and feel his presence – David, in that reckless mood that half scared, half excited her, just beyond her reach in a field of waist-high barley strewn with poppies, calling to her, arms outstretched. And the breeze that riffled the silvery sheaves in a seductive, every-moving wave, carried the echo of his voice. 'Come, Aimée, lovely Aimée – come to me now.' In the dream she always ran towards him joyously, only to stop as the poppies burst into flames, consuming him in an instant.

But this time was different. This time she didn't pull back. Their fingers were on the point of touching . . . the scorching blanket of heat threatened to envelop her, and for the first time she could see his face quite clearly, saw his eager expression change to one of horror, a horror that echoed in his voice as he cried out, 'No, no! Go back! Oh, my dear love, go back!'

Aimée woke in a shaking sweat, her mouth as clogged as the bottom of a cesspit. She opened her eyes to an unfamiliar room, cloaked in darkness except for a shaded lamp beside the bed. A lady was sitting in an armchair nearby, dozing, a pale dressing-gown edged with swan's-down framing a face half turned in to a cushion. She looked familiar, but smaller and frailer than Aimée remembered.

She swallowed experimentally, and her throat grated. 'Mother, is it really you?'

Minna Buchanan shot upright, instantly alert. 'Oh, darling, at last. Thank God!'

It seemed a very strange thing to say. 'Do you think I could have a drink of water?'

'Water – yes, of course.' The jug rattled the rim of the glass. 'No, don't try to sit up just yet, my dearest.'

It was rather like being a child again, mother's hand behind her head, supporting it as she had done many times, while Aimée drained the glass. She felt damp and sticky and slightly light-headed. 'I can't seem to remember . . . am I home?'

'No, dear. You are at your Aunt Felicity's. I came, of course, the moment she sent word. Your father brought me. You have been delirious for two whole days. I . . . we were beginning to wonder . . .' Her mother's lip trembled.

'Heavens! You haven't been sitting here all that time, I hope.'

Her mother laughed shakily. 'Of course not, dear. We have taken turns, your aunt and I – and a nurse. And your father usually drives over in the evening with Frank Lomax. Poor Frank – he is so frustrated, for naturally Felicity called in her own doctor, Andrew Graham, who has looked after you quite splendidly.'

'Oh Lord, I'm sorry. I seem to have caused a lot of trouble.' Aimée attempted to lift herself on the pillows, and was appalled by her weakness.

'Do be careful. You mustn't rush things, dear. You have been very poorly, you know.'

'Yes, of course.' The memories were coming back. 'Major Langley must have wished me far away.'

'Not at all. He was so kind, so considerate. He even stayed to explain to your aunt what was wrong with you, in spite of his own troubles.'

His wife. Of course. But before Aimée could assemble her thoughts, the door opened to admit Aunt Felicity. The lamplight picked out the hint of diamonds in her hair, and she wore a gown of some pale floaty material that swished gently as she came swiftly to the bed.

'So you've decided to come back to us at last. Good.' Aimée caught the faint drift of her perfume as she bent to lay a cool hand on her brow. 'Hmm. Not bad, but you'll feel a lot better after a sponge down, I dare say.'

'I'm sorry, Aunt Fliss. It must have been quite a facer, having a delirious female foisted on you without warning.'

'Oh quite a facer,' Felicity agreed, gently mocking. 'We would have turned you away had Oliver Langley not been so desperate to be rid of you.'

'Felicity!' Minna exclaimed, shocked. 'How can you – even in jest!'

'But it's true.' Aimée suddenly felt very tired. 'I fear I was abominably stubborn and selfish, when all that poor man wanted to do was get back to his wife. How is she, do you know?'

Her aunt's hesitation was answer enough. Tears of weakness rolled down Aimée's cheeks. 'Oh how sad. And the baby?'

'A little on the small side, but thriving, I believe.'

'For goodness' sake!' Minna exclaimed. 'Felicity, I will not have you upsetting Aimée when she's scarcely returned from death's door herself. I am surprised at you.'

'Rubbish, Minna. Your daughter is made of sterner stuff.' But the wan smile this assertion produced, made her add lightly, 'However, I think it's time to fetch the nurse. She will soon have you comfortable and in a fresh nightie, my dear, and then she'll bring you a nice hot drink.'

'Such a fuss over a touch of fever,' Aimée said thickly. 'I shall soon be as fit as a flea.'

But it wasn't quite that simple. Even when Dr Graham pronounced her fit to travel, Aimée remained lethargic, spending many hours alone in her room. She wrote to Major Langley, a polite little note, expressing her sympathy, and her thanks for his care of her. And he replied with equal brevity and politeness. But she seemed curiously reluctant to return to her beloved Crag Vale and her mother's cossetting, and the questions that would be asked. Even when the bells pealed out across Liverpool, across the whole country, proclaiming the end of hostilities, she remained unmoved.

In the nursery of a house in Falkner Square, Oliver Langley also heard the bells that would bring joy and hope to so many people. But for him they had come too late. He stared down at Christopher Charles Langley, asleep in his cot, blissfully unaware of the tragic consequences of his birth. Such a scrap of humanity to be the unwitting cause of so much grief.

There was a peremptory tug at his jacket. 'Dada?'

The child who demanded his attention was so like her mother that he could hardly bear to look at her; the same silver fairness, the same eloquent eyes, more violet than blue, echoing her dress beneath its crisp white pinafore, and the same fragile birdlike build that made her look less than her three years.

'Alice, don't bother your father just now,' her Aunt Jane said sharply.

'But, I want – '

'Nice little girls don't say "I want",' the reproving voice continued. 'Nanny, take Miss Alice into the other room.'

'No, it's all right.' Oliver shook his thoughts free, and stooped to lift his daughter, who promptly wound her arms round his neck. He nodded dismissal to the nanny, who left the room.

'You'll spoil the child,' said his sister, though her eyes softened briefly at the sight of Alice's head tucked into her father's neck.

'We mustn't neglect her. She will be missing Catherine, too – more perhaps than any of us realize.'

Jane Langley uttered a distressed little tut. She was two years younger than Oliver, striking rather than pretty, with soft brown hair, the family nose, which gave her a look of fine-boned hauteur, and a wonderfully practical streak.

'Children are surprisingly resilient. Oliver, do you have to go back to France? I mean, now that the armistice has been agreed – '

'My dear, I can't desert my men. There is much still to be done. But I should be back for good in a month or two, as soon as final details are worked out, and someone can be appointed in my place.'

Alice planted a wet kiss on his cheek. 'Dada come home.'

'Soon, sweetheart.' He ruffled her hair, the thought of home without Catherine suddenly catching at his heart. He quickly turned his mind back to practicalities 'I can't tell you what it means to me to know that you can stay on. Nanny is very efficient, but . . .'

'Oh well,' Jane shrugged. 'I have little enough to rush back to at present. I was so thankful that Mamma decided she was unfit to leave her benighted Welsh spa to attend the funeral. She has Hetty King for company, which means that for a while at least I am spared her constant hints about what she will do when I am gone – as if I were contemplating moving to outer Mongolia instead of Surrey. As for Nick – ' she twisted her sapphire and diamond ring round and round on her third finger ' – Nick is God knows where on his precious ship.'

Oliver felt a pang of sympathy for his sister. Jane had borne the brunt of their mother's imagined illnesses with more patience than he could ever have done. He did not know how he would have got through the last week without her. She was due to be married next year, and he hoped with all his heart that nothing would happen to prevent it. She deserved to be happy.

'Poor Jane. It isn't easy for you either, is it? But for what it's worth, I am grateful that you can stay for a little while longer, at least.'

Minna Buchanan sat in her sister's elegant drawing room, upset and bewildered, a lacy handkerchief fluttering to dab at her eyes. 'I don't understand. She hasn't once asked about Gerald, and you know how close they were – are. He might be dead, for all she . . . Oh, how could I even think such a thing. I scarcely know what I'm saying.'

'We haven't heard from Giles either,' Felicity said soothingly. 'I dare say the armistice has made a lot of extra work, you know, and those young men of ours can be very single-minded. It would never enter their heads that we might be sitting here worrying.'

'Perhaps. But that doesn't explain Aimée's behaviour. She has always loved her home, so I can only think she is deliberately avoiding being alone with me.'

'I think she is doing just that,' said Felicity, regretting her bluntness as it brought forth yet another stifled sob. 'Now don't take on, Minna.'

The thin November sunshine trapped her younger sister in its shaft, turning her fair hair to spun gold beneath the upturned sweep of a stylish lavender hat, and highlighting the softly trembling lips.

'I'm not suggesting that Aimée doesn't love you. Quite the contrary. I'd say she cares too much and is afraid of hurting you. If you ask me, Aimée's withdrawal has nothing to do with her illness, and until she's exorcised whatever's eating at her, emotional pressure is the last thing she wants.'

'You think she's mentally ill, don't you? Like Toby . . .' The accusing words were out before Minna could stop them. She uttered a little gasp, her lower lip trembling. 'Oh, my dear, I'm sorry. I didn't mean – ' Her pretty face crumpled and the handkerchief fluttered again.

For a moment the sunlight blurred. Then Felicity blinked and forced lightness into her voice. 'Of course you didn't.

'How is the poor boy?'

Minna's hushed enquiry was almost harder to take than her initial insensitivity, but Felicity now had her emotions well under control. 'He's coming along slowly but surely. The doctors are quite pleased with him. However, to get back to Aimée – I suspect her trouble is *au coeur*, and if she comes home with it unresolved, she'll simply put on an act for your benefit, and the hurt will get buried deeper.' Felicity saw that Minna was weakening. 'Just leave her here for a few more days, and we'll see what happens.'

But Seth Buchanan was less easily convinced. Big and bluff and ill at ease with his pale shadow of a daughter, who was usually so full of life, he turned to Frank Lomax.

'I don't know what's for the best, and that's a fact,' he grunted, lighting his cigar with unaccustomed clumsiness. The lights in the library were subdued, but Dr Lomax could sense his distress. 'You know, I thought when that church bell rang out across Crag Vale it would perk Minna up no end, instead of which she burst into tears. But then I never did understand how women's minds work.'

'They aren't so different from us, Seth. Tears may simply be a release of tension.'

'If you say so.' Seth leaned across to pour himself another whisky. He pushed the decanter towards Frank Lomax, but he waved it away. 'It doesn't help, of course, that we've had no word from Gerald for weeks. Now Felicity's got my lass convinced that Aimée's better off in Liverpool till she's right. And I can't stand to see Minna grieving.' He sighed. 'Go and see Aimée, Frank. I'm not much with words, and besides, you always could get to the bottom of her better than anyone – except our Gerald.'

So Dr Lomax went to Liverpool. He found Aimée where she mostly spent her time, curled up in a comfortable squashy armchair in her room. And, as always, he was forthright. 'I'm ashamed of you, Aimée Buchanan. Skulking away here, feeling sorry for yourself.'

A faint flush ran up under her too pale skin. 'Maybe I have cause.'

'If you mean that you're physically and mentally exhausted, probably anaemic, and with not a spare ounce of flesh on you, I'd agree. Whatever happened to those first principles I instilled into you?'

'About not being able to look after others properly if you don't look after yourself?' She quoted his favourite maxim, raising a jokey smile to hide her real malaise – the growing fear of her own inadequacy. 'I'm afraid first principles have little relevance in a casualty clearing station crammed to the doors and beyond with men indescribably maimed, and never enough time or people to deal with them.'

He tutted in distress and walked across to look out of the window. If she told him how she really felt, would he understand? The need to unburden herself became unbearable.

'I'm not on leave, Doc,' she said jerkily, meeting his eyes as he turned. 'I was sent home – cracked up and funked an operation. I couldn't take the strain, you see. Now I can't even hold a scalpel without shaking, let alone use one. Some surgeon I turned out to be. Maybe Dad was right after all, not wanting me to become a doctor. Maybe I'm just not up to the job.'

His reaction was explosive. 'That's feeble-minded twaddle and you know it, my girl.' He came to tower over her, and, meeting her eyes, his manner softened. 'Not up to the job, indeed. Give yourself credit, lass. You went out there as a raw recruit, with no more than a brief spell on a surgical ward under your belt after medical school – that's a baptism of fire with a vengeance. And for eight months you'll have worked yourself into the ground, no doubt.'

'Others managed,' she insisted doggedly.

'For a time, maybe. But everyone has a breaking point, Aimée. We're none of us God, more's the pity.' He sighed. 'You've just learned that lesson a bit more dramatically than most.'

Tears of weakness threatened. 'Perhaps.'

'There's no perhaps about it.' The doctor hesitated, then settled his backside against the edge of the dressing-table. 'Who is David?'

For a moment the room spun about her, and she was silent, not wanting to answer; not, with his eyes on her, able to evade the question entirely. 'How do you know about David?'

'When you were feverish, you kept calling his name. Your aunt heard you. She said you seemed distressed.'

'I see.' Aimée stubbed out her cigarette. 'She's never mentioned it.'

'No. Well, the poor woman has troubles enough with that young lad of hers, and I reckon she was afraid of doing more harm than good.' He waited. 'Well?'

She plucked at the arm of the chair, not looking at him. 'David was someone I knew, briefly. A young flier.'

'A friend, or more than a friend?'

Amy felt herself blushing and said defiantly, 'If you mean did I "know" him in the Biblical sense the answer is yes.'

'That's your business lass,' he said dryly. 'I'm not one for prying or making judgements but if you want to talk about it – '

'What is there to talk about?' Aimée's voice was bitter. 'He was twenty-three, and he was gentle and funny and a little crazy, and I loved him. We had exactly two and a half weeks of snatched hours before he was shot down over enemy lines in a bloody great sheet of flames. It was the kind of death he dreaded, though he never mentioned it, except once, in delirium.' She was suddenly alive, eyes blazing. 'And if you tell me that his death would have been mercifully swift, I'll – '

'Aimée, girl, d'you think I'm that insensitive? But there's something I will tell you for nothing, something you should know. It's my belief that you never allowed yourself to grieve for that poor boy. It's festering away inside you, and until you put him to rest, you won't get your other problems sorted.'

He rose to leave, placing a firm hand on her shoulder as he passed her chair. 'Don't stay away too long, m'dear. Your parents are trying hard to understand, but it isn't easy for them.' He cleared his throat. 'And I could use an extra pair of hands. We've a number of cases of this wretched influenza to add to all the coughs and colds – and I'm not getting any younger.'

For a long time after he had gone Aimée remained curled up in the chair, watching the ancient beech tree in the wind, a profligate shedding its few remaining tattered leaves like a wanton before her lover – an unfortunate simile, she thought, as painful memory stirred. But I am no longer ill, merely devoid of purpose – a dry leaf fluttering in the wind.

She rose and went to a drawer and took out a small package. With unsteady hands she prised loose the knots and took out the shabby book of poetry, its pages well thumbed.

David had been brought in from one of the casualty clearing stations with suspected concussion. In spite of his pallor, and the blood already congealing in hair bleached almost white by the sun, her first impression had been: What a beautiful young man – an Apollo brought low.

'Engine chucked it a mile short of home.' He was slurring his words. 'Tried to pancake the poor old Henri Farman . . . went arse over apex . . . bloody stupid . . . knocked out cold.' His voice rose abruptly. 'But no flames, thank Christ . . .'

The long golden eyelashes fluttered and lifted to reveal the most brilliant blue eyes Aimée had ever seen, made more brilliant by stark terror. But as she bent over him, they cleared momentarily. 'Sorry, sweetheart,' he muttered. 'Language unbecoming, and all that.' And he smiled at her so sweetly that her heart turned over.

She had been concerned in case he had sustained a fracture, although the fact that he had regained consciousness, however briefly, must be encouraging. Colonel Grant was of the same opinion, but agreed that he would need watching. When she came on duty the next morning, the blue eyes were turned towards the door, and the moment he saw her, he made as if to raise himself.

'Don't move,' she said sharply, going swiftly to stand beside the bed close to him. 'How do you feel?'

'Rough. As if all the hammers of hell are beating a tattoo inside my head.'

'It was a nasty blow.' She went through the routine tests, all the while aware of his intense gaze. 'But this time I believe you've been lucky, Lieutenant Farrar.'

'I wouldn't argue with that.' His free hand shot out without warning to encircle her wrist as she took his pulse. 'In fact, if I'd known doctors came in such lovely packages, I might have made it my business to pancake the dear old crate sooner.'

She removed herself from his grasp and stood up out of reach, her anger out of all proportion to his misplaced levity.

'That's a stupid thing to say, even in jest – *especially* in jest. We have men dying here every day, some of them in appalling agony, and you could well have been one of them.'

'Sorry. You're quite right. Deuced bad taste. No, please – don't go.'

He looked so contrite, like Gerald used to look, after some

63

particularly horrid schoolboy prank. And then he smiled, and she was lost. In the days that followed, he watched for her constantly, conjuring up fictitious symptoms in order to claim her attention, and shamelessly whispering love poems in her ear under cover of her examination, delighting to watch the blush creep up under her skin. When he was discharged, it was as if a light had gone out of her life.

But two days later he was back, seeking her out just as she was about to take her dinner break.

'Did you think I wouldn't be?' He seemed surprised. 'I won't keep you now if you're busy, but things have gone a bit quiet at our end, so they've put me on light duties for a few days, and I thought you might be able to steal a few minutes from your duties . . .'

It was a beautiful day. She begged some bread and cheese from the canteen, and they walked up the road in the sunshine, swinging hands, doing and saying silly, inconsequential things, like children – no, like lovers. It all happened so quickly. Until that moment, no man had ever equalled Gerald in her eyes. Now suddenly she was giddy with delight, intoxicated. Thinking back, she had no recollection of what they talked about, except that they discovered a mutual love of poetry, in particular the works of Christina Rossetti – a selection of which he carried with him in a small, well-used book. When that first brief encounter ended too soon, he asked, 'Can we do this again?'

They did, as often as possible. And, in spite of his odd swings of mood, each time became more precious than the last. Until the day when he said tersely, 'Is there any chance of your taking more than the odd hour? A whole day or more, perhaps?' And she knew that time was running out.

It wasn't difficult to arrange. With a temporary hiatus in the fighting, the pressure had eased at the hospital, too, and she was given two whole days.

David brought a picnic hamper. He had borrowed a shabby but elegant Hispano-Suiza sports car from a friend, and seemed in excellent spirits, singing at the top of his voice, although as time went on Aimée sensed a more than usually edgy bravura about his gaiety. They drove for miles, and found a small farm hidden away down a country lane that had somehow remained untouched by the fighting. The farmer's wife, Madame Buchard, made them fresh coffee from her precious store, and said, with a knowing look that, yes, she could put them up for a night, if they did not mind the narrowness of the bed. Her husband was away, delivering produce to the nearby town, but she gave them carte blanche to go where they pleased.

They set the hamper down in the shade of an ancient elm tree, and had their picnic, and then fell silent. A little way off there was a field of barley, silvered by sunlight, and ripe for cutting. Poppies dotted it with scarlet. And above it a lone skylark swooped, its song heart-breakingly sweet. With sudden awkwardness they looked everywhere except at each other.

'It's quite perfect,' Aimée said finally, desperate to break the silence. 'A perfect summer day. So perfect, we might almost be in England.'

He answered with a mocking laugh. 'Oh, perfect,' he agreed. 'So let us by all means do the *English* thing, and talk about the weather!'

'David!'

'I know, I know – I'm sorry. It's just that suddenly I feel like a bloody schoolboy,' he said tautly, still without looking at her. 'I brought you here with every intention of ravishing you, and now I'm afraid to touch you.'

She touched his arm tentatively, smiling through tears of relief. 'You think I didn't know that? But I came just the same, didn't I?'

He turned slowly. 'Dammit, I've made you cry.'

'No.' She blinked the tears away. And he, seeing the quiet certainty in her eyes, took her in his arms, his mouth closing on hers with a probing fierceness that took her breath away. At medical school she had made many friends, but there had been no emotional involvement. Now, as every nerve began to quiver, she made the stupendous discovery that clinical knowledge bore no relation to reality. And he, sensitive to her mood, grew gentle, his persuasive tongue coaxing a willing response until, laughing with soft exultance, he lifted his head and she saw that his eyes had darkened and deepened to a midnight blue.

'Oh, Aimée, lovely, lovely Aimée,' he whispered, his wilful smile bewitching her. And taking her hand, he pulled her towards the field of barley.

'David, we can't! We might damage the farmer's crop.'

'Of course we can, sweetheart. Right now, there is nothing we can't do!'

'Ouch! It prickles!'

With a shout of laughter he let her go, ploughing on alone to the centre of the waist-high stalks, where he shed his shirt and laid it across a flattened patch with a ceremonious flourish before turning to her, his arms outstretched. 'Come, Aimée, lovely Aimée. Come to me.'

The sun shimmered on the poppies. For an instant they turned to splashes of blood and she shivered. Then the image dispersed and she ran to him joyfully, abandoning all scruples, to be carried down, down, down, until they were hidden from sight.

And there, in the sweet-smelling barley, cradled from sight, David had slowly, almost reverently undressed her before shedding his remaining clothes with careless haste in order to possess her quiveringly aware body. She had never thought herself particularly beautiful, but that day he made her feel not only beautiful, but desired, as questing lips and fingertips explored the most delicate and intimate places, and she found herself so eager to respond that he dubbed her Jezebel, his laughing taunts rousing her to new peaks of confidence. They made love again, heedless of the occasional shudder of distant gunfire, until the sun went down, and the sky turned to amber, then crimson, fading to a pale purply velvet as the first star appeared.

At last they went indoors, and did more than justice to the *pot-au-feu* prepared by Madame Buchard, and drank her red wine before going up the winding wooden staircase to the attic room with its slanting roof and tiny window. And in the narrow bed, bathed in a shaft of moonlight, they made love again, then slept in each other's arms.

The next morning they drove back in virtual silence. Their parting kiss seemed to hold a particular intensity.

'I'm going back on flying duty,' he said casually as he helped her out of the car – as if he were already, imperceptibly, drawing away from her. 'I'll write when I can, and come back the first chance I get.'

But he didn't write, or come. And when, several weeks later, a fellow officer came to tell her that he had watched David go down in flames over enemy lines, taking an unexploded bomb with him, it only confirmed what she already knew in her heart.

'He asked me to give you this, if anything . . .' The young man was clearly embarrassed as he proferred the small brown package, as if expecting tears. Aimée took it from him, dry-eyed, knowing what it was, and carefully laid it in a drawer, unopened.

The hospital was once more inundated with wounded and there was no time to grieve — no time, after the first piercing agony had dulled, even to dream.

Aimée came back to the present, her fingers feeling for the little book, which fell open at a page he had marked.

> Remember me when I am gone away,
> Gone far away into the silent land;
> When you can no more hold me by the hand,
> Nor I half turn to go yet turning stay.

The words blurred before her eyes. She blinked to clear them, knowing Christina Rossetti's poem by heart, yet needing to read it to the end as he had wished her to.

> Yet if you should forget me for a while
> And afterwards remember, do not grieve:
> For if the darkness and corruption leave
> A vestige of the thoughts that once I had,
> Better by far you should forget and smile
> Than that you should remember and be sad.

The tears rolled down her cheeks unchecked, healing tears. They left her feeling empty, and yet a great weight seemed to have been removed, leaving her curiously light-headed. She knew that the dream wouldn't come back. David was at peace at last, and she could remember him as he was — eager for life and ever young.

There was a tentative knock on the door, and in answer to her muffled 'Come in', her aunt entered.

'I'm not disturbing you, am I?' she asked, noting the sheen of tears.

'Of course not. Take no notice of this.' Aimée scrubbed at her cheeks with a handkerchief. 'I've just been laying a few memories to rest.'

'Good,' Felicity said with a satisfied nod. 'I was wondering if you might feel like taking a drive? Some shopping, I thought. And then there is a small matter I must attend to urgently – a wrong to be righted, if you like. It might interest you.'

7

MATTY HAD JUST finished cutting out a skirt and blouse for Mrs McBride at number 42 when the knocker sounded.

'I'll go, Mam,' she shouted upstairs, laying aside the shears with a sigh of relief. Not to anyone, least of all her mother, had she been able to confess how much she missed the feel of fine wools and silks between her fingers. But cheap cloth was all most folk could afford and it was a case of needs must. At least the sewing machine had been a good buy. She hurried to open the door.

'Matilda?'

Momentarily deprived of speech, Matty stared at the elegant figure of Mrs Mellish swathed in silver fox furs, and the wand-slim young woman at her side, and then beyond them to the familiar gleaming Rolls waiting at the kerb. Bloom Street had never seen its like. Already doors were opening, necks craning to get a good view. She heard Dolly McBride's strident voice: 'Hey, Brenda, come an' gerra load of this fer a motor car – like a ruddy great silver 'earse!' Embarrassment brought the colour flooding to Matty's cheeks. Whatever would Mrs Mellish think?

But not by so much as a flicker did Felicity betray that she had heard. Her charity work frequently brought her into contact with the likes of Mrs McBride. She smiled reassuringly.

'I hoped I might find you at home, Matilda. This is my niece, Aimée Buchanan. If you are not too busy, may we come in for a moment?'

'Yes, of course, madam.' Galvanized into action, she stood back to let them past, her mind seething with curiosity. What could Mrs Mellish possibly want with her? How had she known where to find her? She swiftly shut out the prying neighbours.

'If you wouldn't mind comin' through to the back,' she

whispered. 'Only, me dad has to have the front parlour, 'cos of his bad chest.'

As she hurried down the lobby and pushed open the door, the smell of damp washing mingling with the lingering smell of boiled sheep's head wafted out, and she suddenly saw the cluttered room through their eyes. Cheeks burning, Matty rushed to clear a pile of washing off one chair and Daisy's doll off another and shyly asked them to sit down. Then, remembering her manners, she offered to make them a cup of tea, and felt a great wave of relief when Mrs Mellish, with a glance at her niece, declined.

Aimée rose again almost immediately and squeezed between an armchair and the sewing machine to reach the rocking pram beneath the window, watched with intense curiosity by a bright-eyed child who offered a bald toy dog for inspection.

'That's our little Daisy.'

'Hello, Daisy. What a lovely dog.'

'Gog,' the child repeated.

'The pram takes up a lot of room, I'm afraid, but the lobby's too narrow to take it, and it's too cold for her out in the yard, and if we let her loose, she's into mischief that fast. I'm sorry everywhere's so untidy, but it gets that way, what with all of us coming and going – and now there's my sewing things an' all . . .'

'My dear, it is I who should apologize for coming without warning,' Felicity smiled. 'But I knew nothing of what had occurred until yesterday when I called at Mrs Crawley's house. I am so very sorry. And angry. I have, of course, dispensed with her services.'

'On account of me?' Matty said, awed.

'In part. I had been considering doing so for some time. But, if what your apprentice friend Edna told me is true, and I have no reason to doubt her in spite of Mrs Crawley's protestations to the contrary, I find the reason for your dismissal quite deplorable.'

So that was how she had found out. Matty bit her lip. 'Well, to be fair, I didn't help meself much – I said some terrible things.' Righteous indignation would not be suppressed. 'But so did she!'

The girl's spirit isn't crushed, at any rate, thought Felicity. 'I believe she also tore up your beautiful sketch.'

'Oh, that. I can always draw it again, and I've got plenty more ideas . . .'

Felicity wondered if she should mention that she had seen that tiresome woman Augusta Bennett at last night's charity ball wearing an indifferent copy of Matilda's design, undoubtedly the work of Mrs Crawley, though she hadn't the imagination, or maybe the nerve, to interpret the design accurately. On balance she decided there was little point in upsetting the girl.

'But you still haven't found work?'

Dad had taken a fit of coughing. Matty stiffened and wondered if it would be impolite to leave her guests to go to him. And then she heard Mam come downstairs and go into the front room. She rushed into speech. 'It's not a good time for finding jobs, but now I have the sewing machine, and we've put cards in a lot of shop windows, I'm getting quite a bit of work I can do at home. With people expecting their menfolk home soon, they want something new to wear.'

'Splendid. Because I am now in need of a good dressmaker, and I believe we might suit one another rather well. Perhaps you could come up to the house one day next week?'

Matty's pleasure was almost immediately banished as the painful sounds coming from the front parlour intensified.

Aimée heard them, too – and saw the agony mirrored in Matty's eyes. She had only come to please her aunt, a mere spectator, but their journey had taken them past some of the meaner courts, and the deprivation she had glimpsed had been unsettling: the ground running with filth; children in rags that did nothing to disguise acute malnutrition that had little to do with wartime restrictions; there had been an emptiness in the eyes of the women who watched them pass – people for whom even the barest necessities were clearly an impossibility. And with all her nerve ends slowly coming back to life, something that was not simply conscience began to stir within her. Now, abruptly, she turned away from the pram.

'Is there anything I can do?' she said. 'I am a doctor.'

Matty had read about lady doctors, especially the famous pioneering ones like Elizabeth Garrett, but she'd always imagined them looking very mannish and severe, and a lot older than Mrs Mellish's niece. She was quite attractive, even a bit delicate-looking, in a cossack coat trimmed with fur, with matching fur hat.

'Well, I don't know.' She wanted desperately to say yes. 'He does sound proper bad – but it seems an awful cheek.'

'Not at all,' Felicity said briskly, giving swift thanks for the intervention of Fate, and allowing Aimée no time to change her mind. 'My niece is the very person you need.'

Matty led the way to the next room where her father lay, gasping and exhausted, and small wonder, Aimée thought in dismay. The room, though neat as a pin, was stuffy and airless.

'Mam, this is Dr Buchanan. She's Mrs Mellish's niece and she'd like to help.'

Agnes straightened up from the bed, her small frame rigidly defensive as she eyed the attractive, well-dressed young woman. Doctor, indeed.

'You're very kind, I'm sure, but our own Dr Hutton looks after us very well.'

'I'm sure he does, Mrs Shaw.' Aimée's eyes were sympathetic as they met the older woman's, seeing the strain beyond the indignation. Her glance moved on to the spare, white-faced man hunched over in the armchair near the fire. His bout of coughing was spent, but the aftermath was almost as distressing. 'And I would not dream of interfering. I see you are managing splendidly, but perhaps, between us, we can make Mr Shaw a little more comfortable.' She hesitated. 'Is the room usually this warm?'

'Day and night.' Agnes bristled, sensing criticism. 'The fire never goes out, so there's no chance of my Pat catching a chill, if that's what you're hinting.'

'Mam!' Matty whispered. And then, 'I'd better get back to Mrs Mellish, Doctor. Take no notice of Mam – she's just tired and worried.'

In the back room she found Mrs Mellish standing by the pram, jiggling a toy and regarding Daisy's antics with some amusement. 'A bright child,' she said. 'How many are you in all?'

'Six, not counting Mam and Dad. Our Phil's in the army, though he should be home soon, and there's Irene – she's goin' on twenty-one, and Kevin's fourteen and working on the docks, and Moira's ten. She's at school just now. And there's this little monkey.'

'I can see your mother has her hands full.' Felicity paused. 'Is your father very ill?'

'He has good days and bad days,' Matty said flatly. 'This is one of his worst, but it'll pass. This time of year's not good. So, all in all, p'raps what happened was for the best. It's a help for Mam, having me here.'

'I see.' Felicity did see, only too well. Matilda was a bright child with a talent, still raw, but a talent, nonetheless. But unless something was done, it was destined to be dissipated by the necessity to make a succession of unimaginative garments for women with little to spend. 'So you have given up any idea of finding outside employment?'

'I didn't say that, madam.' Matty's shoulders straightened, her chin lifting defensively. 'As you'll likely guess, the extra money would come in handy, and I'd still be able to carry on with me dressmaking in the evenings. But jobs aren't that easy to come by. Mam keeps saying it'll be better when our Phil comes home, but there's no guarantee he'll walk into a job. There'll be thousands like him in the same boat – and only so much work to go round.'

Again Felicity was impressed by the girl's grasp of events. She said casually, 'I asked because we have just come from Madame Vincente's in Bold Street – I'm sure that with your interest in fashion you will know of her.' Felicity's eyes twinkled. 'She is an excellent modiste. While I was there, it came to my attention that she has a vacancy for a part-time junior alteration hand.' Felicity thought it better not to mention that the volatile Frenchwoman was something of a perfectionist, and did not tolerate fools gladly. 'It is not perhaps what you had in mind, but there is no reason why you should not gain promotion once you have proved your worth.'

'And I'd be working among beautiful clothes!' There was a yearning in Matty's voice; hope leaped like a flame in her eyes, only to fade. 'Ah, but someone like me wouldn't stand a chance. Mrs Crawley wouldn't give me the time of day, let alone a reference.'

'But I would, and I venture to think my recommendation would far outstrip that of your erstwhile employer.'

'You'd do that?' There was awe in Matty's voice. 'For me?'

Felicity lifted her exquisite eyebrows. 'My dear Matilda, you have a talent. If you wish to exploit it to the full, you must begin somewhere. You must also learn not to undervalue yourself.'

'That all went rather well, I think,' Felicity settled her furs as the car began to move.

Aimée chuckled, a sound so long absent that her aunt heard it with profound relief.

'Dear Aunt Fliss, did anyone ever tell you what a formidable character you are when you take up some cause?'

'Nonsense. I'm sure I am the easiest person in the world to deal with, but I cannot abide injustice. Oh, my dear, do look at that poor child. I'm sure I never saw a worse case of rickets.'

Aimee's glance had already been drawn to the little boy in threadbare clothes shuffling along the cobbles on his poor deformed legs – and as he disappeared down an alleyway between two buildings concealing one of those infamous courts, a kind of anger stirred within her.

'Is Mr Shaw very ill?'

'I'm afraid so. Classic symptoms of consumption, made no better by the atmosphere in that room. There is almost no ventilation. I wonder their doctor has not insisted on it, though the fault may not be his. The wife is fiercely protective.'

'Well, you cannot blame her for that, my dear.'

'No, of course not. A sanatorium is the answer, of course, but I suppose that is a virtual impossibility at present, and anyway it would be too little, too late.'

Felicity heard the frustration in her niece's voice with a mixture of emotions, knowing that for the first time since her return home, Aimée was looking outwards. Frank Lomax had begun the cure, and this visit had taken it one step further in a way she could not have predicted. Felicity was truly thankful, for the possibility that Aimée might go the same way as Toby had lingered at the back of her mind. Now all doubt had been removed. The cure, once begun, would soon gather pace, and for Aimée's sake she must be glad. But she would miss her when she returned home.

Although her busy life left her little time to brood, Felicity missed the company of young people. Her elder daughter, Sophie, was married and living in Cheltenham, and, at fifteen, Celia was too young to share her mother's confidences. As for her sons, Giles was her first-born and special for that reason, but somewhere between boarding school and the army, she had lost the closeness that they had once enjoyed. Now, like his father, he was totally self-sufficient, his life dedicated first and foremost to the army. As for Toby – she sighed.

'Are you all right, Aunt Fliss?'

Felicity roused herself. 'Yes, dear, of course. I was thinking of poor Toby.'

'Oh, I'm sorry. How selfish of me not to ask. Is he no better?'

'He is no worse.' It wasn't like Felicity to sound indecisive. 'I just wish I could be sure that everything is being done that could be done. Your uncle insists that he is in the right place, and they are all very kind.' She could hardly air the growing conviction that with George it was a case of out of sight, out of mind; that her husband was in fact ashamed of Toby.

But Aimée needed no telling. It was not uncommon for parents, especially fathers, to reject any form of mental breakdown. And George Mellish was the kind of man for whom the stigma of anything smacking of cowardice would be unacceptable. She remembered what a stickler for discipline he had always been with the boys – and how often Toby had fallen short of his high standards.

Even so, and much as she sympathized, Aimée told herself that it wasn't her problem. And yet, as the Rolls turned in at the gates and bowled up towards the house, she heard herself saying, 'Aunt Fliss, would you like me to go with you the next time you visit Toby?'

There was a flurry of furs, and her hand was grasped almost convulsively as her beautiful aunt, who managed everyone else's problems with such ease, said in a choked whisper, 'Oh, darling, would you really? It would mean so much to me – and to Toby, I'm sure.'

Aimée was less sure. In fact, she was already regretting the impulse of the moment. But looking into her aunt's over-bright eyes, she could not retract.

Before the Rolls had reached the end of the street, Dolly McBride was knocking at the door, her raddled face alive with curiosity.

'I wus wonderin', like, how you'd gorr'on with me skirt an' blouse, Matty, gairl,' she said, easing her bulky figure along the passage. ' 'Cos I could spare five minutes fer a fittin', if you want.'

'Very noble of you, I'm sure,' said Agnes, coming through from the scullery.

'Not at all. I knew yer wus in, with that fine posh motor car parked outside. I said to Brenda – Bren, I said, if that's the kind of customer our Matty's after attractin', I'd better be makin' sure of me place in the queue.'

'Mr McBride comin' home earlier than you thought, is he?' Matty asked, evading her roundabout prying with an ease born of long practice.

'Well, he could be. Yer never know.' Dolly's beaming smile revealed an unfortunate gap in her teeth. 'It's as well ter be prepared.'

'Likely,' Agnes sniffed. 'I hope you've thought to warn that Eric Bagshott. Wouldn't do to get caught in the act, would it?'

The vast bosom heaved. 'Eric's a good friend, an' nothin more, as well you know.'

Matty decided it was time to change the subject. 'I'm sorry about the skirt and blouse, Mrs McBride. They aren't properly cut out yet.'

'Got fancier fish to fry, I dare say. Them sort think they've only got ter crook their little finger, an' everyone else can wait.'

'I said the end of this week,' Matty said, 'and that's when they'll be ready. I'll come over and fit the skirt this evening, like I promised.'

The knocker on the front door rattled impatiently.

'Eh, yer popular today. Who is it this time, I wonder – the Lord Mayor?'

She showed no sign of shifting, so Matty exchanged an exasperated glance with her mother and left the room, closing the door firmly behind her.

'All right, I'm coming,' she called as the knocker sounded again.

'Shaw?' A skinny post boy was holding out a flimsy orange envelope. For a moment her mouth went dry and the world spun dizzily about her. But the war was over. They'd had all the celebrations and everything. God couldn't be that cruel. Most likely it was from Phil, to say when he'd be home.

'Here.' Embarrassed, the boy pushed the envelope into her hand and rode off whistling loudly, his old boneshaker wobbling and skittering over the cobbles.

Still Matty lingered in the lobby, until her father's voice, weak but clear, called out to her. She slipped the envelope into the pocket of her pinafore, closed the door and went to him.

'Is there something you want, Dad?' she asked, making her voice as bright as she could.

Father and daughter looked at one another without speaking. Then he held out a shaky hand.

'Let's be having it then, Matty love.'

'I don't – ' she began, but there was no fooling Dad.

'Lass, I saw him go past the window,' he said gently. 'We don't want your mam opening it in front of Mrs McBride, do we? Just in case.'

Slowly, Matty took the envelope out of her pocket and handed it over: watched him open it and read the contents in a silence broken only by the wheezing in his chest. Then he leaned his head back against the cushion. His eyes were closed, but a tear squeezed out and ran down his ashen cheek.

Terror crawled up Matty's spine as she took the bit of paper from his inert hand. '. . . regret to inform you that Sergeant Philip Shaw sustained injuries in the last courageous action of his brigade, which tragically have proved fatal . . .'

'Why couldn't it have been me?' She had never heard her father's voice so bitter. 'I'm no use to anyone.'

8

CEDAR GRANGE WASN'T as bad as Aimée had expected: a secure nursing home, they called it, and certainly the iron gates set in the high walls were a daunting deterrent to anyone attempting an unauthorized exit.

'This is the part I hate most,' Felicity whispered as a man in uniform, summoned by a bell, came to unlock the gates. 'Like visiting a prison.'

But as the Rolls purred along a winding drive bordered by the majestic trees that gave the house its name, and the building came into view, Aimée was somewhat heartened to see, not a fortress, but a large gracious house blending into the Cheshire countryside, its walls mellowed by time and softened by a sprawl of ivy.

'There is a very pretty terrace at the back,' Felicity said, eager to justify her husband's choice. 'And lawns. In the better weather, the . . . patients are free to go where they please – even garden a little, if they choose to. Toby is developing quite a gift with plants, you know.'

They found him among a dozen or so uninterested patients in a large room with two bay windows through which the pale winter sunlight streamed. He was sitting alone near one of the windows, his pale straight hair flopping across his forehead, his too-thin frame painfully obvious beneath the ill-fitting regulation blue uniform.

'Darling, see who I have brought with me.' Felicity's voice, echoing in the unnatural silence, was so normal that only someone who knew her could know how much the effort cost her.

'Toby, it's good to see you.' Aimée bent to brush his forehead with her lips, and was rewarded by a flicker of recognition in the lacklustre eyes, a hint of colour in the pale concave cheeks.

'Aim – m – mée.'

She had seen many men reduced to this kind of pitiful incoherence – men for whom the horror had all become too much. She had long since schooled herself to accept it, to stand back and be objective. So she was totally unprepared for the wave of quite appalling anger that shook her. For this shambling travesty of a man was Toby, the gentle artistic boy with whom she had played, shared secrets with in the long summer holidays, defended from the bully-ragging Giles, who with the amiable contempt of an extrovert elder brother, mistook sensitivity for weakness. Toby had enlisted, not like Giles from hubristic motives, to lead others to death and glory, but as an ordinary Tommy, subduing his abhorrence of violence in order to do his duty for King and country, oblivious of what was to come. She had met his kind a thousand times – gentle patriots sent out by mindless politicians to become cannon fodder.

Aimée's throat closed up painfully, and it took every ounce of her professional skill to control her emotions and behave in a cheerful friendly way. He stumblingly managed Gerald's name and she was able to tell him that they had heard from him at last, and that he was well.

The conversation was virtually one-sided, but her aunt was quite wonderful, reminding Toby that it would soon be Christmas, telling him about the family, and the baby that his sister Sophie was expecting in the spring – and a fund of amusing anecdotes arising out of her charitable committee work. He would smile occasionally, and attempt some comment, but his inability to frame a sentence without stumbling over the words obviously distressed him. And Aimée noticed that her aunt never mentioned Uncle George or Giles, or anything remotely concerned with the war.

As they left, however, Toby touched her arm. 'You'll c-c-come again?'

And she promised she would.

On the return journey, Felicity leaned her head back against the soft leather squabs and closed her eyes. Aimée was relieved, for she needed time to think. The visit to the nursing home had shaken her badly, made her ashamed of her continuing indolence. Toby and his fellow sufferers had no choice in the matter. But she was deliberately wasting the talents she had been given.

Felicity sighed and sat up, smoothing the back of her hair. 'Give me a cigarette, there's a dear.' And as Aimée flicked open her black enamel case with its little gold monogram, she took one with fingers that shook. 'How did you think Toby seemed?'

She had been dreading the question. 'It's hard to tell on such a brief visit. Has he improved at all, Aunt Fliss?'

'Some days are more encouraging than others. Thank you.' Felicity leaned towards the lighter flame, inhaled deeply and allowed the smoke to trickle out in a gentle cloud. 'Ah, that's better. Today was not one of Toby's good days. He is used to my visits, you see, but although he was undoubtedly pleased to see you, I think it also made him more conscious of his affliction.'

'Yes.' Aimée glanced at the thick glass partition separating them from the chauffeur. 'What does he do all day?'

'Matron says he paints a lot. You remember he used to paint those nice little flower pictures when he was young.' Felicity's brow increased. 'I don't think these are quite the same. In fact, well, she won't let me see them. I gather they are . . . well, the doctor is of the opinion that Toby is working something out of his system.'

Aimée had a good idea what they would be like, but perhaps on her next visit, she would ask to see them. 'Does anyone else go to see him?'

The question seemed to imply accusation. Her aunt flushed and said, 'It isn't that easy, my dear. Sophie is too far away, and Celia is too young. As for anyone else, you know how difficult Toby always found it to make friends. Andrew goes occasionally, of course – '

'And Uncle George?'

Felicity hesitated, not wishing to show her husband in a bad light. 'He is in London a great deal,' she began defensively, but Aimée was not so easily fooled. 'He went once,' she admitted with a tiny shrug. 'When Toby was first admitted, but he was so ill at ease that he did more harm than good. I confess I have never suggested it since.'

'I see.'

'I wonder if you do, my dear? Your uncle has many excellent qualities, and it isn't that he doesn't care. He loves all his children – he simply doesn't understand.'

He never did, thought Aimée.

'It would be different if Toby had lost a limb or – ' Felicity swallowed convulsively and put up a hand to clutch her furs tightly about her neck ' – or suffered some physical disability that one could recognize as evidence of – ' She paused, then stubbed her half-smoked cigarette out, straightened her furs and said defiantly, 'But I'm sure he knows in his heart that Toby is not mad, or guilty of cowardice.'

'Of course he does. I didn't mean to sound critical. Uncle George isn't alone, you know. A lot of people find it difficult coping with mental breakdown in their loved ones.' Aimée heard her aunt sigh. 'But Toby will improve, given time.'

'Oh, my dear, do you really think so?'

It was perhaps foolish to raise hopes that might not be fulfilled, but nor could she bring herself to dash the springing joy in her aunt's over-bright eyes.

'Yes, I really do. Oh, it won't happen overnight, but – '

'Dear Aimée, you are such a comfort. And you will visit Toby again, as you promised?'

'Indeed I will.' There was a positive note in Aimée's voice, something her aunt hadn't heard in a long time.

It came as no surprise therefore when, after a pause, Aimée said, 'Aunt Fliss, you have been wonderful to me, and I shall be forever grateful, but it's high time I stopped malingering – '

A gloved hand came swiftly to cover hers. 'Darling, as if you could ever be guilty of such a thing!'

'Nevertheless, I have to pick up the threads of my life again.'

'Yes. I shall miss you, of course, though I have been expecting something of the sort for several days now. What will you do?'

'For a start I must go home. Mother has been incredibly patient.' Aimée smiled wryly. 'Encouraged by you, I suspect. But with Christmas almost on us and no sign of Gerald getting leave, I must do what I can to make amends. Doc Lomax will be glad of my help, so I can be of use. Beyond that – well, we shall have to see.'

Agnes Shaw let herself in quietly and leaned against the front door in order to master her feelings before facing Pat. The fight had gone right out of him ever since that telegram, no matter how hard she chivvied or coaxed. One day she had almost screamed at him:

'Phil was my son, too, Patrick Shaw! I'm feeling every bit as bad as you, but someone has to keep going, look after you, feed the kids.' And then she looked into his eyes, which were filled with suffering, and bit the words back just in time.

But it was hard, putting on a front when your heart was breaking into little pieces. In trying to be a good mother, she had always told herself it was wrong to have favourites, but Phil was her first-born, and he'd grown into such a fine young man. Now she went to mass for the children's sake, and because it would grieve Pat if she didn't, but she was finding it increasingly hard to believe in a God who could snatch that young life away with nothing to show – not even a grave she could tend. Sometimes she imagined she could hear Phil's voice – 'Don't worry, Mam, when this is over I'll look after you all . . .' She dragged her thoughts back yet again from the abyss.

It had been a terrible few weeks, made worse by the almost daily arrival home of someone's husband or son. And it didn't help knowing that there was hardly a street untouched by tragedy. She'd seen evidence of that only this afternoon. That poor young Mrs Reagan, no one should have to bear a burden like hers!

In the back room Marge Flynn looked up from turning the clothes on the maiden, her eyes like two plump shiny raisins thumbed into a roly-poly face framed by a motley assortment of rag curlers, Friday being her night out at The Anchor with Fred.

'Eh, chuck, yer luk frozen ter the marrow!'

Agnes dumped her shopping basket unceremoniously on the table, pulled off her gloves and began to drag angrily at her coat buttons. 'The snow's freezing hard. I looked in on Pat, but he was asleep. Just as well, perhaps. I don't think I could have faced him right now.'

'You are het up.' Marge moved the maiden to one side and dragged the armchair forward, her rolls of fat, the legacy of ten children in quick succession, quivering with the effort. 'Come an' get yerself warm an' I'll make us a brew while you get it off yer chest, whatever it is.'

But Agnes, unable to relax, took the poker to the fire, stirring the coals viciously, then set about unpacking her shopping, rattling tins on the cupboard shelves as she made room for more.

'Honest, Marge, if someone could prove to me that our Phil

would have ended up like Danny Reagan, I could maybe resign meself to his going. I've just seen his Nellie wheeling him out in a bathchair, and it near turned my stomach. He's only half a man, and them only two years wed and a kiddie hardly out of the pram. It doesn't bear thinking of.'

'So that's what's got yer all worked up. Poor sod. I 'eard they was lettin' Danny home fer Christmas, to see how they gorron, managing him, like.'

'Some Christmas they're going to have! As for us, I never felt less like celebrating. If it wasn't for the kids – '

'Mammy, Mammy!' Daisy was bouncing up and down in her pram, arms outstretched, fingers working.

'Hush, chucky – yer mammy's tired.'

'It's all right, Marge.' Agnes gathered the child close, comforted by the small warm body settling itself against her and the sound of a thumb being vigorously sucked. 'I'm not tired, just flamin' angry. I mean, it's such a waste. There's our Phil dead, and thousands besides him – and there must be tens of thousands more like Danny Reagan, condemned to a living death. And for what? I never have been able to understand what it was all in aid of.'

'Eh, well, it's no good lukin' at me, Aggie, girl. I'm as much in the dark as you. The clever politicians'll give yer reasons till they come out of yer ears, an' yer none the wiser at the end of it. Come on now. Tek the weight off yer feet an' get this down yer while it's hot.'

Agnes lowered herself into the armchair, put her feet on the fender and took the proferred mug. Daisy stirred, nuzzled her neck, then drifted into sleep. 'You're a good soul, Marge. I don't know what I'd do without you.'

A throaty chuckle set the rolls of fat quivering. 'Yer might tell that to my lot sometime.' Marge cocked a thumb at the wall on the lobby side as the noise level rose. 'Yer can hear school's out. Still, they're not so bad, all things considered. Even if they do sometimes sound as if they're 'alf killin' one another.' Marge strode across the room and banged on the wall. 'Hey, shurrup, you lot.'

'Look, if you want to get back, I'll be fine now. Matty should be home any time.'

'Well, if you're sure. Only them little tikes don't always mind our Ethel like they ought.' Marge took her shawl off the hook, draped it over the rag curlers and wrapped it deftly across and round her ample curves. 'Any sign of your Irene gettin' a job yet?'

'No.' Agnes sighed. 'She reckons there's nothing to be had.'

'A pretty girl like her shouldn't have any trouble.'

'That's what I say. Trouble is, there's plenty more like her. *And* she's been spoiled, what with the munitions paying so well, and that Eddie Brighouse givin' her big ideas, goin' on all the time about starting his own business and wantin' her to help him run it. I've told her, I'm not holding me breath.'

'It's a good job your Matty's doing so well.'

'That doesn't please our Irene none, either. She always poohed-poohed my saying that we might one day be glad of Matty's skills, but I was right. We'd be in queer street without her at present, and no mistake.'

Marge cocked her head at the dressmaker's dummy, enveloped in a huge cloth. 'That's a bonny-lookin' frock. I had a quick peek.'

'I shan't have a moment's peace until it's finished and away from here where sticky fingers can't get at it. The material cost a fortune! It's for a lady up Sefton Park way.' A note of pride crept into Agnes's voice. 'Recommended by that Mrs Mellish. When our Matty first started going up to her house to do some sewing, I was afraid she'd be getting big ideas, but the lass has got her head screwed on right, and it's led to one or two more commissions like that one. And it's thanks to Mrs Mellish that she got the job in that swanky dress shop, mornings. So, all in all, with a steady stream of customers answering the adverts we put out, Matty's got as much work as she can handle.'

That evening, after tea, the subject of Christmas came up again. Irene had gone out with Eddie, and Daisy was in bed and fast asleep. Matty was painstakingly tucking the bodice of the frock she was making while Kevin polished the shoes and Moira helped her mother to fold some clothes.

'It's only a week off, Mam,' Kevin said, 'an' we haven't done nothin' about decorations.'

'I've more things to think of than decorations, my lad.'

'Oh, but Mam – '

'Will you stop going on?'

Matty threw her mother a quick look, aware that she'd been

more on edge than usual all evening. 'We'll see what we can do about it this weekend,' she said. 'You and me and Moira.'

'Miss was showin' us how we could make them out of newspaper coloured with crayons,' Moira put in quickly, before Mam could say they couldn't afford it. She was rewarded by a smile from Matty.

'Splendid. And if the weather's fine, we'll maybe take the tram to Aigburth after church on Sunday and see if we can find some greenery.'

'Hey, that'd be great.' Kevin glanced warily at his mother. 'An' we *will* be hanging our stockings up, won't we?'

'At your age? You're a working lad now, and old enough to have grown out of all that nonsense. And if you've finished those shoes, you'd best get to the sink and wash your hands before you get fingermarks on these clean clothes,' Agnes said repressively, pausing in her folding to ease her aching back. 'Anyway, I doubt there be any money to spare for presents this year.'

Kevin and Moira exchanged horrified looks, and Moira's face crumpled as she valiantly tried to hold back tears.

'But, Mam, what about Daisy? She won't know it's Christmas if we don't have stockings.'

'Talk sense, child. Daisy's too young to bother about presents. Anyway, that's not what Christmas is about. It's a holy feast to celebrate the birth of Jesus.'

'Well, I think Jesus'd want us to have presents. An' if he was here with us now, I think he'd be proper fed up, 'cos we never have any fun any more.'

It was so unlike Moira to rebel that for a moment no one spoke, although the air was charged with angry vibrations. In the silence Pat's rasping breathing could be clearly heard through the wall.

'I think you'd better go to bed, miss,' Agnes said, tight-lipped.

'I'm goin' anyway,' Moira cried and rushed from the room.

Matty didn't know who she felt more sorry for, as her mother sank into a chair with something that sounded like a sob, and put a hand to her head.

'I didn't mean to snap the child's head off. It's just – I've been really down all day today.'

'It's okay, Mam, I understand. So does Moira, really.'

'If we're short, Mr Fearn down the pie shop'd be glad of some extra help, evenings,' Kevin offered, embarrassed. He'd taken on the extra job when Irene had left the munitions. 'He reckons I'm gettin' ter be a dab hand with the pastry. And I'll help cook the Christmas dinner. I quite enjoy cookin'.'

'And I'll have quite a bit coming in, what with this dress and the others I've got ordered for Christmas.'

Agnes uttered a great sigh and looked up. 'You're good children. I don't know what I've done to deserve you.'

'Gerrof,' Matty said with a grin. 'You'll have us blubbing next. I'll pop up to have a word with Moira. She's such a practical child, we tend to forget how young she is. But she's not one for holding grudges.'

She found Moira curled up on the narrow bed. She hadn't lit the gas, but moonlight filtering through the frost-encrusted window illuminated the small shivering body. Matty pulled the eiderdown up to cover her sister's thin shoulders, then sat down and stroked back the fine flyaway hair that had escaped her plaits.

'This isn't going to be an easy Christmas for Mam, you know. And it's not just about money. Our Phil's death is still too close, and she's bound to be remembering other Christmases when Dad was fit and we were all together. It's not that she loves any one of us less than she loved Phil. But he was always a bit special to her. Being the eldest, she kind of looked to him with Dad being the way he is, so she must be grieving badly inside.'

'Oh!' Moira lifted her head, her drenched eyes wide with distress. 'I hadn't thought about that. Oh, poor Mam!'

'Yes, but you mustn't let on we've guessed,' Matty said, swiftly, fearing an excess of zeal, for Moira never did anything by halves. 'Let's just pray for a little bit of magic to make everything right. See – ' She drew her sister's gaze to the window where the intricate medallions of frost sparkled like diamonds, each one different. 'If God can make something that beautiful, I expect he can make our Christmas special.'

It was getting on for ten o'clock when Irene came in, by which time Kevin had gone to bed, too, and Matty and her mother were sitting down together, enjoying a cup of cocoa. They heard her slam the door and come running down the lobby.

'That sister of yours!' Agnes lifted her head angrily as the door burst open. 'Irene, whatever are you thinking of? I'll give you what for if you disturb your dad!'

But her eldest daughter was clearly too excited to be repressed. Her face was aglow, her eyes sparkled. 'Mam, oh, Mam! You'll never believe it.'

For the first time they saw Eddie hovering in the doorway. Irene grabbed his hand and dragged him into the room. 'Eddie's asked me to marry him and I've said I will. Oh, I can, can't I, Mam?'

You could have cut the silence with a knife, Matty thought. She broke it by running to hug her sister. 'Trust you to spring a surprise like that! Oh, Irene, I've always wanted to design a wedding dress. I'll make you the loveliest one you ever saw!'

'Well, you'll have to get a move on, 'cos we don't want to have to wait ages.'

'Not so fast, with all this talk of weddings,' Agnes said, eyeing the young man in front of her with something less than enthusiasm.

Eddie Brighouse was a stocky young man in his mid-twenties, with shrewd eyes, an air of confidence, and a full moustache that disguised a thin-lipped mouth. His overcoat was a passable copy of an officer's greatcoat, and he wore it with a bit of a swagger.

He had escaped active service through a knee injury he'd got playing football. It had left him with a slight limp that Irene had always thought glamorous. He'd been courting her on a fairly regular basis for some months, but he'd never struck Agnes as the marrying kind.

'This is all a bit sudden,' she said, getting wearily to her feet. 'No particular reason for the rush, I hope?'

'Mam!' Irene flounced angrily across the room and flung her coat over a chair. 'How could you? As if Eddie and me'd do such a thing!'

But she avoided meeting her mother's eyes and Matty caught a glimpse of the guilty blush that stained her cheeks. Surely Irene wasn't – couldn't . . . That really would put the tin lid on things.

'Stranger things have happened, miss – and I'll thank you to hang that coat up where it belongs. You'd better hang Eddie's up as well. We've got some talking to do.'

'I realize this must come as a bit of a shock, Mrs Shaw – '

'You could say that,' Agnes agreed dryly.

'Eddie's got the chance to buy a bicycle shop, Mam. It's up Walton way, and there's some nice big rooms above we can live in.' Irene's voice had taken on the wheedling note they all knew so well. 'And since I'm going to help him run the shop, there doesn't seem any sense waiting.'

'The place is a bargain, Mrs Shaw. I've had my eye on it for some time. The old fella who owns it has let it go, but I reckon it's a really good spec. I've got big plans for it. And you know how I feel about Rene.'

The nickname grated on Agnes. 'That's as maybe, Eddie, but as to marriage, her father will need to be consulted, and I can't possibly put a thing like that to him this time of night.'

When all was quiet at last, she went in to settle Pat down for the night. He was lying with his face turned to the wall, something that was happening more and more since Phil . . . She shook her head. He had taken it worse than any of them, perhaps because he had more time to dwell on it.

Her heart hollowed with grief and pity, and for a moment she longed to be somewhere far away, where she could let go of her grief, be waited on, not have to be strong for everybody else. As well ask for the moon, she thought, straightening her shoulders.

'Ah, come on now, Pat.' She put down the bowl of water, and spread out the towel on the fender to warm, her voice firm, her manner brisk. 'You know you'll sleep better after a sponge down.'

'Sleep.' His bitter voice, muffled by the pillow, was painful to hear. 'Sure, sleeping and coughing me heart up is all I'm good for. The sooner I'm under the sod, the better off you'll all be.'

'That's a terrible thing to say! I never thought I'd hear rubbish like that coming from you. A right old misery guts, that's what you're turning into.' Agnes sat on the edge of the bed and put a hand on his shaking shoulders, feeling the brittleness of his bones. Her voice softened. 'Listen, Pat. D'you think I don't know what's eating you? I know, right enough, for the same thing's eating away at me. But giving up on yourself isn't going to bring our boy back.' She felt him shudder. 'And there's maybe worse things than dying.' She told him about Danny Reagan. 'You wouldn't have wanted that for our Phil, now, would you?'

After a minute or so, he turned onto his back. In the lamplight she saw the tears, and when he spoke, his voice was choked with them.

'I don't know what I ever did to deserve you, Aggie, my love, but by God, I'm glad I've got you.'

9

IT WAS THE middle of February before Gerald came home to a
Crag Vale powdered with fresh snow. And he did not come
alone.

'Mother, Aimée,' he said sheepishly, stooping to kiss each in
turn. 'This is Megan. I did write to you about her.'

His companion was almost as tall as himself, slim but cur-
vaceous in a soft blue coat that bespoke Paris in every line, with a
matching hat perched on pretty dark hair, and eyes that held a
wariness in their clear grey depths. As if, Aimée thought, she was
not entirely sure of her welcome.

'My dear.' Minna Buchanan rose gracefully from her chair, the
folds of her peach-bloom tea gown settling about her plump figure
as she held out her hands, gold bracelets jingling amongst a flutter
of lace. 'What a lovely surprise. Of course we have heard all about
you, but it was wicked of Gerald not to tell us he was bringing you
home with him.'

Megan had been slow to remove her gloves, and when she did so
the reason was immediately obvious. Aimée saw the wedding ring
before her mother did. Her eyes lifted accusingly to her brother,
and he returned the look with a mute appeal for help.

'Wicked, Gerald, indeed,' she exclaimed, swallowing her indignation and striving for the right degree of enthusiasm. 'But,
goodness, how exciting! Mother dear, isn't this exciting? You
have a new daughter and I a new sister – just like a rabbit out of a
hat! Oh my dear Megan, I didn't mean . . .'

She was talking too fast, she knew, but hopefully it would give
her mother time to recover from the shock and collect her wits.

Minna, however, heard not a word. Her mind was striving to
cope with a whirl of cherished plans and expectations fast
vanishing into a void; of a grand wedding, now destined not to be

realized. She had guessed from Gerald's letter that he was serious about Megan. It had to happen sometime, and as long as she was right for him, a mother could not ask for more. Meanwhile, it was never too early to begin preparations. Now, suddenly, there was no guest list to be pored over with infinite pleasure, no finery to be chosen with exquisite care, no pomp. Instead, a young woman she had not set eyes on until a few moments ago . . .

'Darling, do come and sit down.'

Aimée's voice was gentle, but firm. Minna allowed herself to be led to a chair, and sank into it gratefully. A voice with a soft Welsh lilt was saying anxiously, 'Can I help?' and Gerald was there, too, with a glass of brandy. Her china-blue eyes opened wide as she sat up and waved it away.

'No, no, dear boy. You know I hate the stuff. Tell Joshua to bring champagne – oh, and he must send someone immediately to fetch your father.'

This sudden recovery made Megan blink, but brother and sister exchanged a rueful knowing smile.

'Well, now. Let me look at you properly, my dear. Gerald is very naughty – he knows too much excitement is not good for my heart.'

Minna, quite unaware of the lingering amusement in her children's eyes, had turned her attention to her new daughter-in-law, who was regarding her with a very proper concern. A charming girl, she thought, approving her taste in clothes, her femininity. As one who saw beauty in soft curves and delicate pastels, Minna deplored the passion of the new breed of young women, Aimée included, who seemed to delight in looking like sticks in their stark shapeless tunics that showed a good six inches above the ankle.

'I'm sorry our news came as such a shock, Mrs Buchanan. I told Gerald he should have let you know we were married.' Megan was deferential without being the least ingratiating. 'It was a spur-of-the-moment decision. We were in Paris, you see, and quite suddenly we knew that we couldn't bear to be apart a moment longer.'

'Ah, what it is to be young,' Minna sighed.

'How clever of your bride to appeal to Ma's strong romantic streak,' Aimée murmured in her brother's ear. 'Your suggestion, I take it?'

'What an old cynic you are. Megan isn't like that.' His voice softened. 'Are you angry that I didn't let you know?'

'Furious,' she replied, only half joking.

'My marriage won't make any difference to us, I promise.'

Oh, but it will, dear boy, she thought, with a stab of fierce possessive jealousy. Twin or no twin, your wife will see to that. But men could be very naïve about such things. He was watching her face anxiously.

'You will be kind to Megan?'

'To Megan – yes, of course, but I'm not at all sure I've forgiven you.'

Megan had, as she knew from her brother's letters, been a VAD in France. They had met when he went to visit a fellow officer in hospital, and presumably had fallen in love there and then. Envy and a whole host of other emotions crowded in as memory momentarily swamped Aimée. She pushed them away, and gave his hand a reassuring squeeze.

'She had better make you happy, dear boy – that's all.'

'She will. She does.'

Seth Buchanan arrived at that moment with Joshua and the champagne, his manner abrupt as always, though there was no disguising his pleasure in having his son home, safe and unscathed, or his pride in the distinctive DSO ribbon adorning Gerald's uniform coat. To his daughter-in-law he was quietly courteous and welcoming.

'A dinner party,' Minna was saying, clapping her hands with delight amid the flurry of popping champagne corks. 'These dear children are here for a whole week, and since I have been denied a wedding,' she added playfully, 'we must have some kind of celebration. Next weekend, do you think, Seth?'

'As you please, lass. I leave all that sort of fancy nonsense to you.'

He still looks tired, Aimée thought.

'Dad is all right, isn't he?' Gerald asked under cover of her mother's excited chatter.

'No, but he won't be told – not by Frank Lomax, and certainly not by me. Early in January he had a bad bout of Spanish flu. It's left him debilitated, though he won't admit to any weakness. He just takes refuge in anger if I try to reason with him. To be honest,

I'll be glad when you're home for good to take some of the weight of the business off his shoulders. Do you know when that will be?'

'Not long. We are going on from here to see Megan's family. Just a short visit. Her father has a sheep farm, so it's a busy time for him. The minute we get back, I'll see what I can do to hurry things up – plead extenuating circumstances, if necessary.'

Just for a moment his voice sounded edgy. But before she could pin it down, he was glancing across the room, saying with a kind of smug satisfaction, 'Megan seems to be doing a good job on the parents. I knew they'd get on. Meg's a real country girl at heart.' And the moment was gone.

Aimée also turned her attention to the small group. Megan and her mother were deep in conversation, while her father sat quietly looking on. A perfect family group, and Megan bidding to be a perfect daughter, her face animated as she discussed the forthcoming party. Again jealousy shot through Aimée. I ought to be glad, she thought. It will solve a lot of problems for me – make my decision so much easier to broach.

Since her return home before Christmas she had been helping Frank Lomax. The flu epidemic hadn't struck as hard in Crag Vale as it had in the larger towns and cities. There had been no fatalities, though once or twice they had come pretty close, as with her father.

It had never been said in so many words, but she knew that a partnership with her old friend and confidant, here in her own little corner of the world, was what everyone wanted and expected of her. For a while she had been prepared to settle for that, but now she was herself again and the world beyond Crag Vale beckoned once more.

'You do see, don't you?' she pleaded with Frank Lomax, broaching the subject the next day. 'It isn't that I don't enjoy working with you. I do. But it isn't . . . there isn't . . .'

'Enough challenge?' he suggested dryly.

'Exactly. I knew you'd understand! But mother won't. She'll never be able to comprehend this need in me that has to be fulfilled.'

'She'll come round to the idea, lass. Once Gerald is back for good with his bride, Minna'll be that made up, she won't have time to mope. As for me, it seems I'll just have to put off sitting back with my feet up for a bit longer.'

She laughed. 'That'll be the day.'

'I'll be sorry to lose you, but I've waited a long time to see that light come back into your eyes.' He regarded her quizzically. 'You'll study for your Fellowship, of course. And with the hospitals run off their feet, it shouldn't be too difficult to get a surgical post.'

'No, Frank. Not that.'

He was shaken by the vehemence in her voice. 'Ah. So that's the way of it still? Well now, maybe you should do something about it pretty sharp.'

'What do you suggest?' she demanded bitterly. 'It's not exactly like falling off a horse, is it? There is no magic remedy for loss of nerve. I've finally faced the fact that, the way I feel right now, I wouldn't even pass a preliminary interview.' Her words fell into a pool of silence, and anger drove her to almost childish defiance. 'Anyway, surgery isn't everything.'

Abruptly, he turned away from her and went to stare down into the fire. When he spoke there was a fierceness about his voice that took her by surprise. 'I remember a girl full of fire and enthusiasm, a young woman with special skills for whom surgery *was* everything. And I tell you now, Aimée Buchanan, such skills are not given to us to be wasted.' He turned to face her and she saw the raw emotion in his eyes. 'That's why I fought tooth and nail to get you into medical school – a move you repaid by justifying my faith in you one hundred per cent – and that's why I say now, don't let this thing defeat you. There are plenty of run-of-the-mill doctors like me to tend the masses – '

'You're not run of the mill!' she cried passionately. 'You care, really care about people. And you taught me to care. Surely that is more important than anything else?'

There was an almost desperate note of pleading in her voice. Frank heard it and realized that her shell of confidence was more fragile than he had supposed, and that he had come very close to cracking it, old fool that he was. His expression softened. 'It is indeed, lass. Maybe I was in danger of forgetting that. So, what *will* you do?'

Aimée's cold tremors subsided, and she became positive once more. 'Well, I've spent a good deal of my free time recently walking round Liverpool, and – oh Frank, the conditions I found in some of the worst areas so appalled me that I've decided to open a practice there, specifically aimed at the most needy. I have some money that Grandma Aimée left me – '

His abrupt shout of laughter brought her to a halt. 'I might have known you wouldn't take the easy way.' Then, sobering just as suddenly: 'But think carefully, lass. You could find yourself treading on some sensitive toes, not least among your own kind.'

'I know, but I've made up my mind.'

'Ah well, then there's no more to be said.' He chuckled suddenly. 'Your mother'll have a fit.'

Minna had overcome her disappointment about the wedding, and her mind was now full of the forthcoming dinner party. Aimée decided it would be cruel to upset her again so soon. This decision was confirmed when she arrived home to find her mother with her new daughter-in-law in the drawing room in happy disorder, surrounded by invitations.

She made her apologies and escaped to her room, where she lay on the pink velvet chaise longue, yet another of Minna's additions to the already over-embellished decor, relaxing and enjoying a cigarette.

Presently she heard sounds of animated greetings as Aunt Felicity arrived, and was torn by a desire to see her aunt, and the temptation to remain in peaceful isolation.

Her thoughts turned to Gerald. With his bride usefully occupied, he had taken to spending a considerable amount of time down at the mill office, and seemed outwardly content. But increasingly she had heard him moving about during the early hours of the morning. Nothing was said, and as Megan's brow remained unclouded by worry, Aimée supposed she either slept through her husband's night-time perambulations, or was not troubled by them. The question vexing Aimée was – should she interfere?

Before his marriage, such a question would not have arisen. Now, in subtle ways, she was increasingly being reminded that Megan took precedence in Gerald's life, and it was more than possible that any attempt to voice her concern to Megan might be construed as interference.

A tentative knock disturbed Aimée's thoughts. She called 'Come in', and a pretty blonde girl put her head round the door.

'I'm not disturbing you, am I?' she asked in a breathy voice. 'Only Aunt Minna said it was all right to come up.'

'Of course, Celia. Come in, do.' Aimée drew on her cigarette, and as the ribbon of smoke curled lazily upwards, she was aware of Celia eyeing the ornate ebony holder with some envy.

Felicity's youngest child was very much in awe of her splendid cousin. Celia still remembered with affection the young Aimée who had always found time to play with her when she was small, but once she had become a weekly boarder and Aimée had gone away to be a doctor, their paths had seldom crossed. She had, however, heard her father going on at great length about Aimée's exploits in France, which he dismissed as unsuitable and un-womanly, but which she considered quite magnificent, as did all her friends at school, who had listened wide-eyed to idealized accounts of her cousin's bravery under fire.

A surreptitious glance round the gorgeous cream and pink room provided new delight to feed Celia's fertile imagination – wisps of lacy underwear scattered across the bed and chairs with flagrant abandon, fine silks and slippery satins in the palest prettiest colours, and – wickedest of all – black crepe de Chine that she longed to touch, quite unlike her own black stockinette knickers, liberty bodice and flannel petticoats. Even Mama did not possess anything quite so dashing. Astonishment was tinged with desire as she dragged her gaze away from the finery and cornflower-blue eyes met laughing pansy-dark ones.

'Scrumptious, aren't they? But not for someone of your tender years.'

'Don't you freeze in this sort of weather?'

'Frequently.'

Aimée smiled as she stubbed out her cigarette, and swung her feet to the floor. She stood up and held out a hand.

'Come on. Shall we go down and see how the party preparations are coming along?'

That same day, with the winter sun shining out of a windswept sky, Matty felt her spirits lift as she made her way down the passage from Madame Vincente's back sewing rooms into Bold Street.

She sometimes wondered how she would have managed these

past weeks, busy as she was, without her few hours every morning at Madame Vincente's. Not that she was allowed anywhere near a customer, or permitted to stitch anything but the most basic of seams and hems under the watchful eye of Miss Timms, the senior alteration hand. But in the design of the gowns she instinctively recognized the hand and eye of a true artist, and the materials themselves were a delight to handle.

Matty was very much in awe of her new employer. Madame was tiny, elegant and sharp-featured, with vivid red hair and an explosive temper to match. She talked incessantly in a delightful confusion of French and English that fascinated Matty, and her brilliant dark eyes missed nothing.

Matty was determined to emulate this little woman, who was already her idol, and as the weeks went by, her own creative instincts, which had become submerged, began to revive.

Irene's wedding early in January had caused something of a stir in Bloom Street.

'A bit sudden like, your Irene gerrin' spliced,' Dolly McBride had said with a knowing chuckle when she heard. 'That Eddie give her somethin' a bit extra ter put in her Christmas stockin', did 'e?'

'If you minded your own business half as well as you do other people's,' Mam had said, neatly evading the point, 'you'd not need all that make-up on your face to hide the bruises your Bill gave you for Christmas, and Eric Bagshott wouldn't be sporting the biggest black eye this side of the Mersey.'

Dolly's eyes had flashed with sudden spite. 'P'rhaps not, but bruises soon fade. An' I still say if Tommy Feelan was ter make a book on the date your Irene drops her first babby, I could maybe earn meself a nice bob or two.'

But it had been a lovely wedding in spite of everything. Mam set aside her grief over Phil. Life had to go on, she said, and Phil wouldn't have wanted long faces on his account.

The ivory satin wedding dress, created with love by Matty, made her sister look almost ethereal, and the pale blue brides-maids' dresses for herself and Moira were also much admired. Dad was a bit emotional, but he was smiling as he waved them off from the window, and Kevin, looking very grown-up in a borrowed suit, had given Irene away.

10

THE WINDOWS OF Fernlea were ablaze with light on the night of the dinner party, and the clear frosty air of Crag Vale echoed to the sound of motor cars arriving, doors banging and much chatter and laughter as voices were raised in greeting.

In the drawing room the family assembled to greet their guests. Walter Buchanan, Seth's younger brother, who managed one of the mills, and was a prominent member of Crag Vale Town Council, had already taken up his stance before the fire, his gold watch and albert looped ostentatiously across his chest as visible proof of his prosperity. He could be heard across the room, holding forth about his fears of a depression folowing on from the years of conflict. His wife, Olga, sat close by, rigidly encased in black taffeta, a pained smile pinned to her face.

'Bunions,' Aimée had whispered to her brother under cover of the conversation. And he grinned mischievously, for Aunt Olga's bunions had been a standing joke between them for years.

Only Grandpa Howard was missing, laid low by a particularly bad bout of rheumatism – a sad but fortuitous accident of fate, in Minna's opinion, for her father's presence at a dinner party, though lending it considerable prestige, always made her nervous. And Gerald had already taken Megan on a duty visit.

Now Minna was fluttering happily between the gentlemen – 'a brilliant butterfly amid a flock of penguins,' Aimée observed irreverently to her aunt.

'Oh, my dear, she's loving every minute,' Felicity said indulgently, watching her sister's animated face, her eyes sparkling as they lifted to Giles, who had arrived home unexpectedly two days previously in time to join the celebrations, and was undoubtedly paying his aunt extravagant compliments.

The war had not left Giles wholly untouched, Aimée thought,

eyeing the new harshly drawn lines that now added a touch of distinction to his bland good looks. There was no denying that he was every bit as much of a charmer as his father. He had kissed her on both cheeks when he arrived, looked her over appreciatively and smiled into her eyes.

'My, how you've grown, little cousin. I like the hair. We must talk later. I've been hearing splendid things of you.'

And although she knew his interest to be quite spurious, she smiled back, because it was impossible not to like Giles in this mood. 'And I of you. A Military Cross, I hear, to go with your DSO.'

He shrugged it off with a self-deprecating grin. 'Oh well, you know how it is. Pure luck, being in the right place at the right time. Gerald had a far rougher time than I did.'

He made no mention of his brother, and Aimée, remembering her visit to Toby at Cedar Grange on the previous day, dared not say anything for fear of losing her temper.

Toby had made considerable progress over the past few weeks, so much so that she suggested Gerald might like to see him while he was home.

But the matron, a little tight-lipped, had taken her on one side when they arrived. 'I'm afraid your cousin is not at his best this afternoon, Doctor. His brother was here an hour or so back and the visit seems to have had an unfortunate effect. In fact . . .' she had eyed Gerald with misgivings.

Aimée assured her that Gerald and Toby had always been on the best of terms, but the damage had been done. The visit had been a disaster, Toby a stammering wreck, and all the good work of the past weeks undone. 'If Giles were here now, I'd break his neck,' she had fumed, crashing the gears of the family Daimler as they drove home. 'Of all the crass, insensitive – '

'Oh, come on, Aimée. I dare say Giles meant well.'

'Heaven defend me from well-meaning men! I dare say General Haig and his cohorts meant well when they sent more and more young men to be slaughtered.'

'Don't start on that tack, old thing.' There was an edge to Gerald's voice that pulled her up short. 'What's done is done. You're in danger of becoming obsessed.'

She caught his eye, and smiled wryly.

'Sorry. All right, maybe Giles did mean well. The trouble is, he hasn't a scrap of imagination or sensitivity, and where there's no imagination, there's no compassion. Everything is black and white.'

'Feel better now, do you?'

And she'd grinned ruefully. 'Much.'

Watching Giles now, guiding her mother solicitously through the crush as she took him to meet Megan, Aimée wondered if she had been too hard on him. It wasn't her place to sit in judgement. Giles had many good qualities, not least his ability to make a woman feel special. She saw that her sister-in-law, looking suitably bridal in a simple cream dress, was reacting as predictably as the rest to his practised gallantry.

Felicity also watched the meeting, in particular the way Minna fluttered round her new daughter-in-law. 'How fortunate that you mother seems to have taken so well to Megan. A nice girl.'

Aimée detected a curious inflection in her aunt's voice, though her expression was bland.

'You don't like her?'

'Of course I do, darling. How could anyone not like her when she seems so reassuringly biddable. Which is fortunate, since I understand she and Gerald are to be living here.'

'Yes. It seemed the sensible thing to do with so much room to spare.' It was foolish to feel again that momentary stab of jealousy. 'Aunt Fliss, can I come and see you soon? There is something I want to discuss with you.'

Felicity raised a quizzical eyebrow. 'Of course you may. When did you ever need an invitation? Come next week – stay for a few days, if you like.'

Oliver Langley, entering the room with George Mellish, saw Aimée at once. His initial reaction was surprise, for the elegant creature in animated conversation with Felicity Mellish bore little resemblance to the brusque, obstinate young woman he remembered, and less still to the delirious wraith he had delivered into her aunt's charge not so very long ago. She was still whip-thin, yet there was grace in every gesture; an essential femininity in the way her slender body moved beneath the black silk dress, cut like an oriental tunic to reveal a tantalizing glimpse of ankle, its only adornment a long string of pearls and a vivid red sash loosely tied at the hips. Her auburn hair, cut with almost geometric severity, swung thick and shining against her pale, heart-shaped face. As if, he thought, she were making a statement.

'My wife's niece,' George Mellish said, his glance following Oliver's, his manner amiably patronizing as they crossed the room. 'Odd creature. Unnatural occupation for a female, to my mind – doctoring. Nothing soft or womanly about it.'

His companion's eyes glinted. 'I imagine she would take issue with you quite forcibly, were you to press that point.'

'She would indeed. Aggressively opinionated at times, is our Aimée. But you would know that, of course. Had personal experience of her ministrations, I believe.'

'I did.'

'Any good, was she?'

Oliver had accepted Mrs Buchanan's invitation with reluctance, knowing that it would have been churlish to refuse. He was not a particularly social animal these days. It had been different when Catherine . . . He shied away from dangerous territory, addressing his attention instead to the hint of derision in his companion's voice: just for an instant, the sickening horror of that night in the makeshift casualty station came vividly to mind. His jaw tightened.

'Damned good,' he said abruptly, resenting on her behalf Mellish's patronizing attitude. 'I doubt I'd be here now without Dr Buchanan's coolness and expertise.'

'Really?' George Mellish was unused to being put so comprehensively in his place. He cleared his throat. 'Yes, well, I'm glad to hear it.'

Outwardly composed, Aimée watched through a curl of cigarette smoke as they crossed the room. Uncle George was an older, heavier version of Giles, his greying sandy hair well brilliantined, his complexion beginning to show evidence of too many late dinners washed down with too many brandies, his manner urbane.

But it was his companion who had set Aimée's stomach churning. Half a head taller than her uncle and wearing his most inscrutable look, Major Langley in evening dress looked every bit as formidable as he had in mud-caked battledress; if anything, the severe black and white accentuated his air of authority. I would not care to be cross-examined by him, she thought. And yet there had been moments during that nightmare train journey when he had been incredibly kind.

Her mother had been quite insistent that Major Langley should be invited. 'My dear, it may be a slight exaggeration to say you owe him your life, but your father and I certainly have reason to be grateful to him, and I have been feeling quite guilty that we have not adequately thanked him.'

'There you are, Aimée, m'dear. Looking very dashing, I see.' Uncle George's whiskers brushed her cheek. 'Believe I don't need to introduce Major Langley. Intimately acquainted already, what?'

Her uncle's heavy-handed teasing had grated on her even as a child. Now the jocular insinuation reminded her of things she would rather forget: of a shared intimacy that for a brief moment set Major Langley and herself apart from everyone else in the room.

Inevitably he must be recalling his own moment of vulnerability, his almost aggressive detestation of being obliged to submit to her ministrations. Her own recollection of that first encounter remained vivid, but their second meeting was a blur of disjointed sensations: a quiet firm voice: hands, suprisingly gentle, lifting her legs on to the train seat – and curling up warm and being covered with something warm – a cherished child, head pillowed in soft wood smelled faintly of tobacco.

Yet here, in her mother's pretty drawing room, their previous encounters seemed so far removed from reality that she found it easier than she had expected to meet his eyes.

'Major Langley, how nice to see you again.'

'Dr Buchanan.' His handshake was as firm and impersonal as her own.

'I'm so glad you were able to come.'

'It was kind of your mother to ask me. If I may say so, you are looking much better than when I last saw you.'

'So I would hope,' she said, quick as light, to cover her embarrassment. 'But thank you, just the same. I must have been a great trouble to you.'

There was a decided glint in his eyes. 'Not at all.'

Felicity was intrigued not so much by the formal exchange, as by the unspoken message that vibrated in the air all about them, and the wild blush staining her niece's cheek.

Reluctantly, because she longed to know more, she came to Aimée's rescue. 'Oliver, what a pity Jane couldn't stay long enough to come with you this evening.'

'She has been a godsend, but I really couldn't expect her to stay indefinitely.'

'Another time, perhaps. Oliver's sister is charming, Aimée. You would like one another, I'm sure.'

A swift flash of gratitude from her niece was her reward and for a few moments the conversation became general. Then, her duty done and still none the wiser, Felicity reluctantly gathered up her pale grey ostrich feather stole and linked her arm through her husband's. 'George darling, we really must go across and speak to Walter and Olga. My dears, you don't mind if I drag George away, do you?'

'A delightful woman, your aunt,' Oliver said, watching the graceful figure in pale grey satin, swaying against the dark bulk of her husband, her head uplifted in animated conversation. 'They make a handsome couple.'

'They do indeed. But I would not for the world change places with Aunt Felicity.' Aimée bit her lip. 'That was tactless of me. Do you know my uncle well, Major?'

'Moderately well.' His mouth quirked. 'But not well enough to fly to his defence. And to be strictly accurate it isn't major any longer, Dr Buchanan. I took an early discharge.'

'Of course. You must have had a dreadful time. How is your little boy now?'

'Still frail, but getting stronger every day. My sister has been a great help with young Alice, and we have always had an excellent nanny.'

The 'we' had slipped out, and Aimée saw his mouth quiver momentarily.

'That is good,' she said swiftly. 'Children need stability. I expect you will be glad to get back to practising law.'

'Indeed. I've rejoined my uncle's chambers in Rodney Street. I had just established myself there when the war intervened.'

Aimée remembered Aunt Felicity talking about Oliver Langley when she was convalescing – of the impact he had made in those early days, with his mesmeric charm and sometimes caustic wit –

and of his beautiful wife. She hadn't taken much notice at the time, being too locked into her own misery.

'And you, Dr Buchanan?'

'I've been kept busy helping our local doctor. The Spanish flu epidemic swelled the usual crop of winter ailments, and Frank Lomax isn't all that young.' She knew she was making excuses, justifying to herself her lack of commitment. 'I needed time, you see . . .' Her words were not really for him.

'Naturally.'

Aimée looked for scepticism and found none. She removed her cigarette from its ebony holder and stubbed it out.

'Now Mother expects me to be content to remain in Crag Vale, pursuing medicine as a nice little hobby.'

'Ah.'

'Like Uncle George and a great many other people, she doesn't approve of my calling, being of the opinion that young women should be perfectly content to get married, minister to their husbands and have babies –' She stopped, suddenly stricken. 'Oh, I'm so sorry!'

'Don't be,' he said harshly.

Aimée sighed. 'You see how shockingly self-centred I have become. For a little while I was in grave danger of forgetting that I didn't become a doctor to take the easy path,' she said with sudden passion. 'There is so much to be done.'

'And you want to change the world overnight. I've been down that road, too, Doctor. Our aims are similar, though justice is my particular passion. But idealism isn't enough. One must cultivate patience.'

Oliver watched her anger flare and as quickly fade; a delightful blush crept up under her skin, making her look much younger, more vulnerable, as he remembered her . . .

'You're right, of course.' Aimée straightened suddenly, half laughing. 'Oh dear, I am being a very bad hostess.'

'Oliver, stop monopolizing my beautiful cousin.' Giles had come up behind them, unnoticed, and now put an arm round her waist with an easy familiarity, nuzzling into her neck beneath the shining hair. 'We have a lot of catching up to do.'

'Of course. My apologies.' Oliver's manner cooled instantly. He inclined his head and made to turn away.

Perversely, Aimée did not want him to go.

'Do behave yourself, Giles,' she said sharply.

He stepped back, accepting the rebuff with good humour, but behind the mocking smile, his eyes watched the two of them speculatively.

'Have you met my father, Major Langley?' Aimée asked. 'He hates parties, but adores my mother who loves them, so he is being very stoical about the whole thing.'

To her surprise, he chuckled.

'Come, and I'll introduce you. You'll like him, I think.'

The dinner party was a great success, the bride and groom were toasted in style, and the last guest finally departed leaving Minna exhausted but triumphant, and her husband vastly relieved. It was a long time before Aimée could settle to sleep, and when she did, it was intermittent, so that the sound of Gerald's bedroom door softly closing wakened her at once.

She knew where he would be making for, where he had always gone as a child when anything troubled him. They had dubbed it 'the Den', a small boxroom tucked away at the back of the house above the kitchens, and seldom used.

'Are you all right, dear boy?' she called softly, hearing the painful muffled sounds, but not able to see him at first.

Gerald's breath caught, then his voice came harshly from behind a stack of card tables. 'No, I'm not bloody all right. Trust you to find me out.'

'I'll go away, if you'd rather – '

'No!' There was despair in the abruptness. Then he said less dramatically, 'Don't be an ass. You're just about the one person I don't mind seeing me like this. Because you *know*. Christ, you probably know better than I do.'

He was crouching on the floor in a corner, his arms locked round his knees, which were drawn up tight to his chest. Aimée knelt beside him, threading her arm through his. 'Not better. But I know enough to understand.'

'Which is more than Uncle George does. You should have heard him holding forth after dinner in that holier-than-thou way he has – as though we'd triumphed in some glorious crusade. What can he possibly know about gas and mud, of the agony and the shame of being alive and in one piece when you've ordered so many poor blighters horribly and needlessly to their deaths – '

'Gerald, don't! You mustn't even think that!'

'Why not? It's true.' One hand came to cover hers, his fingers biting into her flesh, though she hardly felt the pain.

'You did what you had to do.'

He laughed bitterly. 'How many of us salved our conscience with that platitude? "Only following orders from above, lads! Over the top you go." And what about the poor buggers who survived, hopelessly maimed in body or mind. What about Toby? Uncle George kept going on and on about me and Giles and Oliver Langley, and the clutch of medals we had between us – singing our praises, for God's sake – but he couldn't bring himself to mention poor Toby, who was braver than the lot of us put together! I don't know how I kept from striking him.'

She cradled him in her arms, cursing her stupidity. The signs were all there if she'd had the wit to recognize them. But his marriage had confused the issue. Had she realized, she would never have taken him to see Toby.

'Uncle George can't help the way he is,' she said, coming unwillingly to his defence. 'It's how a lot of people at home feel. They aren't deliberately insensitive – just relieved that the war's over. They can have no real comprehension of the awfulness and the agony involved.'

'I know. But knowing doesn't help. My head tells me I ought at least to be glad, if not exactly proud of my part in the slaughter. But why, if we won the bloody war, do I feel so *defeated*?'

Her throat ached with unshed tears, but her voice, though husky, was firm. 'A natural reaction. Simple as that, brother dear. You've gone from one extreme to the other in a very short time – from fighting and killing to falling in love, getting married. And no doubt doing your best to hide your feelings from Megan. Give it time. You're still tired – '

'Aren't we all?' he said jerkily.

Amen to that, Aimée thought. ' – and a little off balance,' she added. 'It's a pity you can't arrange to have a longer break – an extended honeymoon with Megan, somewhere quiet and peace-ful.'

Gerald laughed shakily and stood up, pulling her with him, and they stood looking out of the darkened window where the moon sailed serene, casting deep shadows across the valley. 'All the peace I want or need is here. Home, family, the chance to do something constructive with my life. It's all I thought about, lying in those stinking trenches.'

'Well, then,' Aimée said, giving silent thanks that Gerald's particular malady, given time and understanding, would heal of its own accord. 'How about a hot drink before you go back to bed?'

His hand slid down to catch hold of hers, squeezing it painfully tight. 'Thanks, Doctor, but I'll be fine, now.'

Together they stumbled towards the door, trying to be quiet and giggling like children. Before opening it, he turned to her, suddenly serious. 'You won't tell Megan? I don't want her to worry.'

'Finger wet, finger dry,' she promised, going through the age-old childhood ritual.

But in a corner of her mind, she put a small black mark against Megan for not noticing that something was wrong.

PART TWO

MATTY AND IRENE pushed their way through the noisy crowd singing along with the naval airs being played by the band down at the landing stage. They were anxious to get as near as they could to the New Brighton gangway in time to see Admiral Sir David Beatty arriving back from New Brighton where he had been unveiling two bronze tablets, to be placed on the *Iris* and *Daffodil*, which commemorated the part played by the gallant little ferry boats in the raid on Zeebrugge exactly a year ago on St George's Day – a feat for which the King had dubbed them Royal.

The early sleet had gone and the sun was sparkling on the river, so that you forgot how grey and downright mucky it could often look. From where they were, Matty and Irene had an excellent view of the giant grey warship *Queen Elizabeth* moored in midriver.

'I bet our Kevin'll be first on board that when they start the trips after,' Matty said excitedly. 'I wouldn't mind goin', meself.' And then beyond, she saw the two little ferry boats, still scarred with shell holes, but freshly painted with bunting flying in the strong breeze. 'Hey, Irene, there they are, the *Iris* and the *Daffodil*. That must be the Admiral on the top deck. It's just like a film!'

When there was no answer, she looked anxiously at her sister who was nearly five months gone, for all that she still insisted it was four, and showing in spite of the loose dress she had made her in a pretty shade of blue.

'Are you all right, Irene?'

'Of course I'm all right. Don't fuss.'

Matty knew how much Irene hated losing her trim figure, and it didn't help that twins were commonplace on Mam's side of the family. It would be just her luck, Irene had muttered gloomily, if she took after them. For once Mam had been less than sympathetic. 'You should have thought of that before jumping the gun, my girl,' she said. 'It's a bit late complaining now.'

All in all, marriage to Eddie hadn't turned out to be quite the gateway to freedom and independence that Irene had supposed. Almost before the euphoria of the wedding had worn off, and the morning sickness began, she had begun to rue the loss of her freedom. And once the flat was decorated to her liking, her husband let it be known that he expected her to pull her weight. 'We can't afford help in the shop as well as the workshop, Rene, and the workshop's where the money is, which means the shop's down to you, girl.'

'Eddie says it's important for him to be out and about, touting for business. But I'm proper fed up, to say nothing of being worn out of an evening, what with all the housework as well,' Irene confided to Matty.

Matty had grinned sympathetically. 'I dare say you'll get used, given time, though you never were much cop when it came to housework.' She was tempted to add: 'And it's what you wanted.' But her sister wore such a woebegone look that she hadn't the heart to rub it in. Matty thought the shop had a quaint charm. The shelves carried a motley assortment of goods – gas mantles, footballs, mouth organs, bicycle bells – and lots of advertisements for phonograph repairs as well as bicycles. But it wasn't Irene's kind of place at all.

'Are you still being sick of a morning?' Matty asked now, as they stood, squashed up against the rail, with the crowd pressing in on them.

'No.' Irene forced the word out as she felt panic rising up. Why did Matty have to mention being sick? The smell of the river together with the swell of the waves as the two ferries ploughed their way midstream, suddenly made her want to heave. She shivered, and averted her eyes. 'But if we don't get out of here quick, I shall be. I wish we hadn't come. I'd no idea there'd be so many people.'

Matty shot her sister a worried look. She'd gone ever such a peculiar colour. 'Hey, don't you faint on me. Come on. Give us your arm.' And seizing Irene's elbow, she began to push through the crowd amid grumbles, which turned to sympathy as her urgent, 'Let us through, will you, me sister's not well,' communicated itself.

'At last,' she panted, half dragging the now distraught Irene in search of a bench. 'You'd better get your breath back. No use going for the tram in your state.'

At the mention of trams, Irene groaned and leaned against a nearby wall.

'I'm a doctor. Can I help?'

The voice was vaguely familiar, but Matty didn't immediately recognize the vibrant young woman whose shining bobbed hair, unconfined by a hat, lifted in the breeze as she bent over Irene, her fingers seeking out her pulse.

'Put your head down and take several deep breaths. That's good. You'll feel much better in a few minutes.' She glanced up. 'You're Matty Shaw, aren't you?'

'Yes. Oh, it's Dr Buchanan!'

She looked quite different from the tired young woman who had come to the house a few months back. A corner of Matty's mind registered that the coat and skirt of soft green wool was unmistakably a Madame Vincente creation.

'I'm that glad it's you,' Matty exclaimed, stumbling over the words in her relief. 'Irene's my sister. She was taken bad down by the river and I was afraid for the baby. Is she all right?'

'Oh yes, I should think so.' Aimée kept her voice deliberately calm. 'Too many people and too much excitement, I expect.'

'I should never have suggested coming, but Irene needed a bit of cheering up, and I didn't stop to think.'

'You needn't talk about me as if I wasn't here,' Irene muttered, straightening up.

'Well, there's no harm done,' Aimée told her, watching the colour come back into her face. She was a pretty girl, or would be but for that scowl of discontent. 'How far gone are you? Five months?'

'Four.'

So that was the way of it. Another unwanted baby conceived through carelessness or ignorance. Aimée guessed, judging from the surly brevity of her reply that Irene, for all her shiny new wedding ring, was not overjoyed at the prospect of motherhood. Anger flared up and was instantly quashed. It wasn't her business, and at least Irene's child would have a caring family around it.

'Half an hour at home with your feet up and a nice hot cup of tea, and you'll be fine. If you like, I can drive you there. Bloom Street, isn't it?'

'That's me mam's. I live in Walton now.'

'Well, if there is no desperate need for you to get back, I think it might be better if you had an hour or so at your mam's before attempting the long tram ride.'

Irene pictured Eddie waiting on his tea. He'd been grudging enough about her coming out with Matty, but she hadn't had any proper time off in ages. It made a nice change being fussed over, she thought, making up her mind to make the most of it. Do Eddie good to get his own tea for once.

'I wouldn't mind a bit of a rest,' she said with a deep sigh that would have done credit to Sarah Bernhardt.

Matty had never been in a motor car. And this one was special – spanking new, all shiny paintwork and pale leather, with a dashing let-down hood.

'Is it very difficult, learning to drive?'

'Not once you master the clutch and gears. I learned years ago at the same time as my brother. Being twins, we did most things together, and I was determined not to let him outshine me.'

The mention of twins brought another huge sigh from Irene. Aimée helped her into the back where she reclined with as much grace as her bulky figure would permit.

Matty wished someone she knew might walk past as she settled herself in front beside the doctor. 'It's ever so elegant,' she said. 'This leather's as soft as silk.'

Aimée, delighted by their innocent preening, threw Matty a smile that was pure joy. 'It's a recent birthday present from my father. He said if I was set on going into general practice, I would need some kind of transport. To be honest, a bicycle would probably have been more use, but not half so much fun.'

Fancy getting a car for a birthday present! Matty could hardly keep the awe out of her voice. 'Your dad must be ever so rich!'

The smile turned to a chuckle. 'He wouldn't agree with you at the moment. He's always made a point of treating me and Gerald exactly the same, which in this case cost him two cars.'

The silence that followed was palpable, and Aimée realized too late the crassness of such a remark when Matty's father . . . Oh, damn her insensitivity!

'How is your father these days?' she asked quietly.

Matty dragged her thoughts back from her favourite daydream in which she owned a house where luxury was commonplace and two new cars would be a drop in the ocean – a place like Mrs Mellish's. It had certainly been an eye-opener, going there to do the sewing. 'You could probably get our whole house into the housekeeper's rooms!' she'd told Mam. And Mam had told her not to get any big ideas. She sighed.

'Poor Dad. He's not so good. Our Phil's death knocked him for six, of course, though he's perked up a bit since.'

'I was so sorry to hear about your brother. It must have been dreadful for you all, especially when you had been thinking him safe. That dreadful war – so many tragedies.'

She sounded really sad, as if she'd lost someone, too. As the car turned the corner into Bloom Street, Matty changed the subject, saying impulsively, 'I'm working part time at Madame Vincente's now, you know.'

'Yes, I believe my aunt mentioned it.'

'It was her put a word in for me. I was ever so grateful.'

'And you like being there?'

'It's really great. Not that I get to do anything very important, but I've already been promoted from alteration hand to the workroom with increased hours. And I'm getting ever such a lot of ideas, sketchbooks full of them. You'd be surprised how much you can learn just watching someone like Madame Vincente. She's a real artist.'

'Oh, for heaven's sake play another tune, our Matty,' Irene groaned.

But Matty's enthusiasm warmed Aimée's heart, and it was with a fleeting moment of regret that she drew up outside Matty's house, which stood out from the rest with its sparkling windows and crisp lace curtains.

'Will you come in, Doctor?'

'I think not. I was actually on my way ...' Aimée was immediately aware of her disappointment. 'Well, perhaps just for a moment – to make sure that Irene is all right.'

Agnes Shaw was taken aback to see her, but Matty quickly explained, and Irene was scolded and bustled into the back room where she was settled in the armchair. Aimée watched, recognizing the increasing signs of strain in the older woman's face.

Daisy, who was at the crawling stage, had somehow loosed the reins that confined her to the table and was already scurrying across the floor trailing them behind her, one hand reaching up to tug at the beautiful green skirt. Agnes let out a skirl of dismay.

'Daisy, don't you dare put your sticky fingers all over the doctor! Pick her up, our Matty, for goodness' sake.'

But Aimée was already scooping the child up in her arms, laughing as the sticky hands patted her face. 'My, how you've grown! And giving your mam a hard time, I expect.'

'She's a handful and no mistake,' Agnes admitted, her manner softening a fraction. 'I'd forgotten how active they can be at this age.'

Aimée thought of all the wretched lacklustre children she had seen during her recent exploration of Liverpool's black spots – children grown old before they had known the joy of being young. 'What is a little dirt? Daisy's a bonny baby, and that's all that really matters.' She handed the child back to her mother. 'I must go.'

'You'll take a cup of tea, first?'

'I'd love to, Mrs Shaw, but I really can't stay just now. I was actually on my way to visit my cousin when I saw the girls.'

'Oh well,' Agnes's manner cooled again. 'I'm sorry you've been troubled.'

'It was no trouble.' She smiled reassuringly at Irene. 'And I'm happy that there's no harm done.'

All had seemed quiet in the front room but as they moved towards the lobby, there came a great heaving, wrenching sound that galvanized Agnes into life.

'Dear God!' she whispered and, thrusting the child into Matty's arms, she ran towards the front room. But Aimée was before her, grabbing the bowl from the little table beside Pat Shaw's chair, one arm firm around the heaving shoulders as the terrible wrenching cough racked his body. When the bout was over, Agnes took the bowl from her without a word, her face rigidly expressionless as she covered the frightening contents with a cloth, and removed it, returning moments later with a bowl of fresh warm water.

Together, they washed Pat, changed him and got him into bed.

Aimée was disturbed by the difference in him. The skin around his eyes and across his cheekbones was so taut as to seem transparent, giving his face a skeletal look. Did Mrs Shaw realize, she wondered, just how ill he was?

'Does your husband have some medicine?' she asked Agnes, who for the moment seemed to have had all the fight knocked out of her.

The bottle was handed over meekly.

'Better?' Aimée asked presently as a little life came back into Mr Shaw's face.

Pat moved his head fractionally in assent, summoning a travesty of a smile. 'No way . . . to greet . . . a charming young lady.'

'Rest now, Mr Shaw. Don't try to talk.' She eased him round onto his side, with an extra pillow for support, and he sank down with a sigh and closed his eyes.

'You've a good sure touch, Doctor,' Agnes said abruptly. 'He'll be all right now – until the next time . . .'

Her voice broke, and Aimée led her from the room, closing the door quietly behind them. In the back room, the two girls waited apprehensively, Matty holding a now grizzling Daisy who wanted her mammy.

'Is Dad all right?' she asked, white-faced.

A sound – half-laugh, half-moan – broke from her mother.

'He's sleeping,' Aimée said quickly. 'Matty, do you think you could take the little one out of the way for a while – just to give your mother a breathing space?'

'Yes, of course. I'll put her in the pram and walk to the tram with Irene, if she's ready to go.' She made frantic signs to her sister, who had gone ever so pale again. Irene had always been scared of anything to do with illness and dying, though please God, it wouldn't come to that. She'd go in to church on the way back and light a candle. 'Moira's gone out with Emmy Flynn and Kevin won't be home for ages.'

When they had gone, Aimée made Mrs Shaw sit down while she put the kettle on.

'Your appointment . . .' Agnes protested half-heartedly, surprised by the matter-of-fact way Aimée found her way round the kitchen.

'That will keep. Time means very little to my cousin. He's in a nursing home. Another victim of the war, poor boy. I go and see him whenever I can.' She knew that the older woman wasn't really listening, but she talked on, knowing that anything was better than silence at this moment.

Agnes watched, grateful not to be left alone, while her mind skirted round and round the inevitable truth. 'Pat's really bad, isn't he?' she said at last. 'He's never had a turn like that before. I don't know how I'd have managed without you.'

Aimée accepted the grudging admission without comment. 'Has the doctor never suggested that your husband might be admitted to a sanatorium?'

'Dr Hutton did say he'd see what he could do some time back. I was dead against the idea.' Agnes flushed. 'Afraid of losing Pat, I suppose. Anyhow, nothing's come of it – and there's small chance, what with all the soldiers coming back.'

'I think he *should* go away for a while,' Aimée said gently. She set a steaming cup of tea in front of Agnes. 'For your sake as well as his own.'

'There's lots worse off than me.' The reply came automatically, but for once it lacked conviction. 'Anyway, where would Pat go?'

'Well, if you like,' Aimée said, 'I could make a few enquiries of my own.'

She was pensive as she drove away. Was it fair to separate the family when it was clear that even a spell in a sanatorium, always supposing she could find one near to home with a vacancy, would only extend Pat Shaw's life by a few months? And yet, she was convinced that Mrs Shaw was almost at breaking point.

There was, of course, Crag Vale Cottage Hospital. A few years ago her grandfather had built and equipped a splendid new convalescent wing behind the old building where members of his staff could recuperate from illness in comfort. The six private rooms looked out over the valley. They were seldom all in use at the same time, and any one of them could provide exactly the kind of care Mr Shaw needed. Frank would be on hand, and she could also keep an eye on him. The more she thought about it, the more this seemed the ideal solution. It wouldn't take her too far out of her way to call in to see Grandpa Howard on her way to Cedar

Grange, and once she had persuaded him, the biggest difficulty would be overcoming Mrs Shaw's scruples.

Sir Amos Howard was becoming much more frail. He no longer went to the office, and frustration was making him more fractious by the day. But he refused to be confined to his bedroom, even if it meant a couple of the servants carrying him downstairs to his study.

Judd greeted Aimée with a kind of surly relief.

'He's got the devil on his back, good and proper today, Miss Aimée. His screws were so bad he had to admit defeat about coming downstairs an' that really riled him, stubborn old devil! Wouldn't even take his pills – said they weren't doing him no good, and the sooner he was gone, the better. Perhaps you can get him to take them.'

Aimée sighed. It was not an auspicious start. She ran up the beautiful staircase as she had done as a child, remembering with nostalgia a time when the house had been alive with people, her tiny French grandmother, for whom she was named, filling it with her presence, her laughter. Flowers everywhere. Now, although it was kept scrupulously clean and tidy, the house was becoming more and more like a mausoleum.

The master bedroom was heavily wainscoted and hung with velvet curtains, which had been drawn half across the deep bay window as though deliberately to blot out the view of the river that had always been her grandfather's lifeblood, the window from which he regularly looked out towards the docks to watch for the return of his ships. It was this deliberate mental cutting off that troubled Aimée more than his physical condition.

Sir Amos was in his chair beside a leaping log fire, his large frame now as spare and twisted as his temper. 'Oh, it's you,' he grunted. 'About time you came to visit me. Y'r Aunt Felicity whisks in and out to bully me at regular intervals, and y'r mother's visits, thank God, are limited to the times when she don't have a migraine. When she does come, she cries all over me.'

'Goodness, you are in a mood.'

'What if I am? Sitting here like a vegetable. And if that old fool's been on at you about Graham's fancy new pills, forget it. It's a new body I want, not pills.'

'Poor Judd is in despair. I'm surprised he hasn't left you long since.'

'No one else would have him.' Something that might have been a grunt or a laugh rumbled deep inside him. 'I reckon we deserve one another.'

Aimée grinned. 'Maybe you do. I'm not surprised you're bad-tempered with all this gloom.' She went across and flung back the curtains to let in the sunlight. 'That's better.'

'If I want gloom, I'll have it,' he growled, but he didn't insist on having the curtains closed again. 'So what have you been getting up to since I last saw you? Got your life sorted out yet?'

She told him of her plans, her enthusiasm bubbling over. For an instant he remembered what it was like to be young and full of drive and ambition. But the recollection brought a different kind of pain – and by hell, it hurt him more than his damned useless body.

'I thought you were all set on becoming a surgeon – studying for your fellowship?'

'I changed my mind.'

The abruptness of her reply said more than mere words. He peered into her face and decided not to pry. 'Well, as long as you're sure it's what you want,' he grunted, 'though I'm surprised. Never thought you'd be content with treating a procession of spotty children with sore throats, bringing babies into the world.'

His derogatory tone flicked her on the raw. 'I'm surprised at you, Grandpa, after all you've done in your time to press for better conditions. 'Why, I grew up on stories of how, from the moment you became one of Liverpool's youngest councillors, you fought to push through amendments to the 1847 Sanitary Act and got better housing for the poor.'

'Lord, child, how you do go on. That was a long time ago.'

'Yes, but there are still too many people who have no proper sanitation, who can't afford mere necessities, let alone a doctor –too many families who have lost their main breadwinner to the war, children with rickets and other chronic diseases who will never grow to maturity . . . I had no idea of the scale of the problem until I began to look into it.'

His eyes were overbright. 'A chip off the old block. I might have known you'd want to play God.'

Why must everyone think that? Oliver Langley had said something similar.

'If that were true, and it isn't, I've likely caught it from you,' she retorted.

What began as a chuckle turned into a rasping cough. He leaned forward in his chair, and the movement forced a low keening moan from him. She was at his side in an instant, easing him back, wiping the cold sweat from his face.

'Take the pills, Grandpa,' she entreated. 'Just for me. They will help the pain.'

He was in no position to argue. It was some moments before he could speak again, and Aimée had already resigned herself to leaving all talk of Pat Shaw for another day. But she had reckoned without his amazing resilience.

'Just make sure you get proper advice. You'll need a decent house, equipment, all that sort of thing. John Waring'll see you right on legal matters.' He paused, breathing hard. 'And if you're set on using the money y'r Grandma Aimée left you,' he gasped, 'just remember – if it's not enough, you come to me. I'll not be needing money where I'm bound.'

'Don't talk like that!'

'Ah, there never been any flummery between us, girl. You're a doctor. You, of all people, know what's what.'

'Maybe I do, but you aren't finished yet.' Aware that the pills would soon make him drowsy, she gathered her courage and said huskily, 'Grandpa, there is something I wanted to ask – a favour.'

'Well come on then. Out with it.'

And so she told him about Mr Shaw.

It was late afternoon when she arrived at Cedar Grange. She found Toby potting brightly coloured blooms in the conservatory. He was not immediately aware of her presence and she had time to observe him at leisure. He had come on well in the last few months and had put on weight, so that his uniform no longer hung from his shoulders. 'He paints flower pictures, now,' Matron had told her. 'Hopefully, he has worked the other out of his system.' It certainly seemed so.

'Aimée.' He turned and smiled, the gentle smile that had always drawn her to him as a child. 'How nice.'

She kissed his cheek. 'Sorry I'm late.' She indicated the plants. 'You're busy, I see. What beautiful colours.'

'Yes. Pretty, aren't they? *Primula malacoides*.'

No hint of a stammer.

'My word. Your mother told me how good you had become with plants, but I'd no idea you were so knowledgeable. You are going to be worth your weight in gold when you return home. Poor Davenport is getting too old to do very much, so you'll be able to keep a discreet eye on the hothouses and help him keep that lovely garden in order.'

Aimée knew at once that she had said the wrong thing. He pushed the pot away almost childishly and began to struggle with his gloves. 'It w-w-won't be the same. Besides, M-M-M-Matron needs m-me here.'

She cursed her clumsiness in not realizing that his shell of confidence was still so fragile. But instinct told her that she must treat the lapse as normal.

'Of course she does,' she said casually. 'Anyway, all that won't be for ages yet. You remember I told you I meant to set up practice in Liverpool? Well now that Gerald is home for good, and Mother has Megan to fuss over her, I can really begin to make plans.'

Toby had turned his back on her and was busy trimming dead heads off one of his plants. 'I'm g-g-glad for you,' he muttered.

'I'm glad you're glad,' she said, striving to keep her voice light, to ignore the painful stammering. 'And when I've found a house, and am settled, you shall be one of my first visitors.'

He didn't answer at once, but the hunch of his shoulders told her that he had reverted to the old withdrawn Toby.

'Oh, come on, old thing. Cheer up. Tell you what – why don't we take a stroll? The sun is so warm, it's almost like summer.' She tucked a hand under his arm. 'Would we be breaking any sacred rules if you were to show me round?'

Toby hesitated, then shook his head.

As they walked between banks of tulips, and anemones growing wild beneath the trees, Aimée kept up a stream of light-hearted chatter, encouraging him to point out various plants, and to her relief his monosyllabic answers grew more animated as he gradually relaxed. 'I'm impressed, Toby, truly I am. I'm hopeless at remembering the names of flowers, but Mother knows them all. She would love this garden! And, oh, see – beyond that shrubbery. Bluebells and primroses – masses and masses of them.'

'Dear Aimée,' he said suddenly. 'I d-do love you.'

She grinned, and tucked her hand tighter in to his. 'And I love you. What fun we had as children. Do you remember how we used to march through your mother's shrubbery together, singing Gilbert and Sullivan at the tops of our voices?'

She began to sing a lusty version of 'The Flowers that Bloom in the Spring, tra-la' at the top of her voice, and soon he was joining in, making a noble stab at the final tra-la-las, and finally collapsing in laughter among the bluebells.

Aimée sat up first. She held out a hand and pulled him into a sitting position, her eyes dark with a deeper emotion as the laughter faded.

'Toby Mellish,' she said as he wiped his eyes, 'do you realize that all the while you were singing, you didn't stammer once?'

12

THE HOUSE IN Myrtle Street was double-fronted with neat black railings either side of the steps to enclose the basement. The ground floor had a sitting room, dining room, a tiny morning room, and kitchen and scullery, with two bedrooms and a bathroom above and two small attic rooms on the second floor. It even had an entry big enough to take a car.

Aimée had noticed the house quite by chance. It must have only just come on the market, or she would have seen it earlier. When no one answered the door, she went straight round to see the agent.

He told her that the house belonged to the widow of a business man who had died quite suddenly of a heart attack. She, unable to bear the loneliness, had finally gone to live with her married daughter. Dr Buchanan could, if she wished, see round it immediately. The rooms were still furnished, and Mrs Arbuthnot had reserved some items to be sent on to her, but, should she be interested, the remaining furniture and fittings were to be sold.

Aimée followed him round in complete silence, her heart beating very fast as in her mind's eye she converted the dining room to a surgery, and the study to a dining room. The price was right at the top of her range, even with Grandma Aimée's legacy, but the agent had been given power to negotiate within reasonable bounds. She made an offer on the spot, and to her relief it was accepted, subject to the usual conditions.

'Are you always so impulsive?' Oliver Langley asked dryly, when she had entered her aunt's drawing room on winged feet, eager to spill out the good news.

Aimée was momentarily disconcerted to find him very much at home beside the fire enjoying a cigar, a glass of sherry at his side. She had been too preoccupied to notice his car on the forecourt.

They had met on several occasions over the weeks, and after he had called her 'Dr Buchanan' a number of times in his sardonic way, she had been provoked into suggesting that it sounded ridiculously formal, and they had become Oliver and Aimée. But the relationship had never quite lost its prickly edge.

Aimée collapsed into the nearest chair, removing her deep-crowned hat and shaking free her hair, which spun and settled back into its shining bob.

'Impulse implies a lack of thought,' she said lightly, accepting a glass of sherry. 'I hope I am never guilty of that, though I do sometimes have an instinct about things. And the moment I saw the house in Myrtle Street I knew I wanted it. The position, everything about it is exactly right.'

'And do you always get what you want?'

'Don't tease, Oliver,' Felicity said. 'I know just what you mean, Aimée. I dare say I would have done the same thing in your place. Sometimes one just has to grasp the nettle or whatever it is one is supposed to do. I think it's splendid news as long as you are quite sure.'

'Oh, I am, Aunt Fliss. I was never more sure of anything in my life.'

Aimée had told her aunt of her plans to set up a practice after she had confided to her grandfather. Now, just a few days later, Felicity heard something in her niece's voice that she had long prayed for. Aimée had been improving steadily over the months, but with the improvement had come an increasing restlessness. Now, suddenly, it was as if a spark had been rekindled inside her niece.

Minna would throw up her hands at the thought of her daughter setting up the kind of practice Aimée envisaged, and in Liverpool. Only if someone she knew, like Andrew Graham, agreed to take Aimée into partnership, would the idea be anywhere near acceptable. Felicity had casually broached this possibility to Aimée.

'Heavens, no, Aunt Fliss. Pandering to rich people with imaginary illnesses isn't at all what I have in mind.' She had stopped short. 'My wretched tongue. Andrew Graham is a good doctor, as I have reason to know. But there are so many people who can't afford his fees, people in desperate need – and not just of medical care. They need a radical change in the way they are forced to live – better hygiene, better housing. And someone has to show them the way.'

Oh dear, Felicity had thought, fearful of where her niece's zeal might lead, aware that she had been the one who had encouraged her to look outward again. But: 'You will take care, dear?' was all she had said.

Oliver was continuing to play devil's advocate. 'And what if your dream house proves to be less than perfect? A detailed survey could reveal any number of tiresome little drawbacks – rising damp, deathwatch beetle, dry rot in the woodwork.'

Aimée wrinkled her nose at him. 'Now you're talking like a lawyer.'

'Which is precisely what I am.'

'So you are. But I am not the silly featherbrain you seem to take me for. Mr John Waring, of Messrs Waring, Trimble and Trimble, is handling the sale for me.' Her smile was sweetly challenging over the rim of her glass. 'I do hope he meets with your approval?'

'An excellent choice, though it is hardly for me to approve or disapprove. And as for thinking you featherbrained –' Those dark inscrutable eyes glinted momentarily. 'I wouldn't dare. If you had said stubborn, I would wholeheartedly agree, but even your worst enemy couldn't call you featherbrained. I'm sure you know exactly what you are doing.'

Drat the man, and his infuriating habit of damning with faint praise. Aware that her aunt was watching and listening with interest, she kept her smile and her temper firmly in place, took out a cigarette and accepted a light from him, determined to prove herself a woman of sense.

'I do.'

The tip of his cigar glowed red. 'So you will also have taken into account that in putting up your plate in Myrtle Street, you may well meet with some antagonism – not least from those you most wish to help?'

Aimée felt some of her earlier excitement draining away. The fact that there was some validity in his argument – the memory of how suspicious Agnes had been when they first met – did nothing to quell her annoyance. She drew on her cigarette and exhaled slowly, deliberately, taking her time in answering.

'Naturally. Any woman who becomes a doctor must be prepared to encounter prejudice.'

'You are also Sir Amos Howard's granddaughter.'

'Oh how ridiculous! Grandpa is one of the most respected men in Liverpool.'

'I don't dispute that. But the very fact that you enjoy the privileges associated with your background could work against you – particularly among those you most seek to help.'

'Surely not, Oliver.' Felicity sensed her niece's indignation rising to danger level, and intervened hurriedly, 'Aren't you being overpessimistic?'

'It's all right, Aunt Fliss. There is a grain of truth in what Oliver says.' Aimée flashed him a look of defiance. 'But if there is prejudice, I shall work to overcome it. What I won't do is run away.'

'I never for one moment supposed you would.' Oliver tossed his cigar butt into the fire and rose to stand looking down at her, his expression unreadable. 'I remember a young woman up to her ankles in mud who gave me the edge of her tongue when I tried to bypass an urgent need for medical attention.' His eyes held hers. 'She fought her corner then, and I have every confidence in her ability to do so now. However, it does no harm to be prepared.'

Once again he had cut the ground very neatly from under her, leaving her momentarily speechless and embarrassed.

Felicity looked from one to the other. 'My dears, I am intrigued. Do tell me more.'

'There's nothing to tell.' Aimée stubbed out her cigarette and stood up, too, anger struggling against an illogical desire to laugh. In the end, laughter won, though a thread of irritation ran through it. 'Damn you, Oliver Langley. What a devious man you are.' She pulled on her hat and turned to her aunt. 'I must go.'

'Goodness, you're like a whirlwind.'

'Sorry, Aunt Fliss. Grandpa has agreed to let Patrick Shaw spend two weeks in the private wing of the Cottage Hospital, and I have to convince Agnes Shaw that it wouldn't be a violation of her principles to accept the offer.' Aimée's chin lifted defiantly as she met Oliver's sardonic smile. 'Yes, I know what you're thinking, but I have no objection to using my position of privilege for good, when necessity demands.'

She kissed Felicity's cheek, waved a careless hand in his direction, and was gone.

Dr Hutton had offered no objections when Aimée put her proposal about Crag Vale to him. Aimée had met his kind many times and received the distinct impression that he would go along with most things that didn't involve any effort on his part.

Agnes Shaw, however, took a lot more convincing. Aimée had arrived to find her leaning out perilously from the sill of an upper window, polishing the glass as if her life depended on it.

'I'll be down,' she called, and carefully raised the sash to ease herself inside. There were dark rings under her flinty eyes as she faced Aimée a few minutes later across the living room table.

Damn, thought Aimee. 'Dr Hutton has already told you,' she said.

'He came this morning. And I'll tell you now what I told him. We've never been beholden to anyone in our lives, and we don't aim to start now.'

'And does your husband take the same view?'

Colour flared in Agnes's face, and Aimée knew she was struggling to evade the truth without telling an outright lie. 'Pat left the decision to me,' she said stubbornly.

'I see.'

'I'm not sure that you do. It was good of you to take the trouble, doctor, and I hope you'll tell Sir Amos that we thank him for his generous offer, but Pat paid his fourpence a week all the time he was in work, and that entitles him to free treatment, so I reckon we'll wait to see if Dr Hutton can find a place for him.'

'You can't afford to wait that long.' Aimée kept her voice low, holding on to her patience with an effort. 'If Dr Hutton was really trying he'd have found somewhere by now. Oh, for heaven's sake, there are rooms lying empty at Crag Vale, and my grandfather has offered one to your husband for two weeks. It is nothing to him and everything to Pat – and to you. If you don't have a break soon, you're going to crack up altogether.'

She watched stubbornness turn to indecision and pressed home her point, leaning across the table. 'Grandpa is old and in pain, but he has worked hard all his life. He's straight as a die, and if you'd ever met him, you would know that what he is offering is a helping hand to a fellow worker, not charity. But if you can't see the difference, I can't make you accept. All that I ask is that you don't let pride decide for you.'

Agnes sat down abruptly. 'Sometimes pride is all we have to keep us going.' A fit of coughing from next door made her stiffen and half turn. It stopped almost at once, but the timing had been providential. 'But perhaps this time, it's not enough.'

'Well then?' Aimée held her breath.

Agnes sighed and eased herself upright again. 'You'd better come and see Pat.'

Minna Buchanan had a chronic aversion to illness of any kind, though she had always steeled herself to overcome her weakness whenever Gerald or Aimée had need of her.

And if Megan hadn't mentioned TB the afternoon that Pat Shaw arrived in Crag Vale with Aimée in attendance, all might have gone off without comment.

'But, darling,' she exclaimed in alarm, 'you said your Mr Shaw was very ill. You never mentioned that he had tuberculosis.'

'Didn't I?' Aimée swallowed her exasperation, and prepared to be reassuring. 'Well, it doesn't really matter what is wrong with him. Patrick Shaw will be completely isolated. There is no risk.'

'So you say, dear. But I remember how you and Gerald were separated when you had the measles, and he still caught them and was very poorly.'

'That was quite different.' Aimée smothered an almost hysterical desire to laugh.

'Well, I'm sure you think you know best, dear. And I am not worried for myself.' Her lip quivered. 'But we do have Megan to consider.'

Gerald and Megan had been back at Fernlea since the end of March, and Megan was newly pregnant and thriving, so far as Aimée could see. She crouched down and took her mother's hands in a firm clasp.

'Mother dear, I promise you there is no risk. Do you think for one moment that I would place Gerald's unborn child in jeopardy?'

'I suppose not, but –'

'Aimée is quite right, Mother.' Megan's soft Welsh voice ought not to have grated, but it did. 'I nursed a number of cases of TB during the war, you know. And with proper precautions, there is no danger of infection.' She busied herself with the tea tray, and set a cup on the table beside Minna's chair. 'See, here is your tea, just the way you like it. So enjoy it and stop worrying.'

As if she was a helpless child, Aimée thought, biting back her indignation as her mother smiled mistily up at her daughter-in-law. 'Oh well, my dear, if you both think there is no danger, I suppose I must accept that there is none.'

Implying that my word is no longer good enough. Aimée gritted her teeth and tried not to feel a slight where none was intended. 'Yes, Mother, I really think you must.'

This is what you wanted, she told herself. Someone to take your place here, to relieve you of guilt, to enable you to do what you want. It is stupid to be jealous because Megan is succeeding in doing just that rather better than you expected. In fact, now is an excellent opportunity to mention the house, and the plans for the future.

'But I don't understand, dear.' Minna set down her teacup unsteadily. 'I thought you and Frank were getting on splendidly. And now that Gerald and Megan are here, I was hoping we would all be one big happy family.'

'I know, dear, but it wouldn't work.'

'That is ridiculous. We are all reasonable people. I'm sure I don't know what makes you think such a thing. Goodness knows what your father will say.'

'I hope he will understand.' They seemed to have had this conversation a thousand times.

'And Gerald. You and Gerald were always so close.'

'We still are, Mother.' She could feel Megan standing very still waiting for her answer, her gaze unwavering. 'But Gerald's future is here with Megan. Mine is not. Frank doesn't really need me, and I have to go where I am needed.'

Her mother's lower lip began to quiver again. 'I don't know why I should be surprised. You have always done exactly as you pleased, regardless of my feelings,' she said tragically and with a jangling of bracelets, stretched out a hand to Megan. 'At least now I shall not be without a daughter to bear me company in my failing years.'

'Mother! You are forty-six, and your health is excellent.'

'How would you know, dear, when you have spent long periods away? I am sure I have never been one to parade my sufferings – '

'Oh, darling Ma!' The theatrical air of pathos was almost too much for Aimée. Her exasperation dissolved into a sudden uprush of love. She bent to kiss her cheek. 'I know I'm a rotten daughter, but I'm only going as far as Liverpool.'

Her father was in the spinning shed. The noise was deafening, but when he saw her, he took her arm and led her outside. He moved a little slower these days, and his face had never quite lost that grey look, but he seemed happy enough.

'I thought you were going to take things easy once Gerald was home,' she reproached him.

'Eh, you know me, Aimée, lass. What would I do, cluttering up the house? This place is my life. And your brother has taken a lot of the paperwork off my hands. Never did enjoy that side of it. Now he's got some fancy notion in his head of re-equipping one of the factories so as to widen our range. Reckons we should be aiming for the fashion market.'

'Would that be such a bad move?' Aimée said. 'People always seem to crave a touch of glamour after a period of enforced austerity. If you can get into the market early enough, you could well reap the benefit.'

Seth gave her one of his looks. 'You two always did gang up on me. Been talking to our Gerald, have you?'

'No. Honestly, Dad, I haven't seen him, yet. But it makes sense. My young friend Matty Shaw would agree if you asked her.'

'Aye, well, I'm maybe just getting too long in the tooth to change my ideas. We'll work something out, I dare say. At least I know where I am with Gerald. Not like you – ' He shot her a keen glance and she had the grace to blush. 'If you're planning something your mother won't like, I'd better be hearing about it.'

So Aimée told him. He took the news better than she had expected.

'I'm not blind, lass. You've been like a cat on hot bricks for weeks now. And, nice girl though Megan is, it can't be an easy situation for you.'

'You always did see more than you let on, you old bear,' she said, hugging him.

'He was quite sweet about it, really,' she said later, perching on the corner of Gerald's desk.

'The war's changed him. It's changed a lot of us, I guess. He doesn't seem to have the driving ambition he used to have – or maybe I was more in awe of him then.'

'He's older, and so are we,' Aimée said. 'Perhaps it's the prospect of grandfatherhood. Could be a Christmas baby.'

Gerald grinned. 'Mother's in seventh heaven. She and Megan get on so well.'

Only because Megan panders to her every whim. It was an unworthy thought – ungracious, too, to entertain the idea that it perhaps wasn't good for her mother to be indulged to such an extent.

'Aimée?'

She looked up, blushing a little in case Gerald guessed where her thoughts had taken her. He hadn't – quite.

'That isn't why you're going, is it? Because of Megan?'

'Good heavens, no,' she was able to answer with perfect truth. 'Finger wet, finger dry, brother dear. Though I'm sure it wouldn't be fair to Megan if I were to remain here indefinitely.'

Gerald protested that nothing could be further from the truth, but his very vehemence gave the words a hollow ring, and they both knew it.

Matty's experience of the countryside had been confined to the Liverpool parks and woodlands, and occasional trips across the Mersey to Eastham woods, especially in springtime when the bluebells were in full bloom.

Early summer in Crag Vale therefore filled her with awe and delight. Most of the early blossom had gone, though drifts of petals still lingered to be stirred by the breeze. But there was new green shooting everywhere and the hawthorn and horse chestnut trees were in full bloom.

'If I lived here, I'd never want to leave,' she said with a sigh, when she and her mother left Daisy and Moira next door with Marge Flynn and came by train to visit her father on the first Sunday after he had arrived.

Aimée laughed. 'You might not be so keen in the depths of winter. The valley is often cut off for days on end with drifting snow.'

But even this prospect enchanted Matty. The only snow she saw usually turned to grey slush in no time. And then she remembered why she was here.

'Dad looks ever so pale. Mam was that full up, seeing him, I thought I'd leave them on their own for a bit.' She gave Aimée a very straight look. 'He is all right, isn't he?'

There was no point in trying to shield Matty. She was much too intelligent to be fooled. But nor could she or Agnes at present be told the whole truth – that a thorough examination by Frank had confirmed Aimée's suspicions that the increasingly severe bouts of coughing had begun to affect Pat's heart. Agnes would have to know eventually, but professional etiquette demanded that Aimée should first have a talk with Dr Hutton.

'It depends what you mean by all right,' she said tactfully. 'Your father isn't going to get better, but there are lots of things we can do to make him more comfortable.' She smiled to soften the words. 'Look, come along to the house and have hot drink, and I'll try to explain. We can come back here a little later.'

By the time Matty had seen Fernlea, been graciously received by Aimée's mother, and plied with tea and cakes by her twin brother, her spirits were well on the way to being restored.

Gerald asked her opinion about what she thought the trends in fashion would be, and they had talked enthusiastically about fine lawns and muslins in unusual colours. And when he actually offered to show her round one of the mills the next time she came, she was almost in a daze.

'I don't see how you can possibly bear to exchange all this for a house in Myrtle Street,' she sighed, when Aimée finally took her up to her bedroom to freshen up before going back to the hospital to give her mam a break.

The first sight of her husband had shocked Agnes, too. Such a few days apart, and it was almost like looking at a stranger, sitting up all neat and tidy against his starched white pillows and sheets, his sunken face looking almost grey against them. But his eyes were clear, and brighter than she'd seen them in a long time, and the minute he smiled, he was her Pat again.

Her prickly conscience still troubled her a little as she gradually adjusted to her surroundings, the luxurious carpets, the marble washstand, the wide windows looking out on to rolling countryside.

'I can see you'll not want to come home in a hurry,' she said dryly to cover the awkwardness of those first moments. 'Whatever it is they're doing to you, it's working a treat.'

She put up a hand to cover her mouth, which threatened to go awry. Pat noticed the gesture, and swallowed hard.

'Sure, I haven't felt as good in years,' he agreed huskily, his eyes drinking her in. 'And the King himself couldn't have had better treatment.' He reached out a hand. 'But the nurses haven't your touch, girl, good though they are.'

'That's enough of your flannel, Pat Shaw. I tell you what, though – it's no wonder you've got your cardie on. It's terrible cold in here.'

'Ah well, Aggie love, seemingly that's all part of the treatment. You'll have to have a talk with that nice young Dr Buchanan, an' she'll explain.'

'Oh, I'll be doing that right enough,' she said.

The visit to Crag Vale had a curious effect on Agnes. Her tiredness seemed to have vanished and she set about the house with boundless energy and several large tins of distemper. The chimneys were swept and the windows of Pat's room were thrown wide. Daisy was packed off next door and everyone was roped in to help in their spare time without fear or favour. Moira was eager to prove she was every bit as capable as Matty, and the tiny washhouse rang with laughter as curtains and bedding were washed and dollied, and hung out to dry. Agnes scrubbed the lino, and the hearthrug was thrown over the line in the backyard and had every bit of dust beaten out of it before it too was washed.

Kevin was handed a tin of distemper and a brush. He had grown inches in the last few months, and at fifteen already towered over his mother. But he was a good-natured lad and set about the parlour walls with a willing grin.

'The lad's got more energy than skill,' Agnes said when Aimée arrived one evening to find the house a hive of activity. 'By the time he's done the lobby and the kitchen I expect he'll end up with more paint on himself than on the walls, but he's willing enough and that count's for a lot.'

'I thought you were going to take things easy.'

'Oh, I can't abide to be doing nothing, and I want the house all nice for when Pat comes home.' She looked sideways at Aimée.

'I'm not kidding myself, you know. Not any more. Seeing him there in that hospital bed made me realize . . . but I expect you know that. I just want what time he has left to be as good as I can make it for him.'

'You've always done that,' Aimée assured her, and tactfully explained about letting in some fresh air. 'So long as he's not actually in a draught, and he's well wrapped up, Pat won't come to any harm – in fact it will make his breathing a bit easier.'

'I'll take your word for it, though what Dr Hutton will have to say, I don't know. It's a pity we can't have you instead, but what with him being the panel doctor . . .' She straightened up and eased her shoulders. 'You'll be getting close to moving in at Myrtle Street, I expect. If there's anything I can do . . .'

'You could rest, but I don't suppose you will. As for the house, I appreciate the offer, but there isn't much to be done. Mrs Arbuthnot left everywhere spotless. I'm keeping some of the furniture and the rest has already been taken away. I'll be moving in next week and someone is coming in daily to clean and answer the door and the telephone.'

'I can see you've got it all sorted. Still, you never know.'

Aimée thanked her, and promised to ask, should she need any help at all. 'How's Irene, by the way?'

'You know our Irene – making much of little, as always. She says the baby's due the beginning of October,' Agnes's voice grew dry, 'though no one'll be surprised, I'm thinkin', if it comes sooner. And what with running the shop, and Eddie off making deals half the time, married life is proving a bit of a letdown. But her bed's made now, so she'll have to shape the best way she can.'

'Poor Irene. I'll try and make time to look in on her.'

For the next few days, however, Aimée was preoccupied with her own affairs. Gerald came to help her rearrange what furniture remained in her house. The carpets and curtains had all been left, and were for the most part in quiet good taste, so that Aimée was happy to keep them. The green velvet settee and chairs in the sitting room, together with oyster pink walls and a cream carpet, had been a little too reminiscent of her mother's taste, so she had ordered loose covers in a plain soft blue chintz, which gave the room a feeling of serenity.

The surgery was the room that involved the greatest alteration.

Its side wall ran parallel with the entry, and behind it was a small pantry, which had been converted to a waiting room with a doorway cut into the outer wall beneath a prominent sign saying *Surgery Entrance*.

Mrs Arbuthnot had taken the dining room furniture, but had left a huge desk, which had numerous little cubbyholes and lockable drawers.

'It's exactly what I need,' Aimée enthused to Gerald. 'And lots of wall cupboards, of course. My nice builder, Mr Green, seems to be able to turn his hand to most things, or know someone who can – like plumbing in a sink. And I shall need a couch, and some screens to put round it.'

Gerald was used to her single-minded enthusiasm, but this time he feared it might carry her too far. 'Aimée.'

'Hmm?' She didn't look up from measuring the distance between the desk and the door.

'You won't be too disappointed, will you, if at first folk don't come flocking to your door?'

The flutter of nerves that she had so far managed to conceal from everyone threatened to erupt. But she went on measuring and her voice was steady and deliberately matter-of-fact.

'My dear, I have few illusions. Almost everyone I know has spent the last few weeks telling me it won't be easy.' She turned, her chin at a pugnacious angle. 'Oliver Langley reckons I'll meet with prejudice because of Grandpa, and I dare say he's right.' She grinned. 'Though wild horses wouldn't have dragged such an admission from me at the time.'

Gerald came to rest his hands on her shoulders. 'I want you to promise that if things do get difficult, you'll let me know.'

She noticed for the first time that his hair was beginning to recede. It gave him an endearingly earnest look. For a moment she allowed herself to lean against him, drawing strength from his closeness. Then she straightened up. 'Thank you, dear boy. But I'm a big girl now, remember. I fight my own battles.'

13

IN MADAME VINCENTE'S stuffy workroom there was a stunned silence. The girls were all on their feet, crowding round the work table, mesmerized by the zigzag trail of little damp patches spreading down and across the front of the ball gown on which they had been painstakingly working.

A sob finally broke the silence. It came from a pale fair-haired young woman, her trembling hands still clutching the cup whose contents had all but ruined the shimmering ivory silk.

'Oh, God help me! Will yer look at it? The money it cost, she'll kill me!'

'Of course she won't, Vera. Madame isn't a monster.' Matty took the cup from her nerveless fingers and made her sit down. 'This room's like an oven with all the hot weather, I'm not surprised you came over faint. It was an accident. Madame will understand when we explain.'

But Matty's voice lacked conviction. Food and drink of any kind were strictly forbidden in the workroom. Even plain water was bound to leave a tidemark on such delicate fabric. The silk was French and dreadfully expensive. It had been specially bought in for a gown designed by Madame Vincente for Lady Spendlove to wear at the summer charity ball being organized by Mrs Mellish in just one week's time. There might just be enough material left to recut the gown, but to Madame such material was almost a living thing, to be treasured. Matty knew exactly how she felt, just as she knew how furious their employer would be at the waste of time and money.

'Madame will have to be told immediately.' Miss Donald, the head seamstress, was furious, knowing she would be expected to take the blame for this disaster. She had always disapproved of flighty young women in the workroom, even if they were skilled with a needle, and that Vera Lyall, married or not, was little more than a pretty flibberti-gibbet, not solid and dependable like Ethel Higgs and Ruth. As for Matty Shaw – she turned slowly. 'Matty, will you be so good as to go and tell Madame.'

'Me? Why me?' Matty stared in angry disbelief. 'You're head of the workroom. It's your place to tell her.'

'Don't be impertinent, girl. Do as I tell you. And the rest of you, get on with your work.'

Miss Donald's thin features grew even thinner, reminding Matty irresistibly of Mrs Crawley. But she knew better than to argue. It's because Madame has singled me out recently for special praise, she told herself as she clattered up the little spiral staircase and along the corridor with perspiration fast turning to a cold sweat that ran down between her shoulder blades.

'You want to watch out,' Miss Timms of alterations had warned her ages ago. 'Proper jealous of her position, is Miss Donald.'

'That's daft,' Matty had said. 'I'm only a part-timer. She wouldn't lower her nose to notice the likes of me.'

'Don't you be so sure. I've seen that Clara Donald watching you. A part-timer you may be at present, but you've got two things going for you – youth and talent. And she knows well enough that Madame Vincente's spotted the skill you have with a needle.'

Matty had been flattered at the time, and when there was a vacancy in the workroom and she'd been promoted to a full-time junior seamstress, and later to a bodice hand, it seemed there might be something in Miss Timms' words. But so far as she could tell, Madame took no more notice of her now than she had before.

'Well, Mathilde? Why are you not at your work?'

Matty jumped. She'd been noticed now, right enough. With her heart in her mouth she met those penetrating eyes. 'I'm sorry, Madame. I was just . . . I was wondering . . .' It was unnerving, watching her standing there like an elegant inquisitor all in black, except for her frizzy red hair, which seemed to be crackling like fire in a shaft of sunlight. How on earth did you begin to tell someone with a temper like hers that a priceless gown had been ruined?

'Then please to refrain from thinking and not waste my time. *Venez ici* – come, I do not bite.'

Haltingly, Matty explained what had happened, and then found herself running to keep up as Madame set off down the stairs on high clicking heels. 'It was an accident, honest. It's like a furnace in that room. We were all spittin' feathers. I was beginning to feel faint meself . . .'

She might have been talking to the air. She thought she was used to her employer's explosive moods, but in full flow the French-woman was awesome – a tiny volcanic figure pacing the work-room, spilling out a tirade of fractured English that no one dared to interrupt. If it hadn't been so awful, it would have been funny.

'*Merde!* You will tell me *immédiatement* 'oo 'as done this wickedness?' She fingered the gown, revulsion distorting her painted mouth. 'Bah, it is ruin! My reputation will be ruin.' She flung the gown to the floor, stamped on it with vicious finality and kicked it into the corner. 'You will burn this!'

The last dramatic command drew a moan from Vera. The silence was palpable as Madame's sharp little face registered shock.

'Vera? It was you? Oh, this I do not believe! 'Ave I not been good to you? Why you 'ate me so much?'

'I don't, Madame . . . oh no!'

'But, oh yes! Why else you do this thing? Because of you I could lose valued client, reputation, business, everything! *Allez-vous-en!* Go – go – go, before I forget I am a lady and strike you!'

Matty could bear no more. 'Madame, please don't sack poor Vera. Oh, please, if you would just listen . . .'

The bright eyes seared into her. '*Nom de Dieu*, do you dare to argue? There is nothing to 'ear. It is enough that I 'ave eyes to see! Now all will 'ave to be done again, which mean tomorrow and the next day, you will all work extra hours.'

'Honest, Mam, it was awful,' Matty said as she laid the table for supper. 'Talk about a paddy, I thought she'd go off pop any minute. And as for poor Vera – '

'Never you mind poor Vera, my girl. You want to look out for number one, or you could find you're out on your ear, too.'

'But, Mam, Vera can't afford to lose her job. It wasn't just the heat that made her come over faint – she's having another baby, which is why I fetched her the water, even though we aren't allowed. So you see, I'm as much to blame as she is.'

Agnes, busy cutting up some middle neck of mutton for a stew, nearly sliced her finger. 'You didn't tell Madame Whatzit that, I hope?'

'No, but I think I should – when she's cooled down, like. Vera's husband, Tony, hasn't been able to find work since he left the army and what with having two kiddies already, they desperately need her money.'

Agnes's tongue clicked impatiently. 'You'll do no such thing, our Matty. Vera's problems aren't yours. And they're a funny lot, the French. They don't think the same as us.' She put up a hand to brush a strand of hair from her eyes. 'Heaven knows, we've had enough to worry about with Kevin losing his job.'

'I suppose it was bound to happen with skilled men coming back from the war who can run rings round our Kevin. Anyway, Dad reckoned he'd never make a riveter.'

'How could he tell without seeing him at work? Kevin was an apprentice – he needed time. And he'd have had a proper trade at the end of it.' Agnes attacked the meat with renewed vigour.

'It could have been worse if that butcher who supplies the pie shop hadn't taken him on. And we do get a bit of extra meat now and then.'

'It's not what I wanted for him,' Agnes insisted stubbornly. 'But I suppose it's better than this latest crazy notion he has in his head about going to sea.'

'He does seem quite keen,' Matty said.

'Pie in the sky,' Agnes snapped. 'With so many out of work, it's no time for either of you to be playing ducks an' drakes with the jobs you've got. Your friend Vera must shift for herself. As for Kevin, he may be big for his age, but he's still too young to be leaving home. Anything could happen to him at sea.'

'They probably wouldn't take him anyway.' Matty knew that deep down Mam was scared. She was thinking of Phil and Dad, and how Kevin might soon be the only man of the family left to her, even if he was only fifteen. It was enough to make you weep, except tears never solved anything.

Then Daisy was tugging at Matty's skirt, holding up a battered picture book. 'Moira gone out. Want Matty tell,' she insisted.

'All right, precious. But just a little story.' Matty swallowed hard and lifted her up, finding comfort in her small warm body. 'Oh, come on, Mam. Cheer up. Everything'll be fine. You'll see.'

Later, she went to sit with her dad. He had come back fre Crag Vale so much better than when he went, that she might have been tempted to believe in miracles if Aimée hadn't been so honest with them.

'Pat's condition hasn't really changed,' she had told them the night before his return, her eyes compassionate. 'The rest and treatment has gained him a temporary respite, but I can't honestly tell you how long it will last.'

Seeing her father now, with something of the old light back in his eyes as she told him about the drama of the afternoon, she could almost believe that Aimée was being unduly pessimistic. Except when you caught him unawares and realized how thin and drawn his face had grown, or when he got a fit of coughing.

'I'm surprised you're so keen to work for this Madame Vincente. She sounds worse than your mam when she's got a cob on.'

Matty giggled. 'Oh, but she's a brilliant cutter, Dad. I've already learned a lot, just watchin' her. Anyhow, as I was telling you, the upshot was, she told us to burn the gown an' Miss Donald gave me the job of taking it to the incinerator. She gives me all the rotten jobs. But I couldn't burn anything that beautiful, Dad. It would be a sin! Especially if I could think of a way to disguise the stain and making it wearable.' Matty's eyes mirrored the passion in her voice, but as she met his quizzical glance her voice faltered. 'So I hid it in my workbag. That's not really dishonest, is it?'

'Eh, girl, it's not for me to say. I dare say the good Lord would be understanding in the circumstances, but your mam's a different proposition altogether, so I think we'd best keep it a secret between the two of us.'

But the excitement about the silk gown wouldn't go away. All kinds of possibilities were teeming round in her head, and she knew he'd have to get them into some kind of order, or she'd never sleep.

'I'm going out for a walk, Mam,' she said, slipping her small sketch pad into her dress pocket. 'It's too nice to stay indoors.'

'Well, don't be late back. I have to leave at ten to do the offices.'

One day, Matty promised herself, I'll be rich, and then Mam won't ever have to go out to work again.

Outside she almost fell over Marge Flynn who had brought a

chair out onto the pavement, to 'get some air'. She sat like a queen, knitting needles clicking in plump fingers as she effortlessly turned the heel of a sock, her shiny skirt stretched tight across massive thighs to make a comfortable lap for Robbie, her youngest, who scampered up and down with the boundless energy of a three-year-old.

'It's norra bit of use puttin' this little tike ter bed in broad daylight, with every room oven-hot. Like as not, 'e'd sweat hisself into a rash.'

'The heat doesn't seem to bother our Daisy. She's gone out like a light.'

'Ah, the little love.' Marge's eyes twinkled. 'You luk fresh as paint, any road. Goin' somewhere nice, are you, queen?'

'Only to the park for some fresh air.'

'Time you found yerself a fella, a pretty gairl like you.'

'I haven't seen one yet I'd give tuppence for,' Matty said with a toss of the head. 'Anyhow, I've got better things to do with my life than end up like our Irene.'

'Eh, she's gerrin' big, that sister of yours. Early October, is it?' Marge chuckled. 'I doubt she'll last another two months, lerralone three. Still, eight-month babbies aren't that uncommon round here.'

She winked, and Matty blushed and pretended not to notice. But her companion's attention was already being diverted by the sight of Nellie Reagan coming out of her front door.

'She'll be off to her evenin' job – waitress at one of the posh hotels, so she was tellin' us. Now, there's a real tragedy, Matty gairl. Marriage is no picnic for the likes of 'er.'

'I think I'll catch her up,' Matty said, not wanting to get involved in gossip.

Nellie turned when she heard her name called, and they walked to the end of the road together. The air was still and warm, but not unpleasantly so.

'I've been stuck in a stuffy room sewing all day,' Matty said, 'so I thought I'd have a bit of a walk to Sefton Park.'

'I took Danny up there on Sunday. There never seems to be enough time through the week, what with gettin' him ready, an' one thing an' another. And now our Mary's off her food. It's the heat, I suppose.'

She sounded bone weary, and small wonder. A fine figure of a man, Mam had called Danny when he and Nellie got married. Matty had been half in love with him herself in a childish romantic way. She still remembered their wedding day, what a handsome couple they'd been, he with his shock of sandy hair, and blue eyes – and how she'd envied Nellie, who was so shy and scarcely coming up to his shoulder. It was awful to think of Danny now without his legs, almost totally dependent on others. He'd be terrible hard work for anyone as slight as Nellie. It made Matty tired just thinking about it. Dad was only half his size, and he could be quite a handful.

And she had little Mary to look after as well. In a way it was a good job they were living with Danny's mam, except that she was a right frosty-faced old biddy who made hard work of everything. Nothing was ever right for her. So life couldn't be much fun for Nellie. She was only a couple of years older than Irene, and she'd once been ever so pretty. Now her dark hair was scraped back, her eyes had a dead look, and her cotton gingham frock had been washed once too often.

'You should take Mary to see Dr Buchanan. She's just starting up in Myrtle Street, and she's ever such a good doctor.'

'Perhaps I will. We had a leaflet through the door.'

'I know. Our Moira and Emmy Flynn delivered lots of them.'

'Danny's mam says it's just the weather, an' a good dose of castor oil would soon cure her.' Nellie sounded tired, and it was almost as though she was speaking to herself. 'That's her remedy for most ills. Except it won't cure Danny. I suppose that's what makes her so –' She stopped abruptly, a shocked look in her eyes, as if she'd suddenly realized what she was saying. She forced a smile. 'Anyway, I'll think about Dr Buchanan, if Mary's not better soon.'

They parted on the corner, and for a few minutes Matty couldn't get Nellie's smile out of her mind. It was so bleak, it made you want to cry. But her own thoughts gradually crowded in, blotting out the momentary pain she had felt.

There were quite a lot of people in Sefton Park – couples wandering arm in arm with fingers entwined and older folk sitting on benches, watching, dozing, maybe dreaming of a time when they had walked hand in hand. The evening air was still, and heavy with fragrance.

Unable to find a vacant bench, she wandered towards the Palm House, a fairy-tale building made of glass and steel filled with all kinds of exotic plants and trees. Inside the air was even warmer than outside, but moist. As she wandered, her glance was drawn again and again to the delicate tracery of some of the leaves, the sweep of a stem here, the droop of a frond there. And all the scents mingling in the damp warmth – a pungent earthiness giving way to a sweet perfume, and then to the sharp fragrance of a lemon tree.

Later, Matty found a place to sit alone near the lake, and here at last she let her thoughts spill out as she filled page after page of her book with sketches, some quite detailed, others little more than an impression; pages alive with birds and insects; the transparence of a dragonfly's wing, a butterfly, brilliantly marked – and, caught in a brief exquisite flash of blue, a kingfisher, beautiful beyond belief. Beside the sketches she made notes describing the colours while they were still fresh in her memory.

And as she lay wide awake in bed that night, a pattern began to evolve in her mind. Lady Spendlove's dress would be recut tomorrow and no one would ask about the original, supposedly burned. But Matty had plans for that silk.

Aimee's glossy black door now matched the railings, and a neat brass plate on the wall proclaimed that Aimée Buchanan, MD was now in residence.

'This is all splendid, Aimée,' Felicity had exclaimed when her niece took her on a conducted tour. 'You have worked hard. I shall recommend you to all my friends.'

Aimée hadn't the heart to tell Aunt Fliss that her smart friends weren't the people she most wished to encourage, though a few wealthy patients would help to balance the budget. She had tried to cover the area as widely as she could, giving Moira and Emmy a threepenny piece each to distribute leaflets, especially to those for whom the need was greatest. The leaflets listed the surgery hours, and she had tried to emphasize that charges in most cases would be minimal, and expressed the hope that she would soon be opening a free clinic for mothers and young children two afternoons a week.

Mrs Green, the builder's wife, had agreed to come and 'do' for her. She was a formidable woman, half as big again as her husband. Indoors and out, she wore a green felt hat resplendent with a feather — 'I bet she even wears it in bed,' Gerald had whispered irreverently. She also had a large mole on her chin sprouting several black hairs, and a platitude for every occasion.

As the hours passed on the first morning without a single patient, Mrs Green plied Aimée with numerous cups of tea, and came up with an infinite variety of reasons why folk hadn't rushed to break down the door.

'It's always the same with anything new, chuck. No one wants ter be first.' And later: 'Give it time. Remember, termorrow's another day . . .'

Aimée gritted her teeth and told herself the woman meant well. She had plenty of paperwork to do, but couldn't concentrate. Promptly at one o'clock, the surgery door was locked, a poached egg on toast and small rice pudding was laid out for her in the morning room, and Mrs Green departed to get 'her Wilf' his dinner.

Aimée forced the egg down, and was just eyeing the pudding with revulsion when the telephone rang. It was an acquaintance of Aunt Felicity's who wondered if Dr Buchanan could pop along to see her. She made an appointment for two o'clock, trying not to let her eagerness show.

Mrs Fortnam lived in Abercromby Square. She was a lady in her late fifties, plump and pretty except for an expression of discontent, explained by her opening declaration that she was a martyr to migraine.

'Dr Dalywell usually prescribes some of his special medicine, but he's away at present. And as Felicity Mellish was singing your praises at a bridge party last week, I decided to give you a try.' She stared at Aimée with an intensity bordering on rudeness. 'You are very young.' Aimée smiled, but made no answer. 'It seems an odd way for a young gel with your background to go on. Something unwomanly about it. Still, I dare say I am old-fashioned.'

Aimée bit back the retort that sprang to her lips, and, having examined Mrs Fortnum and found nothing wrong with her that a little exercise wouldn't cure, asked if she happened to have a sample of the doctor's special medicine. Mrs Fortnum rang for her maid, who was sent in search of the bottle. It proved to be the standard remedy, though Aimée was wise enough not to say so.

'Rest and a light diet should help matters. You may care to try a paregoric that my mother, who is similarly afflicted, finds particularly beneficial. It is not unlike your present mixture, though it is rather stronger, so it would be wise not to exceed the stated dosage.'

The medicine was in fact identical except for the addition of a little extra peppermint, but the nearest hint that it was something special always worked like a charm with her mother and she guessed it would have a similar effect on Mrs Fortnum. 'I'll send someone round with it later this afternoon.'

Her patient sighed. 'If that is the best you can do. What are your fees? I never pay Dr Dalywell more than a guinea a visit.'

'A guinea will be fine,' said Aimée, who had been about to charge fifteen shillings. Magnanimously, she added, 'Including the medicine.'

The afternoon continued slow, but about three o'clock, she heard the jangle of the bell above the waiting room door. It was music to her ears.

Mrs Green admitted a tired-looking young woman dragging a reluctant little girl of no more than three years old.

Nellie Reagan had thought long and hard before plucking up her courage to come, knowing that Danny's mam would have tried to prevent her if she'd known.

'Do come and sit down, so that I can take a few details,' Aimée said, with a particular smile for the child who shrank against her mother. 'See, Mary, there are some picture books and toys in the box near the window. Perhaps you would like to go and play with them while I talk to your mammy.'

Mary sucked her thumb and pressed closer.

'I'm afraid she's shy of strangers.'

'That's all right. There's no hurry. We can talk while she gets used to the strange room. For a start, perhaps you can tell me a little about yourself, and why you've come to see me.'

The lady doctor was much more friendly than Nellie had expected, and gradually she relaxed and began to pour out all about Danny and his mother, and how Mary wasn't eating. And as they talked, Mary eased away from her mother's side and was soon happily exploring the contents of the box.

'Sometimes hot weather can put children off their food, but in Mary's case, do you think the atmosphere at home might be affecting her, too?'

'It might well be,' Nellie blurted out. 'It's so difficult, you see. Me mother-in-law's a good, well-meaning woman . . .'

'But it can be difficult with two women in one house?' Aimée finished for her, thinking of Megan. 'Especially when, in their different ways, they both love the same man?'

'That's it exactly.' The relief of being able to tell someone who understood made Nellie gabble. 'It's even worse, Danny being . . . you know . . . the way he is. And his mam does go on about him being crippled something awful sometimes. I'm not sure how much Mary understands of what she sees an' hears, but something's changed her – she used to chatter all the time before Danny came back.'

Unbidden, the memory of all those poor broken bodies she had been unable to mend, the shattered limbs she had amputated, came flooding back to Aimée. Nellie Reagan's voice, sounding concerned, seemed to come from a long way off.

'Are you all right, doctor? You've gone quite white.'

'Yes. Yes, of course. I'm sorry.' She pulled her wits together, and the panic receded. 'Do you think Mary will let me take a look at her now?'

The child wasn't very co-operative at first, but a bowl of toffee prominently in view on Aimée's desk made her little tongue quiver with anticipation. The examination over, she was allowed to help herself to a large piece of toffee.

'I don't think there's much physically wrong with Mary,' Aimée said quietly. 'And children are very adaptable, you know. Given a little time, I'm sure she will accept your husband's disability without question.'

'She might if Grandma Reagan didn't keep goin' on about how she must be careful not to bump into her daddy, or touch him in the wrong places.' Again the words burst out.

With difficulty, Aimée told herself not to get involved. 'Perhaps you could encourage Mary to play out more. Does she have many friends in the street?'

'Not really. She seems to like being on her own.'

'It isn't really good for her to be with grown-ups all the time. You live quite close to the Shaws, I see. Isn't there a large family of youngsters next door to them?'

Nellie sighed. Again she could hear her mother-in-law's voice:

'We don't want her mixing with that riffraff brood of Marge Flynn's. Common as muck, they are . . .' She murmured that she wasn't sure.

'Well, see what you can do. As for eating, try to give Mary several small snacks, rather than one large meal, and some fresh fruit if possible, and plenty to drink.'

'Grandma Reagan won't like that either,' Nellie muttered. 'Spoilin', she'll call it. Panderin' to a child's whims.'

Again, Aimée smothered her irritation. 'Perhaps she will, but it isn't for her to say. You are Mary's mother. If you still have a problem, perhaps you'd like me to call round and explain.'

'Oh, I don't think – '

'Well, give it a try,' Aimée cut in, feeding Mary another piece of toffee. 'Actually, I'm more concerned about you.'

'Me? Oh, I'm all right.' Two spots of colour stained Nellie's pale cheeks.

'Are you?'

'Well, just a bit tired.'

Aimée gently pulled down one of her lower eyelids. 'And anaemic. I'm going to give you some medicine. It contains iron, and I want you to take it three times a day, and come and see me again in a week's time.'

'I'm not sure I can do that.'

'Of course you can do it. You owe it to your family to keep your strength up. We can sort something out later if it's a question of money.'

'It isn't.' Nellie spoke abruptly. 'I mean, we're not that flush, but – '

'Well, then.' Aimée handed her the bottle, and moved to the door. 'And if Grandma Reagan has anything to say, refer her to me. I'll see you next week.'

Nellie still hovered as if there was something else on her mind, but after a moment she shrugged, took Mary's hand and left. Aimée stood looking after her, wondering whether she would come back, and what it was she couldn't bring herself to say.

The next day several women, 'front door patients' as Mrs Green called them, turned up with minor complaints, largely, Aimée guessed, out of curiosity. By far the most interesting of these was Mrs Gabrielle Watson. But was a vivacious brunette, well dressed,

148

in her middle thirties, who cheerfully admitted that there was nothing wrong with her.

'We do have a doctor, of course – Dr Dalywell, do you know him?' She smiled wickedly. 'He's a bit of an old fusspot, but he's been doctor to my husband's family forever, and James and I are so incredibly healthy that we seldom have need of him.'

'You have no children?'

She sighed. 'As yet, no. I still hope, but – well, *tempus fugit*, and it does no good to mope, does it? And my work with the Women's Social and Political Union keeps me busy.'

'Ah, I see,' Aimée smiled. 'You've come to check me out.'

'Well, you must admit it is of interest when one of our sex enters a man's world. I have always been a great admirer of Dr Alice Ker – you will know of her, of course.'

'Indeed. I heard her speak several times when I was at medical school and, like you, I greatly admire her, both as a doctor and a suffragette. I also knew her daughter, Margaret, slightly through the Women Students' Suffrage Society, but she left the university the year I joined.'

'So we already have something in common.'

'Perhaps. But I have to say that, much as I admire the courage shown by the Kers and others like them, my own enthusiasm has never encompassed militancy.'

Gabrielle laughed. 'No need to apologize. We all have a role to play. Perhaps you would care to dine one evening soon and we could exchange views. I'll telephone next week if I may.'

'That would be nice. I shall look forward to it.'

In the days that followed, word of the doctor and her bowl of toffee got round, and a steadily growing procession of mothers found their way to Myrtle Street, each dragging a string of children whose complaints ranged from stomach upsets, to racking coughs, while those with rashes were urged to 'Come on, our kid. Show the doctor yer nasty itches'. So with one eye on the magic bowl, they lifted their fraying jerseys to expose skinny blotched ribs, and Aimée dispensed medicine and ointments for pennies, together with good advice, which she had little doubt would be ignored. But one had to begin somewhere. In the mornings she visited some of them in their homes, and was appalled by the conditions under which they struggled to bring up their often far too large families.

'You've made a rod fer yer own back, there,' Mrs Green observed lugubriously one afternoon as she put the snib on the surgery door at five o'clock prompt and reached for her coat.

'A sprat to catch a mackerel, Mrs Green. The word is beginning to spread to those who really need help, so I should soon be able to organize a proper clinic.'

'H'm.' She sniffed. 'Much good it'll do. There's some as'll take all they can get, and go right on their own road. All right if I gerrof now? Only my Wilf likes 'is tea ready an' waitin'. I've left you a nice bit of braised beef in the oven.'

'Thank you, Mrs Green. Yes, do go. I'll see you in the morning.'

'You will, that. If God spares me.'

But within moments she was back. 'I think you'd better come an' luk, Dr B.'

Aimée followed her to the front door, which Mrs Green flung open with a flourish. A message crudely scrawled in whitewash defaced the gleaming paintwork: *Piss off ter yer own kind – yer not gerrin' our good drinkin' money ter pay fer a few toffee an' a lorra soft soap.*

On the far corner she saw a huddle of workmen. The ringleader was handsome, black-haired, and Irish by the look of him. Realizing that he had her attention, he laughed and gesticulated in a way that left little to the imagination.

'Filthy cowards.' Mrs Green dismissed them with a sniff. 'I'll 'ave me coat off in a jiff an' bring a bucket of water. A scrubbin' brush and a bit of elbow grease'll soon fetch this muck off.'

Two spots of scarlet on her cheeks were the only indication of the rage welling up inside Aimée as she said calmly, 'You'll do nothing of the kind, Mrs Green. I shall clean this off myself. You get off home to your Wilf.'

'Well, if you're sure.' She cocked her head. 'I'd like ter use a scrubbin' brush on them. They want lockin' up, idle boozy louts. What little they earn goes down their throats, an' God 'elp their families.' She sniffed righteously as she left. 'But their Day of Reckonin' will come, you mark my words.'

Aimée marched through to the kitchen and returned with the

bucket of water and a scrubbing brush. And there, on the doorstep, stood Oliver Langley.

14

'TROUBLE?' OLIVER ENQUIRED, his expression enigmatic as he observed the angry rigidity of her figure beneath the neatly tucked white blouse and navy skirt.

She turned to face him, bucket in hand, lifted the brush, dripping with water, and brandished it almost beneath his nose. 'If you dare to so much as murmur "I told you so", this is going straight down the front of your beautifully tailored coat.'

'My word, you are cross,' he said.

'Dangerously so,' she agreed, barely able to keep her voice from shaking. 'So, please, I beg you, don't provoke me.'

He glanced over his shoulder. 'I take it the perpetrators are those brave boyos across the road enjoying the spectacle. Would you like me to have a word?'

'Certainly not! I would *like* you to go away. But I doubt you will, so you'd better go through to the sitting room and pour yourself a whisky. You can pour one for me, too – a large one. This won't take long, and I shall need a drink.'

He lifted an eyebrow and went past her without a word.

Aimée scrubbed viciously at the paintwork until not a vestige of whitewash remained. Then she turned, head high, to stare at the jeering group until they began to shift uneasily. Only then did she go inside and shut the door.

She found Oliver standing by the window, glass in hand, his hawkish profile outlined against the light.

'They've gone,' he said without moving.

'Good riddance.'

'Quite,' he agreed dryly, and walked across to the sideboard. 'I like this room. Very restful. Your choice of colour scheme, was it?'

Aimée looked for irony, but his face was bland. 'More or less,' she said.

'How do you take your whisky?'

'As it is,' she said, daring him to comment.

But he took her at her word with only the faintest hint of a raised eyebrow as he put it in her hand.

'You're trembling.'

'Pure bad temper.' She tossed the whisky off too quickly, which made her cough. Her eyes began to water, and she sat down abruptly. 'Damn, oh damn all men. I was doing so well.'

Oliver watched her, a curious expression in his eyes as the fire went out of her and her shoulders began to droop. He walked across and took the glass out of her hand.

'Go upstairs,' he said. 'Have a leisurely bath and change into your prettiest frock. I'll be back in an hour or so to take you out to dinner.'

'Don't patronize me!' Immediately the embers of her temper flared back into life, adrenalin surging through her as she sprang to her feet again to face him. 'How typically male – pat the little woman on the head, offer her a treat to take her mind off her bruised ego, and she'll soon feel better. Well, it won't work. Not with me. And certainly not at this moment. What I actually feel right now is bloody angry with those louts who vandalized my house, so the last thing I want is a cosy dinner *à deux* with you or any other man.'

The silence that followed was palpable.

'I'm sorry,' he said quietly. 'I am not usually so clumsy.'

'Oh!' She put her hands to her cheeks to hide the blush that swept up from her neck, her anger turned in on herself. 'Now I feel even worse! Why couldn't you just tell me that I'm an ill-mannered shrew, scared stiff of failing and lashing out at the first setback.'

'Would that make you feel better?'

'No.' She uttered something halfway between a laugh and a groan. 'But it's probably what I deserve. It was certainly unforgivable of me to vent my spleen on you simply because you arrived at the wrong moment.'

'True,' he said dryly. 'But the hair shirt is quite unnecessary. And the offer of dinner still stands.'

His very calmness flustered her. 'Oh, I'm not sure. I wouldn't be very good company.'

'You might be if you dragged yourself away from here for a few hours – something I suspect you haven't done much recently.'

It was the whisky, Aimée thought, too quickly drunk on an empty stomach, that was making her light-headed. 'Nevertheless, that wasn't why you came. You are not by nature an impulsive man.' Her eyes challenged him. 'Did Aunt Felicity send you?'

Oliver looked pained. 'My dear doctor, people don't *send* me anywhere.' This brought a reluctant chuckle from Aimée together with a muttered 'they wouldn't dare', which he ignored. 'But my reasons will keep. Now, about dinner?'

The prospect was becoming more alluring by the minute, but his clipped assertiveness, so very reminiscent of their early encounters, tempted her to provoke him just a little longer.

'Mrs Green has left some beef braising in the oven – she's even prepared the veg to go with it. "Waste not, want not", she'll say if I don't eat it, but I dare say it would stretch to two.' Her eyes challenged him. 'You'd be very welcome to share my humble repast.'

But he, being trained to read people at a glance, gave her a withering look and picked up his hat. 'Thanks, but I was contemplating something more along the lines of fresh lobster and a bottle or two of Dom Perignon. However, if you have a conscience about your braised beef, so be it. Another time, perhaps?'

'Beast,' she said, acknowledging that her bluff had been well and truly called. 'I'll be ready in an hour.'

It was a curiously exhilarating ending to what had been near disaster. And later, beneath the subdued lighting in the Adelphi's luxurious dining room, at the end of a meal that bore no relation to Mrs Green's plain fare, Aimée sat back, swirling brandy round her glass with a sigh of pure pleasure. Oliver watched her in some amusement.

'I don't believe I've ever seen you so relaxed.'

'Maybe I was in danger of forgetting how,' she said. And looked up. 'You know, I never did find out why you came this evening. And don't tell me you just happened to be passing the door.'

'No, you wouldn't believe that.' He gave a lawyer's unhurried consideration to his answer. 'I was curious to know how you were going on, however, and as I had been working late on a brief, I decided to walk round and see for myself.'

'And picked the worst possible moment.'

'Yes.' He smiled faintly, hesitated, and when he spoke again, sounded almost diffident. 'The dinner invitation, however, was not entirely a fabrication. I wondered if you would care to meet my sister? Young Alice is to have a governess, and Jane is coming to stay for in a few days to interview several women who have applied for the position.' His dark eyes watched her consideringly over the rim of his glass. 'You would like one another, I think.'

In the days following Madame's terrible eruption, it had been easy enough for Matty to collect the scraps of material she needed without being seen by Miss Donald. The far end of the workroom was fairly cluttered with evening gowns on stands in various stages of completion, all ordered for the charity ball, and the waste baskets were brimming with discarded remnants of chiffon and lace, voile and satin, in every hue from palest apple greens and pinks and creams to royal purple, emerald and gold.

'How is Madame Vincente this morning?' she had whispered to Miss Timms when she arrived the day after the incident.

'Touchy,' murmured the older woman laconically. 'It wouldn't take much to set her off again. Seemingly she spent half last night recutting the whole gown from what was left of the material, so just pray that nothing else goes wrong.'

She wasn't the only one, Matty thought. Her own sewing for her regular customers was piling up now she worked full time. Quite a few people had ordered summer frocks and she'd have to work well into the night to have any hope of finishing them.

And then she thought about poor Vera, who would surely be more than glad to have some work put her way – work she could do at home. Matty's spirits lifted. It was a great idea. She could do the cutting out, and Vera the actual sewing. And they could share the proceeds. It would need a bit of thought, of course, and she'd have to pick her moment to broach the idea to Mam. Then perhaps, if all went well, over the weekend she would be able to start making the paper patterns for the designs which she had developed from her original sketches in odd moments. At the mere thought, excitement banished tiredness.

Lady Spendlove had been due for a fitting on the Saturday afternoon, and they all had to work like Trojans on Friday and the following morning. Vera had been sadly missed, though no one dared voice the thought, and Matty was in a real sweat when Madame said she would have to be responsible for setting the sleeve as well as the bodice. But, to everyone's relief, the fitting went well. Her ladyship left, more than satisfied, Madame's mood changed with mercurial speed, and she let them all get off home in good time that evening.

Aimée had promised to go to Crag Vale for Sunday lunch at Bank Holiday weekend. She was not looking forward to her mother's probing questions, but hopefully she and Gerald might manage a good long walk in the afternoon, which would cut short the time available for a full-scale inquisition. And she wouldn't be sorry to get out of Liverpool, in view of a proposed strike by the police force.

Late on Saturday evening, however, she was telephoned by Gabrielle Watson's husband who sounded extremely agitated. His wife had dreadful stomach pains, and their family doctor had gone out on a call and had not returned.

'Gabby wondered if you would come, Doctor. She's not normally one to complain – '

Aimée cut him short and promised to set off immediately. The streets were busy, unusually so for the time of night – drunken men, and some women, stumbled into the road almost under her wheels and peered in, pulling faces and banging on the windows.

In the house in Huskisson Street a grey-faced James Watson led her up to the large front bedroom where she found Gabrielle in great distress, her face bathed in perspiration, her head rolling from side to side.

'Sorry about this,' she ground out through clenched teeth.

'Hush, don't talk, and try not to worry. This won't take a moment.' Aimée turned back the bedclothes and immediately saw that the abdomen was severely distended. Her very first touch brought a muffled scream. Gently she replaced the blankets. 'It's as I suspected. You have a badly inflamed appendix.' She turned to Mr Watson. 'We'll need an ambulance to get your wife to hospital as soon as possible. May I use your telephone?'

The operator said the lines were jammed with calls, but Aimée used her most authoritative manner, insisting that this was a matter of life and death – and was eventually put through to the

Royal Infirmary. When the ambulance arrived, the driver said that the Magistrates had read the Riot Act, and called in the troops.

'Talk about the war – there's near as much blood 'n' guts bein' spilled down London Road as I ever clapped eyes on when I wus on the Somme, I can tell yer. Drunks smashin' shop windows an' lootin', fightin' over the spoils. Ar, an' women, too, cartin' the booty away in prams, bold as brass, and soldiers firin' off guns. There'll be some broken 'eads come mornin'.'

Aimée followed the ambulance in her car. It was a nightmare journey, with people reeling into the road without warning, beating on the windows and trying to climb onto the car. Even the clanging of the ambulance bell didn't guarantee an uninterrupted passage. But at last her patient was safely delivered. The return journey was every bit as eventful, and she arrived back to find a clutch of men and women with broken bones and cuts and grazes, groaning and bleeding at her surgery door.

'It was quite extraordinary,' she confessed to Gerald next day as, with arms linked, they walked the length of the valley, following the line of the chuckling river and using the trees for shelter from the full heat of the sun. 'At times I was terrified, but there was also a curious exhilaration about the whole experience that reminded me in a ghoulish way of driving under fire in France. Does that sound crazy?'

'Not to me.'

'I wouldn't dream of admitting such feelings to Ma, of course. She already thinks I'm mad.'

'So would most people, but I know what you mean.'

He reached for her hand and held it tight. 'We are incredibly lucky, you know.'

Aimée thought briefly of David – the first time in ages that she had done so – and of all those other young men who would never again feel the sun on their backs.

'Yes, I do know, but I refuse to grow maudlin on such a lovely day. Oh, Gerald, look – now all those horrid ranks of vegetables have gone, the meadowsweet is coming back.' She broke off a flower and held it to her nose. 'Nature is surprisingly resilient.' She spoke a little too quickly, but her eyes were quite clear as they met his.

'Speaking of which, how is your patient? Did she come through all right?'

'I telephoned this morning before I left. The appendectomy was a success, but she's very poorly. Still, it's early days.'

'Leave your worries in the surgery,' Frank had told her years ago, long before she qualified. It was sound advice. But then Frank was a wise man. She seized Gerald's hand and dragged him to the bank of the stream. 'First one across and back without wetting their feet gets an extra cream cake at teatime.'

'Idiot.'

But they seized on the spirit of the childhood game with all the old relish, finally collapsing in the grass, weak with laughter amid shouts of 'You cheated!' and 'Me – I won!' before rolling on to their backs to recover.

'A dead heat,' Gerald gasped, and they solemnly shook hands. 'Whew, I'm getting old.'

'Rubbish. You're just out of condition.'

'Yes, Doctor.'

'I prescribe a daily run to Coram and back.'

'Oh, sure.'

They lay in a companionable silence, soaking up the sun.

'Megan looks well,' Aimée said at last. 'Having a baby obviously suits her.' She leaned in to him. 'And you, dear boy, are you truly happy?'

He squeezed her hand. 'Very happy – and busy. That little friend of yours Matty is a bright girl, you know. Our talks have given me much food for thought, as a result of which I've had a long discussion with Dad and we've decided to re-equip the number two mill and turn it over entirely to fashion fabrics.'

Aimée smiled. 'I'll tell her. She'll be thrilled.'

'She must come again, so I can pick her brains. I'm also turning over in my mind the possibility of producing furnishing fabrics, but I won't breathe a word to anyone yet.' He grinned a little sheepishly at her. 'Dad can only take so many innovations at a time.'

'You're growing devious in your old age.' And because she needed to know: 'How is Dad – really?'

'He's all right. A little of the old fire's gone for good, I suspect. And I notice he goes off to sit alone in his study more than he used to, which doesn't always please Ma. Maybe he just needs a bit of peace and quiet.'

Maybe he does, Aimée thought, troubled. Or maybe the reason lies elsewhere. 'And Mother?'

'Oh, she's fine. Megan has been able to relieve her of most of those household decisions she always found so tiresome.'

Aimée longed to retort that their mother had always enjoyed complaining – it was the breath of life to her. And that it wasn't necessarily good for her to be cossetted to such an extent.

Only that morning she had arrived bearing an enormous bunch of flowers, but hardly had Minna finished exclaiming, 'Oh, darling, roses and carnations – my favourites! Now I shall have to find some vases . . .' when Megan was whisking them away with a gentle, 'I'll see to them, dear – and you can talk to Aimée in peace.'

Aimée noticed the faint quiver of her mother's mouth, and came swiftly to the rescue. 'How kind of you, Megan, but I thought we might do them together while we talk. Ma particularly enjoys arranging flowers.'

Megan flushed, and apologized as she put them back in Minna's arms, and Frank, who had just arrived for lunch, gave Aimée one of his looks – and winked.

He managed a few moments alone with her before she left. 'That was very tactfully done,' he said.

'You don't think I offended her?'

'Oh, I doubt your sister-in-law takes offence so easily.'

'You find that so, too?' she said eagerly. 'But what can I do, Frank? How do I explain to Gerald that the woman he loves is taking over the running of the house in a way that amounts to a kind of gentle tyranny? Heaven knows, Mother never was much good at taking decisions, but soon she won't be able to lift a finger in her own home – and that isn't good for her. From what Gerald tells me, I'm not sure that Dad's a hundred per cent happy with the situation, either, but I wouldn't hurt Gerald for the world by suggesting that they should be looking for a home of their own, somewhere nearby. He thinks he's helping.'

'Difficult situation. Perhaps when the baby comes Megan will have more to occupy her.'

'Perhaps.' But Aimée wasn't convinced. She eyed him speculatively. 'No chance of her producing twins, I suppose – or preferably triplets?'

Frank gave a great shout of laughter. 'We all know the Lord

works in mysterious ways, but I'd not wish to raise your hopes. Besides, I'd rather talk about you.'

'Oh, things are going very much as I expected,' Aimée said, trying to sound optimistic as she gave him a blow-by-blow account. He knew her too well not to see through any attempt to gloss over her difficulties.

'I don't mind about those stupid vandals. They just made me angry. It's the frustration of not knowing how to persuade the women to ignore their stupidity and take responsibility for their own health, and the health and well-being of their children.'

'Ah, my Aimée, you were ever impatient. You'll need to understand the way folk live before you can gain their confidence. Opening a new practice is never easy – for anyone. A few weeks is no time at all.' He chucked wickedly. 'Wait till you get your first outbreak of chickenpox or measles – they'll be glad enough to see you then.'

15

EVEN BEFORE THE gates of Cedar Grange closed behind them for this first trip outside, Toby had shown no interest whatever in the world beyond the windows of the Rolls, but as the Cheshire countryside flashed by, Felicity could feel the tension building up in him with every mile that passed.

'Don't expect too much,' Matron had said. 'Your son has been with us for a long time. Even a few hours away are going to seem strange to him at first, perhaps a little frightening.'

Much as she tried to understand, it was hard for Felicity to accept that her son would rather have remained confined in what was, however pleasant, an institution, than visit his own home for a few brief hours. But perhaps once they were home, just the two of them, for Celia was staying with a friend and she had deliberately chosen a day when George would not be there, Toby would relax a little. She had warned all the servants to treat him as naturally as possible. He certainly looked better. The hours spent in the hothouses and gardens at Cedar Grange had transformed his pallor to a light tan.

The day was already warm, but the folds of her voile dress fluttered coolly against her skin as she stretched out a hand to cover his, and found that he was trembling.

'Darling, I've waited so long for this day,' she said impulsively. 'It will be such fun – just the two of us.' Oh, how foolish that sounded. She had always prided herself on being able to handle any situation, but this trial outing meant so much – too much, perhaps. She drew a deep breath and said more calmly, 'Aimée promised she would look in sometime during the day, but you won't mind that.'

'No. I'm g-g-glad.'

The stammer, which had become much rarer of late, was back.

Felicity could have wept for she did so want Toby's first venture into the outside world to be a success. The thought of him spending the rest of his life shut away was not to be borne.

'Otherwise, apart from a dress fitting, which should not take above a few minutes, we shan't be disturbed.'

He turned to her then with his painfully sweet smile that now came more readily. 'Poor Mama. You m-mustn't m-mind about me, you know. I don't. I shall b-be all right.'

'Come in, Mathilde.'

Adeline Vincente watched Matty cross the room, observing her carriage, the way she walked tall and held her head with quiet pride. Not a beauty, but certainly a young woman who would draw glances. One might consider using her occasionally to model gowns.

'She asked for you, special,' Miss Timms had said, loud enough for Miss Donald to hear. 'But she seemed in a good mood, so you needn't get all het up.'

Nevertheless Matty's heart was beating right up in her throat. You never knew with Madame. To distract her thoughts, she glanced around. She loved her employer's room. It stated everything about Madame that she most admired, for all around there was evidence of the Frenchwoman's artistry: a giant sketchpad on a stand near the window conveyed the fluid lines of a gown in a few sweeping strokes, with several swatches of material pinned to one side. More sketches were scattered across a long sloping desk – drawings of sleeves, bodices, collars. And everywhere there were beautiful materials, thrown carelessly across every available surface in a vibrant patchwork of colours.

'How old are you now, Mathilde?'

Matty came back to earth with a start. 'Nineteen, Madame.'

'Nineteen. *Parbleu!*' Madame rolled her eyes heavenward in a dramatic gesture, then she once more became brisk. 'But one must not repine when every moment is precious. I 'ave send for you because Madame Mellish is unable to come for 'er final fitting, which is a mere formality, *bien sûr*. 'Owever, so that we may 'ave no doubts, she wishes you to deliver the gown and fit it.'

'Me?' Matty could feel her cheeks turned bright red. 'But surely it should be Miss Donald or Miss Timms?'

'This is true, but Madame Mellish particularly requests that it is you. She will send 'er chauffeur for you at three o'clock, so you will please to be ready.'

Pleasure was almost immediately swamped by the knowledge that Miss Donald would be livid, and would most surely make her pay somehow. Still, there was no point worrying about anything until it happened.

'That will be all, Mathilde. You may return to your work.'

She murmured assent and turned to leave, and immediately her attention was caught by a ripple of bronze green – soft slippery satin caught in a shaft of sunlight that caused it to change colour with every movement.

'Exquisite, is it not?'

'Oh, yes.' Matty's voice was little more than a breath, for she was already teeming with ideas. The colour would be perfect for Aimée . . .

'So – tell me what it says to you?'

'Me?' For the second time in a few minutes, she had been reduced to a squeak of surprise.

'Yes, yes. Every gown must 'ave a soul – a spirit breathed into it by its creator. So, if I should commission you to design a gown using this material, 'ow would you give it life?'

Entranced by this concept, Matty's hand instinctively went to her pocket. She pulled out the little sketch book and began to draw swiftly, surely, knowing instinctively what she wanted to convey –a lean uncluttered look skimming the figure and reaching to just above the ankle, the neck high at the front, draped low at the back, with a thigh-length overtunic.

Adeline Vincente took the pad from her and studied the sketch in frowning silence.

'It's very rough,' Matty said quickly, 'but I thought how good it would look on Dr Buchanan . . . with her colouring . . .'

'Bien! So tell me, 'ow would you define this tunic line?'

'I thought, perhaps, an inch-wide band of bronze bugle beads, and maybe some round the neck as well . . .' Matty's voice tailed off, the guilty colour surging into her face as she saw that Madame was leafing back through the pad and had stopped at the sketches she had made for the ivory silk gown. Her frown deepened as she looked up, and Matty knew she had recognized it.

'What is the meaning of this?'

The clipped question hung in the air.

Matty began to stumble through her explanation. 'I know what you said, but I just couldn't bear to think of that lovely gown being destroyed. An' then I got this idea, you see, about concealing the mark with leaves and petals – as if they were drifting down across the front, but I didn't know if it would work.' She paused for breath, but the silence continued. 'I was goin' to . . . to own up, an' show it to you when it was finished, honest . . .'

Her employer handed back the book. 'So? For now, take this and go. I will consider. And do not forget to be ready for three o'clock.'

Matty stumbled from the room, confused by Madame's behaviour. She had expected the sky to fall in on her. Instant dismissal. Instead – nothing. Mam was right. They were a funny lot, the French.

It would have astonished her even more to know that in the room behind her, Adeline Vincente was in a ferment, as she came to terms with the discovery that beneath her roof she was harbouring a talent which, carefully nurtured, might one day equal, if not surpass her own. The drawing was crude, but there was imagination, flair, the occasional lightness of touch . . . At first, fear trembled momentarily on the edge of that recognition, fear of being supplanted if someone should recognize the girl's talents and whisk her way – use her talent for their own unscrupulous ends. But she, Adeline Vincente, was above such pettiness. Excitement coursed through her. Mathilde was young, and such a gift must be allowed to develop naturally, so all must be accomplished with discretion. She would in effect make of her a protégée. Next spring, perhaps, she would take her on a visit to Paris, so that Mathilde might absorb its ambience. And eventually, a partnership. Together they would conquer the world of *haute couture*.

Matty, unaware that her future was being mapped out for her, was revelling in the delights of riding in a Rolls-Royce. Aimée's motor car had seemed luxurious, but it was nothing compared to this. The inside was so spacious that you could almost walk into it, and thickly carpeted. And as for the seats – she sank back with a sigh of pure delight, crossed one leg over the other as she had seen some of their younger customers do, and gave her imagination full rein.

Mrs Mellish had a new chauffeur. She could see him now, beyond the window that separated them, with his red hair curling round the edge of his grey uniform hat. He was quite good-looking, really – not much taller than she was, but he had wicked blue eyes and a way of looking at you that brought you out in goose pimples. Matty wished the journey could be twice as long.

'Where is Porter?' she asked as he opened the door and helped her out, hoping the question made it seem clear that she was a regular visitor to the Mellish home.

'Retired last month, miss,' he answered with a knowing grin, as he carried the dress box up the front steps for her and pulled the bell. 'The name's Alec – Alec Gresham,' he said as she took the box from him. 'I'll be waitin' here. I'm to take you back to Bold Street when you've done.'

It wasn't the first time Matty had seen the entrance hall, with its floor of pale creamy marble, and the sweeping staircase that curved away out of sight, like something out of a fairy tale. Effie, the parlour maid, had once taken her through the green baize door when the family was away. But it was quite different actually being ushered in through the front door.

'This way, miss,' said a prim new maid, bringing her down to earth as she led her across the hall to a room at the rear. 'Madam says you're to wait here. She will be with you shortly.'

Matty found herself in a pretty little room, a kind of rear parlour, she supposed. Beyond it she could see a big glasshouse. Intrigued, she set down the dress box and wandered across to peer through the door. It was huge. Further tempted, she turned the handle and pushed. A wonderful smell of earth and greenery rushed out to envelop her – and somewhere close by she heard the faint splash of water.

A man rose up from nowhere, right in front of her and the flowerpot he was holding fell and smashed to pieces at her feet, scattering soil everywhere. She uttered an unladylike squeak and stepped back.

'Oh, you gave me such a fright!'

'I'm s-sorry. That w-w-was c-clumsy.'

He was quite young and thin, with floppy fair hair, and as he hastily tried to brush the soil from her shoes, he seemed so upset that she found herself giving him a reassuring grin.

'It's all right. They're nothing special. And don't worry. I'll tell Mrs Mellish it was my fault the pot got smashed. I'd no business being so nosey, coming in here.' She peered over his shoulder. 'You don't have to look after all this on your own, do you? It's ever so big – almost as big as the Palm House in Sefton Park. I expect you've been there.'

'Yes.' He straightened up with a tentative smile, disarmed by this friendly young woman in her cotton frock, with pretty dark hair framing a face alight with genuine interest, the first person to treat him exactly as she found him, without foreknowledge. 'B-but th-this isn't – I'm only here for the day.'

'Oh, I see. You're part time.' Matty was immediately sympathetic. 'It's not easy getting a job just now, is it? Still, every little helps, as Mam says. I've been ever so lucky. Mrs Mellish spoke for me to Madame Vincente – she's the best dress designer in Liverpool, in the country, I shouldn't wonder – and she took me on.'

'Wh-what is your name?'

Before she could answer, the door opened, and Mrs Mellish was saying, 'Matty, I'm sorry to have kept you.' And then, in an odd sort of voice, 'Ah, I see you have met Toby.'

'I was just having a quick look, madam.' The words tumbled over themselves. 'And it was my fault the plant pot got broken. I took him by surprise.'

Felicity looked from one to the other, and was astonished to find her son smiling faintly. 'I see. Well, perhaps I should introduce you properly. Toby is my younger son. Darling, this is Matilda Shaw, who has come to fit my gown.'

Matty felt herself blushing scarlet. Talk about putting your foot right in it! And then she caught his eye, and was reassured. She giggled. 'You must have thought I was daft.'

'Not in the least,' he said courteously, liking her natural exuberance and the way the flush of embarrassment made her dark eyes sparkle. 'I am pleased to meet you, M-Matilda. You w-were very kind to me.'

Aimée had been kept busy with an outbreak of chickenpox, made more distressing by the warm weather. No use telling mothers to bathe their children with a lukewarm solution of bicarbonate of soda and discourage them from scratching by making them wear cotton gloves, when many of them could spare neither time nor money for the most basic necessities.

Daisy Shaw was more fortunate, but Agnes was finding it difficult to cope with her. Aimée called in to see them while she was on her rounds and found a fractious Daisy clinging to her mother's skirts.

'I know she can't help being fretful,' Agnes sighed above the whimpering, 'but it sets my nerves jangling sometimes. I took it in my stride when the others were young, but now there's so much to be done and I don't seem to have the energy. Her constant grizzling must get on Pat's nerves, too, though he doesn't complain. I've given him one of his pills, so he's asleep just now.'

Aimée went to put the kettle on. 'Well, Daisy should soon be over the worst. Sit down for five minutes, and I'll make us a cup of tea.'

For once Agnes didn't argue. 'I haven't been to see our Irene all week, and I daren't let her come here in case she catches it. Matty goes when she can, though it's not that often. That Madame Vincente's keeping her so busy these days.'

'She's doing remarkably well, though,' Aimée said, hearing the slightly grudging note in Agnes's voice.

'Maybe. She's full of big ideas, that's for sure. I just hope they come to something, because the little dressmaking business she runs on the side is suffering. That Vera – the one who got the sack – has been helping her out, but now her two little ones are down with chickenpox, so Matty's having to work all hours to finish the orders.'

'Oh well, Matty's at the age when one thrives on challenge.' Aimée poured the tea, and pushed a cup across the table.

'Me too,' Daisy whined.

'I've got some of Mammy's special lemonade for you.' Aimée took her on her knee and coaxed her to drink a little. Soon her head began to droop.

'You could do with a break yourself, by the look of you,' Agnes said dryly. 'Have you many more calls?'

'Nearly finished.' She hesitated. 'I thought I might call on the

Reagans. 'Someone told me that little Mary is down with chickenpox, too, and I'd quite like to have a word with Nellie. She didn't keep her appointment – '

'I'm not surprised. With Ada Reagan breathing down her neck every move she makes.'

Aimée had to knock three times at number 20, though she saw the front room curtain twitch.

'I'm sorry you've had to wait,' Nellie said, a painful blush staining her too-white face as she finally opened the door. 'I was upstairs, settling Mary down for a sleep.'

'How is she?'

'Oh, you know – uncomfortable. I didn't like to send for you. I mean, it's only chickenpox, and there's not a lot you can do.'

A well-built woman with greying hair crimped in tight waves, and a pinched expression, loomed in the doorway of the front room.

Nellie became even more nervous. 'You'll not have met my mother-in-law, Doctor. Mam, this is Dr Buchanan.'

'I wasn't told you'd been sent for,' Mrs Reagan said without preamble.

'No one did send for me. But I was passing, and knowing that little Mary has chickenpox – '

'Then yer'll not be expectin' ter get paid.' The bosom beneath the tightly crossed pinafore heaved.

'Of course not. This is an informal call. I like to keep an eye on all my patients.'

'Well,' Nellie said. 'You'd best come upstairs. The rash is going, and I'm trying to keep her from scratching it.'

The bedroom, like the rest of the house as far as she had seen it, was scrupulously neat and clean, almost too much so. The curtains, half-drawn, shaded the little bed.

'Hello, Mary. Remember me?'

Her mouth puckered, and on a sob she whispered, 'The sweetie lady.'

'That's right.' She reached into her bag. 'I've brought a small bag of jelly sweets, just for you.'

The child's fingers reached for the bag, peering into it eagerly, and Aimée signalled to Nellie to leave the room.

'Mary will be fine. As a matter of fact, it's you I really wanted to see,' she said when they were out of earshot. 'Why haven't you been back to the surgery?'

Nellie shrugged, avoiding Aimée's eyes. 'I didn't think there were much point.'

'There is every point. I would still like to arrange for a blood test, but meantime the tonic I gave you will help you to feel less tired.'

'It's no use, doctor,' she burst out. 'Mam tipped the last lot down the sink – said it was money wasted fer coloured water.'

'Right.' Aimée turned to the stairs.

'I don't want Danny worried!'

At the bottom she hesitated. The house was much the same design as the Shaws, and a murmur of voices came from the back room. She walked down the lobby and pushed open the door.

The talking stopped abruptly, and for a moment there was complete silence. Aimée felt the blood draining from her face as her pulse began to race. She had known, of course, that Nellie's husband was a double amputee, but in her fury she had forgotten. For a moment she froze. Danny had a long puckered scar running down beside his eye, dragging the skin down. For a moment she remembered the young man who had precipitated her breakdown and perspiration ran cold on her skin. But Danny had two good eyes, and with his thatch of sandy hair, he was nothing like that other young man.

'What's wrong, Doctor?' Mrs Regan's voice was harsh. 'Never seen a man with no legs before?'

'Mam!' Nellie gasped, and Danny's face turned a dull sullen red.

If anything was guaranteed to restore Aimée's spirit, it was the mother's bitterness.

'Many times,' she said with a calmness that concealed her anger. 'And some much worse off than your son.' She smiled and held out her hand. 'Danny, isn't it? I'm pleased to meet you.'

Still sullen, he ignored her proferred hand. 'How much worse off can a fellow be, fer Chrissake?'

Aimée knew that he was suffering from self-pity, which was hardly surprising, but made worse by his mother's attitude. She ignored the mother, and Nellie's stifled sobs, addressing herself solely to Danny.

'A lot. You have your sight and all your mental faculties, and your lungs have not been destroyed by gas – '

'But I can't bleedin' walk, can I?'

'No,' she agreed quietly, 'but you are young enough to adapt. You have a good strong torso, though it's got a bit flabby through lack of exercise. But I see no reason why you shouldn't be able to strengthen the muscles in your upper body – '

'How dare you!' his mother gasped. 'Downright wicked, you are, talkin' like that to my son who 'as given 'is all for King an' country.'

Aimée turned to her, steely eyed. 'And how dare you throw away the medicine I prescribed for Nellie, Mrs Reagan.'

She flushed. 'Waste of money – fillin' her head with mamby-pamby nonsense.'

'It is not nonsense. Nellie has anaemia. How bad her condition is, I don't yet know, as she hasn't yet been back to see me, doubtless for fear of incurring your displeasure again.'

'Is this right, what the doctor says, Nellie?' Danny's voice had taken on a firmer sound.

'I have been a bit low,' she admitted.

'And I make a lot of extra work don't I?'

'Oh, no!' she cried, running to him. 'I don't mind that, honest! Just havin' you here – '

'No spunk, young women today. Don't know the meaning of hard work.'

'Be quiet, Mam.' Danny's voice was like a whipcrack. 'Nell works bloody hard and you know it.' He nodded at Aimée. 'I'll make sure she comes to see yer. And I'll think on what you said.'

It had been a long day, but Aimée's hopes of having a leisurely bath before evening surgery were dashed the moment she put her key in the lock.

'You've gorra right pair waitin' out there, Doctor.' Mrs Green's whisper was at its most lugubrious. 'Big Liam O'Hara, the great oaf – you'll know 'im when yer see 'im – an' his mate Nobby Nolan. The breath on the two of them'd half paralyse yer. Will I tell them surgery's cancelled an' send them packin'?'

Aimée glanced at the clock – not quite six. It was tempting to take the easy way out, which was, no doubt, what the men would be counting on, so that they could go back to their mates and crow that she'd been too scared to see them.

The number of patients was increasing steadily, but even so . . . She sighed. 'Certainly not, Mrs Green. We can't turn people away. Show them in at once.'

'If you say so.' Mrs Green's sniff spoke volumes.

'I do. And then you can get off.'

'With them two the way they are? That I will not. I'd not have an easy moment. I'm stayin' in earshot, an' the first sign of trouble I'll be away to fetch the constable.'

The two men swaggered in, supporting one another and reeking of drink. The big handsome fellow she recognized as the ringleader of the group who had defaced her front door.

'Sit down, please, while I take some details,' Aimée said crisply, looking from one to the other. 'Which of you is the patient?'

'Well now, me darlin', it's meself. Liam O'Hara is the name,' said the big man. 'Nobby, like the good friend he is, has come to bear me company in me agony.'

So this was Biddy O'Hara's husband, the father of her nine children, not counting two that had been stillborn. Aimée recalled trying to persuade the diminutive Irishwoman that another pregnancy would be extremely dangerous and must be avoided.

'Sure, how would I do that? My Liam'd have six fits if I didn't let him – well, ye know. . .' She had gone pink with embarrassment. 'And anyway, it'd be flying in the face of God an' the teachings of our Holy Mother Church.'

How often had Aimée heard that one. 'Not necessarily. I'm not suggesting that you shouldn't make love.'

Looking now at Big Liam, Aimée owned it would be difficult if not impossible to deny him his rights. He was indeed the epitome of the handsome black-haired Irishman with laughing eyes, which were at present bloodshot, but as blue as the bluest sea, and, she had no doubt, beguiling enough to melt the hardest heart if he chose to give his mind to it.

But if Liam wouldn't take precautions, there were other ways round the problem, as she had tried, very simply to explain to Biddy. She told her about Dr Marie Stopes and her safe methods which, if not infallible, would go a long way towards providing protection. Biddy O'Hara's already pink cheeks had turned bright scarlet.

'A sponge, soaked in oil, you say? And I'd have to put it where? Holy Mother of God! Sure I couldn't be doin' that to meself! It's unnatural – and sinful besides!'

And that had been the end of that. But now Big Liam was here in her surgery and Aimée wondered what fresh michief he was planning. Surely Biddy wouldn't have told him about her contraceptive advice? It would be going right against the little Irishwoman's nature.

'So . . .' Aimée sat back, determined not to let the two men put her at a disadvantage. 'What can I do for you, Mr O'Hara?'

'Well now, it's not something I'd sully a lady's ears with in the ordinary way – ' His companion sniggered. 'But you bein' a doctor an' all, and me wife forever singin' your praises – '

She allowed her glance to lift to the clock. 'If you could just get to the point.'

Nobby doubled up. 'D'ye hear that, Liam? Get to the point. That's rich, tharris!'

'Quiet, you'll embarrass the good *lady* doctor.'

By now Aimée realized that this was precisely their intention, and she had a good idea how they hoped to accomplish it. She stood up.

'I don't embarrass easily, Mr O'Hara, so let's not waste any more time over what is, I suspect, a very routine problem. Just drop your trousers, would you? It won't take a minute, and then we can all get on with our busy lives.'

Big Liam was on his feet, spluttering, his face bright scarlet. 'That's indecent, so it is! Unwomanly, tellin' a fella to drop his kecks! Askin' for ter see a man's . . . privates!'

She sighed. 'My dear man, yours aren't the first I've seen by any means, and I doubt they'll be the last. So, unless they've got bells on, they will be of no particular interest to me. But I can't treat you without examining you first.'

'D'ye hear that, Nobby? Bejabbers, you won't get me exposin' meself to the likes of you!'

'No? Afraid I might do you a mischief, perhaps?' Aimée picked up the small ornamental dagger that she used to open letters, regarded it thoughtfully, and walked round the desk towards him. 'You know, I might be tempted, at that. I'd be doing your wife a favour. Another baby would almost certainly kill her. But I don't suppose she's told you that, has she?'

He spread his big hands protectively across his lower regions. 'You're a witch, so you are! Threatenin' me wid that thing – an' tryin' ter cause trouble between a man an' his wife! Come on, Nobby, we're off.' And clutching his kecks close, as if his very life depended on them, Big Liam charged out of the room with his mate on his heels.

Mrs Green's laughter pursued them up the street. 'Eh, Doctor, I've norr'ad such a good laff in years!' she chortled. 'They'll not be back in a hurry, I'm thinkin'.'

16

MATTY WIPED HER fingers on the cloth at her side for the umpteenth time before picking up the oyster silk bodice. She loved to see the pattern developing, but it was no easy task, trying to work such intricate beading with constantly sweating hands. And Madame could be eagle-eyed when it came to searching out the slightest mark, as poor Vera had learned to her cost.

'It's gotta rain soon,' Ruth said, pulling the neck of her smock forward and blowing down it, grimacing at the great wet patches under her arms. 'An' when it does, I'm gonna walk round an' round in it till I'm soaked through. It's gettin' so everything pongs, including me.'

Ethel Higgs came running in from a visit to the lavvy, her whisper fit to wake the dead. 'Hey, Matty, there's someone wantin' a word with you out front.'

The room went quiet as everyone stopped to stare, thankful that Miss Donald had been called away.

Matty's thoughts immediately flew to her father. 'Who is it? I can't possibly leave what I'm doing unless it's urgent. Miss Donald'd have a fit.'

'Oh well, if yer not interested,' Ethel feigned nonchalance. 'Only it's norrevery day a fella in uniform comes callin' – an' him with eyes as big an' blue as – '

'Not Alec Gresham?' Matty squeaked. Of course, she'd forgotten Mrs Mellish was upstairs this minute having a fitting. 'But I still daren't chance it.'

'Oh go on, fer pity's sake,' Ruth urged her. 'If Lady Muck comes back before you do, we'll tell 'er you've gone fer a Jimmy Riddle like Ethel.' The young ones giggled and the older workers tried to look shocked. 'Only don't take forever.'

So Matty slipped down the back alley, trying to quell her

excitement, and wishing that she didn't feel all hot and sweaty as she saw the distinctive grey-uniformed figure waiting at the end, the sun turning his red hair to flame.

'You'll get me into trouble,' she whispered as passers-by stared curiously.

'I would, too, given half a chance,' he said, bold as brass, and watched her blush with embarrassment and indignation.

'You want to wash your mouth out, Alec Gresham.'

'Sorry.' But his eyes glinted and he didn't look in the least repentant. 'Listen then, it's me night off tonight. Will you come out if I promise to behave meself?'

It wasn't the first time he'd asked, but last time she had already promised Irene she'd go and keep her company, and with Irene finding it difficult to get about in the heat, she hadn't the heart to let her down. This time, for all that there was plenty of work waiting for her at home, she had no intention of letting the opportunity slip. But nor did she want to seem too eager.

'All right,' she said, ever so casual. 'But no funny business.'

'You don't make it easy for a feller.' He grinned. 'So, where do you want to go? Music hall or cinema? There's a good picture on at the Troc. And we could maybe have a little drink after.'

'I don't know about the drink, but the pictures would be nice.' Matty's smile dimpled. A warning whistle came up the crack. 'I'll have to go. It'll be a bit of a rush, so I'd better meet you there, okay? About half-past seven.'

She had a terrible hurry getting ready, and Mam wasn't too keen on her going out with someone who hadn't been given the once-over.

'I'd sooner you'd brought him home first.'

'I'm not a kid, Mam. Besides, there wouldn't have been time, honest. But he's all right – I mean, Mrs Mellish wouldn't employ anyone who wasn't honest and reliable.'

Agnes might have said that it wasn't his honesty she was worried about, but Matty was right – she wasn't a child any longer, and she didn't have half enough fun in her life. Besides which, unlike her sister, she was a pretty good judge of character – except that judgement could fly out the window when a pair of bold eyes smiled down at a girl.

Matty certainly looked pretty enough to turn any man's head as she went flying up the street in her blue dress with its dropped waist, and with her curls bouncing and catching the sunlight as she moved, oblivious of her mother watching her go from the parlour window.

'I'm glad she didn't want her hair very short like Dr Aimée's. It would have been a sin to cut off all those curls.' As Agnes spoke, she absently wiped the perspiration from her hairline with the back of her hand. There'd be a storm before long. She had that pain just behind her eyes that always signalled a storm. 'I only hope she doesn't get soaked through, an' that new frock she's so proud of. I'm still not sure about that hem, though. It shows a bit too much leg for my liking.'

'She's a fine pair of pins on her, right enough.' Pat's chuckle rasped. 'Just like her mother before her.'

'You're a wicked fellow, Patrick Shaw,' she exclaimed, turning and trying to look outraged. But, just for an instant, with the twinkle in his eyes, he looked so like the young man she had fallen in love with all those years ago, that she blushed, her heart melting within her. 'Oh, Pat!' she said tremulously.

Aimée had taken to Jane Langley at once. She was not unlike Oliver in appearance, though her features were less dramatic, her hair a soft brown, and her hazel eyes, picking up warmth from a dress of honey-coloured silk, reflected a good-humoured approach to life.

'You are to be married soon, I believe,' Aimée said, when introductions were over and they were seated in the very pleasant drawing room of Oliver's house in Falkner Square. The windows were open to catch what little air was to be had, and late sunlight filtered through the long net curtains, highlighting a portrait that hung above the mantelshelf. It was of a girl on the verge of womanhood, with laughing blue eyes and a cloud of fair hair framing a fine-boned face so vividly alive that you might expect her to turn at any minute and smile at you. She was dressed in white muslin, closed high at the neck, the embroidered bodice gathered in at the waist, and hinting at the bosom beneath. So this was Catherine. No wonder Oliver felt her loss so deeply. Jane's voice drew her back.

'Next month. They have finally ordered Nick's ship back to

home waters for a refit. Mother is convinced that the Government, in its slowness to ratify the Peace Treaty, has been conspiring with the Admiralty to keep us apart.'

Aimée laughed. 'My own mother has a similar brand of logic.'

Oliver swirled his sherry gently round in his glass. 'If we don't want the same thing to happen again, Germany will have to be tied up good and tight.'

'And we all know the machinery of law grinds exceeding slow,' Jane said, wrinkling her nose at him. 'But I refuse to waste such a lovely evening debating international politics.'

Over dinner their conversation covered everything from the forthcoming wedding, to the excellent governess Jane had managed to secure for Alice, who was to start very soon, to Aimée's meeting with Gabrielle Watson – 'Oh, that woman,' Oliver said disparagingly, to which Aimée replied that she wasn't in the least surprised that he disliked Mrs Watson, but that the country needed women like her, and anyway she was still very ill, so he must be charitable. Finally Aimée told them of the slow but sure progress she was making with her clinic.

'Just one afternoon a week at present, but it's a start.'

'Your women patients haven't been discouraged by those drunken oafs who daubed your front door, then?' Oliver said.

'A few, perhaps, but not for long.' Her eyes began to twinkle. 'One husband, the ringleader, I suspect, tried a different approach, but that didn't get him very far either.' When appealed to, she gave them a brief account of her run-in with Big Liam.

'Taking a bit of a chance there, weren't you?' Oliver said. 'He sounds to be the kind of man who might turn nasty, being made to look a fool by a woman.'

'I doubt he'd want to broadcast his embarrassment. And if my warning about his wife penetrates his thick skull, it will have been worth the risk. In any case, he picked the wrong time. Even Big Liam couldn't compete with chickenpox. Your two were lucky to escape. Sometimes it seemed as if every other family in Liverpool was affected.'

'Nanny didn't allow them beyond the garden until she deemed the air to be no longer polluted,' Oliver said dryly.

Aimée didn't approve of children being so over-protected, but contented herself with a dismissive, 'Oh, but it's relatively harmless in children – more tiresome than dangerous. But it meant I was able to do a lot more home visiting, and frankly I was appalled by what I found.' She pushed her plate away and leaned forward, suddenly full of passion. 'It's a hundred times worse than I remember from my college days. How those poor women manage, women like Biddy O'Hara, having baby after baby in conditions that beggar description – trying to raise them decently, make a home, with no adequate water or sanitation, and in most cases, with little help from their husbands. Small wonder some of them give up.' Aimée stopped abruptly, embarrassment flooding her face. 'I'm so sorry! How rude of me to go on like that. And at the dinner table, too –'

'No, no. Please don't stop. It's so obvious that you care!' Jane exclaimed, putting out a hand. 'We don't mind in the least, do we, Oliver?'

'Not at all,' he said calmly, pushing back his chair. 'But if you've finished, I suggest we would all be more comfortable in the drawing room.'

The sun had set, and a sultry current of air occasionally stirred the curtains. In the distance, like muffled gunfire, thunder rolled and rumbled and there was an occasional distant flash.

'We could do with a good storm,' Jane said.

Aimée sat nursing her brandy glass, struggling to quell the unruly spirit unleashed by her ill-timed outburst. Perhaps it was the stifling heat that was unsettling her. Her glance lifted, not for the first time, to the portrait over the mantelshelf.

'I have often thought,' said Jane, pouring coffee, 'that if only one half of the money wasted by politicians in waging futile wars were spent on meeting the huge areas of need in their own country, the lives of so many people could be transformed.'

'Oh, I do so agree!' Aimée swallowed her remaining brandy in one gulp, and rose, needing to find some respite for her disordered thoughts.

Oliver watched her as she prowled the room, her slim body restless beneath its sheath of peacock blue silk. It was cut low at the back, giving a vulnerability to the curve of her neck. She turned, her dark eyes alive, brightly challenging.

'But politicians are men, Jane, and most of them I suspect know little of what goes on in their own homes, let alone in the country at large.' Her humour had a brittle edge, and although she spoke to his sister, it was to Oliver that she addressed her argument. 'So nothing will change until the franchise is extended to all women. For when one looks at the evils in our society, it is almost always the women who suffer – and the children.'

He met her deliberate provocation with an unruffled calm that made her want to hit him. 'Oh, come – aren't you being a little hard on men? We aren't all monsters.'

'I didn't say you were. But you can't deny that almost all laws are instituted by men for men.'

Jane, sitting quietly beside the coffee table, and quite obviously forgotten for the moment, watched and listened, amused, but also intrigued by their behaviour. She had supposed their relationship to be a slight one, but clearly there was more to it than that, for a curious intimacy ran like an electric current between them, defying explanation. The storm rumbled nearer, but neither seemed aware of it, while the argument which had begun light-heartedly, suddenly intensified.

'At the risk of sounding carping, I would argue that women are not the only victims of man's inhumanity to man.' A harshness had crept into Oliver's voice. 'How many conscripts were shot as deserters, traitors? Their only crime that they were too young, or grossly unfitted to face the horror of the trenches, and the generals and the politicians, who had got it so wrong, could not afford a mass revolt, which would expose the pitiful inadequacy of their strategy.'

With his smooth lawyer's tongue he had very cleverly turned her argument on its head in the one way guaranteed to touch a raw nerve in her. His quiet vehemence would at any other time have surprised and intrigued her. But the image of Toby and the ghosts of others less fortunate were very much before her, and the exhilaration that had spurred her on began to falter.

'A pity you didn't say so at the time, except that you too might have been shot.'

It was a cheap jibe, and undeserved. But he only said, 'I did and I wasn't.'

Her hand shook as she attempted to light a cigarette, and Oliver was at her side, taking the lighter from her, flicking it, guiding the flame. She looked up at him, her eyes stinging slightly from the smoke, and found his expression as inscrutable as ever.

'And now you will remind me that it was often women who, from the comfort of their homes, encouraged those poor foolish boys to take the King's shilling,' she said huskily. 'And handed out white feathers to those who wriggled out of going.'

'I would not be so ungallant,' he said with a faint smile.

He was doing it again, refusing to be provoked. In desperation she sought to justify her original theme. 'But the behaviour of a few foolish women cannot in any way negate the rightness of universal suffrage.'

'I would not dream of suggesting that it should.'

Exasperation filled her. She turned and met Jane's eyes, and was surprised to see herself being regarded with amused sympathy.

'Infuriating, isn't he? I can never win an argument with him either, and I've had a lot more practice. But you mustn't mind him. Unlikely as it may seem, Oliver is on our side. In fact, he is the author of several excellent pamphlets extolling the just cause for woman's emancipation.'

Aimée swung round. 'Is that true?'

His dark inquisitorial eyes narrowed through a curl of smoke as they met the accusation in hers. '*Mea culpa*,' he said dryly. 'However, where you are passionate, my reasons are based wholly on logic. Women form a large part of our population, and as such should be entitled by law to a say in the way the country's affairs are conducted.' A hint of steel crept into his voice. 'But anarchy does little to prove fitness for citizenship, and I shall always oppose anyone, man or woman, who attempts to force change by violent means.'

His views accorded broadly with her own, yet perversely she found herself rushing to the defence of those brave women who had gone against everything in their nature and upbringing to make people listen. 'I could never have done what they did, but I applaud their courage, for without their sacrifice, I doubt Parliament would have budged one inch.'

Again the air was charged, but before Oliver could reply there was a brilliant flash of lightning, and a simultaneous crash, far louder than thunder, which rocked the whole building.

17

OLIVER AND AIMÉE had gone out into the square immediately, leaving Jane to calm the children, to find doors opening all around, people shouting, but no sign of damage. The heat was stifling and, despite the storm, the rain didn't come.

'It's over there,' a young man was pointing to where a plume of smoke was already billowing into the sky. As they watched it was pierced by the first lick of flame. 'Somewhere up the top end of Faukner Street – Smithdown Lane way, by the look of it.'

Aimée didn't wait to hear more. She turned and ran for her car. Oliver followed, grabbing her arm as the engine growled into life.

'Aimée, what are you doing? Leave it to the authorities.'

'Let go, Oliver! I have patients in that area. So either get in or get out of the way.'

He slid in beside her without another word, and she roared away. 'Why doesn't it rain?' she muttered, taking a corner too fast and skidding slightly. 'At least it would damp the fire down.'

Oliver gritted his teeth and said nothing. It took only moments to reach Myrtle Street, and to pull in front of her own house. 'I may need my emergency bag – I won't be a moment,' she said.

In the maze of back streets, it wasn't difficult to find the site of the explosion. A warehouse had been struck by lightning – a thunderbolt, someone said. Already a noisy crowd had collected, many of them spilling out of the nearby pubs, some with pints still in hand, eager not to miss a bit of drama, others afraid for their families or wanting to help. The beat constable was trying to restore some kind of order, but between all the mayhem and the constant crackle of thunder and lightning, it was almost impossible to make himself heard. Smoke and stench filled the street. Aimée was just thanking God that it wasn't a house when she realized the back wall of the warehouse had collapsed on top of

Angel Court where her patients the O'Haras and Bradys, lived.

As she grabbed her bag and climbed out, Oliver said tersely, 'I'll move the car. There are villains in this crowd who'd strip it down to the chassis in minutes, given half a chance. Anyway, the fire engine will need all the room it can get. And don't attempt any heroics. Leave it to the police and firemen.' But he was already talking to the air.

Aimée fought her way through to the lone policeman who was struggling to quell the noise, fend off questions and hang on to his helmet. 'I'm a doctor,' she shouted. 'Is there anything I can do?'

'Plenty, I dare say, if we could get this lot ter shift. Hey, Nellie, move yer backside. They didn't make this entry big enough fer the two of us.'

'Shift yersel', Joe Jenkins. I live 'ere. I'm entitled – '

'Harry, help us get the doctor through in ter the court.'

Above the noise Aimée heard the distant clanging of the fire bell, and almost at the same moment, the skies opened and rain beat down like stair rods.

The constable managed to fight his way up the entry ahead of her. There was rubble everywhere, the privies had been shattered and were giving off an appalling stench. The constable dragged a handkerchief from his pocket and pressed it to his face. His voice was muffled.

'You don't want ter go in there, Doc. It in't fittin' fer a lady.'

Aimée didn't bother to answer. She masked her own face with a handkerchief, and with her dress plastered against her body by the rain, she stumbled on, mingling with others running towards the section that had been virtually destroyed, her worst fears realized as she saw that where the O'Haras' rooms had been, there was only a pile of rubble. Everywhere stunned people were wandering aimlessly, and many times she paused to tend superficial wounds, glad of the extra antiseptic dressings she had thrown into her bag. And then, somewhere amid the rubble, she heard someone coughing, half-choking.

'Over there, constable,' she called, trying to locate the sound.

'Praise be, is that you, Doctor?'

The voice was a thin thread, but Aimée recognized it at once. 'Mrs O'Hara – Biddy? Where are you?'

'Here.' Her breath rasped. 'but I can't seem to move for the life of me. The children . . . I need Liam to find my babbies.'

Aimée located her at last, and saw that the lower half of her body was pinned down by a huge beam, her face bluish white and sheened with rain in the eerie darkness. A plump figure emerged from the shadows.

'She looks bad, Doctor,' whispered Sarah Brady.

'I'll get someone to help me move that beam,' said Oliver, appearing at Aimée's side, but she mouthed, 'Not yet,' and shook her head.

'Listen.' She smoothed back Biddy's rain-drenched hair. 'I'm going to give you an injection to make you more comfortable.'

'No! I'm not hurtin' that bad, honest. An' I must stay awake – till I know all the children are safe.'

'Don't be worryin' yersel', Biddy,' said Sarah Brady, 'I have the three older boys safe. An' aren't your Mary and Eileen forever at the Gallaghers?'

'But Michael was upstairs with Vera Lyall. She was on her own with the babbies an' terrified of thunder. He'd gone up to bring them down . . . such a good kind boy.'

Aimée's glance instinctively lifted to the great gap where upstairs had been. Mrs Brady shook her head as Biddy struggled on. 'But the wee ones were with me. It's them I'm most feared for, young Dec, an' Ally, an' the babby. I thought I heard Dec a minute since.'

As if on cue, a disembodied voice whimpered, 'Mam, Mam, I can't see nothin' an' we can't gerrout.'

'That's him. That's our Dec. He's alive, God be praised! Where are you, me darlin'?'

'I'm under the table, Mam,' he sobbed. 'An' I've gorrour Ally an' Meg, but there's bricks an' stuff all round us. I want me da ter gerrus out!'

'He will so, me darlin', just as soon as he's able.' Her voice rose in sudden anguish. '*Oh, Liam, where are you?*'

'In an alehouse somewhere, with his mates, I shouldn't wonder,' Aimée muttered to Oliver, standing up. 'Well, we can't wait for him. Oliver, will you find the constable? I need to know how badly hurt Biddy is, and she'll not let me touch her until those children are safe.'

'He has his hands full at present.' Oliver bent down and laid a reassuring hand against Biddy's cheek. 'Don't worry. We'll soon have your children out, Mrs O'Hara. If you could just get the boy talking again, so I can work out where he is.'

'God bless you, sir!' she whispered. 'Dec, listen, your da is busy right now . . . but there's a nice gentleman coming to fetch you any minute, so be still an' wait. Are you all right?'

'I aren't hurt, Mam, but I want our da ter come.'

'An' he will, me darlin', just as soon as he's able. But be a good boy now, an' do as the gentleman tells yer.'

Oliver, with the help of many willing hands, had been carefully removing bricks. 'I think that'll do. They sound reasonably close, so with a bit of luck I should be able to get through to them.'

'Oliver, do be careful!'

He flashed Aimée a half-smile. 'A bit like old times, wouldn't you say?'

In the cinema the thunder almost drowned out the music that accompanied the film. Wouldn't it just happen now, Matty thought indignantly. The first time she been asked out properly, and there had to be a storm.

Alec Gresham kept trying to put his arm round her, and when the biggest bang came, she did let him cuddle her, just for a minute, but soon his hands started to wander, and she put a stop to that right away. It was still teeming rain when they came out.

'My frock'll be ruined,' she wailed.

'We could still have that drink,' Alec suggested. 'I know a place close by – norra public,' he said, before she could protest. 'A real classy place, an' when the rain eases off, I'll get us a taxi.'

The thought of arriving home in a taxi with a good-looking young man, and Dolly McBride and her cronies with their eyes out on stalks, decided her.

'All right. But nothing stronger than lemonade, mind. If Mam smells alcohol on me breath, I'll be for it, good and proper.'

'Your mam sounds a bit of a tyrant,' Alec said, seizing her hand and making a dash for the hotel entrance.

'Not really. She's strict, but fair.' Matty looked round the softly lit cocktail bar. There were lots of young people in evening dress, girls no older than herself smoking cigarettes in long decorative holders, and calling everyone 'darling'. It was a bit like being in a film herself, she thought, sipping her lemonade. 'That was a lovely film. Owen Nares! And that Isobel Elson's ever so beautiful.'

'No more beautiful than you.'

'Ah, go on,' she said, but she could feel her cheeks turning pink.

'An' I bet she's not half so talented in other ways.' Alec, into his second pint, waxed lyrical. 'I've heard Mrs Mellish talkin' about how clever you are with a needle – you hear a lot of things when you're drivin' folk. She reckons that with the right backing, you could go far. And if that's one of your own creations you're wearing, I'd agree with her.'

'Oh, you know all about that sort of thing, I suppose,' Matty said provocatively.

'Yeah.' He grinned. 'An' I know that if you've got a talent, you should make the most of it. I certainly don't aim to be a chauffeur all me life. The Mellish's are okay. It's a good billet – and it does no harm to get yer face known in the right places.' He leaned forward, his face suddenly intense. 'But one day, before too long, I mean to race cars – and have me own motor showrooms an' all. It's the coming thing.'

'You ought to talk to our Irene's husband. That's the kind of thing he's always going on about. He's got a shop an' a little garage. It's motor cycles just now, but he's very ambitious.'

'Well, you've got to have ambition if you want to get on. I'm not rushing things, though. I mean to make as many valuable contacts as I can.' He reached forward and took her hand. 'Who knows, if we was to get together, we could both go right to the top.'

Matty's heart was beating very fast, but she wasn't about to let him take too much for granted. She tossed her head. 'Oh, I'm going to do that anyway. I don't mean to get myself tied down for a very long time.'

Alec's eyes narrowed, and she couldn't read their expression.

'You could be right,' was all he said. And then, 'Come on. The rain's easing off. Time to go.'

It wasn't easy to get a taxicab. The rain had almost stopped, but water was flooding the drains, and everywhere smelled damp. Alec finally managed to flag a taxi down. Matty swayed sideways as it turned full circle and he seized the opportunity to pull her close. She offered a token resistance and then succumbed.

'What a night, eh?' The driver, insensitive to lovers' needs, was in a chatty mood. 'I thought the Germans'd decided to 'ave another go at us.'

'As bad as that, was it?'

'Yer must've been havin' a good time if yer didn't hear it – ruddy thunderbolt hit a grocery warehouse up Smithdown Lane way – brought half a dozen houses down in one of them courts. Always said them places needed blastin' ter glory.'

Matty brushed Alec's wandering hand away from her knee and sat forward, her heart skipping a beat. Vera Lyall lived in a court that backed on to a warehouse. 'Whereabouts was it?'

'Blowed if I know exactly. 'Ang on, it had a rum name – kinda religious – Angel Court, that's it.'

'Oh, no! Someone I know lives in Angel Court. Could you take us there, please?'

'Hang on, Matty.' Alec sounded aggrieved. 'This is supposed to be our night out, an' I'm payin' for this taxi, remember.'

'Oh, don't be so petty, Alec. This is an emergency!'

He gripped her arms. 'You're crazy, d'you know that?'

She could feel his exasperation, but it made no difference. 'I have to go, Alec. Vera's expecting soon, an' she has two little ones already. I must find out if she's all right. You don't have to come. I'll pay for the taxi meself.'

'Don't talk daft.'

Matty was halfway down the street before Alec had paid the taxi man. He followed protesting that the air was full of smuts – 'Me good suit'll be ruined!'

'I told you, you didn't have to come.' There was an ambulance pulling up outside the entry to the court as she ran in.

It seemed hours before Aimée heard Oliver's calm, reassuring voice encouraging Dec to hold on tight to his sister and wriggle on his tummy 'like playing trains'. And then he slowly emerged, crawling backwards with the baby in one arm, a little girl clinging to his other hand, and Dec clinging to her feet.

Aimée took the baby from him, blinking back tears.

'They're out and safe,' she told Biddy, crouching to let her see baby Meg. As if to confirm it, the child set up a healthy bawling, and the two older children joined in and had to be restrained from throwing themselves on their mother.

'May God and His Holy Mother be thanked! And you, too, sir.' Biddy lifted a feeble hand.

'I'll look after these three, never fear,' Sarah Brady promised, cradling the baby. 'And those other spalpeens, too, when I catch up with them. You just do as the good doctor says.'

'Not before time,' Aimée said. 'Now, will you please let me give you this injection? The ambulance is waiting and the sooner we get you to hospital, the better.'

'Liam?'

'Don't worry,' Aimée said, injecting the morphine into her arm. 'We'll let him know where you've gone.' If and when it pleases him to put in an appearance, she added in silent wrath.

There were far more uniforms moving about now. Oil lamps had been brought to light the scene, and people who had no business in the court were being firmly ushered out. Suddenly, there was a sound like an enraged bull in the entry and Big Liam burst through, wild-eyed.

'Where is she? Where's my Biddy? Oh God, she's not . . . ?'

Aimée stood up. 'No, Mr O'Hara, your wife isn't dead,' she said crisply. 'But she is hurt – as yet, I don't know how badly.'

'Well, someone'd better find out bloody quick.' He rushed forward. 'Why has no one moved that – that thing? I'll have it off her in seconds – '

The constable stepped in front of him. 'All in good time, Liam. When the doctor says. We don't want to undo all her good work.'

'Liam?' Biddy's voice was a thread. 'Ah, I knew you'd come. The children . . . you'll see them all safe.'

He was on his knees. 'They'll be fine. It's you needs the lookin' after.'

'Mr O'Hara, the ambulance men are here.' Aimée's voice was quiet, but firm. 'Help to move the beam by all means, but it must be done very slowly. Her pelvis may be fractured. If there's room in the ambulance, you may be able to go with your wife to the hospital.'

She supervised as the beam was removed and Biddy was transferred to the waiting ambulance.

'Dr Aimée, is it you?'

Aimée turned, her face begrimed with dust and barely recognizable. 'Matty! Whatever are you doing here?'

But Matty was staring past her at the pile of rubble. 'I heard what had happened. Vera Lyall, a friend of mine, lived up there. Is she, are they . . . ?' her voice trailed away.

'I'm sorry, my dear, they wouldn't have had a chance.' Aimée watched Big Liam walk past like a zombie to the waiting ambulance. 'Poor man. One of his sons was with your friend.'

'You mean she's – that they're all – the kiddies, too? But that's terrible! Isn't there any hope?'

'I'm afraid not.' Aimée put a comforting arm round her shoulder. 'Go home, Matty. There's nothing you can do. Nothing more anyone can do until daylight.'

Aimée watched her walk away with her young man, whom she recognized as her aunt's chauffeur, and Oliver watched Aimée. Her beautiful dress was totally ruined and her face was streaked with dirt and tears, yet there was a strength about her that stirred memories in him of that forthright young woman who had stood in the mud of the battlefield, berating him. Aware of his eyes on her, she turned to smile tiredly at him. The planes of his face stood out, but his features were in shadow. 'Thank you, Oliver. You were splendid. Now, I really should see if – '

'Enough,' he said firmly, taking her arm. He looked around in disgust, as if seeing the place for the first time. 'It's a great pity the whole lot didn't come down, if you ask me. No one should live like this.'

'There are plenty of places as bad and worse than this. And until something is done, those who can't afford better must live somewhere, if you can call this squalid slum existence living, preyed on by greedy landlords who grow fat at their expense – '

'Stop it, Aimée. You can't hope single-handedly to right years of rapaciousness and neglect overnight!'

'Don't tell me what I can and can't do!' She turned on him furiously, her anger trembled on the brink of tears. He saw them glinting in the eerie half-light, and with a muffled oath, he caught her flailing hands and pulled her close. His mouth came down on hers, stopping her protest in mid-sentence. After a moment of fierce resistance, she suddenly gave in, her anger turning to a soft moaning in her throat as his tongue moved against hers. Her mouth widened in response, her body melting against him like a flower too long deprived of rain, clinging as if she would draw strength from his closeness.

In a confused corner of her mind, a voice was whispering 'Oh, David, it has been so long, too long – I had almost forgotten . . .'

And then, abruptly, reality intruded once more and she stood blinking up at Oliver with dust thick in her nostrils and smoke stinging her eyes. His face had such a strange closed look that for one heart-stopping moment she wondered if she had spoken David's name aloud.

Had she but known, he was equally confused. In those brief moments he had not once thought of Catherine. Aimée had filled his senses with her need of him – an Aimée so completely at odds with the practical single-minded young woman she presented to the world that he scarcely recognized her – passionate, all defences down as she yielded to his touch, her mouth betraying an almost unbearable yearning.

'I'm sorry,' he said abruptly. 'That shouldn't have happened.'

His words acted like a douche of cold water. Aimée wondered if it was relief or shame that made her tremble in every limb – or simply the curtness of his apology? To mask her embarrassment, she said in her best professional manner, 'It takes two. Don't give it another thought. It's a natural human reaction to stress.'

Unexpectedly, he smiled. 'Yes, Doctor.' He tucked his hand beneath her elbow. 'Time to go home, I think.'

The fire in the warehouse was out. The rain, combined with the efforts of the firemen, had stopped it spreading. As they walked past, the constable beckoned to them.

'Dr Buchanan.' His voice was respectful. 'Superintendent Manners would like a word.'

They found the Superintendent, with the local inspector and the chief fireman, assessing the state of the warehouse. And with them was a stiff, rather pompous figure in evening dress, beneath an umbrella. Dr Dalywell.

The inspector detached himself from the group and came across. 'This is good of you, ma'am. We have a problem, and wondered if you could help. There was a nightwatchman in the building when the chimney came down – '

'I'm sorry, Inspector, but Dr Buchanan has done enough. She's exhausted – '

'Oliver! I didn't expect to see you here.' The Superintendent greeted him with the familiarity of an old friend.

'I'm with Dr Buchanan.' Oliver drew her forward to introduce her, and she found her hand being firmly shaken.

'This is a bad business, ma'am.'

'Indeed, it is.'

'Do you know Dr Dalywell?'

Aimée nodded. 'Dr Dalywell.' They had in fact met, just once, at a medical function, when he had all but accused her of poaching his patients.

'I was attending a civic reception at the Town Hall when this happened,' the Superintendent continued. 'Dennis was there, too, and he offered to come with me, to see if he could be of any help.' He shook his head. 'A bad business.'

'Quite. But I've already told your inspector, Dr Buchanan is very tired. I am taking her home. I'm sure Dr Dalywell will do all that is necessary.'

'So you have already assessed the nightwatchman's condition, Dr Dalywell?' Aimée asked, ignoring Oliver's intervention.

'There is little to assess.' He spoke with cool superiority. 'A brief glance more than sufficed to convince me that the man's situation is hopeless.'

'We can't move him, see, ma'am,' one of the fireman put in diffidently. 'The old fellow's leg is trapped solid, and if we attempt to free him, that pile of bricks'll come toppling down for sure. In fact, they could come down any time.'

'But if you could free the leg, might there be a chance of getting him out alive?'

'We are talking of amputation, Dr Buchanan,' Dr Dalywell said pompously. 'A difficult enough operation at the best of times, as I'm sure you realize, and in the existing cramped conditions – ' he shrugged. 'Even if it were possible, I have no instruments to hand, and no time to fetch them.'

Little quivers of fear were coursing through Aimée and it took a great effort of will not to turn and run.

'But I have my bag. You are welcome to make use of its contents,

Dr Dalywell,' she said, surprised to find that her voice sounded normal. 'It has everything in it that you might need.'

She heard his swift intake of breath. 'My dear young lady, I am hardly – no, no, it is not possible – '

'Begging your pardon, but time is pressing.' The fire chief cut through his bluster. 'I've got one of my lads in there with old Bill. The poor chap's pretty weak, but his spirit is tremendous. I'd hate to let him go without a fight. But if nothin' can be done, I must pull my lad out now.'

Aimée tried to blot everything out of her mind except the fact that a man was going to die a horrible death unless something was done quickly. But her ears were beginning to thud and she could not quite control her shaking.

'Aimée?' Oliver, touching her arm, had felt it, too. He said tersely, 'This had gone far enough. I'm sorry, but you can see that Dr Buchanan is worn out.'

'I'm all right,' she insisted, knowing that if she took the easy way now, not only would she never forgive herself, she would not be worthy of her calling.

'The least we can do is take a look.' Her eyes challenged her colleague. 'Dr Dalywell?'

He lowered his umbrella with reluctance.

The inside of the warehouse was a shambles, with that choking, acrid smell that only the aftermath of a fire can produce. They stepped carefully over sodden cardboard boxes, blackened and spilling their contents – wet packets, and tins that had exploded with the heat.

'This way.' A fireman beckoned them towards a gaping hole in the walled off end section miraculously left standing.

Inside, in an area no more than a few feet high or wide, a man was lying, the upper half of his body cradled by one of the firemen. Both were covered in brick dust. The fireman turned, his eyes, in their caked sockets, burning with a fear he couldn't quite hide. The old man lay with one leg crooked at an angle, the other being buried to well past the ankle in a mass of crumbling masonry that looked poised to collapse at any moment. The only sounds were the constant drip of water and the laboured breathing of the old man.

'Hopeless,' muttered Dr Dalywell, drawing back. His face was sheening with sweat. 'There is no point in trying to get in, let alone attempt – ' Again words failed him. His glance met Aimée's and slid away, but in that moment she glimpsed blind panic and realized that Dr Dalywell was suffering from claustrophobia. She felt a momentary pity, but his panic gave her strength.

'I can't give up without taking a closer look.' She crawled cautiously over the rim of the hole, and the old man's head turned towards her, his face haggard beneath a coating of brick dust, eyes glazed with pain, his voice a thread.

'Eh up, 'ave you taken a wrong turning, or 'ave I died an' gone ter 'eaven?'

'Neither.' She smiled and said quietly, 'I'm a doctor and I've come to take a look at you. Bill, isn't it?'

'It is, bur' I'm not much cop, gairl, an' that's a fact.'

His pulse was weak, erratic. She reached carefully across him to cut away the already torn trousers. For a good eight inches below the knee, the leg was inflamed, but undamaged. Beyond that, it was crushed beyond help. It wouldn't be easy, working across the body, and the shock of the amputation would probably kill him, but she couldn't just leave him here to die. It would be a betrayal of everything she believed in. Their eyes met, and in that moment she knew that if she ran away she would not be able to live with her conscience.

'You know what I have to do?'

'Eh, I'll not 'ave a pretty lass like you doin' a thing like that – an' riskin' yer life. I've already told yon fireman ter leave us an' gerrout, but 'e's a stubborn lad.'

'Rubbish, Bill. We're not beaten yet.' She forced a smile. 'I'll just be a minute.'

Outside, Oliver was waiting, his face set like granite. As she reached for her medical bag and opened it with hands that shook uncontrollably, he said low-voiced, 'This is madness, Aimée. You're in no state to attempt it.'

'I agree.' Dr Dalywell's voice was scathing. 'Look at your hands, woman.'

'Ma'am, the gentlemen have a point. I shouldn't have asked you to come. This isn't woman's work.'

If anything were needed to stiffen her resolve, the Super-intendent's words did the trick. Her concentration became total as she checked that everything she needed was there: chloroform, artery forceps, scalpel, saw – cold perspiration broke out on her forehead at this last, but she went steadily on – needles, sutures, gauze, antiseptic . . .

'Could you lay a coat or something down here?' she asked the fire chief, feeling suddenly calm. 'It's likely to be ruined, but your men will need to get him out as quickly as possible when I say so. That poor man who's holding him won't be up to carrying him. And we'll need an ambulance – and lots of blankets.'

'Aimée – ' Oliver caught at her arm, but it was as though she hardly heard him, her mind already fixed elsewhere.

Back inside, she suddenly remembered the fireman who was holding Bill. How would he react? He looked exhausted.

'I reckon I can cope, if you can, Doc.'

She smiled briefly, rolling out a small rubber mat and laying out her instruments. 'This won't take long, then your part will be over.'

She worked swiftly once the chloroform had taken effect, faltering only as she picked up the scalpel. For a moment her memory began to play tricks – a faint sickly whiff of gas gangrene seemed to linger obscenely on the air . . .

'Are you all right, Doc?' The fireman sounded concerned.

'Fine, she said, thrusting memory aside.

And suddenly she *was* fine. Her hand became rock steady, the scalpel a part of it as she made the first incision. Her mind was sharp and clear. If she could save the knee, it would help the poor chap later . . .

The grating of the saw made the fireman gag a bit, but the worst was soon over, and with the artery forceps clipped in place, she covered the stump with gauze and knelt back with a shiver of exultation.

Within moments Oliver had changed places with her, and he and one of the constables carried Bill out and laid him down. While she finished off, tidied the wound, ligatured, and drenched it with antiseptic, they went back for the fireman who was suffering from acute cramp. Relief was followed by congratulations, and in all the activity that followed no one but Aimée noticed that Dr Dalywell had not spoken. He stood back a little, taking no part, but even in her extreme weariness, she felt his carefully contained fury.

'I'll go in the ambulance,' she said. 'I need to have a word with the surgeon.'

'If you must.' Oliver was by now resigned. 'I'll follow in your car to make sure that a word is all you do have.'

She turned to him with a smile, and in spite of her acute weariness, there was an aura of peace about her.

Aimée opened her eyes to find that the rain had stopped, the sky had cleared and stars were winking as though nothing had happened. She saw that they were back in Falkner Square.

'Out,' Oliver said, opening the car door for her.

'Oh, no. I won't come in. It must be very late. I'd like to get home.'

'You aren't going home. You're staying here for what's left of the night.'

She blinked up at him. 'But I can't. Someone might call – an emergency.'

'They'll have to look elsewhere,' he said grimly. 'You are going to do as you are told for once.'

Delayed reaction and exhaustion had left her light-headed so that she was reluctant to lift her head from the cushion of soft leather. 'The first time I saw you, I had you tagged as a martinet. I remember thinking: I bet they jump to attention when he barks.' She squinted up at him. 'But I am not one of your underlings.'

She thought he swore as he lifted her almost bodily from the car, and helped her up the steps into the house. Jane was waiting for them, still fully dressed.

'Good gracious,' she said. 'Have you seen yourselves? Do you know what time it is? I thought something must have happened. Aimée, what have you been doing? Your lovely dress is ruined!'

'Never mind the dress. Aimée is staying the night,' Oliver was brusque. 'Perhaps you could organize a bath for her and some kind of nightwear – oh, and a hot drink. I'll explain later.'

The bath was blissfully restorative. Aimée was sitting up in bed in a charming room, softly lit, sipping a cup of delicious hot chocolate when Oliver knocked on the door and came in.

'Better?'

'Much. The bath worked wonders, but I am being ridiculously spoiled, and it really isn't necessary, you know.'

'I'll be the judge of that.' He sat on the bed, and even without the clipped voice, she could sense his anger.

'A short while ago you were outspoken concerning your first impressions of me.' With grim satisfaction he watched the colour creep up under her skin. 'Now I mean to return the compliment with equal frankness. I saw you as a crazy woman, bossy, self-willed and opinionated – and you've done little since to change my mind. If anything, tonight you excelled yourself. What were you trying to prove, for God's sake?'

Aimée put her cup carefully on the bedside table and shrunk down a little in the bed, with hands folded and head lowered. She was still fragrant from her bath, and her hair curled damply into her cheek, but the blush had died away leaving her face pale and achingly vulnerable, which only served to fuel his anger. His glance strayed to the delicate blue-veined skin where it disappeared into the deep V of her borrowed nightgown, and further to the swell of her breast beneath the pale pink satin.

She was at once childlike and all woman, infinitely desirable. For an instant he felt an emotion more powerful than anger – and more dangerous. It had flared into life earlier when he had kissed her – and if he did not leave now, he was in danger of repeating it.

But before he could move, she began to speak in a low flat voice, without looking at him.

'That last time I came back from France, when I was ill and you were so kind to me, I wasn't coming home on leave as I allowed you to think.' She told him the whole wretched story, without self-pity, without excuses. 'Quite simply, I had lost my nerve.'

'Exhaustion,' he said roughly. 'It was a common affliction.'

'True.' She looked up with a faint smile. 'But time and rest will cure exhaustion. It isn't so easy to rekindle a belief in oneself, to stop running away.'

'Is that what you've been doing?' he said, surprised. 'You've always seemed pretty single-minded to me.'

'About medicine, yes. But you see, surgery had always been my goal – and suddenly I couldn't handle it.'

'And now?'

Aimée shook her head, too tired to rationalize her emotions. 'I shan't know for sure until the next time, but I think, I hope I have at last exorcized that particular devil.'

'You're too hard on yourself.' He handed her the cup and stood up. 'Drink your chocolate and go to sleep.' At the door he said without turning, 'For what it's worth, I thought you were bloody marvellous this evening.'

18

Aimée was being prodded, quite gently, but with persistence. She opened her eyes to find a child standing very close beside the bed, a child with hair like golden thistledown trapped in a slim shaft of sunlight, bright inquisitive eyes and the face of an angel. For a moment she wondered where she was – and then remembered.

'Hello. You must be Alice.'

'Alice Mary Elizabeth Langley, and I'm nearly five.' She leaned forward importantly. 'My brother, Christopher, isn't even one yet.'

'Well, I'm Aimée Buchanan, and I'm a lot more than five,' Aimée said, entering into the spirit of the conversation, amused to find herself being subjected to intense scrutiny.

'Auntie Jane says you're a doctor. You don't look like a doctor. *Our* doctor has a bald head and whiskers, and is quite old.'

Aimée smiled. 'I sometimes feel quite old myself.' She emerged from the seductive warmth of the feather bed, leaned back against the pillows, and reached for her watch. 'Goodness. Half-past seven. Time I thought about getting up.'

'I wasn't supposed to disturb you.'

Aimée lowered her voice. 'I won't tell.'

There was a knock at the door and a maid entered bearing a tray. 'Miss Alice! You'll get what for from Nanny, comin' in here.'

'She won't know if you don't split on me,' Alice said, and ran to the door, turning with a huge grin. 'Bye.'

'She's a madam, that one. My mam'd have walloped me, talkin' back like that. Sooner she gets that governess, the better, beggin' yer pardon, doctor.'

The maid put the tray down on the bedside table and went to

draw back the curtains, letting the full glory of early morning sunlight flood in. Aimée had not until now appreciated her surroundings where the restful charm of soft cream walls, and *eau-de-Nil* carpet and furnishings combined perfectly with the gleam of polished mahogany.

'Storm's cleared the air, thank goodness. An' Miss Langley says as you're not to be in any rush gettin' up.'

Aimée was still wallowing in the unaccustomed luxury of tea in bed when Jane came in with an armful of newspapers, which she put down on a chair near the door.

'Well, you don't look too bad, considering the night you had.'

'It was rather like being back in France. Surprising how quickly one adjusts. How is Oliver?'

'Oh, he's already left for chambers. He's got a big fraud case coming up. He sends his apologies and asked me to tell you to take things easy today, and that he'll put a note on your surgery door for Mrs Green to let her know you won't be in.'

Aimée frowned. 'That was quite unnecessary. I'll be home long before Mrs Green arrives.'

'You must do as you think best.' Jane's smile had a wry quality. 'Oliver means well.'

'The world is full of people who mean well.' Aimée saw the hurt in Jane's eyes and was immediately apologetic. 'That was a beastly thing to say. Oliver was wonderful last night. I couldn't have managed without him. It's just . . .'

'I know. But beneath that rather autocratic façade is a deeply caring man. And he wasn't always so brusque. When Catherine was alive – '

'Yes, my aunt once told me what a lively and popular couple they were.'

Jane turned away to stare out of the window. 'Catherine's death hit Oliver very hard. He blamed himself, you see. Catherine almost died when she had Alice, but she passionately wanted a son for him, she said. She was very young, much younger than him, a lovely wilful creature. Oliver could never refuse her anything, so finally, against all advice, he gave in. And Catherine had her son. The rest you know.'

'Fate can be very perverse sometimes.'

'Yes.' There was an odd note in Jane's voice. 'Alice has always been very much her father's favourite. Whereas Christopher – ' she hesitated. 'He is still very young, of course.'

'Yes?'

Jane turned. 'Oh, nothing. It is probably all in my mind.'

'You suspect he has never fully accepted Christopher? That perhaps, deep down, he resents the child, even blames him for Catherine's death?' Jane denied this vehemently, but the truth lay in her eyes. 'There is nothing wicked or even shameful about that,' Aimée said gently. 'It's a very natural reaction in the circumstances, but I'm sure that will right itself in time.'

'I do hope so. It can't be good for him to bottle things up.'

'You are very fond of Oliver, aren't you? I have a brother, too – a twin, so I can understand how you feel.'

'When he first came home I felt so helpless – he was so closed in. That may not seem strange to you, but he hasn't always been so.' Jane came to sit on the bed near Aimée, her fingers plucking ineffectually at the bedclothes. 'You remember how vehement he was last night about the deserters? Well, he told me – after Catherine – that he had acted as defence counsel for some of those men at Court Martial, knowing that in most cases he was wasting his time, thus violating everything he believed in. He said he felt besmirched, unable to look them in the eyes.'

'Poor Oliver. But even the worst memories fade in time.'

'True. But if Catherine had been here at the time to console him, tease him out of it . . .' Jane shook her head and stood up, brisk once more. 'Forgive me, I'm talking too much. Now, are you quite sure you feel up to taking your morning surgery?'

'Dear Jane, it's good of you to be concerned, but I've survived much worse and with far less sleep.'

'Well, perhaps you'd better look at this before you finally decide.' She handed Aimée a newspaper headlined: 'Woman Doctor Heroine of the Hour', and beneath it was a report which stopped just short of high melodrama, together with a photograph, mercifully blurred.

'But this is dreadful!' Aimée hadn't been aware of any newspaperman taking photographs.

'Oh, there are several more, equally graphic,' Jane said dryly. 'And it's not just the local papers. See, *The Times* has a piece about the event and your courage. I very much fear you might find your house under seige.'

'Then the sooner I get over there, the better.'

'But you can't go without breakfast!'

Aimée threw back the bedclothes and then stopped, her face a picture of comical dismay. 'More important than that – I can't go without clothes.'

Half an hour later, she arrived in Myrtle Street to find that Jane's words were prophetic. The street was swarming with people, among them a large number of newspaper photographers. She stopped the car round the corner in Vine Street, and, dressed in one of Oliver's cook's oldest frocks and wearing a hat like a plant pot, with a feather in it to rival Mrs Green's, pulled well down, she shuffled through the crowd and reached the front door.

'Is Dr Buchanan at home?' someone yelled.

'Don't ask me,' she muttered, head bent. 'I'm only the daily 'elp.' And before they realized they had been cheated, she turned the key in the lock and whisked inside.

The telephone was ringing. 'You're thrr-ough,' sang the operator.

'Darling!' Her aunt's voice came crackling down the line. 'Have you seen the papers? What have you been doing?'

'Oh, Aunt Fliss, may I tell you about it later? This place is besieged.' She told her aunt how she had managed to bluff her way into her own house, and Felicity laughed.

'You always did have a talent for amateur dramatics, darling. Still, I won't keep you now, though I'm dying with curiosity!'

The telephone rang again almost immediately. This time it was her mother. Minna described in dramatic detail the agonies she had suffered upon reading the account in *The Times*. 'Darling, you might have been killed! Your father insisted upon sending for Frank who wanted to give me a sedative, but I could not take it for fear you might need me.' There was a hopeful pause, and she seemed almost disappointed when Aimée assured her she was fine. 'You cannot imagine how many people have called already to ask after you and sing your praises!'

Frank himself had been more sanguine about her improvised operating theatre. 'So, you finally overcame your enemy, lass. I'm glad.'

'Don't rejoice too soon, Frank,' she warned him. 'That was just the first battle. I'm not sure that I've yet won the war.'

'You will,' he said. 'One step at a time, eh?'

'Maybe. I must go. There's someone trying to break the door down.'

It was a newspaperman, shouting through the letterbox, wanting a story. 'I'm sorry. The doctor's busy,' she said and called the police station. Within ten minutes help had arrived, the crowd had been moved on, and she had a breathing space.

'I'll leave a constable outside for a while, Doctor, just in case,' said the duty inspector. 'Have you been in touch with the hospital this morning?'

'I really haven't had a chance,' she said.

'Just thought you'd like to know – old Bill's hangin' on.'

'I'm glad. Thank you so much for telling me.' He knew nothing about the others who were injured, though the death toll had gone up to nine.

Mrs Green arrived, huffing and puffing and complaining. 'Talk about takin' liberties! That bobby wasn't for lettin' me in! I told 'im – "you wants ter be catchin' thieves instead of molestin' respectable wimmin." '

In spite of all Mrs Green's efforts to weed out the genuinely sick from the merely curious, surgery was packed that morning. By the time the housekeeper shut the door firmly on the last one at lunch time and left to regale 'her Wilf' with the goings-on, Aimée was exhausted.

'You be all right, will you? I've left you a nice bit of ham, an' a tomato, an' there's bread 'n' butter, an' an apple pie fer afters.'

'Goodness! You're spoiling me, Mrs Green.'

She sniffed. 'Got ter keep yer strength up, doctor.'

As Aimée ate her nice bit of ham, she wondered how best to spend her afternoon. There was no surgery until seven, but she had several home visits arranged, and she wanted to visit Angel Court – was ever any place more grossly misnamed? – before calling in at the hospital.

The telephone rang yet again.

'So, how is the heroine of the hour coping?' Oliver said.

'Don't! I have never read such rubbish. The house was virtually under siege for the first hour or so.'

'Serves you right. You should have stayed put with Jane.'

Aimée ignored the note of censure. 'Well, I now have my very own police guard.'

'So you won't need rescuing?'

Had she not known better, Aimée might have thought he sounded disappointed.

'Not really. Though it's kind of you to offer. My day is pretty well filled, finishing with evening surgery until about nine o'clock. But you are very welcome to drop by any time after that for a drink.'

'Well,' he hesitated, 'my workload is pretty heavy, too.'

'Your fraud case?'

'It opens next week, and my client is decidedly edgy.'

There had been a great deal of speculation about the forthcoming trial in the paper, which Aimée had read with interest, for it concerned a man whom she had more than once heard Grandpa Howard accuse of sharp practice.

'Why do you defend people like Millar?'

Oliver said mildly, 'It is what I am paid to do.'

'But you surely can't believe he is innocent? The man's a rogue.'

There was a small silence at the other end. 'My dear Aimée, it may surprise you to know that the law does not make assumptions of guilt based solely on a man's character or reputation. A rogue has as much right to plead his innocence as a saint.'

'But you are such a stickler. I wouldn't expect you to – oh, I suppose you know what you're doing.'

'Thank you.' His voice was heavy with irony. Again there was a silence. 'Aimée – about that drink. I think perhaps another time?'

'Fine,' she said, her voice bright and brittle. 'I'll say goodbye then, and let you get on. Oh, and, Oliver – thank you.'

'For what?'

'For last night – and everything,' she said, and rang off feeling unaccountably depressed.

Her visit to Angel Court did little to lift her spirits. The fallen masonry had been cleared, but odd remnants of people's lives lay scattered about the cobbles – broken chairs; an odd boot with its tongue protruding in an obscene affirmation of defiance; a bent and blackened pan rolling on its side, the spilled contents drying in the sun, providing a feast for the rats who were ignored by the toddlers playing in and out of the wreckage, and who in turn ignored the people going stoically about the business of salvaging anything that could be of use. Above, the gouged out remnants of what had, however inadequately, been home to several poor families, hung on the brink of collapse.

Aimée found Mrs Brady, red-eyed, but solid and dependable, surrounded by an assortment of children busy devouring thick wodges of bread and dripping.

'It'd break yer 'eart if you'd let it,' she sniffed. 'The friends I've lost, and all them poor kiddies. Vera Lyall's hubby's in a permanent drunken stupor, an' who can wonder at it?' She wiped her eyes with the corner of her pinafore. 'But life has ter go on.'

'What of the O'Hara children?' Aimée asked.

'They're all safe with me excepting young Michael. Such a young rip, he was, but a heart of pure gold.' A fresh tear rolled down and was defiantly brushed away. 'Liam's hauntin' the hospital, near mad with grief and blamin' hisself. I tried tellin 'im it wus an Act of God, an' his being' here wouldn't have made any difference, but I doubt 'e 'eard me.'

'Perhaps not.' Aimée laid a hand on her shoulder. 'But you're a good friend to him just the same, Mrs Brady.'

'Mind you, it's that Frank Prentice, the landlord, livin' in comfort up Woolton way, what's really ter blame. Coinin' it in, he is an' mostly from the likes of us who can't afford better, an' never a penny spent on repairs. But if I'd said that ter Big Liam it would've sent 'im right over the top.'

'Very likely. I must go now, but I'll keep in touch.'

Mr Whittan, the senior surgeon who had dealt with the admissions from the previous night, was gloomy in his prognosis. Biddy O'Hara had, as Aimée had suspected, sustained a severe fracture of the pelvis and a damaged hip, together with some severe bruising. But it was the internal damage that was causing most concern.

'The bladder was badly ruptured. I've repaired it as best I can – but she's very shocked.' He shrugged. 'We shall have to wait and see –'

'That poor family. One of their young sons died, you know.'

'So I believe.' Mr Whittan hesitated. 'I would be grateful if you could persuade the husband to moderate his behaviour. I appreciate that he is distraught, but he's causing a lot of disruption on the ward. We don't want to curtail his visits.'

'I'll do my best,' Aimée said, though with little hope of being heeded.

'On the brighter side,' said the surgeon, 'that old fellow you did such a good job on last night is holding up remarkably well. He's not out of the wood yet, of course. As you know, at his age, anything can happen.' He eyed Aimée curiously. 'Done much surgery, have you?'

Every instinct urged her to retreat instantly into the safe cocoon she had made for herself. But last night had changed a lot of things.

'Quite a lot towards the end of the war,' she admitted with a calmness that surprised her. 'More amputations, in fact, than I care to remember.'

'Ah.' He nodded, seeming to understand without further explanation. 'Well, I hope you aren't lost to us forever. We need good surgeons.'

'One day. Who knows?' She quashed the sudden leap of hope that came unbidden. 'But I seem to have my work cut out for the foreseeable future. Is it all right if I look in on Bill, and poor Biddy O'Hara before I leave?'

'Sure. I'll take you along myself.'

Bill was very drowsy, but he seemed to recognize her voice as he smiled and pressed her hand. Biddy, however, was deeply unconscious, her cheeks paper white and sunken. It was a look Aimée knew well. But someone, probably Liam, had put Biddy's rosary in her hand, and Aimée had long ago learned not to discount the power of prayer.

Trying to reason with Big Liam, however, was almost impossible. Aimée intercepted him as he was about to blunder in through the gates of the hospital yet again.

'You really must stop badgering the nurses,' she said firmly, having coaxed him into her car and driven him back to Myrtle Street. 'There is nothing more they can do, and Biddy needs peace and quiet if she's to have half a chance.' But he seemed incapable of coherent thought.

Mrs Green was silently disapproving as Aimée asked her to make a good strong pot of tea. 'You want ter be careful with that one,' she muttered darkly. 'A leopard doesn't change its spots –an' grief can do funny things to a man.'

At first Liam seemed determined to take upon himself the whole of the blame for all that had happened. Even the death of his son. Aimée sat quietly at her desk and let him rant and rave as God and the landlord came in for equal tongue-lashings.

'It was the drink was me downfall. Always it's the drink. If I had half the money I've poured down me throat, we'd have been out of that stinkin' crumblin' cesspit of a place years ago.' He raised a haggard face from his hands. 'An' that soddin' landlord wants hangin' for murder, an' will if I catch 'im, squeezin' folk of their last few pence fer rat-ridden property as'd fall down if yer tapped it with the toe of yer boot! An' didn't it do just that night, takin' our Michael with it – as bonny a lad as you'd hope ter see, an' full of fun. Laid in the cold ground he'll be, an' my poor Biddy close ter joinin' him. What kind of a God is it as'd let the innocent suffer?'

Aimée listened with a lump in her throat, but when she judged that he had gone far enough, she poured a large strong cup of tea, well laced with sugar, and put it down beside him.

'Now,' she said, 'drink that, and pull yourself together. We have to talk about you – and how best you can help Biddy and your family, which for a start means staying sober. You'll need to find somewhere to live, and I don't want to hear any nonsense about you attacking the landlord, and ending up in jail. That won't help anyone.'

Matty had finally finished the appliqué on the gown, but it took her several days to pluck up the courage to approach Madame Vincente. When she did so, the little Frenchwoman was silent for so long that her lip was bitten nearly raw.

Until that moment Matty had been quite proud of her efforts. The design had worked out beautifully – the leaf and flower motifs, in subtle shades of palest green and shell pink, appeared to drift quite naturally in a soft diagonal across the ivory bodice and down the skirt, each one different and each hand stitched. Above one flower a dragonfly hovered, and elsewhere a bee. The silence stretched, and her confidence began to drain away.

'This is entirely your own idea?'

'Yes, Madame. I got it mostly from visiting Sefton Park and makin' sketches. You saw some of them.'

'So I did. *Incroyable!*' Again her employer fell silent.

'You don't like it.' Matty's flat statement was thick with tears of disappointment.

'Like it?' Madame Vincente seemed to come out of a trance. She sighed. 'It is quite beautiful. The time 'as come when we must talk.'

And talk they did – or rather Madame Vincente talked at great length. Matty's head was in a spin.

'Honestly, Mam, I couldn't take it in at first.' The words tumbled out of Matty almost before she got inside the front door. 'Madame Vincente wants to train me properly – I'm to work with her on my own, three evenings a week, learning to cut and design for *haute couture*.'

Agnes looked up from a shirt she was mending to see her daughter's face lit up like a candle. 'Matty love, calm down. You're making me dizzy with all this talk. I'm not sure I approve of Madame Vincente filling your head with all this fancy nonsense. I mean, where's it going to get you?'

'It'll get me right to the top one day, Mam. You'll see.'

'Not round here, it won't, girl. There's not much call for your *haute*-whatsit in these parts.'

'Well, of course there isn't. But I've a lot to learn. It'll take years an' a lot of hard work, but I don't mind that so long as I get there in the end. Alec says you have to seize your chances when they come.'

'Alec would.' Agnes had her doubts about Mrs Mellish's chauffeur. He was polite enough, but a bit cocky and a bit too smooth-spoken for her liking. And he had an eye to the main chance, that was for sure. She didn't want him encouraging Matty. 'You don't want to believe all Alec Gresham says.'

'I don't. But he's right in a way. If you've got a talent, you have to make the most of it. And you know it's what I've always wanted.' A note of awe entered Matty's voice. 'Madame says she's going to take me to Paris, maybe next spring, to see the collections at all the big fashion houses!'

Alec says – Madame says – never mind what Mam says. Agnes looked into her daughter's shining face, heard the passion in her voice, and her heart went hollow with fear. Suddenly it seemed as though her own life was slowly draining away; Phil had gone, and Pat was on borrowed time and Kevin was forever haunting her about going to sea, though he'd got a really good job with the butcher. Now it seemed she might soon lose this most treasured of daughters, too.

'Mam? Are you all right?' Matty's voice came from a long way off.

Agnes pulled herself together. 'Yes, of course I'm all right,' she said shortly. 'It's just been a long day, that's all. And I've had our Irene here half the afternoon, full of moans and groans. She'll not be so long now, I'm thinkin' – and a good job, too. It's no fun carrying at this stage, and her so big. And that Eddie's no help.'

As the end of August approached, Aimée's list of patients was growing steadily, and the mother and baby clinic was well established on Tuesday afternoons.

After some consideration she decided to visit Gabrielle Watson, who was now well on the way to recovery. They had spoken on the telephone, but Aimée had at first demurred when Gabrielle invited her to take coffee with her one morning.

'Surely you can spare half an hour from your busy schedule?'

'It isn't that, though I am busy.'

Aimée wondered whether it would be wise to become more intimately involved. But she did like Gabrielle Watson, and there were few enough people in Liverpool she could call friend. She decided to be completely honest.

'The thing is, Dr Dalywell has already accused me of laying claim to his patients. And I would not like him to get the wrong idea, should he hear that I had visited you.'

'That old windbag!' Gabrielle's infectious laugh had trilled down the line. 'If that is all, I shall take the first opportunity of setting him straight. Good heavens, a fine thing it would be if I let him dictate who is to be my friend.'

And friends they did become. Aimée found her company stimulating. It was some time since she had enjoyed the cut and thrust of intelligent discussion with another woman whose views broadly coincided with her own, and unlike her exchanges with Oliver, which frequently had an edge to them, with Gabrielle they always ended amicably. Aimée was sorry when she and her husband left to go on a long cruise to complete her recovery, but her steadily growing practice kept her busy.

Old Bill continued to improve, but it had been touch and go with Biddy for the first few days. She was now out of danger, but the problems of rehousing her family had not been resolved. Liam, to everyone's surprise, had remained sober, but as yet he had not managed to find anywhere for them to live that he could afford. In the end, it was Sarah Brady who came up with a solution. She put it to Biddy, who was too listless to argue.

'Starin' us in the face, it was. Here's me, with me last chick flown the nest, an' two rooms goin' beggin'. Sure, amn't I already lookin' after the kiddies an' Liam givin' me their keep, an' dossin' down hisself in the kitchen most nights? What's one more? An' I'd be able to give you a hand till you're stronger.'

Aimée was glad to have them settled, but soon came to know the frustration of battling with corporation departments to try to get some help for the other people made homeless. Tony Lyall had, according to Matty, left town, heartbroken and bitter, and wanting to make a new life as far away as possible from the scene of the tragedy. But there were others trying to pick up their lives with the tragic remnants of their families.

'You need cheering up. Why not get away next Sunday – have a picnic at Crag Vale before the summer ends?' Gerald suggested on one of his visits, when Aimée aired her grumbles to him. 'A big one down by the stream, the way we used to in the old days. Bring some friends – as many as you like. Make a day of it. Joshua will supervize the arrangements. The weather's settled again, and Megan can organize the food if you give her some idea of numbers.'

'Oh, Gerald, what a wonderful idea.' She had seen her parents only once since the thunderstorm, when her mother, while preening in the reflected glory of her daughter's exploits, had reproached her constantly about the danger she had put herself in. 'It won't be too much for Megan?'

'No fear. She thrives on work. And there's Cook and Dora to help. Why not bring young Matty? I'd like to pick her brains again – especially if, as you say, she's likely to be a famous designer one day.' He grinned. 'Bring the rest of the Shaw family, too, if you think they'd like to come. It would give them all a day off.'

'And Aunt Felicity could bring Celia and Toby. He's so much better, and it's just the kind of informal party that would do him good – something he remembers from his childhood.'

'I'll leave it to you, Aimée.'

Aimée's invitation was received with enthusiasm in Bloom Street. She found the whole family at home that evening when she called after surgery.

'You mean all of us?' Moira said, her eyes sparkling. She was growing fast, and would soon be as tall as her mother – a mousy-haired gangly child, practical rather than pretty.

'If that's all right with your mam,' Aimée said. 'Give her and your dad a bit of peace.'

'I've never been on a real picnic. Emmy Flynn and me sometimes take a bottle of water and some sarnies to the park, but that's not the same.' She swung round. 'We can go, can't we, Mam?'

'It's very good of Dr Buchanan,' Agnes said. 'But I'm not so sure about letting Daisy go. She can be a bit of a handful.'

'I'll look after her,' Moira said eagerly.

'We'll all look after her,' Matty said. She smiled at Aimée. 'It's ever so kind of you. Crag Vale's such a lovely place. I can't wait to see it again.' And to tell Gerald about Madame Vincente – and the chance she's given me to make something of my life, she added silently. He would understand what it meant to her.

'Good,' Aimée said. 'What about you, Kevin? Is a picnic too tame for you?'

Kevin was at that awkward stage – no longer a boy, but not yet a man, and prone to spots. Perhaps because Agnes was quick to quash any initiative on his part, he had confided in Aimée, and perhaps because she knew what it was like to have her ambitions thwarted, a kind of rapport had grown up between them.

He blushed and kicked his feet. 'I might come.'

'Kevin!' His mother's voice was sharp.

'It's all right, Agnes. I shan't be in the least offended if Kevin doesn't like the idea. I just wondered if a ride in the car might appeal. It'd be handy having you to crank it for me, too.' She saw the sudden spark of interest and grinned. 'See how you feel come Sunday.'

Aimée looked in on Pat before she left. At first she thought he was asleep, but his eyes opened as she hesitated.

'A pity you can't take Agnes on your picnic,' he said, when she explained the reason for her visit. 'Do her the world of good, it would.'

There was a weariness in his voice that made her look at him more closely. He was very pale. Unobtrusively her fingers sought his pulse. 'Are you feeling all right?'

His smile had a tired quality. 'The heat's been a bit wearing, but I've felt worse.'

'Pain in the chest?'

'A bit. But I've got them pills the doc gave me.' Agnes came bustling in and his voice changed. 'I've been saying to Dr Aimée, it's a pity you can't go on this picnic.'

She sniffed. 'I never did care much for eating in the open, as well you know -- all them nasty flies and creepy crawlies.'

Aimée laughed. 'Oh well, the children will enjoy it.'

Perhaps it was the mention of the children that made her think of Oliver's Alice and Christopher. She hadn't spoken to Oliver since that unfortunate telephone conversation concerning the fraud trial, though she had many times tried to screw up her courage to get in touch.

Unknown to him she had sneaked into the back of the public gallery on the last day of the hearing. It had been a revelation to her, for this was a side of Oliver she scarcely knew existed. In a way that was nothing short of masterly, he had demolished the prosecution case with a brilliant combination of wit and passion, that left her breathless with admiration, and Millar had been cleared of all charges against him.

The newspapers had made much of Oliver's eloquence when, in his closing address, he had exhorted the jury to set aside all knowledge of his client's reputation and to reach their verdict on the facts as presented to them without prejudice. And Aimée could not but agree with them.

She had sent him a brief note congratulating him at the time, but now might be a good time to mend bridges. She called at Falkner Square on the way home.

'Mr Langley is working, I believe, Doctor. If you'd care to step into the drawing room, I'll tell him you are here,' said his manservant, Grove.

'Please don't disturb him if he's busy,' she began, but already the study door had opened and Oliver came across the wide mosaic hall, struggling into his jacket as he came.

'Aimée.' He sounded surprised, but not unwelcoming. His hair was slightly dishevelled, as though he had been running his fingers through it. It was the first time had seen him looking anything less than immaculate. The effect was at once pleasing and slightly disturbing.

'I've come at a bad moment.'

She was wearing a white dress of some floaty material. With her thick shiny hair and her clear dark eyes, she looked fresh and cool and wholesome, and he noticed that her face, uplifted to him, had acquired a faint dusting of freckles.

'Not at all.' His grin was almost mischievous, and made him seem years younger. 'You have rescued me from a very tedious brief. Come into the drawing room and let me get you a drink. I could do with one myself.'

Soon they were comfortably seated, the room bathed in soft lamplight as they exchanged news. Still good humoured, he thanked her for her letter.

She bit her lip. 'I was in court on the last day to hear your summing up.'

'I know. I saw you.'

'You did?' Aimée saw his eyebrow shoot up in that inquisitorial way. 'It's just – well I'm surprised. You seemed so totally engrossed in what you were doing. It was a superb performance,' she added, determined not to be cheeseparing.

'That's what it is, in a way. A performance. There are many people who believe that barristers are frustrated actors. And who's to say they aren't right?'

They both laughed, totally in accord. By the time Aimée got round to explaining about the picnic, the atmosphere between them was more relaxed than she could ever remember.

'So, you see, there'll be lots of people, including children, and I wondered if you would allow your two to come – with Nanny to keep an eye on them, of course.'

'Your parents must be very long-suffering. But it seems to me you'll have more than enough. You can't want to saddle yourself with my children, too.'

'I wouldn't ask if I didn't want them. A picnic isn't a picnic without lots of children running about the place. Aunt Felicity is bringing Celia and maybe Toby. He is home for good now, you know. She is looking forward to it.' Aimée eyed him speculatively over the rim of her glass. 'Can't I tempt you to come? A dose of country air would do you a power of good.'

'Is that the doctor speaking?' He smiled and shook his head. 'Sorry. The children may go, of course, but it's not my kind of thing at all.'

'Alice would love you to be there,' she suggested, and with great trepidation: 'and I'm sure Christopher would, too, small as he is.'

'Nonsense. They'd both be much too busy enjoying themselves to miss about me. Besides, I have other plans for Sunday.'

Oliver's voice was pleasant, but his eyes warned her not to meddle. And yet she felt compelled to continue, her voice persuasive.

'Oliver, when did you last spend time with your children? Really spend time with them, purely for pleasure?'

'With respect, that is none of your business.'

The atmosphere was suddenly crackling with tension. Leave it now, every instinct told Aimée, or you will regret it. But her impetuosity had already carried her too far to stop.

'Perhaps not, but however excellent a nanny or a governess may be, children need to be constantly reassured that they belong and are loved, and when there is only one parent, it is doubly important – '

'Enough!' Oliver was on his feet. 'How dare you presume to lecture me on my shortcomings as a parent.'

'I wasn't!' She, too, sprang to her feet. 'Of course you love your children. I know you do. If I appeared to imply otherwise, I'm sorry.'

'So you should be.'

'But do *they* know it?' she persisted. Everything was going wrong, but by now she was desperate to make him understand.

They faced one another, the lamplight throwing up deep shadows to accentuate the antagonism in Oliver's tight-drawn face. Unshed tears stung Aimée's eyes, but he saw only their defiant brightness.

'The trouble with you, Aimée Buchanan, is that you're too opinionated for your own good. And you never seem to learn – '

'That's unfair – '

'What you need, of course,' he swept on, ignoring her interruption, 'is a husband and a few babies of your own to keep you out of trouble. Then at least you would be able to talk from experience.'

'Oh, how pathetically chauvinistic!' Aimée could feel the angry colour flooding her face. 'I thought you knew me better than that. But you are as prejudiced as everyone else!' She turned on her heel and marched, head high, to the door. She thought Oliver called her name, but she was too angry to heed it. Grove appeared as if on cue to usher her out, and the front door closed silently behind her.

'Damn!' she whispered, her throat constricted. 'Oh damn!'

19

IT WAS ONE of those mellow days in late summer. The sun shone in Crag Vale from early morning, drying the heavy dew long before anyone arrived.

By the time Aimée came, announcing her arrival with a joyous honking of horns, the rugs had been laid out in the field beside the stream, and servants were already scurrying up and down the terrace steps with cane chairs and tables.

'It's like something out of a storybook,' Matty sighed, watching the ordered procession and waiting for Aimée to come back from saying hello to her parents. 'Moira, do keep hold of Daisy, or she'll trip someone up.'

She smoothed down the skirt of her blue dress, wishing she could have made a new one specially for the occasion. But Moira was growing fast and desperately needed a new frock, and with Madame working Matty so hard, there wasn't time to make both. Matty remembered how it felt to be eleven, going on twelve, and resolved that she would make her sister something really pretty. And Moira did look nice, she thought, watching her helping Daisy up the shallow steps leading to the huge lawn belonging to the house, to pick a buttercup and twirl it under her little sister's chin to see if she liked butter. The printed cotton was crisp and fresh and youthful, with just enough of a dropped waist to make her feel fashionable and grown-up.

She hoped it was all right for them to be there. Everyone else seemed to be making their way down to the picnic area.

'Your sisters, I take it?' Gerald said, coming up behind her. He nodded towards the lawn where Moira was on her knees engrossed in making a daisy chain – 'Daisies for a Daisy,' she heard her chant. 'They seem to be enjoying themselves.'

Matty jumped and then smiled, feeling ridiculously nervous,

and thinking how smart he looked in his striped blazer. 'It is all right, isn't it?' she said, suddenly anxious as voices drifted up from the picnic area interspersed with children's laughter. 'Them being there, I mean. Everyone else seems to be down by the stream.'

'Good Lord, don't worry about that.' Gerald smiled back, setting her at ease. 'It's open house. And Mother left the lawns uncut deliberately so that the children could play buttercups and daisies.'

'We don't have a lawn.' Matty thought how silly that sounded, but Gerald didn't seem to notice.

'Aimée was telling me how well you are doing with Madame Vincente – on your way to becoming a famous designer, in fact.'

'Oh, I don't know about that.' She tried to sound modest. 'I've an awful lot to learn.'

'You'll make it,' he said. 'You've already got flair, a love of beautiful material and the instinctive knowledge of how best it can be used. Those are the things that can't be taught. The rest will come with time and practice.'

She couldn't believe he was talking about her. 'You really think so?'

'I'd put money on it. I've been doing quite a bit of travelling round myself recently, gathering ideas for our new ranges of cloth. When the machinery is in and working, I'll get Aimée to bring you along – see what you think of them.'

'Oh, yes, that would be lovely,' she said breathlessly, overcome by the thought that he might value her opinion.

'Gerald darling, do be an angel and ask Joshua to hurry those tables along.' Megan's voice was sugar-sweet. 'Mathilda – it is Mathilda, isn't it? – would you do me a great favour by taking these napkins down and putting them with the rest on the long serving table.'

'Yes, of course,' Matty said eagerly. 'And if there's anything else I can do . . .'

'I'm sure Cook or Joshua would find something for you – oh, and you could perhaps take your sisters down to the field before the other children follow their example. We don't want them getting under the servants' feet, do we?'

'Darling, Matty is a guest.' Gerald's voice was a bit clipped, though he smiled wryly. 'My wife loves to organize us all. Reckons it keeps us out of mischief.'

'Oh, I don't mind. I like to be doing things,' Matty said quickly. But she could tell that he minded. As she hurried back to the house, she heard him say, 'Darling, was that really necessary?' and wondered if she had imagined the look in Megan's eyes, as if – it was ridiculous, of course – she surely couldn't be jealous of her?

'M-Matty?'

She jumped, and turned to see Toby Mellish, shoulders a little hunched, coming across the terrace towards her with a kind of grim determination in his loping stride.

'I'm so g-glad to see you.'

Matty smiled as she took the hand he offered, and felt herself blushing.

'Aimée never said you'd be here,' she said awkwardly, remembering her awful gaffe. 'But then, I don't suppose she knew we'd met.'

'You don't m-mind me ac-c-costing you like this?' There was anxiety in the question. 'Mother told me you w-were coming, and I w-wanted to m-meet you again, to thank you.' Little beads of perspiration stood out on his forehead. 'You w-were the first p-person to treat me normally, you see, because you didn't know my problem and that m-meant a lot to m-me.'

'Well, I'm glad I didn't make a complete fool of myself,' Matty said quickly, sensing the effort it was costing him to get the words out. She'd asked Aimée about him and now understood why he was so nervy. 'I thought I'd put my foot right in it, mistaking you for the gardener.' She giggled, and saw relief flood into his eyes.

'You could never be that clumsy,' he said.

On the far side of the terrace, Felicity caught Aimée's arm. 'There, you see that I mean? Just watch how easily Toby is chatting away to young Matty. They seem to be developing a curious kind of rapport.'

'Matty's a thoroughly nice girl. I expect his stammer has aroused her maternal instincts and, coming as she does from a biggish family, she's probably treating him like a big brother.'

'That's just what he needs.' A capricious breeze tugged at the dipping brim of Felicity's fine pale straw hat, and she lifted a hand to clutch at it. 'I do hope everything will work out now that Toby is home for good.'

Her voice was muffled, but Aimée heard the note of uncertainty.

'I'm sure it will. He has made great progress. His presence here today is proof of that.'

'Of course, making that separate apartment for him, close to the conservatory, has made all the difference. He has ordered a great many books on the history of great gardens, and his confidence is growing daily. It is just that – ' Felicity turned to her impulsively, lowering her voice – 'Oh, my dear, not a word to a soul, for it wouldn't do for word to leak out before he has informed Lloyd George – only I must tell someone and I know you can be completely discreet. Your uncle is giving up his parliamentary seat to come home and take control of the business.'

'Goodness. That's a bit sudden,' Aimée exclaimed, and then chuckled. 'I'd love to be a fly on Grandpa's wall when Uncle George tells him.'

'Oh, he'll hate the idea, of course, but the plain fact is he can't cope any more and decisions have to be taken before the firm sinks into a decline. Besides, George has plans.'

'His fleet of luxury liners?'

'You know? Well, I'm sure he has the right idea. The world is changing fast, but Father's too entrenched in the old ways of commerce to see it. However, having your uncle at home will change a lot of things. Toby is my chief worry. It would be too awful if his progress were to suffer a setback. As you know, George has never really understood Toby.'

Aimée did know, only too well. But it wasn't like her aunt to be pessimistic. 'They don't have to see much of one another,' she said. 'Besides, Toby has found a sense of purpose at last, Aunt Fliss, and that might make all the difference. Given time, he could well surprise us all.'

'Oh, I do so hope you are right,' Felicity exclaimed, relieved, her laughter suddenly self-mocking as she watched the determined way her young daughter, who was growing up much too fast, was preening herself in her pretty floral voile and affecting not to notice that Matty's young brother couldn't take his eyes off her. 'Oh dear, children! It seems there is no end to worrying about them. And speaking of children, my dear, however did you talk Oliver into bringing the children today?'

Aimée flushed and avoided her eyes. 'He's brought them

himself? He was entirely set against the idea – in fact, we almost came to blows about it . . .'

'Did you, indeed?'

Clearly her aunt was eager to know more, but it was not something Aimée cared to confide.

She continued lightly, 'He said he had other plans and wouldn't be persuaded. He really can be an infuriating man.'

'Do you think so?' Felicity opened her eyes very wide. 'How interesting. I've always found him to be quite charming.'

'Dear Aunt Fliss, to you, everyone is charming,' Aimée said, carefully avoiding those all-seeing eyes.

Suddenly, she was dreading meeting Oliver, but in the end nothing could have been simpler. He was looking unfamiliarly casual in a suit of light grey flannel, and in the general bustle of greetings and introductions of the children to their hosts, the merest formalities sufficed – the only moment of embarrassment being when Alice tugged her hand away from Nanny Grey's and ran across to Aimée with the frills of her muslin dress bouncing up and down, shouting, 'Dr Aimée, Dr Aimée! It's me!' and had to be prised away by her father, who seemed surprised that the two had met.

Oliver was already wishing he had not come. He still wasn't sure why he had changed his mind – except that he couldn't rid himself of the memory of that stricken look in her eyes when he had virtually accused her of being unfulfilled as a woman. It was completely against his nature to stoop to petty spite as a defensive weapon, and this, together with the uncomfortable suspicion that she had come a little too close to the truth for comfort, obliged him to make amends.

But it seemed he had worried unnecessarily, for this Aimée, looking cool in lavender silk that skimmed her hips and floated tantalizingly round her calves, was very much at ease, her manner so friendly that he wondered whether he had imagined her earlier distress.

Matty was leaving the kitchen with a tray of Cook's special little pasties when Alec practically jumped out into her path.

'That was a daft thing to do!' she exclaimed, vexed. 'I might have dropped this whole lot.' He stretched out a hand. 'And keep your fingers off them. They aren't for the likes of you.'

Unrepentant, he selected a pasty and put it in his mouth. 'They're not very filling. Anyway, I thought you were supposed to be a guest. You wouldn't catch me skivvying when there's servants to do the work.'

'Helping out's not skivvying,' she insisted, flushing at his implication that she was toadying to her rich friends. 'Aimée's helping, too. And no, you can't have another,' she said, moving the tray out of reach.

He grinned. 'Hey, listen, if you can get away, we could go for a walk. There's some woods over the other side of the road. Nice and private.' He winked.

'Don't talk daft,' she said, though a part of her was tempted. 'I'm a guest. I can't go sneakin' off to meet you. What would Aimée's folk think?'

His mood changed abruptly. 'Afraid to be seen slumming with the servants?' Angry colour flooded his face. 'Who cares what they think. We don't have to kowtow to them just 'cos they live like lords.'

'Now you're just being stupid,' Matty snapped. 'I've got to go.'

'That's right.' He threw his taunts at her retreating back. 'Go and be nice to the ladies and gentlemen. Wait till I'm up there with 'em. Then we'll see.'

Minna loved parties. Even amid the austerities of war, she had managed to entertain with some degree of style, and although the shortages had been a nuisance, she had been fortunate in that most of her servants were past the age of conscription, and were sufficiently well treated not to wish to seek more lucrative employment in the cities.

'Darling, who are all these people?' she had asked Aimée when they first arrived. 'I'm sure I don't know many of them.'

But she moved among the guests like a queen greeting her subjects: — 'So nice to see you — so pleased you could come — delightful children,' her pale pink chiffon flounces fluttering in the light breeze, her bracelets tinkling as she stretched out a gracious hand here, paused to speak to a relative there.

'Isn't Mother wonderful, Pa?' Aimée chuckled as she linked her arm through her father's. 'She's in her element.'

'Aye, she likes a good party, does Minna — always did.' There was love and pride in his quiet voice.

She brushed her cheek against his. 'But you'll be glad when they've all gone home.'

'Well, you know it's not my cup of tea, lass. But we must all learn to give and take in this world.'

There was something in his voice that made Aimée glance at him. She saw he was watching his daughter-in-law, who was also busy talking to people, making sure that everyone was comfortable and had plenty to eat.

'Is it a strain, Pa, having Gerald and Megan living with you? Be honest now. I won't tell.'

Seth's face creased into a frown of concentration. 'It's a big enough house for us not to get under one another's feet,' he said, one hand going instinctively to his pocket for his pipe. 'I'm at the mill a good part of the day, so I reckon Megan's company for your mother.'

'And the evenings?' she persisted. 'Don't you miss those nice quiet dinners together?'

But: 'As long as your mother's happy, I'm content,' he said, and she could draw him no further.

Minna, having done her duty as she saw it, had taken her rightful place in the most comfortable chair in the shade of an ancient spreading cedar, and was graciously holding court.

Oliver, with one ear tuned to a heated discussion about a recent cricket match, had also watched Minna's progress with some amusement. He was still smiling as he looked up, straight into Aimée's eyes, and saw them widen in uncertainty tinged with embarrassment. When he could do so without attacting attention, he moved across to her.

'Aimée, we can't spend the day avoiding one another. It's too absurd.'

'I suppose it is.' She bit her lip in vexation. 'What do you suggest?'

His mouth twisted. 'Call quits?

'No recriminations?'

'No recriminations,' he agreed gravely.

'Agreed.' A cloud drifted across the sun, and she sighed. 'Though I should never have – '

'Aimée Buchanan!' He laid a finger briefly against her mouth, leaving an imprint that lingered. 'It's time you learned that you can't always have the last word.'

'I don't – ' Anger flared momentarily, and then she blushed, and smiled at him, and it was like the sun coming out again. 'Oh well, maybe,' she admitted. And then, with genuine pleasure, 'I'm glad you came.'

'So am I,' he said, and was surprised to find he meant it. It was too long since he had socialized for any reason other than business. There was little incentive to a round of pleasure now.

But he had watched a little earlier as Aimée and her brother, and Toby Mellish and the young girl Matty had gone running down the field, laughing and leaping the stream, and had come back, arm in arm, singing 'She Was Only a Bird in a Gilded Cage' at the top of their voices. Their gaiety had unsettled him, making him feel suddenly dull and staid.

'The children are enjoying themselves, too,' Aimée's voice broke his train of thought. 'Alice seems to have taken complete charge of little Daisy.'

'She's getting precocious,' he said, half-frowning.

Aimée laughed. 'Little girls often are at that age. Just wait until Christopher gets a bit older. He'll sort her out.'

'You think so?' Oliver turned to watch his son nearby, scurrying across the rug towards them in pursuit of a bee, struggling with silent dogged persistence as Nanny attempted to restrain him. And fatherly pride began to stir in him as Christopher refused to be turned from his goal. 'He's certainly got more spirit than I supposed.'

'Give him time.' Christopher put on a sudden turn of speed, leaving the rug and coming to a halt at their feet. As Nanny Grey hesitated, Aimée scooped him up, lifting him high in the air. He chuckled and wriggled for more. 'Oh, no, my lad, once is enough – you're too heavy for me.' And on a sudden impulse, she said, 'Your father can swing you,' and put him into Oliver's arms praying that he wouldn't cry or struggle.

Oliver's hands closed instinctively round the tiny warm body, his heart beginning to thud as anger gave way to a welter of conflicting emotions. In that moment Catherine felt very close. He could almost her her whisper, *This is our son, Oliver*. His eyes blurred and he turned away from curious glances and walked towards the shelter of the trees. A damp hand patted his face, and he became aware of liquid-dark eyes gravely studying him. At that moment the last barrier melted away, and he pressed the hand to his lips.

'Oliver?'

It was Aimée's voice. There was surely no way she could have known that he had never until now held Christopher in his arms? Oh, he had dutifully visited the nursery from the first; been scrupulous in his determination to ensure that his son's every need was catered for, but he had avoided physical contact – still, deep inside, blaming him for Catherine's death. As if anything so small and defenceless could incur blame.

'He's still got some catching up to do, of course, but it's often the late starters who surprise us,' Aimée said.

He cleared his throat, but his voice was still harsh as he asked without looking at her, 'What are you – witch or wise woman?'

'Neither, I hope. Oliver, I didn't plan this – '

'Didn't you?'

'Of course not,' she cried indignantly. 'What kind of devious creature do you take me for?'

'You made your views very plain the other evening.'

'Even so, I would never – Oh, Oliver, it wasn't like that, truly.' She laid a hand on his arm. 'Yes, I have noticed a reticence in you whenever you speak of Christopher – and, given the circumstances of his birth, it wasn't difficult to guess at your state of mind. But I would never have presumed to interfere . . .'

As her voice died away and the laughing voices of the picnickers seemed a distant mocking echo, he gave no sign of having even heard her. Her throat ached with tears of disappointment.

'Ugh,' Christopher grunted, and sighed deeply.

Oliver came out of his reverie to glance down at his son. Slowly, he turned to Aimée with a look of disbelief bordering on acute distaste.

She guessed at once what had happened. 'Oh, Christopher Langley, you do choose your moments!' she exclaimed, mortified. His lower lip began to tremble and she held out her arms for him.

Oliver remained standing with one hand outstretched as though he didn't know what to do with it. Aimée strove for gravity – and failed.

'The cloakroom is just off the hall,' she gasped, her peals of laughter ringing out until the merriment in her eyes finally found a reluctant echo in Oliver's.

'Witch,' he called after her as she carried the grizzling child back to his nanny. But she didn't care, for she knew a barrier had come down that would never be re-erected.

Felicity, sitting under a shady tree, gently fanning herself, watched – and wondered. What was it about those two that so often made the air seem charged? Something more than a simple clash of personalities. She had never been able to fathom it. Her glance moved on to her young daughter, who was all too easy to read. Sixteen was an awkward age. Girls developed so much quicker than boys in some ways. And Kevin Shaw was growing into a handsome lad. It would be so easy for him to get the wrong impression.

Keven wasn't used to wearing a suit. It had been Phil's best and Mam had altered it to fit him.

'Phil only wore it a few times,' she'd said, smoothing the coat lovingly. 'And you're growing so fast, it'll only need a bit of taking in.'

'Mam! I'll look a right fool dressed up. The one you borrowed fer the wedding was bad enough. Albert Finch said I looked a right twit.'

'And who's Albert Finch to pass opinions? Great lump of lard, he is. You'll wear this an' like it, my lad. Everyone'll be wearing their best, and I'm not having you sticking out like a sore thumb.'

But he did.

The suit didn't feel like it belonged to him, and he knew everyone was starin' at him, especially that pretty girl who was Dr Aimée's cousin – the one in the flowered frock that seemed to float as she moved. Every time he so much as glanced her way, she tossed her head and pretended not to see him.

'Hello.'

He turned and there she was. He could feel his neck growing red. 'Hi,' he mumbled.

'I'm Celia Mellish.'

'Yeah, I know.'

Celia waited, and then grew impatient. 'You're Kevin Shaw, aren't you? Matty's brother.'

'Yeah,' he said again.

Celia moved impatiently so that her skirts fluttered. He was a tiresome boy – but good-looking in a rough sort of way, as if there were real muscles beneath that awful suit. Not like any of the boys she knew, who were mostly brothers of her friends.

'Which school do you go to?'

In an effort to impress, Kevin tried to sound superior and scornful. 'I don't. Left ages ago when I were fourteen. School's for cissies.'

'I'm sixteen and I still go to school.'

He blushed again. 'I expect it's different for girls. Any road, I'd sooner be workin'.'

'So, where do you work?'

'You en't 'arf nosey,' he said, reverting to his natural self. 'You're as bad as me sisters. As it happens, I'm learnin' to be a butcher, an' soon as I can gerra berth, I'm goin' ter sea. You stand more chance if you've some kind of trade or a skill.'

Celia was impressed in spite of herself. 'My father might be able to help you. He owns lots of ships.'

Kevin stared, and then began to laugh. 'That's rich, tharris.'

She tossed her head. 'You're very rude.'

'I'm sorry, gairl, honest. Only the thought of your dad botherin' with the likes of me – well, it's like me mam says – pigs might fly, but they're unlikely birds.'

Celia tried to maintain her air of offended dignity, but the phrase tickled her sense of humour, and she too began to laugh.

'It's been a lovely day,' Aimée told Gerald, watching the long shadows already encroaching on to the lawns. Matty was rounding up the young ones. Everyone else had gone, Oliver included, his manner at parting ambiguous.

Gerald put a companionable arm round her shoulder, and she rested her head against it. 'Like old times.'

'Mmm. I hope it hasn't been too tiring for Megan.'

'I'm sure Megan will be fine. She can rest this evening.'

Aimée wondered whether she might drop a hint about them finding a place of their own, but it would be a shame to break this mood of tranquillity.

'Mother enjoyed herself.'

Aimée laughed. 'She did, didn't she? I was delighted to see her taking Toby round the garden. She has always rather shied away from him, but he's come on so much. I think his knowledge of plants surprised her.'

'Perhaps he's found his niche at last.'

'I do hope so.' Matty was making her way back from the stream with two reluctant little girls in tow. Kevin was already sitting in the car. She sighed. 'On evenings like this, I wonder why I ever wanted to leave Crag Vale.'

'To seek your destiny?'

The jokiness concealed something in Gerald's voice that a less keenly attuned ear might have missed. Could it be envy? Surely not. He loved the valley and all it stood for.

'While we're alone, Aimée, can I ask you something?'

She turned, half smiling, to meet his eyes. 'Problems?'

'I hope not. Aimée, do you think Mother would be hurt if we moved out? Bought a place of our own?'

'Goodness!' Was there something in the air this afternoon, or was she, as Oliver had inferred, a witch? 'What brought this on?'

'Oh, a lot small things. In many ways we have the best of all worlds here – comfort, room enough to be private whenever we wish, our every need catered for, everything, in fact, except . . .'

'Independence,' she finished.

'Exactly. I knew you'd understand. Army life was frequently uncomfortable, but one learned to be – self-sufficient, I suppose. I hadn't appreciated how important that is until now. When I came back, I needed somewhere secure, protected, to lick my wounds. Megan never knew, but she seemed happy with the arrangement.'

'Does she know how you feel?'

'She does now.'

'And?'

'Megan would like her own place, too. She does her best to please Mother and make everything easy for her, but Ma can be a bit trying sometimes, as you know all too well.'

It was on the tip of Aimée's tongue to retort that it was, after all, Mother's home to do with as she pleased. But she would not for the world cause friction between Gerald and his wife.

'And when the baby comes . . .' he grinned sheepishly. 'Well, Ma was never very maternal, even with us.'

'That's true.' She laughed. 'So what will you do?'

'As it happens, the Abbotts are moving. Their place would be ideal – only a mile or so away. We could still keep an eye on the old folk. Megan would be able to pop in most days.'

'I think it's an excellent idea.' Aimée paused. 'And I shouldn't worry too much about the parents. They survived perfectly well without us during the war, for all that Mother complained bitterly. But then she rather enjoys having something to complain about.'

On the first of September, after a night of gales blowing straight off the Mersey, during which she had been called out to a bad case of colic, the telephone woke Aimée long before breakfast. At first she couldn't make head nor tale of what the caller was babbling about, then she realized it was Irene's Eddie.

'You'll have ter come to Rene, Doctor. It must be the gale set 'er off – carryin' on somethin' awful, she is, screamin' an' that! An' the midwife's out on another call. Rene's friend from next door's with 'er, but she says she wants you and 'er mam . . .'

Aimée looked at the clock, and felt a little like screaming herself. There was no surgery this morning and she had hoped for an extra hour's sleep. 'Eddie, just calm down. How often are the contractions coming?'

'Hell's teeth! I don't know anything about bloody contractions! Dor-een!' His shout vibrated through Aimée head. 'Come an' tell the doc what's what.'

As a result, she went downstairs to put the kettle on, swallowed a cup of weak tea while she dressed, and left a note for Mrs Green. Then she drove round to Bloom Street.

She found Agnes already hard at work, perspiring over a load of washing.

'Oh, mercy on us!' she cried, whipping off her pinny. 'If you could just wait while I take Daisy round to Marge, and get her to listen out for Pat until Moira comes home for dinner?'

'Slow down, Agnes. From what Irene's friend said, the baby's nowhere near ready to come.'

While she waited, Aimée looked in on Pat. 'Did you hear?'

'About our Irene. Sure, it's grand news – a new babby. Give Aggie something else to think about.' His smile had a tired quality.

'Him up there – ' he nodded his head – 'He has a marvellous way of arranging things, don't you think?'

'Are you all right?'

'Fine. I'm just fine, girl.'

And then Agnes came bustling in. 'I'm not sure how long I'll be away, Pat. Babies have no respect for time, but Marge'll pop in regular. She knows your dinner's on the hob, and our Moira'll be back . . .'

'Fuss, fuss, fuss. Away with you, woman. Our little girl needs you more than I do just now. Give her my love, eh? And don't be hurrying back.'

By the time they got to Walton, the midwife had arrived and was berating Irene with a mixture of firmness and kindness for screaming fit to lift the roof off and frightening all the customers away from the shop.

'Oh, Mam!' Irene cried, throwing herself on Agnes, 'I didn't know it would hurt so!'

And Agnes, with surprising mildness, told her to be a brave girl, and do exactly as the midwife said, then it would soon be over. So, having checked that all was going well, Aimée, was able to leave Irene in safe hands and get on with her rounds, with Eddie's parting plea ringing in her ears.

'I hope you've given Rene somethink ter stop 'er screamin'. She's frightenin' me customers away – them as aren't clutterin' the shop up, makin' a book on when she'll drop the baby.'

Aimée called into Madame Vincente to leave a message for Matty, and Madame, in benevolent mood, magnanimously agreed to let Matty have the afternoon off. 'This new *bébé* is very special to you, eh? So, you will go to support your sister during 'er *travail*.' Her bird-bright eyes twinkled. 'And you will make up the time later.'

'Oh, yes, I will! Thank you, Madame,' Matty exclaimed. And she quickly tidied her work away, under the disapproving eye of Miss Donald and to the envy of her companions. 'I'll be an auntie,' she said excitedly. 'I wonder what it'll be?'

The tram ride seemed to take forever. It was a real bone-shaker, but for once she hardly noticed. When she arrived, the shop was in a shambles with a harassed Eddie trying to cope with several customers at once.

'Matty! Thank God! I've got a bloke comin' back fer his motor in a couple of hours, an' I've hardly looked at it. Give us a hand 'ere, fer pity's sake!'

'Can I go up and see Irene first?'

He groaned. 'Must you?'

A large blowsy woman pushed her way to the counter, clutching six candles, a gas mantle and a box of matches to her chest. 'Give us these, lad. I 'aven't gorr-all day.'

'Matty?'

'Oh, all right.' She grudgingly took the woman's money.

'Don't fret, gairl. It's 'er fairst, innit?' The woman chuckled and everything about her shook. 'Tek it from me, she won't be in any mood fer a chat right now.'

As if to confirm her judgement a piercing drawn-out scream came from upstairs. 'Christ!' Eddie dropped the box of assorted fuses he was carrying.

Matty bolted for the stairs, and Eddie wasn't far behind her, his feet thudding on the wooden treads. But as they reached the top, a different sound greeted them, the shrill bawling of a healthy newborn child.

Eddie paused, out of breath, to pass his arm across a sweating brow. 'An' about time! He's gorra healthy pair of lungs, that's fer sure!'

But Matty had already run into the room in time to hear Irene's tearful sob, 'Please, not now – it's too heavy!' and saw her mother lifting a crumpled wriggling bundle, arms and legs flailing: a red face screwed tight with indignation, wet and streaked with blood, the tiny round mouth emitting lusty staccato cries.

She wasn't entirely ignorant about the act of birth. She remembered Daisy being born, though Marge had kept her out of the bedroom until her mother was decently covered and Daisy wrapped in a shawl. Even then she had been excited. Now Matty sensed a kind of raw energy about this miracle of life that made her want to shout with joy. As she watched in awe, the sound ceased momentarily and two bright blue eyes appeared.

Agnes wiped the little face clean, and swiftly wrapped the child in a blanket. She looked first at Matty, then turned to her son-in-law, her own eyes bright with unshed tears. 'It's a little girl, Eddie – you've got a perfect little daughter,' she said huskily, and put her into his arms.

'Great!' Eddie said, holding the baby gingerly, his disappointment fading away as the bright eyes stared back at him. 'Hey, you're a bit of all right, you are.'

'Can I hold her a minute?' Matty begged.

Eddie handed the baby over and turned to the bed where Irene lay, her hair dark with sweat against the pillow, her face almost as crumpled as her daughter's and streaked with tears.

'Yer a clever girl, Rene,' he said, the awkwardness of the words muffled by a clumsy kiss. 'Listen, I can't stay. The shop's full. I'll be up later when you've had a rest, eh?'

'Very sensible. Now then, Mother,' the midwife said, shooing Eddie out of the room, 'we've not quite done, yet. Just hang on while we get rid of the afterbirth and tidy you up.'

Agnes had brought a bowl of warm water, and as Matty handed the baby over to be washed, and her sister began to cry and complain, she wondered if she was the only one who had seen Irene turn her head away as Eddie kissed her.

In the weeks that followed, Matty spent as much time as she could each evening at Irene's, in the little room behind the shop. And when he had time off, Alec took her in the sidecar of his new motor cycle. He and Eddie had got on well from the first, sharing as they did a mutual interest in motors, and most times they left the girls to their own devices and retired to the garage to talk about cylinders and valves and engine capacities, emerging covered in grease in time for supper.

Matty didn't know what to make of Irene. It wasn't just that she was tired and her lovely fair hair was all lacklustre. You'd perhaps expect that, though Irene usually set great store by her appearance. Mam said having a baby could be a very draining experience, and she should know. It wasn't easy for Mam to get over often, and although Doreen from next door had been quite good, she had her own kiddies to see to first.

What surprised and secretly worried Matty was her sister's attitude. If it had been her, the baby would have been the main topic of conversation. In fact, she would probably have driven folk mad going on about how beautiful she was. But Irene couldn't even raise any enthusiasm for the christening. The name had been decided long ago – Patrick for a boy, Patricia for a girl, after Dad.

'She's such a darling baby,' Matty cooed as she sat by the fire, nursing her.

'You wouldn't say that if you heard her screamin'.' Irene ducked past the maiden with its row of steaming nappies, and attacked the coals viciously with the poker, sending the sparks and smuts flying. 'She's got lungs on her like a pair of bellows!'

'Oh, but she looks so peaceful,' Matty said, smiling down at the sleeping child.

'She is, now. Evening's her best time. But you should hear her at one o'clock in the morning, and again at five, and afternoons. I can't seem to satisfy her. Eddie says he's fed up with havin' his precious sleep disturbed. Honest, I could hit him!'

'Oh dear, I suppose it can't be easy for him when he's got a long day's work ahead of him.'

'And I haven't, I suppose? Honest, Matty, you don't know what it's like.' The easy tears started. 'I mean, just look at me. Sometimes I think I'll never look pretty again! It's all cooking and washing and cleaning, and Patsy's feeding time comes round that fast, I'm getting to dread it. She fastens on so hard sometimes, I'd swear she had teeth. I'm that sore, see?'

She undid the buttons of her bodice.

Matty was horrified at her red swollen breasts. 'Oh, Irene! I thought you were just tired. I'd no idea you were having such a horrid time. I'll ask Aimée to come to see you.'

'Would you?' Irene desperate voice brightened. 'Perhaps she'd let me put Patsy on to a bottle, then Eddie could take his turn getting up to do the night feed, and I'd be able to get a proper night's sleep.'

'And you need to get out for a change. You've not been out in the three weeks since Patsy was born. Why not make an effort and come over for tea on Sunday? Dad's longing to see his grand-daughter. Surely Eddie could bring you – he's got enough cars sitting out there in his garage.'

'It would be nice to get out,' Irene sighed.

'Well, then.'

Aimée was annoyed with herself for not keeping a closer eye on Irene. The girl wasn't sensible like Matty. In fact, sometimes she reminded her of her own mother – a pretty butterfly who was used to getting her own way by devious means. But in this case, the poor girl had cause to complain.

'You've got a nasty dose of milk fever,' she said. 'Those nipples must be very sore.'

'Oh, they are,' Irene agreed with a swiftness that amused Aimée. 'I've been in agony.' She paused for dramatic effect. 'I was wondering if perhaps I should put Patsy on a bottle?'

'Well, neither of you is getting much pleasure at the moment. And Patsy certainly isn't getting the nourishment she needs. But you will have to take the greatest care in preparing the bottle feed.'

'Oh, I will! Just tell me what I must do, and I'll do it faithfully!'

By the time Irene arrived in Bloom Street on the Sunday, she was well on the way to being her old self. Aware that all eyes would be on her, she had taken trouble with her hair and had even managed to squeeze into one of her best frocks – a nice soft blue woollen one that Matty had made for her.

'You look lovely,' Matty said, hugging her.

'Well, I haven't got my figure back yet, but I'm working on it.'

'I don't know why you bother,' Eddie murmured lasciviously. 'I like you all cuddly.'

'Well, I don't.'

'Oh, for goodness' sake, come along all of you and stop cluttering up the lobby.' Agnes chivvied them towards the back room all except Irene. 'Your dad's been on pins all morning,' she said quietly. 'Just let him have a sight of the little love.'

Irene hesitated, half afraid. She hadn't seen him for weeks, and then he had looked dreadful. But, smiling encouragement, Mam was already pushing open the door, and beckoning her in.

'Hello, Dad.' He'd gone so thin. In her effort to sound cheerful, her voice seemed squeaky. 'How are you?'

'I'm fine, girl. And all the better for seeing you.'

Irene pushed back the shawl, and held her daughter up. 'Well, here she is at last. Patricia Mary, named specially for you. We call her Patsy.'

The baby seemed to Pat to be looking right at him as if she knew who he was, and fixed him with her bright blue stare. Tears blurred his vision, but he blinked them away.

'Well, aren't you a sight for sore eyes, then?' he said huskily. 'As pretty as your mammy was all those years ago. I'd love to hold you, but that wouldn't do at all. Your grandma will have to give you a kiss for the both of us.'

His voice was already growing weak, and Agnes knew that he would start coughing any minute. 'Come along,' she said. 'Daisy is waiting to give you a big hug. We'll pop in and see Grandpa again later.'

Aimée came by during the afternoon, and found the family gathered in the back room, replete after an excellent dinner. And Marge, who had dropped in for a sight of the baby, had the little one comfortably enfolded in her plump arms.

'She's gorra lovely smile,' Marge cooed.

'Me want to feed Patsy,' Daisy demanded, as Agnes came through from the back kitchen with the bottle.

'You can't. You're too little,' Moira retorted. 'You'd probably push the bottle half down her throat.'

'I not.' Daisy's mouth quivered.

'You'd berra let 'er mam do it, chuckie,' Marge said. 'Babbies are happier with their mam.'

'Patsy's certainly popular.' Aimée laughed. 'I suspect she knows it, too.'

While everyone was occupied, she slipped into the next room to have a word with Pat. He was lying peacefully on his side with his eyes closed and a smile on his face. And even without touching him, she knew. A good brave man, his loss lay like a weight against her heart.

I must fetch Agnes, she thought. But before she could do so, the door creaked behind her.

'Gone to sleep, has he?' Agnes said softly. 'He was that made up, seeing little Patsy . . .' And then her eyes met Aimée's, widened and reached past her. 'Oh, no!' she whispered and hurried across to sit on the bed. Her throat ached as she smoothed Pat's face from which all the lines of pain had eased, and folded his hands in hers.

'I think he did just that,' Aimée said. 'He went quietly to sleep.'

'You're right. I've known for a day or two he was only hanging on to see the baby.' A dry sob shook her. 'Oh, but I wish I'd been with him.'

PART THREE

20

THE MONTHS FOLLOWING Pat's death had not been easy for the Shaw family, though Agnes inevitably suffered the most. For so long the daily routine of the house had revolved around Pat and his needs, and his going had left a vacuum that no amount of activity could fill.

After the funeral, Agnes had closed the door on the front room, and for a whole week no one had been allowed near. Then one evening Matty arrived home to be waylaid by Marge Flynn on the doorstep.

'Yer mam's gone berserk,' she said, her chest heaving with the drama of it. 'She brought Daisy round to me first thing – an' she's been at it ever since, in a right frenzy of scrubbin' an' scourin'. Old Fred, the totter's took yer da's mattress an' stuff on his cart ter be burned, an' as fer the bumpin' an' bangin' that's gone on – had your Moira round here fast after school, I can tell yer. Well, you'll see fer yerself . . .'

What Matty had seen when she got in was her father's door thrown wide, the room stripped bare, the bedstead dismantled and scrubbed along with the bedding and the curtains were flapping on the line in darkness. The desolation of it all made her want to weep.

'Oh, Mam, it's so final!'

'Maybe, but it had to be done,' Agnes said, stony-faced.

'You didn't have to go so mad at it. You'll be ill yourself if you carry on like this.'

'I never was one for putting off till tomorrow. And there's no sense having a good room going to waste. Pat would have been the first to say so.'

'It's almost as if she was trying to sweep all trace of Dad away,' a distressed Matty had confided to Aimée.

'You mustn't think that, my dear.' Aimée sought for the right words. 'We all have our own way of coping with grief. And your mother has lived with uncertainty for so long that perhaps this is the only way she can come to terms with the fact that what she dreaded has actually happened.' She saw that Matty wasn't wholly convinced. 'But I'll keep a discreet eye on her.'

This turned out to be easier than expected, for early in October, Providence stepped in. Mrs Green slipped on some wet leaves when leaving the surgery.

'That leg's broke,' said one of the passers-by who were already gathering like vultures. 'Yer can see the bone stickin' out.'

'Pride goes before a fall, Dr B,' Mrs Green said through gritted teeth, as Aimée knelt beside her to pad and bind the good leg to the broken one to ease the journey to hospital. 'I were more keen on gerrin me brolly up ter save me hat than luk where I was goin'.' Her white face crumpled. 'An' how you'll manage without me, I can't think.'

'Don't worry about me,' Aimée had reassured her.

But only when the ambulance had gone clanging on its way did the truth of Mrs Green's words come home to her.

And that was when she thought about Agnes Shaw.

She had gone straight round to Bloom Street, where she found Agnes alone, sitting apathetically in front of the range in the living room.

'I wouldn't trouble you,' she began, choosing her words with care, 'but I didn't know where to turn. Evenings I can manage, but I really do need someone on the premises during the day, to take messages, and keep on top of the housework. And I would prefer someone I know and can trust.'

At first there had been no reaction, but gradually Agnes straightened up, and a gleam of interest had come back into her eyes.

'I'll do it, and gladly, if you think I'm able. Heaven knows, you've been a good friend to me, and I'll never forget all you did for my Pat.'

'That cuts both ways. I admired and respected Pat. He was a good and brave man – what my father would call "a bonny fighter".'

'True. Y'know, I'd not have believed how empty this house feels

– like a part of me had died, too.' Her mouth went a little awry. 'Pat always said I was the strong one, but it was him, so gentle and patient, that kept me fighting.' Her chin came up, and there was a glimpse of the old pugnacious Agnes. 'So, I can't let him down now, can I? Besides the more I'm occupied, the better I'll be.'

She had proved to be an inspired choice, and by the time it became clear that Mrs Green would not be able to return in the foreseeable future, Agnes had made the job her own, and with what Aimée paid her, she was able to give up her night job.

Early in December, Nellie Reagan came to the surgery. Aimée was surprised to see her. She had been so much better since taking the iron, and she certainly didn't look ill – a little nervous, perhaps – her cheeks were certainly more flushed than usual.

'How nice to see you,' Aimée said with a smile. 'Do come and sit down. Is everyone well at home?'

'Fine. Danny's doing ever so well with them exercises you gave him. He's gettin' really strong in his arms an' that . . .' she tailed off, biting her lip.

'Good.' Aimée kept talking, to try and put her at ease. 'I can't promise anything as yet, but I may be able to put some work his way before long.'

Nellie's eyes lifted eagerly to her. 'Oh, if you could! That's what he needs, more than anything – well, almost anything.'

'So?' Aimée paused. 'Would that *anything* be what you've come to see me about?' she asked gently.

And then the words rushed out in a torrent. 'Dr Aimée, do you think it would be possible . . . that is, is there any chance of me and Danny being able to have a baby?'

It was the last thing she expected. Aimée took a moment to answer. 'Is this something you and Danny have discussed?' she asked, playing for time.

'Oh, no! But I know that, much as he loves Mary, he always wanted a son, and he's lost so much. And I thought it might give him back his . . . oh, I don't know, his pride, his – '

'Manhood?' Aimée suggested gently.

Nellie flushed. 'Yeah. I suppose that's it. Only it's . . . I mean, since he came home we've never . . . he's never suggested . . . So, I don't know whether it's that he can't, or whether he thinks it might . . . you know, disgust me.'

'And would it?'

'No! Oh, I dare say it'd take a bit of getting used to, like, but I'd do anythin' as long as it was what he wanted – as long as it'd make him happy. Only I'm too embarrassed to ask. Even if he said yes, it wouldn't be easy, with them walls like paper an' his mam in the next room, but . . .'

That bloody woman, Aimée thought.

'Well, if you really think you could manage a baby, on top of everything else.'

'Oh, I wouldn't mind that. With workin' evenings, I'd manage somehow.'

'Then you will just have to overcome your embarrassment, and talk to Danny. There's no reason to suppose that his injuries have made him impotent,' she affected not to notice the wild blush that stained Nellie's cheeks. 'And you realize that if you do decide to try for a baby, you will have to take the initiative – help Danny.'

'I'm sure I could,' she said hesitantly, 'as long as it was what he wanted.'

'Would you like me to come along and discuss it with you both – sometime when you know your mother-in-law will be out?'

Nellie's eyes lit up. 'Oh, would you? She goes to a meeting at church on Monday evenings, so I don't go to work Mondays.'

'Well then. The first thing you must do is talk to Danny. Let me know how he reacts, and we'll take it from there.'

There was feverish activity in the Mellish household as preparations got under way to see out the old year and welcome in 1920. Cook and her minions were hard at work long before daybreak, and above stairs Meredith ensured that the finishing touches were put to the guest rooms, overseeing the dining room himself so that everything might be just right.

It was some years since they had accommodated above twenty people, but: 'We shall be twenty-four for dinner, Meredith,' Madam had told him, and from the look in her eyes, he deduced that the event was to be something special. Perhaps it had something to do with Mr Giles bringing a young lady home. He had recently resigned his commission in order to join his father in the family firm. So it could be that he was thinking of settling down in more ways than one.

Whatever the reason, it was with a sense of occasion that Meredith produced the winding handle to extend the gleaming rosewood table to its maximum length, so that the extra sections could be added, after which it would be covered in white damask.

'Just like the old days, Mr Meredith,' Cook had exclaimed, upon being told that a party of six were travelling up from London. Except, he thought ruefully, that in the old days they had been able to muster almost twice as many servants. He had been on to a local agency to hire extra staff, but he had grave doubts about their ability to meet his requirements.

'If there's anything I can do to help,' Matty had offered shyly when Mrs Mellish had half-laughingly declared during a fitting that with so many people to accommodate, chaos would probably reign.

'My dear, I'm sure you would rather celebrate the New Year with your own family and friends, than wait on mine.'

'We've nothing planned,' Matty said. 'Mam never did reckon much to New Year. The last two Christmases have been bad enough, though she's made an effort for the little ones.'

'Of course. How tactless of me.'

'Oh, no, you've no call to feel bad,' Matty said quickly. 'But I've always wondered what it would be like to see the New Year in properly, and I can't go out anywhere with Alec, because he says you'll be needing him.'

'Ah.' Felicity's eyes had twinkled. 'Well, in that case I'm sure Meredith can find something suited to your talents. And be sure to bring your prettiest frock. There will be lots of music and dancing later, and the celebrations won't be confined to the family and guests.'

Felicity's reputation for entertaining on a grand scale was well known, but this, with the addition of a few chosen friends, was to be a family affair, and she had been most insistent that the whole family should be at the dinner, which immediately aroused Aimée's curiosity.

'She's up to something. I can always tell,' she told Oliver, who had come to visit after afternoon surgery one day.

Oliver looked quizzical. 'Your aunt takes an almost childish delight in springing surprises, so whatever she's hatching, she'll keep it to herself.'

'I know. I've asked her outright, but she just smiles and looks enigmatic. It's quite infuriating.'

Aimée's relationship with Oliver had undergone a subtle change since the picnic. He hadn't exactly lowered all his barriers, but his attitude towards the children was different, and she sensed that he was gradually coming to terms with his situation and beginning to look outward again.

In social circles they were more and more accepted as a pair, and Oliver seemed content to go along with this. Aimée supposed she ought to feel flattered. His looks, his presence, not to mention his growing prestige as a barrister, made him a formidable escort. It also made him a prime target for marauding mothers, whose marriageable daughters had been deprived by the war of the degree of choice they might overwise have enjoyed when seeking a husband.

There were moments when she wondered whether Oliver was simply using her as a shield. Apart from that disturbingly passionate incident on the night of the storm, which embarassed her even now when she remembered it, he had made no attempt to commit himself, while for her part, she had no wish to become emotionally involved. But she enjoyed the challenging cut and thrust of their relationship, and would be loath to lose it. So it would be churlish to feel aggrieved, whatever his motives. It might even be deemed quite flattering, she told herself, that many a young woman would give much to be in her place.

There were other, blindingly vulnerable moments, when the loss of that something more precious left her feeling barren, as at Jane's wedding, when Aimée had watched her come down the aisle on Oliver's arm, radiating joy as her eyes met those of her handsome naval officer. Just for an instant, her own body had recognized that joy, and melted with the remembrance of its own brief and glorious flowering.

And when, in mid-December she had become godmother to Jonathan Amos Buchanan, who made his appearance early only two weeks after Gerald and Megan had moved into their new home, and she had held her brother's child in her arms, her happiness for him had again been tinged with a sense of her own barrenness. But this time, her foolish thoughts were more easily banished.

On New Year's Eve she and Oliver arrived together to find the Mellish house as brilliantly lit up as the huge tree, which dominated the entrance hall. Already a subdued buzz of conversation was drifting out from the drawing room.

Matty, neatly dressed in black, with a frilly white apron, moved forward to say demurely, 'May I take your wrap, Dr Buchanan?' And then, lowering her voice, 'You look lovely.'

Aimée's eyes danced with amusement. 'Matty! Is this yet another new strand to your career?'

'Your aunt's got a house full, so I'm helping out,' Matty whispered. 'An' I tell you what, that Meredith's a right stickler.'

'Well then, we'd better make sure you create a good impression.' Aimée slipped off her sable wrap. 'Thank you, Matty,' she said clearly. She was wearing the bronze green that Matty had fallen in love with months ago. Madame Vincente had taken her ideas to heart and had designed it very much on the lines she had suggested with Aimée in mind.

I was right about that colour suiting her, Matty thought with pride as Aimée crossed the hall to the drawing room with Oliver. The silky satin was exactly right for the simple lines of the gown, skimming her figure in a way that was both daring and becoming – worth every minute of the hours she had spent sewing those bronze bugle beads round the neck and hip line. Matty's glance flickered briefly to Mr Langley, who had been relieved of his coat by a young footman. Douglas Fairbanks had nothing on him! She daydreamed briefly about what it would be like to be escorted by such a handsome man. Maybe one day . . .

'Matty!'

The butler's clipped voice brought her back to earth.

'Coming, Mr Meredith.'

The drawing room was already filling up as Aimée's eyes scanned the elaborately coiffured heads in search of her mother's pretty blonde waves. There were a number of people she didn't know. London friends, she supposed. Gerald caught her eye and waved to her to come over. Megan had been reluctant to leave Jonathan, even for a few hours. Only his promise to drive her home the moment they had seen the New Year in made her relent.

'Aimée darling!'

Sophie Westbury, who was very much Felicity's daughter, came rushing to meet her, hands outstretched. The two cousins hadn't met for some years, but it was obvious to Aimée that life had treated Sophie well. Her black pleated jersey skirt, overlapping, harem style, well above the ankles, was topped by a daringly cut silver tissue blouse with a narrow band of the same tissue confining her blonde curls. The whole ensemble screamed Paris, as did the musky perfume that wafted beneath Aimée's nostrils as they touched cheeks.

'Darling, isn't this fun! I can't remember when we last had a real family get-together. My wedding day, I suppose. It's worth every moment of that dire journey with the children and Nanny and the luggage, though Charles wouldn't agree.' Her plucked brows shot up, and her mouth made a little moue of amused dismay. 'He has vowed never again!'

Aimée laughed as she drew back. 'Do you know Oliver Langley?'

'Yes, of course.' Sophie offered her hand. 'Though I was still in pinafores when we last met, so you won't remember me.'

'I remember you very well,' he said gallantly. 'You were remarkably pretty even then.'

'What a charming man! Talking of pretty – Aimée, your mama has scarcely altered in years. How does she do it?'

Aimée resisted the temptation to say 'by sitting back and permitting others to wait on her', and instead, laughed and said, 'I have no idea. I only hope it's hereditary.'

'I'm sure it is. You look ravishing, darling. Love your hair. I remember when you had pigtails. Such a pity Gerald is going bald. But his wife seems a nice girl. Welsh, I believe.' She lowered her voice. 'Have you seen Giles's young lady? Face like a well-bred horse, but fearfully rich, and an honorable, so I'm told. Do you suppose it could be serious?'

Before she could reply, Aimée saw Uncle George bearing down on them. He was in a particularly jovial mood and she felt her smile beginning to set in anticipation of his heavy-handed humour. But for once no facetious references were made to her calling, and she wondered if he was at last beginning to take her seriously.

'All got drinks, have you? Good.' He beamed. 'Seen your parents yet, Aimée? They're taking advantage of the fire. Minna tells me she feels the cold, but then we're none of us getting any younger. Still, it's a great night, this – all m'family round me.' He lifted Sophie's hand to his lips and looked across at Oliver. 'Our good friends, too, of course. A great night.'

Aimée finally caught up with her own family, linking her arm through Gerald's and giving it a little squeeze as he eyed her approvingly. Her mother, wearing her favourite pink, was talking animatedly to Aunt Felicity, who was looking even more elegant than usual in black lace, while her father tried not to look as though he would rather be at home.

Megan had something of the same look. She was still a trifle plump following her pregnancy, and had made little effort to mix. For once Aimée found herself in sympathy with her sister-in-law. It couldn't be easy, being a relative stranger amid such a large gathering of people who had known one another forever.

'How like old times this is,' Minna was murmuring emotionally. 'Do you remember, Felicity? Such parties we had at Hightowers when we were girls, and our dear mama there to see that all went as it should.'

'A pity Grandpa couldn't be here tonight,' Aimée said mischievously. 'He always enjoyed the big occasion.'

'Darling, don't!' Felicity exclaimed dramatically. 'For one dreadful moment yesterday, I feared he would insist on making the effort, but Andrew absolutely forbade him. Besides, an extra man would have completely ruined my table plan,' Felicity concluded. Her eyes clouded momentarily. 'Which is a horrid thing to say, of course. We are so blessed in having our full complement of men. So many parties these days are tragically one-sided – so many young women doomed to spinsterhood.' She felt rather than saw the faint shiver that passed through her niece, and at once realized what she had said. 'Oh, darling, I didn't mean – I am sure that won't be your fate.'

Aimée looked past her aunt, straight into Oliver's eyes. It was hard to read their expression, to know whether she had betrayed that moment of bleak recognition. 'Dear Aunt Fliss, don't give it a second thought,' she said lightly. 'I am well content as I am.'

By tradition they sat down to dinner later than usual, the time being contrived so as to take them up to midnight. The table was a delight, a sea of sparkling silver and glass, of greenery and flowers, and in the centre, Felicity's beautiful gleaming epergne, its fluted vases containing sprays of red and white carnations from the glasshouses, their theme repeated at intervals along the table.

Aimée had wondered how Toby would cope, and was pleased that she had been seated next to him, with Minna on his other side. So far he seemed to be managing better than she had expected.

'W-with so many people here, I can fade into the background,' he told her. 'It's an art I am acquiring w-with practice.'

Aimée wondered if his growing preoccupation with garden design was responsible for his increasing confidence. As one of the favoured few, she had been allowed a glimpse inside his office, and had been amazed at the number of carefully drawn plans adorning the walls. He had explained to her how he made a basic drawing of an area, and then superimposed upon it variations in terms of trees, rockeries, water. It was a skill that no one realized he possessed – until he received his first commission to redesign a garden for one of his mother's friends.

'I know Mrs Knightly only asked m-me as a favour to M-mama,' he said with his gentle wry smile. 'But I m-mean to create something very special – something that will m-make people take notice.'

Aimée grinned. 'Good for you.'

'In fact, I have decided that w-what I most w-want to do is design beautiful gardens for a living, if possible.'

His face was a little flushed, and for a moment she wondered if he had been drinking rather more than he was used to. But his eyes were clear and steady. He glanced round to see if anyone was listening, and lowered his voice.

'I really need a house of m-my own – a small one w-would do so long as there's enough land at the b-back for hothouses and so on. If I found the right one, do you think P-Pa would lend me enough to b-buy it?'

'Oh, Toby! I don't know.' Would his nerves stand the strain? Did he have the necessary business sense? Desperate not to disappoint him, she tried to visualize her uncle's reaction to such a proposal. 'You'd have to sound him out. If he won't, perhaps Grandpa Howard would come up trumps.' Apprehension flickered in Toby's eyes at the thought of approaching his grandfather, so she added hastily, 'Anyhow, let's wait and see, shall we? You'd need help – you couldn't run something like that alone.'

'I've got ideas about that, too. A couple of men I knew at Cedar Grove might be interested.'

At this point, Minna touched Toby's arm and with a whispered, 'You w-won't tell anyone?' he turned courteously to listen to what his aunt was saying. Oliver was by now engrossed in conversation with a dark-haired beauty on his other side, which left Aimée to reflect with mixed feelings on what Toby had told her.

As the meal drew to a close, Giles rose to perform a duty that had been his by tradition for many years – to propose the toast to The Family. And then, with the hands of the ormolu clock on the mantelpiece showing ten minutes to midnight Uncle George got to his feet.

The candlelight flickered, the room was warm and Aimée was pleasantly replete, though she longed for a cigarette – a luxury still only accorded to the gentlemen with their port. She prepared to sit back and let his words flow over her. Over the years he had gained a reputation among his children for 'boring on', and when he began, Giles looked across at her and solemnly closed one eye. Her lips twitched, and he turned to murmur something to his young lady, who had the misfortune to be called Gwendoline – a name that really didn't suit her.

Uncle George began with the usual platitudes concerning the family in its immediate and wider sense, which they had all heard countless times, and then he paused – a ploy he had long ago perfected and doubtless used to great effect in the House of Commons – and Aimée suddenly noticed that Aunt Felicity was looking like the cat that got the cream. She sat forward.

'You may wonder why we were so keen to have all the family and our special friends present on this particular night. It is my very pleasant duty to inform you, my nearest and dearest, that His Majesty has been pleased to confer a knighthood upon me in recognition of my – ' The rest of his words were lost in a babbling chorus of cheers.

'Well, I'll be damned!' Aimée heard Giles exclaim. 'The sly old bugger!'

'As you must realize,' Uncle George continued when the first wave of sound died down, 'we have known of this for some weeks, but were sworn to silence until the official announcement was made on the first of January 1920 – ' He glanced at the clock, and then drew his gold hunter watch from his waistcoat pocket – 'which, by my reckoning, should be exactly ten seconds from now.'

A hush fell as they waited. In the hall beyond, the grandfather clock could be heard gently whirring as it gathered itself to chime the hour.

'Beautifully timed,' Aimée murmured as they listened to the bell-like notes of the four quarters. The first stroke coincided with the popping of the first champagne cork and everyone began to congratulate her uncle.

Below stairs the clearing up was all but complete, any remaining dishes being banished to the scullery, to be dealt with later. In the servants' hall the gramophone was blaring out a ragtime tune, and the younger servants were enthusiastically doing the chicken reel when Meredith arrived to proclaim the news.

When the oohs and aahs and 'Good luck to 'im!'s had died down, Meredith announced that Sir George and Lady Felicity would be down later to wish them all a happy New Year, and, in addition to the barrel of stout already being broached, Sir George had provided a case of champagne, so that they might drink his health in style. It was not vintage, which would be wasted on palates unaccustomed to such luxury. Alec, however, had been around posh houses enough to spot the difference.

'Non-vintage. Big of 'im, I'm sure,' he muttered. 'I suppose he thinks anything's good enough for the workers.'

'Don't you be so ungrateful, young man, bitin' the 'and that feeds yer,' Cook reprimanded him. 'Say what yer like, there's many not so lucky as us, an' that's a fact.'

'Ah well, vintage or not, it's all the same ter me,' someone said, and 'Mighty generous of *Sir* George,' other voices were quick to shout out.

Matty had already changed her frock, as had the other girls. She had made herself a new one for Christmas in a pretty shade of pale green, with a scalloped hem much envied by some of the younger maids as it showed off her legs when she kicked them up – which seemed to happen quite a lot, she and Alec being pretty nifty dancers.

By the time the family came down an atmosphere of jollity prevailed. Matty hadn't seen Sir George until tonight, but she was impressed when, after Meredith made a little speech of congratulation, he had popped the champagne and then one-stepped Cook round the table to the delight of all, leaving her pink and breathless.

There was dancing upstairs, too. The music was provided by a trio of jazz musicians, with one-steps and foxtrots to please the older guests, and turkey trots, chicken reels and bunny hugs, for the younger, more energetic dancers. And when everyone else stopped for breath, Giles and Gwendoline entertained them with an exaggerated version of the tango.

'Wildly energetic, but no finesse,' murmured Oliver.

Aimée laughed up at him. 'I suppose you could do better.'

'He can actually,' Felicity said. 'I watched him many times when the tango first came out. He was in great demand at parties.' And then she stopped abruptly, remembering with whom she had seen him.

Oliver was also cursing his careless tongue as memories crowded in. But, rather to his surprise, they were less painful than he expected. He was able to recollect, if not in tranquillity, at least without bitterness, how he and Catherine had been the envy of all their friends; she, as light as thistledown, with a natural grace; he, possessing the strength and suppleness to complement it.

Perhaps the time had come, not to forget Catherine – he could never do that – but to set her in her appointed place, and look outwards again. His eyes, meeting Aimée's, were enigmatic.

'I'm totally out of practice. But Felicity does not exaggerate – I was once reckoned to be the Valentino of the dance floor. Would you care to take part in a small experiment?'

Aimée's heart was pounding, making her ears feel strange, blurring her eyes. Too much wine too quickly drunk, the doctor in her was quick to proclaim. She blinked, saw the mute appeal in his eyes, and was unable to resist.

'Why not?' she said lightly.

They had danced before – impersonal little one-steps and foxtrots – but never like this. Aimée was no Catherine, but she had a litheness, an instinctive sensuality that responded without reserve to the tango's exacting rhythm, to the pressure of Oliver's hand. Her body felt at one with his, aware each time they turned to glide forward, thigh to thigh, of a *frisson* that sent her emotions spiralling, increasing in intensity as the music's beat gathered itself towards the dramatic climax.

They were both oblivious of the crowd that had gathered to watch, until applause greeted the final flourish, and there were shouts of 'bravo' and 'encore'. Aimée found that she was trembling, and knew it was not simply from the physical pressure exerted on every nerve.

'No more,' she gasped, laughing to conceal the shake in her voice. 'I don't know about Oliver, but I'm exhausted.'

'My word, you were wonderfully well-matched,' Sophie exclaimed, wide-eyed.

Oliver said nothing. He was equally shaken by that curious illusion of oneness, for it was an illusion, he told himself, or at best pure coincidence that their two bodies should be so perfectly attuned.

In the end he was spared comment by the arrival of refreshments, taking advantage of the enthusiastic surge towards the long side table, where they were being laid out under Meredith's watchful eye, to say quietly, 'Thank you, that was quite an experience.' And his eyes were telling Aimée quite plainly that he wasn't referring to the dance.

While everyone else ate and drank and talked, Toby, his fine fair hair flopping down over his eyes, moved aside and began to play the piano, very softly, just for himself. No one noticed except Matty, who had brought a platter of fruit up from the kitchen.

She set it down, and slipped unnoticed between the various groups to listen. It was a song that everyone was singing these days – sad, but very beautiful, and there was something about the way he played it that brought the tears to her eyes.

Toby looked up, his hands hovering above the keys as he saw her.

'M-Matty!'

'Oh, don't stop, please! It's sad, but ever so beautiful.'

He smiled gently and his fingers took up the refrain again. 'Do you know it?' He began to sing very softly, '*Roses are shining in Picardy . . .*' and after a minute she joined in. Gradually the conversation came to a halt as, one after another, people began to hum, or sing until a gentle swell of sound filled the room, and there was a lump in many a throat. With the final chord came a moment of complete silence. Then everyone began talking again as though nothing had happened.

'That was lovely,' Matty whispered.

Aimée wandered across to drape an arm casually across her young cousin's shoulders, and briefly rested her cheek against his. 'Thank you, Toby dear. It's nice to know you haven't lost your touch.'

She smiled at Matty and moved on, and Matty found herself envying them their closeness.

'I shouldn't really be here,' she said. 'I'd better go.'

'M-must you? I'd like you to stay.'

He sounded as if he really minded. 'That'd cause a bit of a stir,' she said with wry humour. 'Having the hired help join their party. I only came up to bring some food.'

'You're p-pretty enough to p-put m-most of them in the shade,' he declared gallantly – and blushed.

The compliment left Matty momentarily speechless. She turned to watch Aimée and her friends laughing and talking, their wrists sparkling with jewels as they caught the light. How could anyone think she was prettier than them?

'Can I come downstairs with you?'

He was behaving very oddly tonight, Matty thought. 'Oh, but you surely don't want to leave all this, Mr Toby?' she nodded towards the crowded room. 'Wouldn't everyone think it a bit odd?'

He ran his fingers lightly over the keyboard and stood up.

'They w-won't even miss me,' he said simply. 'And, Matty: Do you think w-we could drop the "Mr"?'

Her heart leaped and steadied. 'I don't think they'd like that.'

'W-well, just between ourselves. We are friends, after all, aren't we?'

'I'd like to think so.'

'W-well, then. That's settled. Come on.'

Downstairs in the servants' hall, the celebrations had grown noisier as the crate of champagne emptied, and the barrel of stout went the same way. Someone was winding up the gramophone and the tinkling sound of Scott Joplin penetrated the babble of voices, so that Toby's arrival was hardly noticed at first. But Meredith, seeing him with Matty, looked startled, and then endeavoured not to show his disapproval.

'You don't m-mind m-e being here, do you, M-Meredith?' Toby asked anxiously.

'It is not for me to say, sir. This is Cook's province.'

Toby turned his gentle smile on Mrs Blackwell. 'I m-may stay, m-mayn't I, Cook?'

Fortified by several glasses of champagne, she beamed at him. 'Why, bless you, Mr Toby, of course you can stay, if you've a mind to, an' welcome.' She had always had a soft spot for Mr Toby, even when he was a boy, for a gentler, sweeter nature you could never hope to find in a child. And, not taking anything away from Mr Giles, who had done wonderful deeds in the war, an' had got hisself a whole string of medals to prove it, she reckoned that this young lad had been every bit as brave in his way – an' had suffered more than most.

Alec had consumed more than his share of the drink, and the mixture of champagne and stout made him light-headed and more extrovert than usual. He had been chatting up one of the girls from the agency – a pretty redhead who giggled a lot and was a nifty little dancer – and was preoccupied in showing her some new steps he'd learned from a dancer friend of his. They got so carried away that he hadn't realized Matty was back until the music stopped, and he found himself coming to a halt in front of her, still with his arm round the girl.

'Oh, there you are. I thought I'd lost you.' He was slurring his words. 'This is Penny, and, oh boy, can she do the bunnyhug!' He suddenly became aware of Matty's companion, and frowned. 'Wha's he doin' here?'

'None of your business, Gresham.' Meredith frowned. But Mrs Blackwell was full of peace and goodwill to all.

'Bless 'im, he's come to have a bit of fun, and to see his old friend, Cookie, haven't you, Mr Toby?'

Alec didn't like the way he was standing so close to Matty. He thrust his head forward aggressively. 'That 'ow yer get yer kicks, is it – comin' slummin'?'

'Alec!' Matty's voice broke the sudden embarrassed silence as she saw the painful colour flood Toby's face.

'Why, you nasty ignorant little toerag!' Cook cried, incensed. 'I won't 'ave talk like that from no one in my kitchen, least of all when it's addressed to one of the family!'

Alec swayed, staring round at all the shocked faces. 'Aah, you're all the same, bowin' and scrapin' to yer lords and masters. Well, not me, nor'any more. Them days are over, far as I'm concerned . . .'

'Be silent, Gresham.' Meredith was awesome in his anger. 'You will apologize to Mr Toby, and then you will go to your quarters. And, if I were you, I would pack my things. When Sir George is informed of your behaviour, you will be out on your ear faster than you can think.'

'Oh, p-please!' Toby looked distressed. 'I d-don't w-w-want any trouble! It's m-my fault. I'll g-g-go.'

'Your fault, indeed! You'll stay right where you are!' Matty cried, eyes flashing, arms akimbo, like a tiger defending her young. 'You've got more right to be here than him, any day. As for you, Alec Gresham – ' she swung round in disgust ' – you ought to be ashamed of yourself. You're falling-down drunk!'

He thrust his face into hers. 'And you're a jumped-up little snob, makin' up ter the gentry!'

Before he knew what was happening, he was flat on his back, with Toby standing over him, nursing his fist. It was impossible to say who was the more surprised.

'You w-will apologize to M-Miss Shaw, Gresham,' he said, with a quiet authority no one present had ever heard in his voice before.

Alec scrambled ignominiously to his feet and muttered 'Sorry.'

'I suppose that will have to do,' he said dryly. 'I'm sorry, too, M-Matty. I hope I haven't ruined your evening.'

'Oh, no, not you.' She glared at Alec.

Toby turned to the butler. 'M-My fault, M-Meredith. Let it end here – forget the whole thing. No sackings, eh? New Year, spirit of goodwill, and all that.'

To everyone's surprise he held out a hand to Alec who took it grudgingly. 'Start w-with a clean slate, what?'

'Which is more'n you deserve, my lad,' Cook muttered.

As Toby passed Matty, he paused. 'I'm sorry it all w-went wrong, m'dear. B-Be happy.'

But Matty didn't feel happy. She wanted to cry.

They drove home in silence through a landscape sharply etched in black and white. The air was crisp, a three-quarter moon sailed across a sky pricked with stars, and Aimée lay back in the passenger seat, cocooned in sable, her body filled with a wondrous languor, while her every sense was singingly aware of Oliver close beside her.

In Myrtle Street, he drew up at the kerb, and came to help her out. He took her key from her and slid it into the lock, but didn't immediately turn it. She looked up, and studied his profile, the formidable brow and Roman nose finely etched in silver moonlight. She didn't want the evening to end.

'Will you come in for a nightcap?'

'At half-past three in the morning?' His lips moved in amusement. 'What would the neighbours say if they looked out and saw my car parked outside? Isn't a doctor's behaviour supposed to be above reproach?'

'Mmm,' she murmured regretfully. 'A barrister's, too, I suppose. A pity.'

'Another time, perhaps.'

'Yes.'

His mouth was cool on hers – a brief salute. And then he was gone.

Aimée wandered through the hall and up the stairs, trailing her wrap. In the bedroom, she threw it across the bed and decided to indulge in a leisurely bath. She was on her way downstairs again when the doorbell rang.

Oliver stood on the doorstep, bathed in moonlight, his overcoat unbuttoned, his white scarf hanging loose. His face wore an enigmatic expression as he eyed her softly flowing pyjamas and loose robe.

'I'm not keeping you from your bed, I hope?'

'What is a few minutes here or there?' Aimée took the ends of his silk scarf and drew him inside, a smile curving her lips as he kicked it to behind him.

'I left the car in Falkner Square and walked back.'

'How very sensible.'

She pulled gently on the scarf and allowed it to slide through her fingers and slither to the floor. 'I'll show you where to leave your coat,' she said, taking his hand and leading him towards the stairs. 'Your drink is ready and waiting.'

He laughed softly. 'You were that sure?'

'We're wasting time.' The pressure on his hand increased.

'Aimée Buchanan, am I being seduced?'

Her eyes were luminous. 'Yes, Oliver, I rather think you are. Do you mind?'

21

SPRING HAD ARRIVED. It wasn't immediately obvious in the grey back streets, but in Sefton Park the daffodils were already in bloom.

'I sometimes wonder how long it'll be before there's only Moira and Daisy left at home,' Agnes said, coming in with Aimée's mid-morning cup of tea. 'It's bad enough keeping up with Matty. Now, it's our Kevin. He's forever hauntin' the Cunard offices, hoping to get taken on. A few months with that Mr Eyre, the butcher, and he thinks he's God's gift.'

'He's a bit young, isn't he?'

'Barely sixteen, scarcely dry behind the ears. But, being on the big side, he'll likely lie about his age and get away with it.'

Aimée thought she was probably right. However, it would be prudent not to say so. 'But Matty's Paris trip has been on the cards for some time, surely?'

'Oh that! I'll believe that when it happens. This latest piece of nonsense is closer to home. You know that fancy frock she's always on about – the one she and Madame Whatsit have designed between them? Well, now it seems Madame wants her to model it at a Grand National Night ball at the Adelphi. What next, I ask you!'

'Oh, but that's a wonderful opportunity for her!'

'Maybe, though I'm not convinced.' Agnes bustled across to the fire and attacked it viciously with the poker, sending the sparks flying up the chimney. 'All this mixin' with the nobs could easily turn a girl's head.'

'Not Matty. She won't get carried away that easily. She's got too much of both Pat and you in her, and that's a formidable combination.'

'Well, I hope you're right,' Agnes muttered, mollified by the compliment.

Outside, the March sun shone deceptively bright in a pale washed sky. She threw some more coal on the fire.

'Anyhow, it's no use meeting trouble,' she said, pressing a hand to her back as she straightened up.

'Quite right,' Aimée agreed. 'And speaking of trouble, when are you going to let me take a look at that back? I've seen you favour it more than usual just lately.'

Agnes hurried to the door. 'I've told you, it's nothing but a touch of lumbago. The March winds have set it off.'

'Coward,' Aimée called after her.

She hadn't seen Nellie for several weeks, but when she did come later that morning, there was a look about her that Aimée had seen many times.

'I can't be absolutely certain, Doctor, but I think I might be . . .'

'Pregnant? That's wonderful. Do sit down, and we'll see if we can be more definite about it. How long is it since you had a period?'

'About seven weeks and three days.' Nellie laughed nervously. 'I suppose I have been counting pretty regular. And me breasts are sore like they were when I was havin' our Mary, and I've been feeling queasy of a morning.'

After examining her, Aimée said with a smile, 'Well, there's not much doubt about it. Does Danny know yet?'

'Oh no. I couldn't risk telling him until I was certain.'

'Well, I think you can safely tell him now.' She smiled as Nellie's eyes lit up like twin stars. 'And I want you to take things easy for a while, and keep on with the iron. That's most important.'

'Oh, I will!' Nellie said fervently. 'I'm not taking any chances with this one.'

The contrast between Nellie and Biddy O'Hara could not have been more marked. It still grieved Aimée to see the bright, birdlike Biddy so changed. She could get around on her two sticks, and with Sarah Brady's help managed to look after the little ones and do a small amount of cooking, though she couldn't stand for long. Mostly she took care of the sewing and mending, which was no small task with the children growing out of their clothes faster than she could deal with them. This, at least, gave her a sense of purpose.

Liam was a changed man since the accident. He seldom took a

drink, and it was deeply touching to see him carrying Biddy around like a child. Occasionally, he made half-hearted attempts to find a place of their own, out of pride as much as anything else.

'I wish you'd give over trying,' Sarah was saying one evening when Aimée called. 'Sure, aren't we managing just fine? I wouldn't know what to do with meself if you weren't here. It's like havin' me own lot back again.' She nodded towards the corner where three young O'Haras were locked in mortal combat. 'And isn't it the kiddies that keep you young? Give over now, Dec, or yer'll have yer brother killed fer sure!'

Liam rose from his chair and put an arm round her shoulders. 'Just one big happy family, Sarah gairl,' he agreed, a shade too heartily. 'An' Sean and Frankie earning the odd shillin' here an' there.'

'That toad of a landlord sent his agent round earlier this evenin'.' There was a note of disgust in Sarah's voice. 'Said I'd need to be payin' extra fer takin' in lodgers – the brass nerve of the man!'

'Ah well, I was able to show him the error of his ways,' said Liam with deceptive amiability.

Sarah began to laugh. 'You did that, right enough – oh, oh!' She held her sides as the rolls of fat quivered. 'You should'a seen it, Doctor. Liam hauled him up by 'is collar an' the seat of his kecks, and 'e went arse over tip into Aigburth Street. I've never seen anyone so took aback. He went harin' off like the hounds of hell wus after him!'

'It was no more than the little creep deserved.'

'To be fair, Liam, he was only doin' his job.'

'And what kind of a job is that?' Liam growled. 'The man's little more than a landlord's pimp.'

'Liam! The children!' Biddy glanced fearfully at the three, who seemed oblivious of what was going on.

'Well, what else would you call it when he spends his time procuring folks' hard-earned shillin's fer his lord and master?' He laughed harshly. 'No wonder someone purra couple of bricks through the windows of Frank Prentice's fine house last night. 'E's lucky that's all they did. There's many'd like to string 'im up by 'is – '

'Enough, Liam!' Biddy clamped her hands over her ears. 'I

don't want to hear any more! Just so long as you weren't mixed up in it.'

'Not me, me darlin',' he said softly, crouching down in front of her. 'If it'd been me, it wouldn't be his windows. I'd have smashed 'is bloody head in fer what he done to you an' my boy.'

'Ah no, Liam, me darlin! It's a sin to even think such things! 'Twas an accident,' she cried, wrapping her arms round his neck and pulling his head down onto her breast, her tear-filled eyes lifting appealingly to Aimée.

'Liam wouldn't be that stupid, Biddy,' she said calmly, her words directed at the big man. 'He knows how much you would be hurt.'

Liam lifted a face twisted with bitterness. 'Yer right, Doctor. An' isn't that the pity of it all?'

Aimée should have been reassured. She knew that Liam, sober, meant every word, but what if he were ever to go back to drowning his sorrows? He was still very bitter about what had happened, and with work at the docks hard to come by some days, his anger had plenty of time to fester. She occasionally wondered how they would have coped if there had been no Sarah Brady.

There were many less fortunate as she was constantly discovering on her rounds; too many children with rickets and scurvy; too many apathetic mothers, worn down by years of never having enough, of huge families living in one room. She finally grew tired of badgering officials, and appealed instead to her aunt.

'You and your charitable committees did so much during the war, Aunt Fliss. Could you possibly persuade them to raise enough money to enable me to provide at least a few of the necessities these poor people need? The winter has left them desperately vulnerable to illness.'

'Well, of course I'll do all I can, darling.' Felicity had eyed her niece with some concern. 'But you really mustn't take it so much to heart, you know, or you'll make yourself ill, too.'

'I'm fine. Just frustrated by officialdom.'

Gabrielle Watson, now back from her cruise and fully fit, helped, too, throwing herself into the cause with enthusiasm. With the money collected from all sources, Aimée was able to buy quantities of cod-liver oil for the children, and margarine, rice and tapioca, Skipper sardines and tinned meats, cheese, eggs and potatoes, and Sunlight soap – and anything else that would be of use. They made up assorted parcels and Aimée took them round in the car. It was disheartening to discover later that many of the recipients of her bounty promptly sold the goods to those who could afford to buy.

'Well, what did you expect?' Oliver said. 'You can't blame them for making money out of what they would consider luxuries, when they are more concerned with simply staying alive.'

'I don't blame them,' she snapped. 'I blame the system which makes it impossible for them to live with any degree of dignity.'

Oliver had come to take her to a concert at Crane Hall, and found her resplendent in crushed wine velvet, struggling with the lock on the front door.

'Damn this stupid thing!' she muttered, jabbing at it viciously with a screwdriver.

'Trouble?'

'It was perfectly all right when Agnes left. But now the lock's jammed and I can't shift the screws.'

'Let me,' he said.

'You?' Aimée exclaimed. 'Why should you suppose you can do any better? Because you're a man?'

He lifted a laconic eyebrow. 'Not necessarily. But I'm not in a filthy temper.' Tight-lipped, she handed him the screwdriver and he had the screws off in no time. 'It could use some oil, if you have any,' he said without looking up. 'And, by the way, you've got a smear of grease on the end of your nose.'

She marched into the kitchen full of self-righteousness, and stood on tiptoe to peer in a small mirror above one of the cupboards. Damn, he was right! She unearthed a small oil can, and marched back, to find that Oliver had laid her copy of *The Times* out on the hall table and had the lock in pieces.

'I hope you know what you're doing,' she said, determined not to unbend. But the sight of him in his evening clothes, working away with the total absorption of a schoolboy, weakened her resolve, and she found herself suppressing a chuckle.

'Thanks.' He looked up with a laconic grin, and reached for the can, applying the oil to strategic points and giving the key a few experimental turns. 'That should do it, I think,' he said with satisfaction. In minutes the lock was put together again and back on the door.

'Very professional,' Aimée said with a hint of irony. 'Except that I'm not the only one smeared with grease.'

He held up his fingers. 'I see what you mean.'

'Come into the surgery.' She led the way, amused by the fleeting look of apprehension. So he had an Achilles heel! 'It's all right, I'm not going to chop them off.'

She took a large bottle of surgical spirit from the cupboard, unscrewed the cap and cut a square of lint. 'This should do the trick.'

'Let's see, shall we?'

Before she knew what he was about, he had tipped some onto the lint and was gently dabbing the end of her nose. 'Very effective,' he agreed.

Aimée slid under his arm, and made for the door. 'I'll get my wrap while you clean up.'

'In a moment,' he said, and his voice sounded quite different. 'Tell me why you were really in such a filthy temper when I arrived.'

'You know why. The food parcels – '

'No, I can understand your frustration over the failure of your scheme, but that isn't why you were stabbing away at that lock as though you were trying to kill someone.'

'We'll be late for the concert.'

'There's time enough.'

For a moment their eyes locked in a battle of wills. Then, with a shrug, she crossed to her desk and took out a letter.

Oliver read it through in silence, his expression giving nothing away. When he looked up, he had his lawyer's face on.

'Is this true? Have you been treating these patients?'

'They came to me for advice,' she prevaricated.

'Which you gave them, knowing them to be Dalywell's patients?'

'Stop cross-examining me. I'm not on trial.'

'You gave them advice,' he repeated inexorably.

Why am I being so defensive? she thought. Her head came up. 'They were frightened and I reassured them. What else could I do? Each of the three women came to me independently, each complaining of the same classic and distressing symptoms of the menopause.' She looked him full in the eyes. 'Perhaps you aren't aware how difficult some women find it to talk about such things to a man – even if he is a doctor.'

He inclined his head. If she had hoped to embarrass him, there was no evidence of it.

'I simply explained to each of them in the clearest terms exactly how the changes taking place in their bodies could produce a variety of symptoms, and I gave them some practical hints on how best to alleviate the worst effects. That is all. And they went away reassured.'

'And promptly complained to their husbands that Dr Dalywell didn't understand them, and they wished to change doctors.'

'At no stage did I suggest any such move.'

'Hmm.' Oliver glanced at the letter again. He didn't much like the pompous physician, but the man had been in practice for many years. 'Surely, if they had consulted Dr Dalywell – '

'They had already done so. He as good as told them that they were silly spoilt women with too much time on their hands, that most women accepted the changing cycle with its slight discomforts as inevitable, and the best thing they could do when they felt down, was to go out and buy a pretty new hat.' Aimée's head lifted, as if challenging Oliver. 'I don't know about you, but I view that as an insult to their intelligence.'

He frowned. 'Dalywell is not the most tactful of men. And the young girl he mentions?'

'The same problem but in reverse. The poor child began to menstruate and thought that something terrible was happening to her. Coming as she does from an inhibited middle-class background, she was too afraid to tell her mother, who had given her no warning of what to expect, and too shy to approach Dr Dalywell. So she came to me.' When Oliver said nothing, she challenged him. 'What was I supposed to do?'

'Unfortunately, ignorance is not the prerogative of the poor,' he said slowly.

'I agree. But until it is eradicated, a lot of people are going to suffer unnecessarily.' When he didn't answer, she said less confidently, 'Dalywell can't possibly suppose he has grounds for an official complaint?'

Oliver glanced again at the letter. 'I think this was meant more to frighten you.' He looked up with the ghost of a smile. 'Clearly he doesn't know you very well. I suppose there's no chance of you becoming less of a firebrand?'

'Not while there are doctors like Dalywell around.'

'Hmm.' He folded the letter. 'Will you leave this with me?'

'Yes, of course,' she said, relieved. 'I had been trying to make up my mind to tell you about it.'

'Good God! Don't tell me you were afraid?'

'Certainly not.' She blushed wildly, wishing her tongue had been less quick. 'But you can occasionally be quite formidable.'

Oliver gave a great shout of laughter. 'Now I've heard everything. Go and get your wrap, Aimée Buchanan. We have a concert to attend.'

It was one of those moments when she wished she knew where she stood with Oliver. At New Year, high on champagne and celebration, he had been exactly the kind of lover she had guessed he might be, passionate, dominant, even exultant, but also tender, allowing her to enfold him with her own lovemaking. Afterwards they had drifted for a while between sleeping and waking, loosely entwined, her own body still singing, the last lingering echoes of David finally and lovingly laid to rest.

But she had woken later, when it was still dark, to find him sitting on the edge of the bed, his head in his hands, and she knew that for him the healing process would take much longer.

'Oliver?'

He gave no sign of having heard her. Aimée gathered up the feathered quilt and wrapped it round him. 'Oliver, don't. Don't blame yourself. We celebrated too well and got carried away, and it was fun. Perhaps we both needed to prove something.' He moved slightly, but said nothing and she sought for the right words. 'You see, I once loved someone with all the sweetness and desperation of a first love doomed by war.' She hesitated, and made herself go on. 'David was a flier, and when he was killed, he left me his cherished book of Christina Rossetti poems – and one in particular, he had marked. Perhaps you know it?'

She had recited it softly to him and when she came to the last lines: 'Better by far you should forget and smile, Than that you should remember and be sad.' Oliver had turned to her, burying his face in her shoulder.

'Come back to bed,' she said softly.

But he had sat up, shaking his head. 'Not a good idea.' His voice had sounded strained, but there was a hint of humour as he added, 'The neighbours would have a field day if I arrived home on foot, in daylight and in full evening dress. But thank you.' He kissed her once, lightly on the mouth, and stood up. 'You make powerful medicine, Dr Buchanan.'

In a sense it had been a turning point. But nothing was ever that simple with Oliver. He had come to her more than once since that night, but their lovemaking had never again tipped over into abandoned passion. It was as though he needed to be in control at all times – as though he were afraid to lose himself in love ever again, and because her natural instinct was to heal, not to hurt, she had been patient.

She had tried to analyse her own feelings; was what she felt for Oliver love? It was different from the heady joy she had known with David, but the need for him had certainly grown over the weeks and months, as the thought of losing him became more painful. Maybe patience would not in the end be enough.

But meanwhile their relationship progressed in an erratic, not unpleasurable fashion. On Sundays, she often went to Falkner Square for afternoon tea. The children would join them, to the delight of Alice, who clearly adored her daddy, and could wind him round her little finger. And, 'Dr Aimée is my bestest friend,' she told everyone who would listen. Oliver's relationship with his son had undergone a complete change, and it pleased Aimée to see them together. Christopher was now toddling, and though he said little, he was a very loving child.

For Matty, life was changing so fast that she sometimes felt it was all a bit unreal. She didn't mind Madame Vincente working her hard. It helped to dull the pain of having no Dod to confide in when she came home of an evening. He had always believed in her, encouraged her to strive for seemingly impossible goals, and she hadn't realized until now just how important that had been.

Mam cared, just as much – of course she did. But hers was a practical love. It was Dad who had been the dreamer. And she wished with all her heart that he were here now, so that she could tell him about the Grand National Ball, how excited she was about going – and how terrified in case she made a pig's ear of it.

'Of course you will not make this *pig's ear* – such a droll expression – because I 'ave put my trust in you,' Madame declared sternly. 'We 'ave create this gown together, and me, I will not permit you to fail.'

'But folk would take much more notice if you wore it,' Matty insisted, while a part of her waited for the emphatic denial she was almost sure would come.

'Me?' Madame's raucous laugh rang out. '*Mais non!* Twenty years ago, per'aps. You know what they used to call me then? *Jolie laide* – "pretty ugly".' Again the laugh rang out. 'Oh, but I 'ad much chic. All the 'eads turned when I walk in a room.'

'They still do, Madame,' Matty assured her eagerly. 'You always look so elegant.'

She shrugged neat narrow shoulders, not displeased by the young girl's compliments. 'Ah, but I am no longer so young, eh? It needs your height and figure to show off this beautiful gown. You will see that I am right. And I shall be there to make sure that everyone knows that Madame Vincente is supreme.'

It was beautiful, Matty thought, turning yet again to admire the finished gown on its stand, still scarcely able to believe she was partly responsible for it. Not that she could ever have created anything anywhere near as beautiful on her own. It was Madame who had been so taken by Matty's original experiment in appliqué that she had carried it several stages further, and with a few tentative ideas from Matty had designed something that was at once simple and exquisitely complex.

The gown, expertly cut by Madame, was in palest sea-green chiffon over a deeper green satin slip. It was sleeveless, falling slim and straight from a simple neckline cut low at the back, to just above the ankle, the bodice appliquéd with tiny delicate snail-shaped shells fashioned from turquoise beading and silver net. The motive extended to the skirt in curving lines of scallop shells graduating in size, of silver and gold lace that rippled like the sea with every movement, the space between each line widening. It had taken Matty hours over weeks, sewing until her fingers were sore, and now, with barely another three weeks to go, it was almost finished, with only the largest scallops along the hem to complete. But it was worth all the blisters and the cramps, and in a curious way it helped to exorcize her grief.

And if she was completely honest, she couldn't bear anyone else to wear it.

'It's the most beautiful thing you could ever dream about,' she had enthused to Alec, when he took her dancing to the Imperial on his night off. 'I wish you could see me in it.'

'And who's to say I won't? I'll be leavin' me job at the end of next week,' he said cockily, adding a few intricacies of his own to the foxtrot, 'and I'm thinkin' I might get meself a ticket fer the ball.'

Matty's relationship with Alec had been very shaky for a week or two after the New Year fracas, but he had finally charmed her into giving him another chance. He was good company, and now that he was definitely going into partnership with Eddie, it would have made things very awkward if they hadn't been on speaking terms.

'Are you sure? It won't really be your kind of a do.' Matty was surprised to find that she didn't really want him to be there, pushing his way in. She despised herself for being snobbish, and tried to force more enthusiasm into her voice. 'And you'd probably need to wear evening dress.'

'No problem. I can borrow one from a mate. He gives demonstrations of all the latest dances from America at parties.' Alec grinned. 'An' I'll have to start puttin' meself about a bit, build up connections. Eddie and I are goin' places, girl, and you too, now yer startin' to make an impression on that Madame Vincente. Hey, it'd be great, Matty, you and me rubbin' shoulders with the great *Sir George* – ' he bowed with a flourish – 'on equal terms, stuck up old miser that he is.'

'You shouldn't talk like that,' Matty said. 'The Mellishs have been good to you – to both of us. You'd have been out on your ear after that business at New Year if Toby hadn't smoothed things over.'

Alec flushed, not wanting to be reminded. 'That feeble little twirp.'

'He's nothing of the kind!'

'Ah, they're all the same, that lot, lookin' down their noses at the likes of us. Well, we'll be up there with 'em soon. Then we'll see.'

Matty hated it when Alec got on his hobby horse. She owed everything to Mrs Mellish – Lady Mellish she was now. And nobody was more of a real lady than her.

22

M ATTY WOKE ON the morning of Grand National Day to lowering skies. The weather had been so lovely yesterday. Why did it have to change now? Her special evening would be ruined.

'Lord, child, it's not the end of the world,' Agnes said, bustling round to get everything straight before she went out. 'Daisy, the jam goes on your bread, not on the tablecloth. Moira, give her a hand, for pity's sake, or it'll be another one for the wash.'

'I can do!' Daisy screamed as Moira leaned across to help.

'Well, let's see you then,' Moira said with a firmness beyond her years. And Daisy tossed her blonde curls and applied a three-year-old's concentration to the task. 'That's better. Now, put your tongue away before you bite it off. It's Friday, and we don't eat meat on Friday.'

Daisy chuckled and pushed it in.

Agnes sighed. 'You'll need a bath before I take you to Dr Aimée's.'

'But I've never had my hair done properly, by a hairdresser, before,' Matty wailed, unable to think of anything but the ball. 'and Maison Julie is one of the best. What'll I do if it's ruined before I get to the hotel?'

'For goodness' sake, Matty!' Irritation made Agnes sharper than she intended. 'I'll tell you something for nothing – you're starting to act like one of them prima donnas. Come down to earth, do.' Then she saw Matty's face, and cursed her rough tongue.

It was times like these that she missed Pat. He would have had exactly the right words to encourage his daughter without making her big-headed. And she did need a bit of encouragement. It was a big day for Matty – something that meant an awful lot to her. But it must be frightening, too – the thought of being gawped at, and prayin' you wouldn't trip over your feet at the vital moment. Pat would have understood all that, and known how to calm her down. Agnes swallowed hard. Help me, Pat, she pleaded silently.

'Listen,' she said, 'your Madame Vincente says you'll be fine, and she should know. So, just be yourself, Matty, and you won't go far wrong. That's what your dad would have said.'

'Oh, Mam!' Matty threw herself on her mother, enveloping her in a stifling hug.

Agnes struggled free and cleared her throat. 'Get on with you! I've got things to do.'

In spite of the weather, there were crowds outside Fazakerley Station to watch His Majesty, King George V arrive, to be greeted by Lord Derby. More crowds lined the rain-drenched streets to watch him drive with Lord Derby in an open carriage pulled by two lovely bay horses, with a mounted police escort, on his way to Aintree Race Course to watch the Grand National. His Majesty, wearing a dark grey overcoat, didn't seem to mind the sharply falling rain, as he raised his hard felt hat to acknowledge the cheers.

Lord Derby, who was his host for the day, had invited Sir George and Lady Mellish to be among those privileged to share the Royal Box.

When Aimée had called two days earlier, she had been whisked upstairs to approve her aunt's outfit – a softly tailored suit in her favourite pale grey, with silver fox collar and cuffs. And the matching hat had a dipping brim adorned with a single full-blown pink rose.

'It's lovely, Aunt Fliss. The King will be enchanted. Are you nervous?'

'I try not to dwell on it, and keep telling myself he's only a man beneath all the trappings,' Felicity said with a chuckle. 'But when the time comes I shall probably be as overcome as anyone else. Your uncle has met him before, of course, which must be a help.'

'Well, I'm sure you'll carry the day splendidly.'

'Oh well.' Felicity shrugged, but there was a twinkle in her eyes. 'He can't eat me.'

'Don't be so sure. You'll be looking good enough to eat.' Aimée picked up her bag.

'Darling, before you go, can I have a word about Toby? I know you persuaded George to advance him the money for that old farmhouse at Gateacre he'd set his heart on.' Aimée heard the worry creep into her aunt's voice. 'I do so want him to succeed, but suppose it's all too much for him? Once the place has been decorated and the glasshouses built he'll be moving in, and I can't help worrying how he'll manage on his own when the time comes.'

'Toby won't be on his own, Aunt Fliss. That nice young man, Bill Watts from Cedar Grange is coming to help him.'

'Yes, but that's why I worry, don't you see? What sort of asset can a young man with half his lungs blown away possibly be to Toby, who,' Felicity's breath caught on a painful sob, 'has never had to fend for himself?'

Aimée put a comforting arm round her shoulders.

'Darling, I do understand. But you can't go on cushioning Toby forever. Perhaps this is the moment to let go, to allow him to stand on his own feet. I may be wrong, but I believe that for the first time in his life Toby has found something he can do really well. It's given him a sense of purpose – the chance to prove himself in his own way as much a man as Giles.'

'But he has absolutely no business experience.'

'No, but Bill Watts has. He trained as an accountant, which is just the kind of help Toby will need. All we have to do now is find him a nice housekeeper. I may be able to help there, and do someone else a good turn at the same time, if you don't think I'm already interfering too much.'

'Of course I don't think anything of the kind,' Felicity said, blowing her nose. 'I'm just a broody old hen, fussing over her lame chick. It isn't like me to get things out of proportion, but life has been so hectic recently – with all the fuss that has surrounded George, the Lord Mayor insisting upon a Civic Reception, and so many dinner invitations.'

'Poor you!' scoffed her niece, unimpressed. 'I might feel more sorry for you if I didn't know how you love being at the centre of things.'

Matty couldn't eat a thing before the ball. Madame had ordered her to rest during the afternoon on the chaise longue in her own apartment above the salon, but that was easier said than done, fascinated as she was by all the beautiful things that surrounded her.

The room was very like Madame, small but uncluttered, every item chosen to blend with or complement another: neat velvet chairs with gilded legs; a lamp shaped like a flaming torch, held aloft by a beautiful female form in a kind of milky luminous glass that Madame called Lalique; a picture of the Champs-Elysées in the rain, gay with umbrellas beneath the trees. This last set her mind off on a train of new ideas for designs, and at last she drifted into sleep, to be woken by Madame who said it was time for the hairdresser.

The workroom girls had all promised to be there to see her leave. They had been very good about her changed status, all except Miss Donald, who was, according to Ruth, 'pig-sick'. 'Not tharrit takes much ter make 'er behave like a porker. She'll be gerrin 'er marchin' orders if she's not careful. Madame was quite sharp with 'er yesterday.'

Aimée had previously had a quiet word with Madame Vincente, and as a result, Agnes was invited to the salon to watch her daughter depart in all her elegance. She was a bit overawed by Madame, but that was forgotten the moment she saw Matty.

She had talked a lot about the famous gown. Now, stunned into silence at the sight of this elegant creature who was her daughter, Agnes at last began to comprehend the scope of Matty's burgeoning talent. Her hair had been gathered up and threaded with sea-green ribbons, her dainty silver-strapped shoes made her taller, more graceful than usual. The gown itself was a thing of beauty, and it seemed incredible that it was Matty who had done so much to make it what it was. Agnes's throat dried as she sought for the right words, and then, out of nowhere, they came to her.

'Eh, Matty love, Pat would've been proud of you this night.'

'Oh, Mam!'

Matty stretched out her hands, and for once her mother wasn't shocked to see she had painted pink nails.

'We will 'ave no 'ugs and no tears, if you please, Mathilde,' Madame Vincente ordered imperiously. 'Your make-up will be ruined!' A motor horn sounded outside. 'Come, 'ere is your wrap.' She quickly fastened the shell clasp round Matty's neck and folds of sea-green satin slithered and settled round her.

'I feel a bit like Cinderella,' she gasped, waving to the small crowd that had collected, the workroom girls well to the fore, before stepping into the luxurious limousine ordered by Madame Vincente to take her to the Adelphi.

'Ah, an' yer look like Cinders, an' all,' Ethel shouted back. ' 'Ave a great night, gairl – we'll be wantin' ter 'ear all about it termorrer.'

It was a night that Matty would never forget – an unbelievable magical night. There were more jewels on display than she had ever imagined existed, though Aimée had assured her they were real. And she was too innocent, too naïve, to realize that her lack of adornment gave her a freshness that many a gilded lily present that evening envied. At one point, when passing a long mirror, a beautiful stranger had looked back at her – too tall and too elegant by far to be Matty Shaw from Bloom Street.

Her gown, named 'Seascape' by Madame, was a sensation, the appliqué work pored over with sighs of delight. Lady Mellish was particularly impressed, and Madame Vincente was approached by many beautiful women with pleas that something of a similar nature might be designed specially for them.

In the intervals between such sessions Matty was in constant demand, her first dance partner being Mr Langley, who she was sure had been coaxed by Aimée into setting her at ease. He had always seemed rather aloof, which threw her into a panic. But he couldn't have been nicer, and she saw at once why Aimée liked him so much. Within minutes he had her chuckling with some quite outrageous comments about one of their fellow dancers. She also foxtrotted with Toby's brother, Giles, who spent the whole time flirting outrageously with her, in spite of having recently become engaged. Of Toby himself there was no sign, which was a pity for she would have loved him to see her looking like a real lady.

It was well into the evening when Alec appeared. Matty had been half hoping that he would be too busy to come, with all the work he and Eddie had on, getting their new premises ready for business. Much as she despised herself for the thought, this was her evening, and he could so easily ruin it for her.

However, he looked very smart in his borrowed evening suit,

and although he was in high good humour and she could smell whisky on his breath, he didn't seem to be drunk. Perhaps becoming his own boss had made him more responsible. Something had certainly made him happy. The moment he opened his mouth she knew that he was almost bubbling over with excitement.

'It's all right, I'm quite sober. But listen, can we go somewhere quiet for a minute? There's somethin' I've got to tell you before I bust.'

Curious, though a trifle piqued that he hadn't seemed to notice how nice she looked, Matty said, 'We-ll, I don't know. Madame expects me to be – well, available. It's why I'm here.'

'Oh, stuff Madame!' He took her arm in a tight grip and hurried her, protesting, towards an anteroom. 'This is more important than impressin' a few snobby women. For the first time in my life I've made a real killing.'

'Keep your voice down, Alec!' She was the one who was hurrying now, panic in her voice as she pushed the door shut and she faced him. 'What's this about killing? You've never done someone in?'

'What *are* you goin' on about? Come down off that pretty pink cloud, will you, and listen to what I'm saying. I'm rich, Matty, richer than I ever hoped to be! I've made a pile today!'

Perhaps she'd been wrong and he was drunk. 'Keep your voice down, Alec. People will hear.'

'Sod people!' His voice croaked with excitement, and there was a triumphant glint in his eyes. 'Listen, I did a treble early in the day, and it paid off. I usually take me winnings and scarper, but today I went mad and put the whole bleedin' lot on Troytown in the National at six to one, and the bugger won! What a time to choose, eh?'

Matty understood nothing about betting, or what a treble was, but from the way Alec was going on, it had to be special. 'That's great,' she said. 'How much did you win?'

'You'd better sit down, kiddo,' he said, pushing her into a chair, his eyes almost wild with excitement. 'Guess. Go on, just have a guess.'

'Alec, I don't know. A hundred pounds?' It seeemed rather a lot, but it had to be a biggish amount to get him so excited.

He laughed. 'Not even close, lovely Matty.' He put his face close to hers, so that she could smell the whisky on his breath. 'All in all, it came to just short of three and a half thousand quid.'

'Alec!' Her voice rose in a squeak. 'That's a fortune!'

'Isn't that what I've been tellin' you? It means I've got real money to put into the motor business. An' it'll soon make more, you'll see. I'll be able to take up racing, like I've always wanted to. This is an omen, Matty – you an' me both goin' places at the same time! We'll make a great partnership, with your connections and my – '

'Alec, calm down! Everyone's looking!' She stood up and drew a deep breath to calm herself. 'Alec, I'm delighted for you, really I am, but please, if you're talking about marriage, don't – not here, or anywhere else, for that matter. This is only a beginning for me. I've got a long way to go to get to the top, and I can't do that if I'm wed. It wouldn't be fair to either of us.'

'Mathilde – what is this? Why are you 'iding yourself away in this corner?' Madame Vincente had flung back the door, her sharp eyes raking Alec, taking in the suit that she saw at a glance was of inferior quality. Her voice was like chipped ice. 'You are not 'ere to make cheap secret assignations. We 'ave clients to woo – '

'Don't you call me cheap, you over-painted old trollope!'

Madame's outraged screech carried beyond the anteroom, above the music. Couples nearby stopped dancing and hurried across, with the manager just ahead of them. Matty prayed, Oh dear God, don't let her throw one of her tantrums – not here, not now!

Alec pushed his face close to Madame's, his expression like thunder. 'I don't 'ave to be pushed around by the likes of you – ' he looked up to see the manager approaching – 'or anyone else. I'm leaving. As for you, Matty Shaw, you don't know a good thing when you see it. You could well live to regret turning me down this night!' He swung on his heel and slammed out, shrugging off the manager's restraining hand.

It was all over in minutes. Only those closest to the door had witnessed Matty's embarrassment and distress. But Madame, her own dignify swiftly restored, would not allow her to indulge in tears.

'I forbid it – *absolument*! Men – pah! They are not worth that!'

She snapped her fingers. And as Matty struggled to regain her composure, the little Frenchwoman's face softened. 'You 'ave a great future, my Mathilde, so now you will lift up your pretty head and we will return to the ballroom as though nothing 'as 'appened – eh?'

Nellie Reagan had hoped to get away without telling anyone about the baby for a fair while, but so slight was her figure that by the time she was into her fourth month, the tongues were already beginning to wag.

'The sly little cow. Who'd've thought it – 'avin' it off behind 'er poor crippled 'usband's back?' Dolly McBride leaned against her open door and watched the slight figure hurrying down the road. 'An' 'im norr able ter take 'is belt to 'er.'

'Ar,' Brenda from next door agreed, her head nodding. 'Bur 'is mam will, soon enough, if she 'asn't already.'

Dolly laughed, a cackling sound that caused Nellie to look back momentarily as she turned the corner. 'Nah, the whole street'd 'ave known about it if she'd set about Nellie. In my experience, it's them that's closest as don't see what's under their nose.'

Brenda nudged her. 'Maybe we'd best do the Christian thing, then, an' drop 'er a hint.'

Their voices drifted across to Marge Flynn, who was out giving her mats a good shake. She stopped what she was doing and joined in. 'Well, you should know, Dolly – there's plenty goes on under your Bill's nose, an' e's about as useless as a blind man in a fog with 'is nose bunged up when it comes ter smellin' rats.'

'You want ter wash yer mouth out, Marge Flynn.'

'Aye, an' I could say the same t'you, Brenda Fisher, fer there's norra Christian bone in your body – and, what's more, before you start spreadin' ugly rumours, you want ter get yer facts straight.'

'What's that supposed ter mean?'

'It's not for me to say, but if I were you, I'd keep me gob shut, if yer don't want ter end up with it full of you know what.'

They couldn't get any more out of Marge, but a few days later, Danny's mother, outraged beyond the bounds of caution, so far forgot that she considered herself a cut above them as to let the news slip out.

'Yer mean it wus she as did ... you know what ... to 'im?'

Dolly's eyebrows almost disappeared into the bunch of peroxided frizz not confined by the scarf hiding her curling pins. 'That little mouse! Who'd have thought it?'

Distaste turned the corners of Mrs Reagan's mouth down. 'Well, she must have, egged on, no doubt, by that woman who calls herself a doctor. Our Danny certainly couldn't 'ave managed it on his own. I didn't know where to look when 'e told me.' The well-confined bosom heaved as, already regretting her loose tongue, she sought to exonerate her son. 'I've never trusted Nellie, too meek to be true, an' then carryin' on like that behind my back. Downright deceitful, I call it.'

'The quiet ones are always the worst,' Brenda said, trying to imagine how they'd 'done it'.

'I think it's disgusting!' Dolly added, fanning the flame.

'It's certainly not the way I brought Danny up ter behave.' Mrs Reagan's voice took on a sanctimonious whine. 'Of course, he's never been the same since the war. I sometimes think 'is injuries 'ave scarred more than 'is poor body – an' he get terrible 'eads, sometimes.'

'Ah,' they said in chorus.

Nellie knew what they were all thinking and saying, but she made no attempt to defend herself. Let the miserable cows think what they liked. She was proud of what she'd done. It meant a lot to Danny that she was now carrying his child, and that was all that mattered to her.

But as time went on, it wasn't that easy, and the strain began to tell. Even the wholehearted support of Marge Flynn and Mrs Shaw, and Matty's enthusiastic 'Well, I think it's wonderful news!' failed to lift her spirits. It was all going wrong. Even Danny, angry with his mother, his nerves rubbed raw by his own helplessness in a situation he could do little about, grew short-tempered and reverted to sullen despair.

'Honestly, Aimée,' Agnes banged the pans around in the sink. 'I could ring their necks, those stupid ignorant women, Ma Reagan's most of all. How that poor girl sticks her, I'll never know. She's got more courage and sheer guts than I would've had in the same situation.'

'I'd no idea things were so bad. I'll go round there this evening,'

Aimée said. 'It's Monday, so Mrs Reagan will be out, and we can talk. I believe I may have a solution to their problem.'

She didn't get the most gracious of receptions. Nellie was quietly polite as she removed a pile of clothes from a chair so that Aimée could sit down. And Danny was downright sullen.

'I gather your present situation has become a bit trying,' she said, coming straight to the point.

'I suppose that Mrs Shaw's been blabbing,' Danny muttered.

'She is concerned,' Aimée said. 'And so am I. So how would you like to move from here?'

Nellie's laugh betrayed a touch of hysteria.

'Pigs might fly,' muttered Danny, his shoulders hunched. 'But with my luck, I'd be the one they'd shit on as they passed over.'

'Danny!'

'It's all right.' Aimée laughed. 'A very natural reaction in the circumstances. But don't despair just yet. I have a proposition to put to you. See what you think.' She told them about Cousin Toby, a little about his background, and his current venture. 'What he is going to need is someone to keep house for him – someone like you, Nellie. A young couple would be even better, he's sure to need extra help in the hothouses.' She looked steadily at Danny. 'I'd say that potting up plants could be accomplished quite as well sitting as standing up.'

'Oh, Danny!' Nellie breathed.

His face flushed brick red, and then the blood drained away, leaving him deathly pale so that the scar on the side of his head became livid. If he heard Nellie's gasp of hope he gave no sign, his eyes and all his attention seemed to be fixed on Aimée.

'And does your cousin know you're making all these fine plans for him, Doctor?'

'Good heavens, no.' Aimée kept her tone very down to earth. 'Toby hasn't the least interest in anything as mundane as the nuts and bolts of living. His head is filled with grand vistas, with plants and trees and waterfalls. Trifling details such as meals and housework simply happen at regular intervals.'

'So he wouldn't know about me being a cripple, then?' Danny persisted doggedly.

'Don't!' Nellie pleaded. 'You mustn't call yourself that, Danny.'

'Why not?' Bitterness grated in his voice. 'It's what I am.'

Aimée hesitated, then said with quiet passion, 'Danny, you don't have to lose a limb to be crippled. For the best part of a year, Toby couldn't string two words together without becoming hopelessly tongue-tied and confused and ashamed. For a victim of war, that is almost worse, for with neurasthenia there are no visible signs of injury, so thoughtless people label you a coward. So you see, there is nothing you can tell Toby about being crippled that he hasn't already experienced.'

For a long moment no one spoke. Then Nellie said softly, 'Oh, the poor young man.'

Aimée smiled. 'The mind takes as long to heal as the body, sometimes longer. But Toby has been lucky. His family could afford the right kind of help, and in the healing process he is discovering a talent he never knew he possessed.' She paused to let her words sink in. 'Of course, you may hate plants, or you may not want to move from the city – Toby's place is rather isolated, though the farmhouse is fairly close to the village, and there is a small school within walking distance.'

'It sounds like heaven to me,' Nellie whispered.

To her dismay, tears began to fill Danny's eyes and roll down his cheeks. She ran to him, cradling his head against her breast. 'Don't! It's all right, Danny, we don't have to go if you don't want!'

He sniffed and wiped a hand across his face.

'Don't be daft,' he said thickly, pulling away and looking across at Aimée. 'Of course we'll go, if your cousin's agreeable, that is. It's just – well, I was thinkin' – fancy havin' summat like this droppin' into our laps, an' it's not even bloody Christmas.'

23

ON A SUNNY day in June, Uncle George completed the first stage of Howard and Mellish's new venture, when his first luxury liner, *Lady Felicity*, was launched. Aimée took time off to watch her aunt perform the honours, and Celia, who had been allowed time off school to attend the ceremony, was there, too.

The shipyard was festooned with flags in the company colours of purple and gold that danced in the breeze coming off the river. The same breeze gaily teased the ladies' skirts, and gulls whirled and shrieked overhead as if trying to outdo the applause from the enthusiastic onlookers.

Kevin had sneaked into the shipyard when no one was looking and stood on the fringe of the crowd, his eyes devouring the majestic lines of the huge white ship as it cleaved the water for the first time, sending back curling plumes of spray. His heart was instantly enslaved by this most beautiful creation. He was still standing, rapt in adoration, when he heard his name called.

Aimée knew he ought to have been at work, but from his expression she guessed that, at this moment, work came very low on his list of priorities.

'Why, Kevin,' she said, as the official party made its way slowly back to the waiting limousines. 'I didn't expect to see you here.'

He blushed scarlet and mumbled some garbled explanation that she did not for a moment believe.

Celia had also seen Kevin. She whispered something to her father, and as they came abreast of Aimée and her young companion, Sir George, in genial mood, paused to look him over, this fine strapping fellow.

'So, young man, what d'you think of my new liner, eh?'

Kevin twisted his cap between nervous fingers. 'She's . . . she's beautiful!'

'My daughter tells me you've a fancy to work aboard her.'

His glance flew to Celia. She was all in white, as dainty and pure as an angel, except that her eyes, surveying him from beneath the brim of a straw hat, turned back to frame her face, had more of a laughing devil in them. Well, if she'd hoped to embarrass him, he'd show her. Dad always said you had to take your opportunities when they came.

'I'd give anything fer a chance like that,' he said boldly, looking Sir George squarely in the eye. 'I've got me trade as a butcher, an' I'm not afraid of work.'

'Well, I like a lad who knows what he wants,' Sir George said with a laugh. 'I can't make promises, mind. Not my province, hiring crew. But in a couple of months' time, when she's fitted out, we'll see what can be done, eh?'

'There'll be no livin' with him now.' Agnes, who had been given chapter and verse of the whole incident several times, was by now resigned to the inevitable. 'I just hope Sir George hasn't got our Kevin's hopes up for nothing.'

Aimée hoped so, too. Uncle George wouldn't deliberately lead Kevin on, but he had been in a particularly good mood that day, and his own ambitions for a fleet of liners to rival Cunard, must inevitably take precedence over the dreams of one insignificant boy.

'I'm sure he'll do what he can,' she said.

Grandpa Howard had been predictably scathing about the *Lady Felicity*. 'That's George all over. Everything for show. Commerce ain't good enough for him, though he wouldn't be where he is today without it.'

Aimée was surprised to find herself coming to her uncle's defence. 'I don't think for one moment that he means to abandon that side of the business –'

'You don't, don't you?' he growled. 'And since when has y'r uncle started taking you into his confidence?'

'Don't bully me,' she said, pulling a face at him. 'It won't work.'

'No. You're too much like your grandmother. She never let me get away with anything, either.' He hunched deeper into his chair, and sighed. 'Why don't you give it to me straight? Tell me I'm out of touch, becoming senile – an irascible old fool who's tired of living and too stubborn to die.'

There was enough truth in the final comment to bring a lump to her throat. His white hair was thinning and turning yellow, and hung almost to his shoulders. And the lines in his face were many and deep. Only the unquenchable spirit remained, but for how much longer? Aimée desperately wanted him to go on fighting.

'Now you're just feeling sorry for yourself.'

'True.' His chuckle turned to a wheeze. 'I should practise what I used to preach. "If you can't stand the heat, stay out of the engine room," I used to tell the young whippersnappers. They listened, too, in those days – by God, they did! Now they know it all, and given half a chance, they tell me what to do.'

'Perhaps. But to be fair to Uncle George, he's been at the hub of things long enough to have his finger on the country's pulse. In spite of recession and unemployment, there are still plenty of very rich people, and even I am aware that soon more and more of them will be wanting to travel abroad. And with these big luxury liners able to reach America in four days or less – '

'Yes, yes, I dare say you're right.'

His attention span was getting shorter daily, and already his head was beginning to nod. She kissed the top of his head and left him to doze.

Two days later, in the middle of surgery, Aunt Felicity telephoned in considerable distress. 'Andrew has just called me from Hightowers. Your grandfather has had some kind of heart attack. I've been on to your mother, and Gerald is driving her in with Seth.'

'I'll come as soon as I can,' Aimée said.

She could see the change in him the moment she walked in. Sir Amos was propped up on pillows, looking, at first glance, more dapper than a man close to death might expect to look, in his wine-coloured velvet smoking jacket, with his chin freshly shaved and his hair brushed smooth.

'He gave me his orders, Miss Aimée,' Judd had told her with quavering voice on that last visit. 'Said as he wasn't goin' to meet his Maker lookin' shabby and unkempt, an' when his time came, I was to do all as was necessary to send him off in prime style.' Judd had followed his orders to the last word, and now stood in the shadows, looking suddenly older, awaiting the inevitable.

Also in the shadows near the bed, she saw the stooped figure of the Reverend Aloysious Crank, who had been his confidant and friend for so long, and Grandpa's brother, Great-uncle Albert, an insignificant little man, who had never been more than a fleeting figure in their lives. Uncle George stood behind Aunt Felicity's chair with a hand on her shoulder.

Aimée's parents had already arrived. Minna was sitting on the couch near the window, quietly sobbing, with Seth's comforting arm round her shoulders, and Gerald standing at her side. Aimée went to greet them all quietly, and her mother's sobs intensified as she clung to Aimée's hand. Gently, she released it, and glanced at Andrew Graham, who shook his head.

'Darling!' Her aunt rose from the chair near the bed and came to take her hands. 'He's been asking for you.'

Aimée went to perch on the bed beside the man who had taught her so much about integrity and persevering against all odds, who had shown her love without mawkishness – a man of his time, fully aware that its span was fast running out. The eyes that met hers still held a hint of that stubborn spirit. It was a bravura performance and she must not let him down.

'Going out in style, I see, Grandpa,' she said steadily, touching the velvet before taking his hand in hers. She heard a faint gasp from her mother, but Sir Amos's eyes gleamed with momentary appreciation.

'Never could . . . abide . . . sentiment,' he breathed, the words barely discernible. And as her mouth slipped a little: 'No tears. One . . . watering pot . . . enough.'

For a while after that he didn't speak, though his eyes remained fixed on her. She held his gaze steadily, saw the dawning smile.

'Aimée,' he murmured, and she knew it was not her he was seeing. And then he slipped quietly away.

Sir Amos Howard was buried with full civic honours. St Nicholas' Church was crowded to hear the Reverend Aloysious Crank deliver his panegyric, in which he praised Sir Amos as a true son of Liverpool, the city for which he had done so much throughout his life, not only as one of its most prestigious merchants, but as an alderman, an honour which he never took lightly.

'So moving,' sighed Minna. 'People take so much for granted these days. They forget that men like Papa have helped to improve their lot.'

Aimée glanced at Gerald and saw his lips twitch, remembering their mother's gentle complaints about the way he had so often ridden rough-shod over his family. They had all gone to Aunt Felicity's for a light luncheon after the burial, and when the guests had left, Mr Waring, the family solicitor, stayed on to read the will.

In subtance, there were no great surprises, he said. Aside from a gift of five thousand pounds to Liverpool charities, a few minor bequests, and a thousand pounds and a small cottage in Seaforth to his faithful servant, Judd, Sir Amos had divided his estate equally between his brother, and his two surviving children, with substantial annuities to all his grandchildren until they reached the age of twenty-five in the case of his grandsons, and his grand-daughters, thirty, at which time the principal would become available to them.

'There remains only the disposal of Hightowers.' Mr Waring cleared his throat. 'Sir Amos has left the house and all the contents therein, together with the adjoining land, to his granddaughter Dr Aimée Buchanan – ' he ignored the faint hiss of indrawn breath and continued – 'to be used as a holiday refuge for needy families, together with sufficient monies to be invested for its alteration and upkeep.'

A murmur ran round the room.

'Well!' Minna said, and fell silent at a touch from Seth.

'Good for Grandpa,' Gerald whispered, giving Aimée's hand a squeeze.

Aimée said nothing. She couldn't speak for the constriction in her throat, but her eyes blazed with a brightness that defied all criticism, encompassing as it did a fierce and joyous gratitude and love for the grandpa who, by this gesture, had proved how well he understood her.

'Sir Amos has left you a letter, Aimée,' Mr Waring said quietly, placing it in her hand. 'No doubt you will wish to read it when you are alone.'

With her emotions in turmoil, it didn't immediately register with Aimée that Grandpa Howard's quixotic gesture had not gone down well with everyone. Felicity tried to lighten the atmosphere, but Megan's manner remained distinctly odd.

Aimée, guessing that her sister-in-law was almost certainly

pregnant again, asked Megan gently if she was feeling unwell. 'Funerals can upset some people more than others.'

'There's nothing wrong with me.' Megan was tight-lipped, the Welsh lilt very strong in her voice. 'You had better ask Gerald how he feels. And everyone else. Furious, I shouldn't wonder.'

Still mystified, Aimée swung round to meet Gerald's eyes.

He was clearly embarrassed, as he reached out a hand to her, shaking his head at Megan. 'I have no complaints,' he said quietly. 'Grandpa knew exactly what he was doing, and I entirely approve.'

Uncle George cleared his throat, Giles and Sophie exchanged mildly amused glances and Toby looked uncomfortable, as Felicity assured her, kindly but firmly, that no one had anything to add.

But Megan refused to let the matter rest. 'It's all right for you,' she swept on, ignoring Gerald's 'Stop it, Megan', her voice rising. 'But that house and the land is worth a great deal. It should have been sold and the money divided up. But, oh, no – Aimée was the old man's favourite – '

Felicity stepped across the room and slapped her face – not hard, just enough to silence her. She began to cry and Felicity turned to her embarrassed nephew. 'Gerald, perhaps you would care to take Megan up to my room to lie down for a while. She is obviously overwrought. Meredith will direct you.'

'Yes, of course.' His eyes pleaded with Aimée.

'Don't give it a thought,' she said quietly. 'I do understand.'

When the door had closed, there was a moment's silence. Then Giles said in his droll way, 'Well, that livened things up a bit.'

His mother glared. 'Thank you, Giles, we can do without your levity at this moment.' She went across to Aimée. 'My dear, I am so sorry.'

'For what, Aunt Fliss? I don't blame Megan for feeling aggrieved. I dare say I should feel exactly the same in her place. But I promise you, I was as surprised as anyone.'

'Darling, of course you were,' Minna reassured her with a tearful sigh. 'I'm sure you had no thought of ending up with the lion's share. Your grandfather, God rest him, always went his own way.' A note of aggravation entered the soft voice. 'It would not have occurred to him that his family might care to be consulted on a matter of such delicacy.'

'Mother, the house isn't *for* me! Oh, this is ridiculous!'

'I suggest we all change the subject,' Seth said in his gruff abrupt way. 'No sense getting heated. Sir Amos was entitled to do as he pleased with his own estate, and there is no more to be said.'

'Quite right, Seth.' Uncle George, recovering swiftly from the bombshell, was at his most urbane. 'And you know, Minna, I'd say Amos knew exactly what effect his little bombshell would create, and that, wherever he is, he'll be enjoying a good chuckle at our expense.'

Minna fluttered her lacy handkerchief, and looked about to dissolve into fresh tears, but Felicity, with a tut of exasperation, managed to distract her attention.

A little later Gerald came back alone, rather subdued, to say that Megan was feeling better. 'I'm sorry, Aimée,' he said, drawing her to one side. 'It isn't at all like Megan to – '

'Please, dear boy, say no more,' she said swiftly. 'I do understand that she's a little sensitive at present.'

His eyes widened. 'You know?'

She smiled. 'An educated guess. But I shan't let on if you want to keep it to yourselves for a while.'

He pressed her hand.

From then on, the atmosphere lightened, but Aimée was glad when she could take her leave without arousing comment. When she arrived home she kicked off her shoes and took a bath before settling down to read Grandpa Howard's letter.

The letter was so like the man – uncluttered by sentiment – that the tears she had been unable to shed before came freely. He explained why he had left Hightowers to be used as a holiday home. It was, he said, as much a Victorian monstrosity as himself, but unlike the man, the house could still be put to good use. Considerable alterations would be necessary to make the project viable, and he had already engaged a firm of architects to draw up plans for her approval.

I can think of no one who would make better use of Hightowers than you, my Aimée – you who have so much to give, and are never afraid to fight for what you believe to be right. I'm not sure if I ever spoke of my great pride in you for having the courage to break the mould. You have great gifts, child – be sure that you never compromise them – or worse, become complacent. Always remember, it is not what we achieve in life that matters, only how we achieve it . . .

'Are you all right?' Oliver asked that evening, finding her red-eyed.

'Yes, of course,' she said, too quickly. And then, 'Oh, Oliver, I am going to miss that awkward old cuss. I never realized how much until now.'

And Oliver, without a word, but with a warmth and perception that took her by surprise, drew her down to the couch, where he gathered her into his arms and allowed her to weep out her grief.

Life had taken a new turn for Matty since the night of the ball. Alec had not been near, though she heard more than enough about him from Irene.

'I think you're daft, ditching him,' her sister had said, soon after Alec had walked out of the Adelphi in a rage. 'He's ever so good-lookin', and he knows how to make a girl feel special.'

'And you're a married woman, so don't you go falling for his charm. Your Eddie won't stand for any hanky-panky.'

'As if I would!' But Irene had blushed. 'I just think you should stick with Alec. He still fancies you, you know, and he's got big ideas for the business.'

'He's welcome to them. I've got ambitions of my own, and I don't want Alec or anyone else meddling in them.'

But for all her brave words, she did miss Alec occasionally, though she wouldn't admit it, even to herself. And Madame kept her more than busy enough to subdue any lingering disappointment.

'Now you will see 'ow it really is to be a designer,' Madame Vincente told her, as one after another the clients came, new as well as established ones, each wanting an exclusive Vincente creation, appliquéd in the style of 'Seascape'.

'But how are you going to please them all? I mean, they won't want to meet anyone else wearing the same gown.'

Madame's laugh trilled out. 'Of course not. This is where one must employ skill and imagination. The challenge for a designer, *ma chère Mathilde*, is to create as many variations employing appliqué work as possible. Not everyone will wish to pay for a gown such as "Seascape", but you demonstrate with your very first attempt, how a small amount of decorative work and a great deal of imagination in the use of cut and colour can achieve much.'

'Oh, I've got lots of ideas!' Matty's eyes shone. 'I've been thinking about beadwork, too. In fact, there's something special I'd like to try.' She drew a half-frightened breath. 'Oh, Madame, I've got so much to learn!'

'Indeed, you 'ave. You must work to perfect your cutting skill until you are able to look at material and feel in your fingers what is required. It is a little like sculpting.'

It seemed an impossible task. And all the extra work meant that Matty hardly went near the downstairs workroom. In lots of ways she missed the company and the chatter of the other girls, but inevitably, much as she tried to preserve that spirit of friendship, an awkwardness developed, fostered by Miss Donald whose envy of Matty made her particularly spiteful.

'Here comes Lady Muck,' she'd say when Matty did pop in. Matty tried to ignore the barb, but there was the odd stifled giggle, and Ruth and Ethel looked embarrassed. On one such occasion, Madame Vincente overheard, and called Miss Donald to her room to reprimand her.

'You 'ave served me well,' she said coldly, her tiny figure rigid with anger. 'But do not imagine for one moment that you are indispensable to me.'

The reprimand did nothing to help Matty's cause, for the insults merely became more insidious. After one particularly trying day, she was walking home up Bold Street, feeling despondent, when someone gently, almost diffidently, called her name.

'Why, Miss Helen!' she said, turning to see her former colleague from Mrs Crawley's workroom. 'Oh, what a nice surprise. How are you?'

'Fine, thank you.' She didn't sound fine, even allowing for her rather reserved nature. And as Helen had always been kind to her, Matty suggested that they might go into a nearby café for a cup of tea or coffee.

'There's one near us, run by a terribly chic French lady who is a friend of Madame Vincente. It's called the Café Candide.' Matty grinned suddenly, looking more like the young apprentice Helen had known. 'Do say you'll come.'

Soon they were sitting a cosy corner table of the café which managed to combine cool elegance with a friendly atmosphere. And Candide's husband, a nice young man with sandy hair and a droopy moustache, brought them a whole pot of coffee, a jug of cream and a plate of delicious-looking cakes.

'My, but you've come on,' Helen said, watching the confidence with which Matty handled everything. 'I hear about you occasionally. I always knew you had something more about you than most of the others.'

Matty blushed. 'I don't know about that. Here, have one of these gorgeous cakes. Candide will be offended if we don't eat them. She makes them herself. Besides, if Mam were here, she'd say you look as if you could do with feeding up. Are you still with Mrs Crawley?'

Helen stirred her coffee, not looking up. 'Yes, I'm still there. Most of the girls you knew have gone, but – well, Mrs Crawley kind of depends on me. She hasn't been at all well for some time. In fact, I don't see her carrying on much longer. We've lost a lot of the regular customers, and with so many ready-made clothes now available, business has dropped off badly.'

'I'm sorry.' She'd never liked Mrs Crawley, but from her present happy position she could afford to be generous. 'What would you do, if . . .'

Helen sighed. 'Try for a shop job, I suppose, though it's not easy these days. If I didn't have my mother – '

A thought came to Matty, almost unbidden. She said casually, 'Listen, would you let me have your address? I can't make any promises, but there's just an outside chance I might be able to help. I always reckoned it was your cutting that kept Mrs C in business.'

When they parted, Matty had the address safely tucked in her purse. She reckoned that Miss Donald's days were numbered, and if she went, Miss Helen had as good a chance of succeeding her as anyone else.

She was eager to tell Mam about it, but when she got home, she found Moira with her tongue between her teeth, darning socks, and her mother, tight-lipped and obviously in no mood to listen, black-leading the grate like there was no tomorrow.

'Mam, whatever's got into you? You shouldn't be working so hard at this time of night.'

'It's got to be done. I can't abide a dirty range. There's some people seem to think this house runs itself.'

'Oh, come on, Mam. That's a bit unfair.'

'Yes, well, we can't all be paragons of virtue.'

It was Moira who enlightened her sister. 'It's our Kevin. He's been for an interview fer that job on the boat – '

'Ship.' Kevin, from the doorway, corrected her, his voice truculent. 'It's a ship, our Moira – a luxury liner, and a right beauty she is, too.'

'Oh, Kev, have you got it? The job you wanted?'

'You'd better ask our Mam.'

Matty, seeing him standing there full of sullen pride, suddenly realized how much he'd grown up in the last few months. Also, how much like Phil he was becoming. She'd never really noticed before. Could that be why Mam was so loath to let him go?

'Mam?'

Agnes turned, surprised by the gentleness of Matty's voice.

'Yes, yes, I know what you're going to say. And I suppose he'll have to go. There'll be no livin' with him if I say no.'

'Hey, Mam, that's great!' The change in her son was nothing short of dramatic. He dashed across the room, lifted her off her feet, tin of blacking, brush and all, and swung her round.

'Give over, Kev! Put me down this minute!' She straightened her pinafore, saw the great streaks of black where the brush had been pressed. 'Just look what you've done now, an' I only washed it yesterday.' She tried to sustain her anger, but the look in his eyes was her undoing. 'Think on, it doesn't mean I approve.'

'No, Mam.' Kevin grinned. 'But wait till I come home with all them exotic prezzies.'

'Never mind prezzies. Just come home in one piece; an' I'll be satisfied.'

'So when do you go, Kev?'

'Not for ages yet. They're still fittin' her out. I don't know if Sir George did put in a word. No one said, an' in a way, I'd rather he hadn't. I mean, it'd be nice to think I'd gorrit off me own bat.' He looked sheepishly at his mother. 'The thing is, though, I'll need ter buy quite a bit of stuff, clothes and the like.'

'I wondered when we'd get to that,' Agnes said dryly.

24

JULY HAD BEEN an uncomfortably sticky month, with a series of thunderstorms that never quite managed to clear the air, and the usual outbreaks of measles and chickenpox. And August promised little better.

Aimée longed for Hightowers to be completed, so that it might be possible to get the needy families away for a break. But it would be some weeks before the builders had finished. In one way it was sad to see rooms like the beautiful drawing room disappear, as it was sectioned off to make several smaller rooms. But the plans had been sensibly drawn up, and when it was all decorated, the house would accommodate a great many people. To her joy, the staircase was to remain. She couldn't wait to see the children come whizzing down the bannisters as she and Gerald had done.

And at least the Reagans had settled in wonderfully well with Toby. It was a good to see them so happy.

'I have to keep pinching meself,' Nellie said. 'And our Mary's a different child. She trots round after Mr Toby, chattering in a way she's never done before. And he's that patient with her. I think he really enjoys her company.'

'Mary's just the kind of medicine he needs,' Aimée said with a smile. 'In fact, I'd go so far as to say that you'll all do him a power of good.'

Nellie blushed. 'It works both ways. I can't tell you what it means to us, being here, Dr Aimée. It's such a lovely old house – and there's so much room, it was like a dream at first. I still 'ave to pinch meself sometimes. And Mr Toby's got Danny doin' things he wouldn't 'ave dreamed of a few months back.'

'I'm glad it's all turned out so well. I know Toby appreciates all you do for him, including the delicious meals he's been telling me about.'

'It's a pleasure to cook for him. He's such a gentleman.'

'Has your mother-in-law accepted the move, yet?'

'We've not had so much as a word. Mind you, I don't care if we never hear, but that wouldn't be fair to Danny. She is his mother when all's said and done. I dare say she'll come round in 'er own good time.' A sudden grin lit up her face. 'Driven by curiosity, if nothing else. She never can keep her nose out of other people's business for long.'

Aimée laughed. 'And no problems with the pregnancy?'

Nellie shook her head. 'I've never felt so well.'

The weeks were flying past for Matty. There was a different atmosphere at work since the day Miss Donald had finally been sent packing. And what a day that had been.

'You should have heard them, Mam,' she had said, coming home in triumph. 'In fact, I'm surprised you didn't. At times it seemed like the whole of Liverpool must have heard them. Madame shrieking like a banshee, and Miss Donald givin' back as good as she got. She'll not be getting any references, that's for sure.'

'Well, there's no call for you to gloat,' Agnes had said severely. 'It's no joke for a woman of her age, being thrown out of work.'

Matty sobered. 'I'm sorry, Mam. I didn't mean – but she's been asking for it for ages. Anyway, there's nothing to stop her working for herself like I did.'

Agnes shook her head. 'It all sounds so easy when you're young, Matty. Still, what's done can't be mended.'

'Anyhow, the good thing is, I've put in a word for Miss Helen. I'm sure she and Madame would get on.' She began to giggle. 'I've just had a thought. If she does get the job, perhaps they could do a straight swop. I reckon Mrs Crawley and Miss Donald were made for one another.'

'You should have more respect for your elders, my girl,' Agnes reproved her, but there was a smile lurking in her eyes. 'And when you've got a bit of time to spare from all these grand plans, you might give a thought to your sister.'

'Irene? Why, what's wrong with her?'

Agnes shook her head. 'There's nothing wrong. It's just – well, you've been that full of yourself lately that you haven't been near.'

She looked closely at Matty. 'Or is it maybe that you don't want to risk bumping into that Alec?'

'I can't say I look forward to meeting him, but I really have been too busy.' Matty gave her mam a peck on the cheek. 'I'll go over to Walton this evening, straight from work.'

Irene was a bit cool when Matty arrived. 'It's good of you to make the time, I'm sure. I thought maybe you'd got too grand for the likes of us.'

'As if I would.' She wondered if she'd come at a bad time. Irene was done up to the nines, with make-up and everything. 'I won't stay if you're going out.'

'No,' Irene said, rather too quickly. 'Eddie may be bringing people back later.'

'I see. Well, I can't stay long, in any case. Can I have a peep at my goddaughter?'

Matty gazed down at Patsy, who was all pink and soft in sleep. She felt a pang of envy. 'She's beautiful!'

'She's quiet at present, which is a relief,' Irene said sharply, closing the door. 'All her baby talk, there's no end to it some days. It wears you out. You won't have seen the flat since we finished decorating. You might as well look round while you're here.'

It had been enlarged to include the next-door property and was now surprisingly spacious, and modernized to include a bathroom. Eddie had decorated it throughout, and she noticed that a lot of the furniture was new – on tick, if she knew her brother-in-law.

'I don't know about me being grand. You're getting pretty grand yourself.'

'Oh well, Eddie says we have to live up to our new image. He sometimes brings prospective buyers upstairs to discuss terms, and we entertain a lot more, too.'

Matty hid a smile, listening to Irene's carefully enunciated vowels. And because the question lurked at the back of her mind, 'And Alec? Where does he live?'

Irene blushed. 'As a matter of fact, he's livin' here with us at the moment. Just until he finds something he likes. He's gone out just now, looking at possible properties.'

'Properties, is it?' Matty's eyebrows rose. 'The business *must* be doing well.'

'There's lots more people wanting cars these days,' she said with a toss of her head. 'Besides, Alec's got that money he won on the National. And he's been on a really good winning streak ever since. They say much makes more, and it seems he can't go wrong at present.' She bit her lip. 'Are you two still not speaking?'

'I don't think we've got anything more to say. Maybe we just outgrew one another.'

'Well, I've said it before – I think you're daft. Especially now he's got pots of money.'

'Money isn't everything,' Matty said, and thought how pious she sounded.

It was well into evening when she finally left, and there weren't many people about as she walked to the tram, the setting sun warm on her back. She smiled to herself, remembering how Irene had enjoyed showing off.

'Hey, Matty! Hang about.'

Oh drat! Her heart gave a little jerk of apprehension as the luxurious open-topped motor drew alongside and Alec leaned across to the passenger side. She affected not to notice him and walked on, her heels clicking on the pavement.

She heard the car door slam, running footsteps. He took her arm and swung her round.

'Let me go, Alec.'

She attempted to free her arm, but he only gripped it tighter.

'Don't be bloody silly. What happened's past and gone. Can't we be friends?'

That sounded like the old teasing, coaxing Alec, and for a moment she almost weakened. But she had been down that road before. He'd used up his chances.

'You're lookin' good, Matty. That green frock really suits you. Makes you look all cool an' fragrant. Silk stockin's, too. You always did have great legs.'

'Don't be cheeky.' But she blushed. The frock in question was fashioned in soft crepe that fell to mid-calf in deep scallops. And she was wearing a neat hat the same shade of green. She knew it suited her, but that wasn't the same as having someone else tell you. And Alec always did have a way with words when he wanted to.

'Listen, it's not far to Stanley Park.' His voice softened

persuasively. 'We could have a bit of a stroll and exchange news – an' I'll run you home in the new motor.'

'Oh, I don't know.' She was tempted. 'It's ever so big, and very smart.' Like Alec himself, she thought. He was wearing a smart tweed suit and driving cap, and carried a pair of leather gauntlet gloves. On his little finger he wore a heavy gold ring with a small diamond set in it.

'It's an American motor – a Packard,' Alec said smugly. 'I bought it off a bloke who wanted to exchange for something smaller. Everything's going my way now. I can't go wrong on the gee-gees. So why don't we take that walk an' I'll tell you about it?'

It was a lovely evening, too nice to be indoors, and if she went home, she'd probably end up working. She glanced at the little watch that hung round her neck on a silver chain – a present from Madame Vincente.

'Ten minutes, then,' she said pertly. 'And no nonsense.'

He grinned. 'You drive a hard bargain.'

The park was fairly quiet. The children had all gone home and the older folk were moving towards the gates. Soon, only the courting couples would be left. Still, she had said only ten minutes.

Alec was his old self, bragging about his winnings, and all the plans he was making. In fact, he was getting a bit over-excited about it. Matty couldn't help noticing that Irene's name cropped up quite often, though Eddie was hardly mentioned. 'A great little girl, your Irene – got the right ideas about how to enjoy life.'

'She's also got a husband.'

'What? Oh, Eddie. Yeah – good old Eddie!' He laughed.

Matty suddenly realized that they had left the main path, and there was no one in sight. 'It's time we went back,' she said. 'I promised Mam I wouldn't be late.'

'Just a few more minutes, eh?'

'I'd rather go now.'

Before she could protest further, he had her up against a thick tree trunk, the bark pressed into her back, and there was a harsh note in his voice. 'An' I said a few more minutes.'

'Alec! Stop playing the fool. I'll yell me head off if you don't let go.'

He laughed. 'Go ahead. No one takes much notice of a bit of scuffling behind the bushes.' One hand began to grope for the hem of her skirt, the other pinned her against the tree. 'It's time you an' me got a few things sorted. You're a tease, Matty Shaw. You lead a fella on, and then play hard to get.'

'I don't! I've never – '

'Come off it! How often have you let me get a hand up yer skirt as far as yer stockin' tops, and then slapped me down? Well, from now on, no one's going to push Alec Gresham around. I reckon you owe me, an' I'm in the mood to collect.' His breathing was becoming ragged, and his hand was already pushing her skirt up. 'So, what are we wearin' tonight, eh? Garters or suspenders? Your Irene favours suspenders.'

Horrified by what was happening, she only dimly registered his comments about Irene as she fought to push him away.

'Stop it! Take your hands off me! I should never have trusted you!'

'It's a bit late ter say that now, Matty girl. Thought you were a bit too high an' mighty for the likes of me, didn't yer? Someone to be kept in his place – you an' yer fancy Mr Toby, and the like. Well, I'll tell yer somethin', darlin' – them highfalutin types won't give yer half such a good time as I will.' Alec's hand was pushing right up her leg now. She screamed, and he slapped her, back-handed, across her face. His fingers dug in hard round her throat and she almost choked. 'Scream again,' he muttered, his mouth wet against hers, 'an' I'll really hurt you.'

He lifted her almost bodily from the tree, and pushed her to the ground, knocking the breath out of her, his full weight landing on top of her, his face close to hers. 'If yer hadn't played hard ter get, you could have had it all nice and romantic.'

Mattie tried desperately to think as she gasped for air, her one free hand uselessly hitting at him. He was pulling at her underclothes, doing unspeakable things that pierced her like a knife, fumbling with his own clothes.

Her hat was half covering her face by now, and in a final act of desperation she reached up and pulled out the hatpin. It was about four inches long and she sank it into his backside, desperation giving her strength.

Alec screamed and flung himself backwards. It was all she needed. She scrambled to her feet, pushing down her skirt, and ran.

Aimée was spending a pleasant evening alone, catching up on some reading – the first chance she'd had in a long time, though it was always possible that Oliver might drop in. When, just short of ten o'clock, the front doorbell rang, she laid her book aside. If it was Oliver, he was past his usual time.

She did not at first recognize Matty in the distraught creature with the bruised face and clothes in disarray, half sagging against the wall. Only when she muttered, 'Aimée?' did she realize who it was.

'Matty! My dear girl, whatever – '

'I hope you don't mind – only I couldn't go home to Mam like this.'

Aimée wouldn't let her talk, not then. She took Matty upstairs to the spare bedroom where, as gently as possible, she attempted to gauge the extent of her injuries. Matty's cheekbone had been cut and would need a stitch, as well as a degree of random scratches, and bruises. More worrying, there was some evidence of interference, though Matty seemed confused about whether Alec had actually raped her.

'I'll try not to hurt you,' she said, 'but it really is important that we should know as soon as possible.'

But after a few uncomfortable moments, Aimée was able to assure the distraught girl that all was well, and a long soak in a hot bath went some way to soothing the worst of Matty's aches and pains.

'It was my own stupid fault,' she insisted when she was at last tucked up in bed in Aimée's pretty blue spare bedroom, wearing a silk nightdress that would have made Mam blink, and sipping hot milk laced well with brandy. 'I need my head looking at for believing a word Alec said! Only it was an awkward situation with him and Eddie – and I thought this time he really did seem quite genuine about wanting us to be friends.' She made a sound halfway between a hiccup and a sob. 'I'm a rotten judge of character.'

'No, you aren't. There's nothing wrong in looking for the best in people. You were just unlucky.' Aimée got up off the bed. 'I'd better slip round to tell your mother you're staying with me for tonight.'

'She'll want to know why.'

'Oh, I'll think of something – enough to satisfy her.'

But Agnes wasn't that easy to fob off. 'There was trouble, wasn't there? I know she wasn't keen to go, with that Alec around. And I made her feel guilty for not keeping in touch with Irene.' She braced her hands against the edge of the table, and gave Aimée one of her straight looks. 'You'd better tell me what happened.'

So Aimée told her, in the simplest terms and with the instant reassurance that her daughter had not been raped.

'Oh, my poor Matty!'

'She's all right. A bit shaken, but the bruises will soon heal, and the cut on her cheek should leave only the faintest scar. In fact, she was almost asleep when I left.'

'If I hadn't talked her into going to see Irene – '

'Agnes, it's no one's fault.'

'Except that worthless article Alec Gresham. If I could just lay my hands on him for five minutes!'

'He isn't worth it.'

She looked stubborn. 'I'd still like to go over to Walton first thing tomorrow morning – if you can spare me for an hour. There are things that have to be said. If nothing else, Eddie needs to know what kind of creature he has working with him.'

'Well, it's up to you,' Aimée said.

When she got home, she checked to see that Matty was sleeping, and then telephoned Oliver. Somehow, just hearing his voice was immensely comforting.

'Someone is going to have to teach that fellow a sharp lesson,' he said.

'I think Matty already did.' Aimée told him about the hatpin and heard him chuckle. 'It would be extremely unethical of me to hope that blood poisoning sets in. Even a local infection, enough to make sitting down painful for a few days, would suffice.'

Agnes arrived in Walton the following morning to face an even greater shock. The showroom wasn't open, nor was the garage with its little shop that Eddie had built in to it. She banged on the door to the flat, and eventually Eddie came down to open it.

'Great heavens, lad, whatever's wrong with you?' she exclaimed, for he was unshaven, dishevelled and almost incoherent with rage.

'I'll tell you what's happened. That good-time-seeking little cow of a daughter of yours has gone an' run off with Alec Gresham.'

'Irene, gone? Dear God, is there no end to that young man's shamelessness?' Agnes pushed him inside and shut the door, her eyes widening in fear. 'Patsy? What's happened to Patsy?'

Eddie laughed harshly. 'You don't think they'd saddle themselves with a kid? Doreen from next door's upstairs seeing to her.' He sat down abruptly on the stairs, and sank his head in his hands. 'How could Rene do this to me, after I've given her everything she wanted? Doreen says the two of them've been carrying on behind my back for weeks, an' me too full of plans to see it! I've put everything into this place, borrowed money – '

'Pull yourself together, lad,' Agnes said. 'Do you know where they've gone?'

'Norra clue. Just a note, if you can call it that, sayin' Alec had to leave suddenly an' she couldn't bear ter be parted from him.' He began to sob noisily. She patted his shoulder awkwardly.

'Eh, pull yourself together, lad. Tears never solved anything.' Sorry as she felt for him, she was more concerned with the immediate future of her grandchild. 'I'd better take Patsy home with me until you get yourself sorted out. Then we can talk.'

The day after Irene left, Agnes also received a letter from her. It said little more than the one she'd left Eddie – that she couldn't bear to be parted from Alec, that she did love Patsy, but it wasn't practical to take her, and she was sure Mam would look after her, and that Alec meant everything to her. The postmark was smudged, so they were no nearer knowing where the two had gone.

Irene's decampment was the talk of the street for a few days. Dolly McBride and her cohorts had a field day. 'She were always a flighty one, your Irene, always an eye fer the fellers.'

'It takes one to know one,' Agnes snapped. But at least it kept the limelight off Matty.

She had suffered no long-term ill effects, except that she was more subdued than usual. Irene's behaviour had shocked, but not surprised her, when she remembered how Alec had hinted that there was something between them. But she couldn't forgive her sister for abandoning Patsy.

Madame was wonderfully kind to her in the weeks that

followed, and fortunately the beautiful new autumn materials began to arrive – fine wools in rich autumn tints and wonderfully soft tweeds for day wear. And for evenings, jewel-bright silk and crepe, and slinky satins, imported from Paris, and pale drifts of chiffon and net. Matty couldn't wait to get her hands on them.

'I'm going to concentrate on my work from now on,' she told her mother, and there was a hardness in her voice that Agnes had never heard before.

Matty had persuaded Helen to apply for Miss Donald's job, and Madame seemed impressed with her qualifications and her quiet, ladylike personality. The advance orders for the new autumn lines were already coming in steadily, and she soon discovered that she could safely leave the less exclusive customers to Helen, and concentrate her energies on those who commanded special attention.

Aimée persuaded Matty to visit Crag Vale with her on the following Sunday afternoon. 'I know Gerald is keen to show you some of his latest patterns for furnishing fabrics. He has decided to concentrate on that area of the business.'

Gerald, primed by Aimée, was kindness itself. He had arrived at Fernlea alone, Megan having pleaded tiredness.

'Such a pity,' Minna exclaimed, when Gerald had taken Matty off to the mill. 'She is usually so fit and energetic. I do hope this baby isn't going to take too much out of her.'

'Rubbish,' muttered Frank, who had dropped by for tea, as he often did. 'Megan's as fit as a flea. You know why she isn't here, of course.'

Aimée did know. And she felt the time had come to do something about it. 'Mother, would you mind if I disappeared, too, for a short while? There are some books I want to borrow from Frank.'

Her father looked up from his paper, and Frank gave her one of his looks. Then he tamped down his pipe, gave it a few experimental draws, and obligingly heaved himself out of his comfortable chair.

'You do as you please, dear,' Minna's thoughts were already dwelling blissfully on the prospect of putting her feet up and closing her eyes for half an hour or so. 'Don't be too long, though. We shall be having tea in about an hour.'

'So what are these books you're so desperate to borrow?' Frank enquired as the front door closed behind them.

Aimée put her face up to the sun as the breeze lifted her hair. 'Blissful country air,' she sighed and threw him a roguish look. 'Do you mind being dragged away from your Sunday snooze?'

'Not if it means I get you to myself for a while. But you're up to something.'

'I'm going to see Megan. This situation can't go on – tiptoeing round one another – it's childish and ridiculous, and it's time something was done about it.'

'Fine. As long as you don't expect me to referee the bout,' he said laconically. 'Just tread a mite carefully.'

'Honestly, Frank! Give me credit for a little common sense.'

He chuckled. 'Your car or mine?'

'We'll take yours. It'll look better if Mother happens to look out. As a matter of fact, I did want a word,' she said as they drove up the road towards Gerald's house. 'How would you like to squire me to a dinner being given by the Medical Faculty at the university next month? Colonel Grant is coming to open a new surgical unit, and the local association is keen to make the most of it, in view of his exemplary war service and the OBE he received last year, by giving this dinner in his honour.'

Frank threw her a look. 'Is this *the* Colonel Grant? The one you served with?'

'Mmm.' Aimée bit her lip. 'Part of me is petrified at the thought of meeting him again, but I would very much like to hear him speak. He is a fine doctor. But I don't fancy going alone, and I thought it might be a treat for you, too.'

He grunted, but she thought he looked pleased. 'I haven't had a decent evening out for a long time.'

'You could stay with me overnight.'

'Then I'd be happy to come.' The car drew to a halt outside Gerald's house. 'It's over to you,' he said. 'I'll wait here.'

Megan looked taken aback when she opened the door and saw Aimée. She had an apron over a floral dress, and wore gardening gloves. Her figure was just beginning to thicken, and she looked the picture of health.

'I haven't got very long, but it's time we talked,' Aimée said without preamble.

After a moment's hesitation, Megan opened the door wider and allowed her to pass.

Megan's pretty drawing room overlooked a circular lawn surrounded by herbaceous beds, and the pram in the middle of the lawn rocked slightly as Jonathan Buchanan exercised his limbs. The two strong-willed young women faced one another.

'You'd better sit down,' Megan said, less than graciously.

'Thank you.' Aimée chose an upright chair. 'Megan, do you love Gerald?'

She was again taken by surprise. 'Of course I do. What a stupid question.'

'It's not stupid at all. Because the way you're carrying on you could well lose his love.' Her sister-in-law's face paled. 'Jealousy is a very destructive emotion. And there is no reason for it in your case. Gerald and I are twins, and we have always been very close. Nothing can change that. The more you seek to come between us, the more likely it is that you'll be the loser – and though you may find it hard to believe, that is the last thing I want.'

Megan sat down abruptly, pulled off her gloves and stared down at her hands. 'At home,' she began in a toneless voice, 'I was a middle child. There was only about eighteen months between my two elder brothers, then a five-year gap, then me. And then there was another big gap before my twin sisters.' She looked up bleakly. 'I wonder if you know what that was like? I never seemed to fit in anywhere, but because I was shy and wanted to be liked, I spent my whole childhood trying to please them all. Perhaps I tried too hard.'

'You must have been very unhappy,' Aimée said softly. 'And your parents?'

'They were – are – busy people. I suppose I learned to cover up so well, they never noticed. When I met Gerald, and we fell in love, it was the first time I felt I really had someone of my very own to love.' There were tears in her eyes. 'I knew about you, of course, but this time I thought things would be different. Only when I saw the two of you together, I knew I'd lost out again.'

'Oh, Megan!' Aimée went across to crouch down in front of her, taking hold of her hands. 'It isn't like that, truly it isn't! All I want is for you both to be happy. Gerald really loves you. But although he has said nothing to me or anyone, I know he is hurt and bewildered by your antagonism towards me, and everything connected with me.' She gave the hands a final squeeze, and stood up. 'And there is no need for it. Can't we be friends?'

Megan sniffed. '*Duw*, you must think me a right stupid woman, carryin' on like I have been.'

'Not stupid, no. Insecurity is destructive. Don't give a chance to take hold.' Aimée smiled and stood up. 'And now I'd better go. Why don't you forget the gardening, and wheel young Jonathan up to Fernlea for tea? Mother thinks I've been to Frank's, so we won't say anything about this meeting.'

Aimée drove home by way of Gateacre, so that Matty could see Toby's smallholding, and have a chat to Nellie. On the way, it became obvious that the day so far had done her good. She talked more freely than she had done for days, about her visit to the mill and how impressed she was with the progress Gerald had made in his bid to add a new strand to the business.

But all that was as nothing compared to her first impressions of Toby's farmhouse. It was looking at its best in the mellow sunlight of early evening, and she fell in love with it at first sight.

Toby greeted them with a smile of pure pleasure. Matty, who had not seen him since New Year, was amazed at the change in him. Gone was the pallor, the hesitancy of the rather lost young man he had been. Now there was a sense of purpose about him. The sun had turned his skin to a healthy golden brown, and bleached his hair almost white, but his smile had the same gentle warmth as he took her hand.

'Matty, w-what a pleasant surprise.' As Aimée went in search of Nellie, his glance dwelt briefly on the scar, and for a moment he looked almost angry. 'I w-was sorry to hear about your distressing experience.' Adding, as surprise flared in her eyes, 'Mother told me. I hope you don't m-mind?'

'No, of course not. She's been very kind to me.'

'Perhaps,' he suggested diffidently, 'it's all for the best. Gresham w-was never good enough for you,' he added boldly, and blushed.

'I'd already decided that, only I let him talk me round. But not any more. No man's ever going to hurt me like that again.'

There was a hardness in her voice that shocked Toby. It was so foreign to the Matty he knew. And he cursed the man who had made her like that. Gently, he put his hands on her shoulders.

'Don't let one bad experience make you bitter, M-Matty. There are good men in the world, too. And one day you'll m-meet one who will love and cherish you as you deserve.'

'Maybe, but I'm not holding my breath. I've made up my mind, from now on I'm concentrating on my career.' She saw the hurt in his face. 'Oh, I know you mean well – an' if all men were like you, there'd be no problem. Only, like Mam says, God broke the mould after he made you.' On impulse, she reached up on tiptoe and kissed his cheek, and saw the faint colour come up under his tanned skin. 'And now I've embarrassed you.'

'No. No, you haven't.'

There was an odd little moment of silence. Then Matty said with a sigh of pure envy, 'This is a lovely house.'

He smiled courteously. 'Nellie keeps it beautifully. W-would you like a conducted tour?'

There was a gentle tug on his hand, and he smiled down at Mary. 'Me, too?'

'Yes, of course. You, too,' he said.

Matty's admiration increased as they went from room to room. The walls were thick, the rooms all different, but beautifully proportioned. There were wonderfully craggy oak beams everywhere, and lots of odd nooks and crannies crammed with bowls of flowers, and the floors were flagged and slightly uneven, so that everwhere seemed cool and fragrant, a haven from the warmth outside.

Toby's office took up the whole of one end of the building. The walls were lined with plans and small paintings of flowers and plants, all done with exquisite delicacy.

'Did you paint these?' Matty asked in awe.

'Small things, but mine own,' he admitted. 'I've been painting flowers since I was quite small. It was my one accomplishment.'

'But they are beautiful,' she said. 'You could make a fortune selling them, I shouldn't wonder.'

He seemed pleased. 'Perhaps, but I like them where they are.'

'I'm not surprised you're happy here,' she sighed. 'You'd have to be hard to please if you weren't. An' all that out there – ' She gazed through the window towards the glasshouses and the rich earth, with plants in neat rows. 'You must have worked ever so hard to get it all going in such a short time,' she said.

'I've had a lot of help from Bill. And Danny's worth his weight in gold.' He nodded towards one the glasshouses. 'Come and see.'

Danny had changed out of all recognition. He looked up from the tray on his lap which held a number of small seedlings, and grinned at her. 'Come to give us a hand, have you, Matty?'

She laughed, partly from the pure pleasure of seeing him so happy. 'Oh, I wouldn't know where to begin.'

'You must be ever so proud,' she said as the time came to leave.

'W-well, just a little bit.' Toby grinned. 'I think the b-best part was seeing my father's face when he came to inspect the place last w-week.'

'Oh, he was certainly impressed,' Aimée assured him. 'I heard him at a party the other evening, telling someone that his younger son was on his way to becoming a rising star in the horticultural world.'

25

IT WAS ROGER Whittan from the hospital who had first mentioned the dinner to Aimée.

'Colonel Grant's quite a character by all accounts. His war record is legion, of course, and somehow the title stuck. I believe he's recently made some quite radical advances in colonic surgery. All the teaching hospitals have been after him, but not surprisingly he's decided on Edinburgh. So we had best make the most of him while we have him. I mean to attend his lecture, too, if work permits.'

Aimée remembered the larger-than-life man with hands as nimble as Matty's. She was reluctant to admit that she knew him, and yet she was tempted – and not only by the dinner. She would dearly like to attend the lecture.

'You wouldn't be the only woman at the dinner, if that's what's worrying you,' Roger said, noticing her hesitation. 'There are a couple of interns from our hospital going, and maybe the odd one or two from elsewhere.'

That was when she had thought about Frank, and having been assured that he would be welcome, her mind was made up.

When they arrived, the reception was crowded with doctors of all shapes, sizes and ages, ranging from fresh-faced interns to grey-haired general practitioners and doyens of the various hospitals, and at first Aimée couldn't see a soul she knew.

She had dressed with care, only too aware that she would be subjected to the scrutiny of her peers. Her simple long black dress could surely not be faulted, and a handsomely braided bolero jacket made for her by Matty for the occasion, covered her bare arms. Her only concessions to jewellery were the pretty jewelled fob watch on its long gold chain, given to her by her parents on her twenty-first birthday, and a pair of long gold earrings.

'Very elegant,' Frank said, when she presented herself for inspection, and found him struggling with his tie. 'Which is more than can be said for me. Ridiculous nonsense, all this dressing up like a dog's dinner.'

'You're worse than Pa. Here, let me,' Aimée said, taking the tie from him and tying it swiftly and neatly.

'I don't smell of mothballs, do I? Mrs Meadows said she'd had the suit out on the line to air.'

'You're fine,' Aimée laughed.

She was glad of Frank's support, but he quickly discovered a friend he hadn't seen for years, and was soon engrossed in reminiscence. Andrew Graham saw her and came across to have a few words, before he too was called away.

'Aimée,' Roger Whittan was at her side, and with him a cheery-looking young woman with a mop of sandy hair. 'How charming you look. May I introduce Elsie Sprague. She's one of our interns on Surgical, and she's Scottish. Elsie, this is Aimée Buchanan.'

'For intern, read humble dogsbody. But, then, you'll remember, no doubt.' She grinned. 'Pleased to meet you. I've heard all about you.'

'Oh dear.' Aimée laughed ruefully. 'Nothing too terrible, I hope.' As they shook hands, she took an immediate liking to the slight young woman whose emerald green dress matched her eyes. 'Thank heaven for a friendly face.'

'I know what you mean. Roger bullied me into coming, but I was half terrified at the thought of it. And then I thought, ach, why worry? They can't eat me!' Her laugh spilled out, causing several heads to tun.

'Would you like a sherry, ladies?' Roger asked. 'There should be waiters coming round, but I'll see if I can find one.'

'He's a nice wee man, isn't he? He never makes you feel you should be home, washing the dishes – if you know what I mean.'

'Yes, I do.' Aimée laughed. And looked up to see Dr Dalywell watching her.

She hadn't seen or spoken to him since the incident of the letter. Once Oliver had assured her that the matter had been settled – she suspected, grudgingly – it had been dismissed from her mind. Now, uncomfortably aware of his hostility, she hoped he would not be seated anywhere near her.

'Sherry, Aimée?' Roger was at her side again, glass in hand.
'Thanks.'

'Were you watching Dalywell? Pompous old bore.'

'He doesn't like me very much.' She sipped her sherry. 'Or, rather, he doesn't like what he calls my feminist approach to medicine, whatever that is.'

'Oh, I shouldn't worry,' Elsie said. 'He's well known for his dislike of women doctors – and for having a big opinion of himself. They can't stand him on Medical. He's always dropping in, offering unwanted advice on how to to treat his admissions.'

Aimée didn't tell them about her own clashes with Dalywell, but she could hardly fail to be aware that the group surrounding him turned more than once to look at her.

'That must be Colonel Grant, over near the door with the bigwigs,' Roger said, and Aimée bit back 'Yes, it is' just in time.

The shock of red hair was unmistakable, and from a distance, seemingly untinged by grey. In evening clothes, he looked younger, more relaxed and rather more flamboyant than she remembered. He looked up and their eyes met. She saw his brow crease in a frown, as though he was trying to remember where he had seen her before. But almost at once he was surrounded, and his view was blocked, so that she was spared the embarrassment of being recognized. Then they were being called to take their places.

Frank was in mellow mood. 'Haven't enjoyed myself so much in years,' he said. 'Excellent meal. I should do this sort of thing more often, but it's fatally easy to become a stick in the mud in a country practice. You were right to strike out on your own, lass, even if it wasn't in the direction I'd have chosen for you.'

'I know someone who wouldn't agree with you,' Aimée said, glancing further down the table to where Dr Dalywell, now rather red in the face and, she suspected, a little the worse for drink, was holding forth.

'What?' Frank followed her look. 'Oh, yes.' He cleared his throat and pushed his plate away. 'I hoped it wouldn't have come to your ears.'

'Why? Has he been slandering me?'

He looked even more uncomfortable. 'Oh, nothing more than you'd expect after that little run-in you had with him. I heard him going on soon after we arrived, but I didn't want to spoil your evening by telling you about it. A case of too much whisky loosening his tongue. No discretion, some people.'

Before she could discover more, the toastmaster was banging his gavel, the loyal toast was drunk, and then he announced, 'Gentlemen, you may smoke.'

From further down the table, Elsie raised an eyebrow at her. For answer, Aimée opened her evening bag and took out her Turkish cigarettes, the ebony holder and matching lighter. Impervious to stares ranging from interest to downright disapproval, she lit up, inhaled and blew a slow curl of smoke.

After a tedious and heavy-handed introduction, Colonel Grant got to his feet and, having thanked the present company for inviting him to Liverpool, he proceeded to electrify his audience with a speech that was both witty and hard-hitting. There had been much talk, he said, of his recent paper on the treatment of colonic surgery. 'In deference to the excellent meal we have just consumed, I don't propose to go into detail at this moment.' There was a sustained burst of laughter. 'Those of you who attend the lecture tomorrow will be given chapter and verse. All I will say is that a lot of nonsense is talked about fancy clinics, wonder treatments and gimcrack techniques. My most valuable lessons were learned under fire, borne of sheer necessity, in the worst conditions known to man. And, if I am not mistaken, there is a fine young doctor here this evening who would bear witness to that.'

Aimée swallowed the wrong way and almost choked, but her distress went unnoticed in the general stir and scraping back of chairs as heads turned, seeking the identity of the said doctor. She kicked Frank under the table. 'Not a word,' she mouthed.

'However, I'll not embarrass the person concerned,' the colonel concluded mischievously, and passed on to other matters.

'He's rather gorgeous, isn't he?' Elsie whispered, as Colonel Grant went ahead of them into the other room. 'I wonder if he's married.'

'I have no idea,' Aimée said, keeping well away from the group surrounding him. 'Listen, Elsie, I must find Frank. It's important.'

'Dr Buchanan – ' The bark of authority was so familiar that she almost stood to attention and rapped out 'Yes, sir?' as she turned to meet those acutely penetrating eyes. 'So I wasn't mistaken.' Her hand was swallowed up in his firm grasp.

'No, Colonel, you weren't mistaken.' It was a banal reply, but she could think of no other.

'Well, this is an unexpected pleasure. It's a long time. I almost didn't recognize you. You look quite – different.' His eyes dwelt on her appreciatively. 'Tell me, now, what are you doing these days?' But his attention was already being claimed. 'Och, we can't talk now. Perhaps we can have dinner together while I'm here. You'll be at the lecture tomorrow?'

'I'm looking forward to it,' she said. Or, rather, I was, she thought, aware of ears all around them, out on stalks, and Dr Dalywell looking daggers at her.

'Good. We'll arrange something, eh?'

As he strode away, the conversation, which had almost ceased, broke out again.

'Let's get away from here,' she muttered, grabbing Elsie's arm, and pushing a path through to the far side of the room, where, hopefully, no one had heard or seen anything.

'You're a close one, right enough? Fancy not letting on you knew him.'

'Ssh. Do be quiet.' Aimée saw Frank, and made for him.

'Well, that's got a few tongues wagging,' he chuckled.

'Frank, it's awful. I shouldn't have come.'

'Don't talk daft, girl. You don't suppose it would occur to anyone that it was a woman he was on about? Anyone who saw you talking later will assume you were one of his students. But you should be proud, for all that. I was, I can tell you. Mind you, Dalywell's all but doing a dance of rage, seeing the two of you so cosy together.'

She laughed ruefully and drew a deep steadying breath. 'Oh, Frank! You always did know how to cut me down to size.'

But Elsie had been listening with growing excitement. 'It was you, wasn't it? The one he – '

'Hush, for goodness' sake! I'll tell you later.'

But that evening, and the lecture the following day, left Aimée in a strangely restless state of mind, which hadn't resolved itself by the time she was due to have dinner with Colonel Grant. He immediately disconcerted her by insisting that she should call him Fergus.

'No need to observe the formalities, now,' he said, his glance openly admiring, so that she was glad she had made a particular effort with her appearance. The bronze green dress always made her feel good, and she had brushed her hair until it gleamed. 'My, but you've grown bonny, Aimée Buchanan.'

Embarrassed, she murmured something banal in reply.

He was a charming host, unobtrusively solicitous, the dynamic energy that had been so essential to his survival in France, now wholly devoted to ensuring that her every whim was satisfied. And, warmed in the glow of being pampered, she soon relaxed.

But whilst she learned little more about him, he skilfully drew from her a great many details concerning the last two years of her life. And she responded, the words tumbling out in her eagerness to convey the scope of the task she had taken on – and the bureaucracy and prejudice that so often dogged her every step. He watched her shining eyes, the determined set of her chin, and smiled.

'Well, you've been busy, right enough,' he said genially, when they had reached the coffee and brandy stage. 'And from all I've been hearing, you're doing an excellent job, and raising a few of those hackles you've been talking about.'

He leaned forward, suddenly intent. 'But I remember a young impassioned doctor facing me across a table, fair begging me to let her go on operating when she was almost droppng with fatigue. Whatever happened to her?'

'She lost her nerve,' Aimée said baldly.

'For a wee while, maybe. But she found it again, so I heard, in a warehouse fire.' An accusing finger pointed straight at her. 'So why is she doing nothing about it?'

Aimée had asked herself the same question many times. She smoothed the tablecloth with nervous fingers. 'There are reasons,' she said defensively. 'For one thing, I can't simply abandon my patients. There is so much to be done. They need me – the women and children especially.'

'Excuses, Aimée,' Fergus Grant said dismissively. 'Make time. Take on a partner if necessary. Another woman, maybe.' His large hand reached out to still her agitated fingers. 'You have a talent, my dear girl, and you're not using it. In my book, that's waste –and I abhor waste.'

Frank had said as much a long time ago. But coming from

Fergus Grant, whose own work she so admired, the words had an added impact.

'There is nothing to stop you studying for your FRCS in your spare time, and you know it.'

Very much aware of his imprisoning hand, she met those inquisitorial eyes with a mixture of candour and embarrassment. 'Yes, I do,' she said with incurable honesty. 'And I have been giving it a lot of thought recently. Your lecture intensified those thoughts.'

'Good.' He sat back, geniality restored, and signalled to the waiter to bring more brandy.

Now that she'd given voice to the restlessness that had plagued her of late, she was half-afraid, half-excited. 'Oh heavens, this will turn my life upside down. And I'll need to compile a list of books.'

He laughed aloud. 'Books! Aimée, let that be the least of your worries. I've got more books than I know what to do with. I'm away from home for a week before taking up my teaching post in Edinburgh, but if you give me your address, I'll sort out the ones you'll need to begin with, and pack them off to you. And we'll keep in touch, eh?'

She wasn't quite sure what he was suggesting; from the look in his eyes, she wasn't even sure that she wanted to know. He was too disturbing.

'Fergus, why are you being so kind?'

'Am I being kind?' Disconcerted, he ran a hand through his hair, destroying its unaccustomed neatness and suddenly looked much more wild and Scottish – as she remembered him – except for the sudden gleam in his eyes, which certainly hadn't been there before. 'You're a very attractive young woman, Aimée. It's no penance to be kind to you, m'dear.'

She blushed, bit her lip. 'That isn't what I meant.'

'No. I know fine what you mean.' He looked rueful, then said abruptly, 'I suppose I've always had you on my conscience. I treated you harshly – '

'They were desperate times.'

'Aye, they were. But maybe I could have shown more under-standing – '

'No,' she interrupted him. 'You were quite right to behave as you did. I was at the end of my rope. I just refused to admit it.

Almost any other doctor in your position would have sent me packing right from the start.'

'Well, I always pride myself on knowing a good thing when I see it, even if it is disguised in skirts.' He chuckled. 'After all, the kilt is a noble garment.'

On the far side of the room, Oliver was enjoying a pleasant working dinner with a lawyer friend, when he looked up and stopped speaking in mid-sentence. Surely it wasn't? But yes, it was Aimée, holding hands across the table with a large, distinctive-looking man with flaming red hair. They seemed totally wrapped up in one another. Indeed, there was an intimacy, an intensity about them that jolted him to the core, and jealousy – an emotion he had not experienced since the callow days of his youth – seared through his veins. And as he watched, the man lifted Aimée's hand to his lips.

'Our Kevin's off any day now,' Agnes said, easing her back for a moment before mounting a fresh assault on the windows. 'Mercy on us, you'd think these hadn't been done for weeks, the dirt they've collected!'

'Hmm?' Aimée looked up from delving into the packing case that had earlier arrived from Fergus. 'Don't overdo things, Agnes. You've got enough on your plate just now, with Patsy as well as Daisy. A bit of dirt on the windows is no great matter.'

'It is to me,' Agnes retorted. 'I can't abide dirt, wherever it is. Anyhow, a fine thing it would be for a doctor to be showing dirty windows to the world. As it is, the man you have to do the outside has left terrible streaks. I suppose you'd not let me – '

'You're right. I wouldn't,' Aimée said, glancing down at the letter she had just picked out from amongst the straw. She smiled and laid it aside to read later. 'Is Kevin excited?'

'Like a cat on hot bricks. Lord, you'd think he was settin' out to discover America single-handed.'

'Well, it is quite an adventure.'

'Maybe,' Agnes said dourly. 'But I prefer to have my feet on solid ground, thank you very much. And what's so wonderful about America, I don't know.'

Aimée knew she was still upset after receiving a letter from

Irene, to say she and Alec were leaving Southampton for America. They must be well on their way now. Eddie, by now resigned to the worst, had left the flat and was bunking down behind the shop, and trying to negotiate further loans to keep his business afloat while he sought a new partner.

'How is Matty? I haven't seen her since we went to Crag Vale.'

Agnes clambered up the steps to reach the tops. 'Well, it seems to have done her good. Whether it was the country air or the company, I wouldn't know, except she's never stopped talkin' about your cousin's place, and how lucky Nellie and Danny are. Really taken with it, she was.'

And with himself, too, Agnes thought. And sighed. She didn't want more trouble for Matty, but to her way of thinking, no good ever came from mixing chalk with cheese. All this over-familiarity, like calling him Toby, even if he had asked her to. She shook her head and rubbed extra vigorously to remove a stubborn mark.

'There's some talk of Madame takin' her to Paris next month at last.'

'Oh, that would do her the world of good!'

'If you say so. Madame things the trip might be just the thing to perk her up.'

As Agnes folded the steps, the front doorbell rang. 'Now, who's that, I wonder? Not expecting any of your paying patients, are you?'

'No.'

'I'd better go and see.'

A few moments later Jane was being ushered in – a Jane, stylishly dressed in a tan broadcloth coat, generously cut to accommodate the evidence of advancing pregnancy – and wearing a deliciously frivolous black hat with a tan feather.

'Oh, what a lovely surprise!' Aimée hurried to kiss her. 'Oliver didn't tell me you were coming.'

'He didn't know.' Jane chuckled. 'He still doesn't. It was a spur-of-the-moment decision, and he'd already left for chambers when I arrived.' She indicated the box. 'If I'm disturbing you . . .'

'What? Oh, no. Just some books – rather exciting, actually, but I'll tell you about them later. Come into the sitting room.' Aimée held out her hand. 'We'll be more cosy there, and I don't have to go out for a while. Agnes, would you bring tea?' She turned to Jane. 'Or would you prefer coffee?'

'Tea will be fine.'

'So,' Aimée said when Agnes had relieved Jane of her hat and coat, and they were comfortably settled in front of the fire, 'how long are you here for?'

Jane shrugged, and then laughed. 'Oh, a day – a week – a month, who knows? Until Oliver gets tired of me. The baby isn't due for two months, and Nick is away on manoeuvres for several weeks. I was suddenly bored with my own company. And as the alternative was to go to Mother's – '

'Yes, I do understand,' said Aimée, who had met Mrs Langley. 'I bet the children were excited to see you.'

'Yes. And as it happens, my visit is most opportune. Miss Galton has been called away to her mother's sickbed. It's extraordinary how children grow up when your back's turned for five minutes. Alice, in particular. She'll be a little madam, if they don't watch her.' Jane's eyes were warm with affection. 'And Christopher is an absolute pet. I'm so happy that Oliver seems to have lost all his inhibitions where that child is concerned. I have a feeling you had something to do with that, but you're not going to tell me, are you?' she said with a vexed laugh as Aimée shook her head.

'Some wounds take longer to heal than others.'

'Quite. And I can take a hint. So, how is Oliver?'

'Oh, he's much the same. Busy.'

'I sometimes despair of you two.' Jane held up her hand. 'No, don't protest. I've heard it all before. Tell me your news instead. Those books. Are they something special?'

That evening, when Jane and Oliver were sitting in front of the fire in a companionable silence, she said casually, 'Did you know that Aimée has a beau? Scottish. He sounds rather splendid, I must say – some bigwig in the medical field. They met years ago – during the war. Aimée seems quite smitten – she turned decidedly pink when I quizzed her about him. I've never seen her so – so glowing, but I'm glad. It's time someone brought a little romance into her life.'

She stole a look at her brother in the firelight. His profile might have been carved in granite, but in the curve of his neck, a pulse beat very fast. She decided to jolt his composure a little more. 'Fergus – that's his name – has been reading the riot act to her. He thinks she's wasting her talent in general practice, and is encouraging her to go back into surgery — study for a Fellowship.'

Oliver tossed his half-smoked cigar into the fire. 'If that's what she wants, good luck to her,' he snapped. 'So long as she doesn't let herself be persuaded into it by some smooth-talking know-all. She works hard enough without sitting up half the night studying.'

Jane smiled, well-satisfied, and changed the subject.

In all the excitement of getting Kevin ready to go to sea, there was little time for Matty to dwell on her own imminent trip. Paris. She still couldn't believe it was finally about to happen.

'Aren't we too busy to be away now?' she'd said anxiously, praying that Madame wouldn't agree with her.

'It is true that there is much work, but you 'ave almost completed Lady Spendlove's gown, and there is nothing so urgent, I think, that a week will make a problem. Your friend Miss Helen is most reliable. She will 'old the fort,' Madame's laugh tinkled. 'Such an expression! But we must see that you 'ave a wardrobe that does Vincente credit.'

The Shaws had gone down with hundreds of other people to see the *Lady Felicity* off on the evening tide, on her maiden voyage. Agnes wheeled the two little ones in the pram, though Daisy insisted she was big enough to walk. Matty and Moira waved and waved, though Kevin was somewhere down below, probably getting the dinner ready for all the folk on board.

'Seems daft, having yer dinner at night,' Moira had said when he told her.

'Posh folk always have their dinner at night,' he insisted, feeling superior. 'You ask Dr Aimée. They have luncheon at dinner time.'

'An' I suppose they have their supper fer breakfast,' she'd snapped, still unsure if he was pulling her leg.

Moira wouldn't admit she was going to miss Kevin, but it wouldn't be the same without him there to tease and occasionally slip her a few extra sweets.

Everything had changed since Mam had starting working at Dr Aimée's all day, and taking the little ones with her. Matty was hardly ever home, and Moira seemed to be spending more and more time next door, playing with Emmy. Not that she really minded. The Flynns' house was always full to bursting, but although Mrs Flynn shouted a lot and the place always smelled of stale cooking, and washing, it did have a lovely homey feel to it.

Moira sighed, but waved with the rest as the huge ship began to move, its sirens drowning out the cheering, and the shouts of good luck from the crowds of people who'd all come down to the dock to see their friends and relations off to America. It was strange to think that Irene was there, too. Perhaps she and Kevin would meet.

Matty's leave-taking the following week was much less dramatic. She was travelling by train from Lime Street Station with Madame Vincente, and staying in a posh London hotel overnight before going on to Dover to take the boat to France. But they were travelling everywhere first class, and as far as she was concerned that was almost as good as going by liner to America. Not only that, she had a brand new suitcase filled with Vincente creations – nothing too elaborate, but beautifully cut. The ambition to succeed now overwhelmed all other considerations. And the trip to Paris was an important step on the way.

Given a year or two of hard work, she'd be every bit as successful, and a lot more important than Alec Gresham. That she would.

26

'PLEASE, DOCTOR, ME mam says can you come?'
Aimée, her breakfast disturbed by the urgent ringing of the surgery bell, looked down into Dec's tearful face, and thought, Oh dear God, that poor family. What now? There was scarlet fever about, and she had recently had two youngsters die of whooping cough.

'Yes, of course. Is someone ill?'

'Norr ill, exac'ly.' Dec swallowed, and then burst out, 'It's me da – e's been took by the police.'

'I'll fetch my coat.' Agnes hadn't arrived yet, but she had a key, so Aimée left her a note.

She found Biddy in tears, rocking backwards and forwards in her grief, with the younger children huddled against her, and Sarah banging pots and pans about in the sink, grim-faced.

'What happened?'

Biddy's wails grew louder.

'What, indeed?' Sarah said, pausing with one hand on her hip. 'You've not heard, then? That swine of a landlord's been found with his head smashed in, not before time – and they've arrested Liam for it.'

'My Liam would never do such a terrible thing!' Biddy sobbed. 'He likes ter talk big, and he's not above going looking fer a fight when the drink's on him, but he'd not kill a man!'

She sounded so much like a woman trying to convince herself that Aimée turned to Sarah, the unspoken question hovering between them. Sarah beckoned her close.

'I'm not sayin' he did it,' she said, low-voiced, 'but he was mad as fire when he stormed out of here last night, an' there was surely murder in his eyes.' Her voice sank to a whisper. 'They say he had blood on his hands.'

'But why? What happened to make him so angry?'

'Frank Prentice sacked his agent and brought in a new bully boy – big as a barn door, 'e is, and hard with it. 'E was here earlier this afternoon, tryin' to put the frighteners on us – an' as the great lunk wus leavin', he knocked Biddy down – '

'Oh, no!'

'Ah, she wasn't hurt, praise be, an' I don't think 'e meant fer it ter happen, but one of the little ones let it slip to Liam when he come home, an' he wus out of here again like an enraged bull.'

It sounded bad. 'So where have they taken Liam?'

' 'E's at the police station fer now, but he'll be charged this morning, and then he'll be remanded to Walton until 'is trial.'

She had spoken quietly, but Biddy heard the mention of Walton and her sobs broke out afresh. Aimée kneeled beside her, gathering up her hands.

'Listen to me, Biddy. You must be strong for the children's sake. I have a friend who'll know exactly what we must do, and as soon as I've spoken to him, I'll come back to tell you what's happening.'

Oliver was finishing his breakfast when she burst in on him. He put down his paper.

'Aimée? A bit early for visiting, isn't it? Jane's having breakfast in bed.'

'It's you I've come to see,' she said, and without preamble, without even sitting down, she poured out the story of what had happened. 'Oh, Oliver, if you'd seen Biddy – she's distraught. So I promised I'd see what I could do – what you could do,' she amended awkwardly.

He frowned. 'My dear girl, it sounds as if there's very little anyone can do. The man was, as they say, caught "bang to rights". He is plainly guilty, and I can't say it surprises me.'

'Oh, don't be so pompous, Oliver!' and as his mouth tightened, 'Yes, pompous. And self-righteous! How can you possibly know Liam is guilty, just like that?' Aimée leaned towards him, her hands braced against the table, her eyes blazing. 'Yes, he used to like his drink; yes, he defaced my front door and came to the surgery and made a nuisance of himself, but that was a long time ago. He's changed. And furthermore, if he was one of your rich clients, you wouldn't make such sweeping assumptions.'

Oliver's mouth tightened and a faint flush ran up under his skin.

Without a word he drew a spare cup across the table and poured some black coffee. 'Sit down and drink that.'

'I don't want – '

'Aimée, don't be tiresome. It's too early in the day.'

She sat down, and sipped the coffee, which burned her tongue. And gradually her agitation evaporated. Perhaps it had been thoughtless of her to burst in on him at breakfast – a time sacrosanct to most men, it seemed – but surely he must see that time was of the essence?

'Now,' he said, 'tell me everything you know that might be relevant.'

He watched her face as she spoke, its myriad expressions revealing anger, compassion and fear on behalf of this ragbag family who clearly meant so much to her – and impatience with him for not leaping into action.

'I know Liam can be hot-headed when he's been drinking,' she pleaded. 'But he's been so good since Biddy had the accident. If you'd seen him, as I have, so protective of her – '

'Protective enough to take revenge on anyone who tried to harm her?'

'Perhaps, but – ' Aimée remembered that, not so long ago, Liam had indeed threatened to kill Frank Prentice in precisely the way he had been killed. Too late she saw the trap.

'Yes?'

'Nothing.'

Exasperated, he said, 'Aimée, if I don't know everything, how can I possibly assess the man's chances in law?'

She looked up, wondering if she had misheard. 'You mean, you might consider – '

'I assumed that was why you had come,' he said laconically.

'Well, yes. Though realistically I suppose I thought you'd put one of your juniors on to it. But, if you would . . . Oh, Oliver! I'd pay the costs, whatever they were.'

'Don't jump the gun,' he said, bringing her down to earth. 'Just tell me what threats O'Hara made against the murdered man that might incriminate him.'

She told him. 'But he was frightened for Biddy. It was just words,' she concluded lamely.

'So long as he didn't repeat them elsewhere,' he said. 'If the prosecution were to get hold of any such statement of intent, it would require a miracle, at the very least, to save him. And I'm not into miracles.'

Liam O'Hara's appearance in the Police Court was brief and to the point and he was remanded to Walton Prison to await trial at the Crown Court.

Aimee was allowed to see him before he was taken away. He was a sorry sight, a broken man hunched up on the crumpled palliasse. Aimée sat beside him.

'Try not to despair, Liam,' she said gently. 'We are doing all we can.'

'But it won't be enough. D'ye think I don't know it? Ah, Doctor, how is my poor darlin' Biddy?'

'She's bearing up. She sends all her love, but I wouldn't allow her to come.'

'You did right.' He suddenly turned and seized her hands and his voice rose in a paean of despair. 'Promise you'll look out for her, if . . . when . . . Ah, Holy Mother of God help me! I didn't do it, Dr Aimée! Oh, I meant to kill him, right enough, for what he done to my Biddy. But, as God is my witness, someone had been there before me!'

Oliver, a silent spectator near the door, watched O'Hara with a professional eye. The man was a rogue, and not short of a word or two, yet every word had the ring of truth.

Proving it, however, could be well-nigh impossible.

'I don't know why you're all bothering to defend him,' Agnes said. 'That fellow Houdini would have his work cut out to escape from the pit Liam O'Hara's dug for himself, innocent or not.'

'Even so, we have to try, for Biddy's sake. The priest is being very supportive, but she's almost worn out her rosary beads. I don't know how long she can keep going. I wanted her to take the children and go to Hightowers for a week or so, but she won't budge. She's convinced that if she stays put, he'll come back.'

'Ah, the poor soul. Some have all the trouble, and others get off scott free. If they hang Liam, it'll kill her for sure.'

A cold shiver ran through Aimée. 'It won't come to that, Agnes. Even Mr Langley believes Liam. The solicitor he's recommended already has private detectives asking questions all over the area.'

'Well, good luck to them, that's all I can say, though they'll need more than luck, I'm thinkin'.'

Aimée deliberately changed the subject. 'Is Matty back, yet?'

'Came about teatime, yesterday,' Agnes said. 'Never stopped talking since. Madame's given her the day off to get over the journey. I reckon I could do with a day off meself, to get over her chatter.'

Aimée laughed. 'It's a big experience in a girl's life. There's nowhere quite like Paris.'

'Maybe, but Liverpool's exciting enough for me. Even Blackpool has never appealed, though Pat and I did go to Southport once – one extreme to the other, that was.' She sighed. 'I still miss Pat something dreadful. And after doing that front room out, I still can't bring myself to use it. The kiddies play in there sometimes.' She sighed again. 'But with half the family gone, it's not the same.'

'You aren't finding Patsy too much for you?'

'Not a bit. She's a comfort, to tell the truth, and with you letting me bring her here, it's not much different than being at home. Eddie sees her most Sundays, but he's got his work cut out, building up that business.' Her voice hardened. 'The least I can do is see the child doesn't suffer, but I find it very hard to forgive our Irene.'

'Oh, Aimée, Paris is the most beautiful place you could ever imagine!' The dreamy note in Matty's voice suggested that she hadn't quite come down to earth yet. 'Everyone talks about Paris in springtime, but it couldn't possibly be more beautiful than it was last week, with the trees in the Champs-Elysées all gleaming like polished copper in the sunshine – and the sky so blue. I could have stood there looking at it all forever.'

Aimée had popped in to see Matty on her way home from her visits, and found her still drifting round in a pleasurable daze. After all the dramas of the day, it was refreshing to watch Matty's revealing face, and listen to the sighs and superlatives falling from her lips. 'I take it you had a good time?'

Matty laughed. 'That obvious, is it? Mind, Madame didn't give me much time to stand an' stare. I'm sure me feet didn't touch the ground half the time. She whisked me from salon to salon, and to factories where we saw some beautiful materials being made. And I saw some of the famous designers, for Madame seemed to know them all. Not Paul Poiret,' she added regretfully. 'He's not around much now, Madame says, though she did show me the school for the poor young seamstresses that he started years ago. It's still there, and lots of them have been successful.'

She stopped abruptly. 'Am I being terribly boring? Mam said last night that I made her dizzy with all me talking.'

'No, I'm not bored. Quite the opposite, in fact. It's good to see you so happy.'

'I liked Vionnet best of all. She has some wonderful ideas. I can't wait to try them out. A lot of what she said was in French, so I couldn't understand, but she was demonstrating as she talked. It's all to do with draping the material on the figure and cutting on the bias. Of course, you waste cloth that way, but it follows the line of the body in quite a different way – like sculpting. Madame once said something about sculptures – oh, I can't explain, but I'll try it out on you one day.'

Aimée laughed. 'You do that. Now, it's time I went home.'

As she was leaving, Matty said, 'Hey, you'll never guess who I saw getting off the train at Lime Street with us last night. Vera's Tony. You remember Vera Lyall – the friend of mine who died in that storm? Tony left Liverpool shortly after and I haven't seen him since, but going away doesn't seem to have done him much good. I asked how he was, but he seemed so strange, not all there, if you know what I mean – '

Before she had even finished speaking, Matty found herself being hugged with a fervour that mystified her.

'Matty, you're an angel!'

'Why, what have I done?'

'I'll explain later. But you might – you just might have saved someone's life.'

To Aimée's intense frustration, she discovered that Oliver had been in court in Manchester all day, and wasn't expected back until quite late, though Jane promised to let him know she had vital information. The solicitor, Mr Field, was also unavailable. She certainly couldn't tell Biddy.

Surgery that evening seemed to drag. Aimée knew the waiting

room would be a hotbed of gossip, murder being a much juicier subject for speculation than the goriest of medical symptoms – and Liam O'Hara was well known for flying into a rage when he'd a few under his belt. But she refused to respond to even the most innocently worded enquiries.

She hadn't expected Oliver to be in touch before morning, so it was a surprise to find him on the doorstep well after the end of surgery, having received the message she had left with Jane.

For Oliver, it had been a long and frustrating day, endeavouring to get the best deal he could for his client in a case he never had a hope of winning. And it did little for his temper when he arrived in Myrtle Street, to find Aimée comfortably ensconsed on the sofa in front of the fire, sorting through the books that man Grant had sent her.

While Aimée poured him a large whisky, he glanced at the books, and in so doing, a few lines of a letter lying open beside him caught his eye: '. . . delighted to receive your letter. I, too, enjoyed our evening together – the first of many, if I have my way . . .'

'Oliver? Your drink.'

Aimée's voice made him jump. He took the glass from her, watching with unreasoning annoyance as she unobtrusively retrieved the letter, folded it and tucked it in her pocket.

'Do sit down, Oliver. You look tired. I didn't expect you to turn out again tonight.'

'Jane thought it sounded urgent.'

'Well, it could be important.' She told him about Matty having spoken to Tony Lyall. 'Don't you see? We'd all forgotten about poor Tony who lost his whole family when the warehouse collapsed. He had every reason to want to kill Frank Prentice. And Matty said he seemed strange, not normal.'

'Aimée, I've had a long and frustrating day. This would have kept until morning.' Oliver regretted the words the moment they were out.

But she, too, was tired. And before he could apologize she was telling him so in no uncertain terms. 'You're not the only one who's had a long day. Heavens, I didn't expect you to turn out this late.'

'If you're so tired, you should be in bed instead of trying to study. It's ridiculous, letting that man Grant talk you into all this nonsense.'

She flushed at the rebuke. 'Don't tell me what I should or shouldn't do. Keep that for your clients. And as for nonsense, I'm very grateful to Fergus – *very* grateful! He forced me to stop shillyshallying and pursue a talent that I was in danger of squandering.'

'And what's in it for him?' Oliver's lip curled. 'A little private tuition, perhaps?'

Incensed by the thinly veiled implication, Aimée struck out at him, but he caught her wrist high and held it, the force of the impact jarring her whole body. Her eyes blazed, and his blazed back, but when she made no attempt to struggle, he released her.

'I'm sorry,' he said abruptly. 'That was a cheap jibe – and quite uncalled for. I must be more tired than I thought.'

If he had taken her in his arms at that moment, Aimée would have succumbed and forgiven all. But he was already tossing off his drink, preparing to leave. And she couldn't let him go without knowing what he meant to do.

She said stiffly. 'About Tony Lyall?'

'I'll get Field's man on his trail first thing in the morning. He'll need a description. But, at best, it's a long shot.'

'It's the only real hope we have – and he might leave Liverpool again any time. He might already have gone.'

Oliver's head was pounding. 'I've said I'll get on to Field first thing in the morning. Satisfied?'

'Thank you,' she said with scrupulous politeness.

Aimée had little time to brood. The outbreak of scarlet fever kept every doctor in the city working at full stretch. The greatest concentration, of course, was to be found in the poorest areas, and here, the mortality rate was at its highest. Aimée was run off her feet for two weeks, and closed her mother and baby clinic for fear of spreading the disease.

'I don't think I shall ever come to terms with the death of a child,' she had once said to Frank during a similar epidemic. 'Young lives snuffed out before they've had a chance to find out what it's all about.'

It was during this period that Elsie Sprague had come to see her, having expressed an interest in joining the practice.

'You could hardly have come at a worse time,' Aimée said ruefully, as she took Elsie out on one of her rounds.

'Ach well, at least it'll give me an idea of what I'd be in for,' she said.

It was a particularly distressing day, and Aimée feared she would be put off for good. But, far from discouraging her, Elsie seemed to relish the challenge. 'I've never been one for sitting back,' she said with a grin. 'And there's surely a lot needs to be done here. I don't know how you cope single-handed.'

'I now have a nurse, Betty Reid, who is a tower of strength. She knows, as I do, that until living conditions are radically improved, there is no hope of eradicating disease. The best we can do is to contain it, and fight on for the abolition of all slum dwellings.'

'Well, I'd surely like to lend my weight to that. We've plenty of slums in Glasgow, so I know the score. And I always did relish a good fight.' Elsie hesitated. 'You know I'll not be finishing my year on Surgical until the spring?'

'There's no hurry.' Aimée was so delighted that Elsie actually wanted to come that all other considerations seemed trivial. 'Getting the right person is more important than time. So long as you're interested, I'm prepared to wait.'

Matty was surprised to meet Toby in Church Street one afternoon when she had slipped out to buy some particular trimmings she needed for an evening gown – something she couldn't delegate to a junior.

'I wouldn't have expected to find you here,' she said shyly.

'No. But Nellie's baby is due any time now, and she really wasn't fit to come in herself.' Toby smiled ruefully. 'So I said I'd have a stab at the shopping. I've got a list, but . . .' He looked lost and helpless.

'Here, give it me,' she said. 'I'll get them for you, and you can call in to Madame Vincente's later and pick them up. Would about an hour be all right?'

His relief as he handed the list over was so comical that Matty began to laugh. 'It's a good job men are handy in other ways, for I never saw one yet as could shop.'

'It's nice to see you laugh,' he said shyly. 'Mother told me how much you enjoyed Paris. Perhaps you'll come out and tell us all about it sometime. I'm sure Nellie would be glad to see you – and so would I.'

27

WITH THE TRIAL set for early December, the search for Tony Lyall had yielded many false trails, and by mid-November they were no nearer finding him.

Oliver was pessimistic. And Aimée, aware that this case was driving a further wedge between them at a time when their relationship was already fragile, still felt compelled to fight Biddy's corner for her, since she was quite beyond helping herself.

'He could be anywhere by now,' Oliver said, after another fruitless search. 'As matters stand, O'Hara's chances of being found innocent are nil. And with no mitigating circumstances – '

'The landlord's agent attacked Liam's wife – a frail invalid,' Aimée protested.

Oliver shook his head. 'As evidence, that cuts two ways. It may quite justifiably have enraged O'Hara, but it also provides him with the perfect motive for murdering Prentice.'

'So you're giving up?'

'Of course I'm not giving up. I am merely being realistic. If all else fails, I will attempt to get the sentence reduced to life imprisonment, on the grounds of provocation, though I can hold out no real hope of succeeding.'

'Much good that will do Biddy!' Aimée snapped, and then bit on her tongue. She was being unfair and she knew it. It wasn't Oliver's fault that there was so little to go on. She knew he had put himself out more for the O'Haras than she had any right to expect.

But he didn't have to face Biddy, who, with the treacherous November fogs seeping into every corner of the building, had succumbed to bronchitis. Mercifully, her children had all escaped the scarlet fever, but even this failed to register with her as a blessing. She had convinced herself that Liam was doomed. And her children, much as she loved them, could not compensate her for the loss of that giant of a man who was her strength.

Sarah was almost in despair. 'I'm not wanting to lay more trouble on the poor soul – though I doubt she'd notice, the way she's turnin' in on herself,' she said. 'But I'm not sure how much longer we'll even have a roof over our heads. I heard tell that a distant cousin of Frank Prentice has inherited this pile of stinkin' rubble, and is considerin' pullin' the whole lot down – which, God knows, is what's needed, except we'll be out on our ears – an' no help for it.'

'But you'll be able to find somewhere before that happens?'

'Ah, Doctor, if it were that easy, wouldn't I have done it before now? Not that I'll stop looking, mind.'

'Of course I told Sarah they could all go to Hightowers if the worst happened before she could find anywhere,' Aimée said when she called in on Jane later that morning. 'But that would only be a temporary solution. It isn't the answer.'

'It does seem unfair that life is so cruel to some, while the rest of us have more than we need,' Jane sighed. 'I wish I could stay longer, or that I wasn't so far away, though there's nothing I can do – nothing any of us can do. Ideally, I would like to have stayed until Miss Galton got back. Such a pity her mother was taken ill now. Alice without a governess can be a handful. But Nick is due home next week.'

'It's very selfish of me to bring my troubles to you,' Aimée said. 'You have lots of happy things to look forward to, with the baby due in a week or two. You mustn't let anything spoil your lovely time.'

Jane's eyes shone. There was a bloom about her that – just for a moment – Aimée envied. 'Well, I must say I can't wait to see Nick.' She laughed. 'Oliver has taken the day off specially so that he can see me safely on to the train.'

'So I should hope.'

'He'll be here in a minute. Do stay and have some coffee with us.'

Aimée stood up. 'I won't, if you don't mind, my dear. I still have some calls to make.'

'Not entirely convincing.' Jane laughed, half-vexed, and kissed

Aimée. 'I do wish you and Oliver would stop being so polite to one another. I would love to have you for a sister.'

Aimée shrugged and hurried out. She had almost reached the car when she heard Grove calling her back. There was an urgency in his voice, and she turned to see him running down the steps – a thing unheard of – his face distorted with panic.

'Come quickly, Doctor! It's Master Christopher – he's choking!'

Aimée took the stairs two at a time, meeting Oliver on the landing.

'Nanny says he's swallowed something. A small wheel off one of his engines, she thinks. God knows how it happened.' They were running to the nursery as he spoke, past worried servants, and even before they arrived, she could hear the terrible whistling, choking sounds.

A distraught Nanny Grey had Christopher upside down on her knee, thumping him on the back, and Aimée could see that he was already turning blue. Alice was screaming hysterically and Jane was trying to calm her and master her own fear.

'Bring him to the table, quickly, Oliver,' Aimée said, sweeping everything off it. 'Jane, take Alice into another room, and I'll need another strong pair of hands.'

Grove stepped forward, white-faced, his voice shaking. 'I'll do anything for the little 'un, Doctor.'

She already had her bag open as Oliver lifted his son onto the table, the small body threshing, his head jerking from side to side as he fought for breath. She held Christopher's head still, not daring to look at Oliver's face, and saw at once that the metal wheel was firmly and awkwardly wedged. To try and dislodge it in haste might prove disastrous. And time was running out.

'I'll have to make an opening in his throat, to enable him to breathe,' she said briskly. 'So, he'll need to be held as still as possible. Nanny, you take his legs, Grove, his shoulders – close your eyes if you don't want to watch, but don't let him move. Oliver, will you hold Christopher's head? Slide him back so that it just drops over the edge. That's fine. There's no time to anaesthetize him, but he won't feel anything.'

All the while she was speaking, she was laying the instruments and everything she might possibly need in readiness, praying that she wasn't already too late.

It was by no means her first tracheotomy. In fact, they had at times become almost commonplace under the thud of the guns. But this was a two-year-old child – a very special child, his neck so tiny, his skin so delicate. She mustn't think about that. Concentrate. She worked swiftly, her hand steady as she made the first incision over the cricoid cartilage. No time for any ligatures. The trachea was opened – double retractors, to keep the wound open and check any haemorrhage. Yes, now she could feel the rings of the trachea – so tiny – her heart lurched. Don't think. Keep going. Small transverse incision – pass the director down between the cartilage and the deep layer of cervical fascia. Is he still alive, this once wriggling, chuckling tiny boy? Don't *think*!

Oliver, holding his son's head immovable, hardly took his eyes off Aimée, except to glance down occasionally into his son's blue lifeless face. How calm she was, how totally engrossed. He saw at last why Grant had been right to insist that she return to surgery, though all reason told him that this time she must surely fail. And what would that do to her? It would be up to him to see that she did not blame herself. Yet still he prayed, as never before, to that same God who had taken his wife from him, that He would spare her son – his son; for his own sake and for Aimée, who he realized with blinding suddenness meant more to him than he had ever believed possible, and who was now so totally engrossed in her task.

There was a spurt of blood, quickly wiped away, and a sound almost like a cough. Aimée was working swiftly now, inserting a small tube, securing it, and cleansing the surrounding tissue before applying protective gauze. A faint whistling noise disturbed the total silence of the room. Oliver looked down and saw that some of the blueness was already fading from Christopher's face, leaving it deathly pale. But he was alive – and breathing.

'Aimée?'

'There is still the obstruction,' she said, her voice tired, and very husky. 'But we're halfway there. I would feel happier if the remainder of the operation were carried out in hospital. You can drive us there. It will be quicker than waiting for an ambulance. I'll telephone to let them know we're on our way.'

Much later, they were sitting in the drawing room, Aimée, Jane and Oliver, drinking coffee – Aimée had refused anything stronger. She had telephoned Agnes from the hospital to explain what had happened, so that she could cancel the family clinic.

Aimée sighed and stretched. 'I'll have to go – evening surgery calls.'

Jane stared. 'You surely won't be taking a surgery this evening?'

'I admit I'll be glad if Agnes manages to curtail the numbers, but I can't abandon people who are ill. Besides, this coffee has more or less revived me. I'm more concerned about you, with your baby due so soon. Setting aside the worry, you must be exhausted after coping with poor Alice.'

'I'm perfectly fit, just a little tired. But I've decided I'll stay on for another day or two. I couldn't possibly leave until I'm sure Christopher's out of danger. Alice will need reassurance, and Nanny Grey is very shocked.

Aimée glanced at Oliver. He had hardly spoken since they'd come back from the hospital. In many ways, his had been the hardest role of all – having to stand helplessly by and watch, knowing there was nothing he could do.

'Children are remarkably resilient, you know,' she said, to no one in particular. 'In a few days, Christopher will be up and running about as if nothing had happened.' She saw the muscles in Oliver's face tense convulsively, and concluded lightly, 'However, you had better tell Dr Thornton what has happened, Oliver. I don't want to be accused a second time of poaching clients.'

'Oh God!' With something halfway between a gasp and a sob, he bent forward, his head in his hands. Jane stared at Aimée, wide-eyed, deeply distressed. Then, at a sign, she rose quietly and left the room.

Aimée, her heart beating painfully fast, went across to perch beside Oliver. She put her arms around him, drawing him towards her. 'My dear,' she whispered. 'It's going to be all right. I'm here. I'll always be here, if you want me.'

And with a muffled cry, he turned his head into her breast, and wept.

Much later, composed, his face still ravaged by his recent distress, they sat together on the couch in front of the fire, his arm tight abound her, as though he would not let her go.

'We need to talk, Aimée,' he said, his voice steady, but still lacking its usual strength and certainty. 'You must know I can never – Dear God, words are my living and I can't even begin to tell you – ' She stirred to protest, but he laid a finger across her mouth. 'Dearest girl, let me finish, please! I just want to say, to insist that any promises you made in *extremis* – '

'I meant every word,' she interrupted softly, turning her face up to him.

He let go a small sigh. 'And that fellow Grant?'

'Fergus?' She stared, and then began to chuckle. 'Oh, Oliver! Fergus Grant is a wonderful man in many ways, and is not averse to a wee flirtation, but he's wedded first and last to his work.'

'Well then?' Oliver said, gathering her close.

Agnes was in the kitchen washing dishes when Aimée came through from the surgery. Patsy was in the pram nearby, and Daisy was entertaining her by 'reading' from a much battered picture book.

'All finished, are you?' she asked, lifting the last plate out of the water and propping it against the pile on the draining board.

'The last patient's just gone. Could I have a word when you've got a moment?'

'D'you want me through there – ' Agnes cocked her head, 'or shall I get on with drying the pots?'

'Well – ' Aimée glanced at Daisy, who was very quick to pick up snippets of conversation and relate them to anyone who would listen.

'I'll come through.' Agnes got the message and reached for a towel to wipe her hands. 'No nonsense, mind, you two. I'll be back before you can wink.'

In the morning room, Aimée seemed loath to come to the point. 'I have a suggestion to put to you, Agnes. If you don't like the idea, say so. I shan't be offended.'

'Fair enough.'

'But first, there's something you should know.'

'Oh, aye?'

Agnes gave her a look that made her blush.

'You've guessed.'

'Well, it wouldn't take a genius. You've been walkin' round with that silly look on your face for days, specially since that little laddie picked up – and Mr Langley's never away from the place. He actually smiled at me this morning when he called.'

'Oh, Agnes!' Aimée began to laugh.

'About time, too,' she asserted. 'You've been skirtin' round one another for long enough. So, has this suggestion you're on about got something to do with you and him getting wed?'

'In a way, yes. You were talking a while ago about how empty your house seemed now, with the family gradually breaking up, and I was wondering how you'd feel about moving in here to live?'

For once, it seemed, she had succeeded in silencing Agnes.

'It's a big step, I know, but it would be more convenient for you, and you wouldn't have any rent to find. There's plenty of space, with two spare rooms on the first floor and two smaller ones above going to waste.' Aimée hesitated, then added, 'I shall be living in Falkner Square, of course, when we are married, but you'll remember Dr Sprague who came to see me a while back? Well, she will be joining me as a junior partner next March, and she'll be living here.' Still there was no answer. 'You don't have to decide now.'

Agnes was thinking: no more traipsing back and forth, no damp coming through the ceiling, no rent man of a Friday, a proper bathroom with an indoor lavvy and all . . .

'It seems I'd be getting the best of the bargain,' she said, lest Aimée might think she was too eager.

'What rubbish! This place would fall apart without you. You know how helpless I am about the house, and I doubt Elsie will be much better.'

'Well, our Kevin won't care either way. He's just gone off on his second trip, and we're only likely to see him between times, and I'm sure Matty won't mind. But it's Moira I worry about. She's at that awkward in between age. I'll need to put it to them.'

'Of course.' Aimée hesitated. 'Do you ever hear from Irene?'

Agnes's face quivered, then tightened. 'Not a word since that one short note. I sometimes – ' She stopped, straightened her shoulders. 'I'll let you know tomorrow.'

But they both knew what the answer would be.

Aimée's parents were delighted to hear of her engagement to Oliver, as was Gerald. Her mother in particular was at last to be granted her dearest wish. The grand wedding, denied her by Gerald's *fait accompli*, could now be sighed over and planned for with even greater pleasure.

'Such a splendid match,' she sighed to all who would listen. 'Of course, I would have liked longer notice. And January is not the ideal month for a wedding. But they are so much in love that one cannot deny them.'

It had swiftly been decided that Celia would be chief bridesmaid, together with Matty and Alice, who had gone pale with excitement on being asked. Vincente were to provide the trousseau, with Matty specifically commissioned to design the wedding dress.

'Only three attendants, dear?' Her mother had looked vaguely apprehensive. 'Your cousin Sophie had eight, as I remember, and – '

'Three will be quite sufficient, Mother,' Aimée said firmly, much to her aunt's amusement.

'I couldn't be more delighted, darling. How is Oliver taking all the fuss?'

'With fortitude,' Aimée replied with a wry smile.

'Are you quite sure you won't hate it?' Aimée had asked him anxiously, as she regaled him with her mother's latest plans. 'I would just as soon slip off somewhere quietly, to be married without fuss, but it means so much to Mother, and I don't think I could bear her to be disappointed a second time.'

He had drawn her close into his arms. 'My darling girl,' she still blushed with delight when he called her his darling, 'I couldn't care less how we marry, so long as it's soon.'

Nellie Reagan's baby was born at the end of November. It was a fine boy – the boy that Danny so wanted.

Aimée took Matty over to see the new arrival, and was intrigued, though not really surprised, to learn that she had been several times by train on her own during the last few weeks, drawn back again and again by the particular aura of warmth and companionship that existed in Toby's home – for a true home it now was, where class differences didn't exist and everyone played their part.

'I mean, everything's so real, there.'

'How do you mean – real?'

'I don't know if I can explain. Perhaps it has something to do with the land and growing things, that gives it a kind of meaning and purpose. And Nellie's baby is now a part of that – new life, and all. Does that make sense?'

'Maybe it does.'

'It sometimes makes what I do seem unimportant – designing expensive dresses for rich women who've nothing better to do – ' Matty uttered an embarrassed gasp. 'Oh, I don't mean you or Lady Mellish!'

'Of course not.' Aimée said reassuringly, but she was puzzled. 'You surely aren't having second thoughts? You have so much talent.'

'Oh, no. I still want to make beautiful clothes. My mind's teeming with ideas – and in a curious way, some of them have come from visiting Toby's home. He's very artistic, you know.'

'Yes, I did know, actually.'

The amused note in Aimée's voice made Matty blush and fall silent. But the frequency with which Toby's name kept cropping up interested her. Those two may not be aware of it yet, but she suspected they were growing fonder of one another with every meeting. What would Aunt Fliss make of that? she wondered. Or, more interestingly, Uncle George?

They found Danny filled with delight about young Daniel Tobias Reagan. 'Did you ever see anything so perfect?' he exclaimed, cradling the tiny infant close. 'He makes me feel a man again. You know what I mean?'

Aimée glanced at Nellie, and smiled. 'Yes, I know exactly what you mean, Danny.'

'An' it's all down to you, Dr Aimée – encouraging us, an' that.'

'No, it's Nellie you have to thank. It was she who was so determined to give you a son.'

'Oh, aye.' Danny's gaze dwelt lovingly on his blushing wife. 'I know what I owe to her, right enough.' He cleared his throat. 'Hey, and when he's grown, I'll be able to take 'im out in the trap. Did Toby tell you, I can get meself up into the trap now. It's a bit of a job, but the pony's real patient. I take our Mary to school sometimes, though most days she goes with the folk from the farm just along.'

'And your mother?'

'We've not had a word,' Nellie said, not sounding too disappointed. 'Mind, curiosity, if nothing else, will nag at her till she comes.'

Before the two young women left, Toby drew Matty to one side. 'There's something I w-want to ask you,' he said, blushing with embarrassment. 'I know you'll w-want to spend Christmas with your family, but w-would you consider coming to stay here for a night or two – to see the New Year in? It w-would make me very happy.'

Matty's heart was beating very fast as she looked up into his earnest face. His baby-fine hair was falling across his forehead, and she had to curl her fingers tight to stop them reaching up to push it back.

'I'd like that very much,' she said breathlessly. 'If you're sure. I mean, won't your mother – your family want . . .'

'I'm quite sure,' he said, with that odd gentle smile that warmed every little bit of her. 'Mother knows – and approves. I shall come and fetch you myself.'

28

AIMÉE'S HAPPINESS WAS obvious to all, though always at the back of her mind was Liam's trial. She had given up any hope now that they would find Tony Lyall, and as the opening day of the trial approached, the worry lay like a stone in her breast. She had been allowed to see Liam, and had found him so calm, the imp of devilment so utterly expunged, that she would have given anything to see the old rip-roaring, infuriating Liam back. He had seen the priest, he told her with quiet dignity, and was resigned to his fate.

'You've done all you can, Doctor,' Sarah said, when she called in. 'Only the good God and his blessed Mother can save Liam now, and Biddy knows it. It's a funny old business, but now the time's come, she seems to have found a new kind of strength. Says she's determined to go to the court, come what may.'

'Oh, Sarah, it will be very distressing. I really don't think she should!'

'No more do I, but she's been real strange the last day or two – fatalistic, yer might say, as if by being there, she can somehow swing the verdict.' Sarah lowered her voice. 'I'm thinkin' she may be goin' a bit queer in the head. Last night she was convinced that picture of Our Lady of Sorrows there on the wall nodded at her and smiled.'

It wouldn't be surprising if poor Biddy's mind had reached the end of its tether, but Aimée thought it more likely that now the moment had come, she only had faith left to her – that and the need to be close to her man in his hour of greatest need, to add her feeble strength to his.

'Well, if she's adamant, I'd better take her myself. I doubt the proceedings will take long, and at least I'll be on hand to look after her when she collapses, as collapse she will.'

Aimée had left the opening day of the trial clear, so that she could stay with Biddy throughout. The worst moment came as they pushed through the crowds waiting outside St George's Hall to be admitted to the Crown Court. Biddy was recognized by many who shouted words of encouragement, but her progress up the steps was painfully slow, the ordeal almost too much for her.

The prosecuting counsel made the most of the unprovoked brutality of the attack, of the defendant's known reputation for becoming aggressive when drunk. The police constables who arrested him gave evidence that, when apprehended, Liam O'Hara was in an extreme state of inebriation, and that blood was found on his hands. Also, that he had been heard threatening to 'do for' the man whose agent had attacked his wife.

Oliver had never been more eloquent. He was forceful, dazzling the jury with a display of incisive oratory, quick to seize on the weaknesses, few though they were, in the prosecution's case – making much of the fact that when his client was arrested, he was nowhere near the deceased's house, and that he could produce several witnesses who would swear that Liam O'Hara had been with them around the time when the murder was committed.

But he had always known that it wasn't enough. By the end of the third day, all the witnesses had been called and the outcome was inevitable. Biddy was in a state of near collapse, but refused to be moved.

The judge was about to sum up on the final day when there was a slight disturbance at the back of the court. He paused and frowned as Oliver's junior, who had been called out a few minutes earlier, so far forgot himself as to come rushing back in, ignoring protocol. He whispered something in Oliver's ear.

Oliver rose slowly to his feet, and Aimée could tell from his bearing that something quite extraordinary had happened.

'If I may crave your lordship's indulgence,' he said with a calmness that scarcely concealed his inner exultation, 'I have this moment received word that a man, who has been sought by the police for some weeks, has just walked into a nearby police station and signed a sworn statement, confessing to the wilful killing of Frank Prentice.'

Pandemonium reigned, and above it rose Biddy's trimphant

voice: 'Liam, me darlin' man, God and our Blessed Lady have heard me prayers! Didn't I always know it!'

It was some time before all the formalities were completed, and Liam, a paler and thinner man, was free. Biddy was there, waiting – and only when he picked her up in his arms, with the tears streaming down his face, and carried her outside, and the crowd who had collected as crowds do when news travels fast, cheered them down the steps and into Aimée's waiting car, did the truth finally sink in.

The celebrations in Angel Court that evening were something to behold, with oil lamps hung about outside and the children rushing around like mad things, and everyone singing and dancing and the ale flowing. Biddy took little part. Now it was over, she was dazed by the swiftness of the events, and Liam was never away from her side for more than a few minutes.

'That's a good man you have there,' Liam had said of Oliver, his voice deep with emotion, when Aimée called in to see that they were both all right. 'I'll never stop thankin' God fer all you've done.'

There was little pity being wasted on Tony Lyall, who had let a man go through hell before owning up, but Aimée was more sympathetic. She had seen him only briefly, but what she had seen convinced her that he was in need of treatment rather than punishment.

'Just what I'd expect you to say,' Oliver said in mild exasperation when he called that evening. 'But that's not for us to decide, so don't ask me to defend him, too.'

'I won't.' She reached up to kiss him. 'Darling, have I told you how wonderful you were?'

'A mere half-dozen times,' he said complacently, winding his arms about her. 'But if you have nothing better to do, you might care to demonstrate your appreciation in a more satisfactory way.'

'Mmm,' she sighed. 'The O'Haras are still singing your praises. I've said that they and Sarah are to spend Christmas at Hightowers – no argument.'

'Enough,' he said, lifting her off her feet and ignoring her laughing protestations as he moved purposefully towards the stairs. 'Do what you like with the O'Haras at Christmas, but I would be grateful if you would put them right out of your mind for the next couple of hours, or three.'

Among the crowd of last-minute Christmas shoppers plodding wearily home, no one noticed a young woman hurrying from Lime Street Station, head down against the chill wind, each pool of lamplight illuminating a pale hand clutching a fur collar tight about her neck, a small case in the other.

Agnes left the surgery early to get the children settled. They'd been at Marge's all day. She'd have given them their tea, so, with luck, they'd be worn out and ready for bed. Moira was a great help, which was just as well since Matty would be late home. She didn't know what to think about Matty getting so thick with that strange Mellish lad. She wondered what Pat would have said, mixing with gentry – and thought she heard the echo of his voice: 'Stop frettin, girl. Our Matty's good enough for anyone.'

She shook her head and hurried on. No use meeting trouble halfway. At home she found Daisy in danger of becoming overexcited, and her mood was already affecting Patsy.

'Moira love, put their nightclothes to warm on the guard, would you, while I unpack the shopping? Then we can get them washed and packed off to bed quick sharp.'

'I don't want to go to bed,' Daisy declared, standing red-faced with indignation. 'I'm not a baby like Patsy.'

'Don' want,' echoed Patsy.

'If you aren't good, Father Christmas won't come,' Moira said sternly. 'And then there'll be no presents.'

Daisy considered this. 'Well, p'raps I will.'

They were washed and standing, pinkly bundled into flannel nightdresses and Moira was buttoning them into woolly dressing-gowns when the door knocker rattled.

'Drat!' Agnes said under her breath. 'I'll go.'

It was dark outside. A figure moved slowly from the shadows and the light from the lobby picked up the fair curls.

'Irene?' For a moment Agnes leaned against the door, the chill mist of faintness washing over her.

'Mam!' Irene was inside, supporting her. 'I've come home.'

Still dazed, Agnes pulled herself together. 'Dear God, you almost frightened the life out of me! For goodness' sake shut the door before we all freeze to death! Just like you, no consideration, landing up on the doorstep without a word of warning.' The words were spilling out without thought or coherence.

'Oh, Mam!'

'Never mind, "Oh, Mam," my girl. Into the back with you.'

She's too thin, Agnes thought, as Irene stood stock-still, unable to take her eyes off her daughter, who was regarding her with sleepy interest, thumb in mouth.

'Irene!' Moira ran and threw her arms round her sister. 'Oh, what a lovely Christmas present. Patsy, it's your mammy!' She stroked Irene's collar. 'Is that real fur?'

Irene couldn't speak for the tears that choked her.

'I'll put the kettle on,' said Agnes.

Later, when the children were in bed, and Moira had gone into the front room to wrap her parcels, it all came tumbling out – how Alec had given her a great time at first and everything had gone right, until he got in with a really fast gambling set – slick men and beautiful women, and she realized he expected her to behave as they did.

Agnes watched in silent disapproval as Irene pulled a cigarette pack from her handbag, lit up with trembling fingers and inhaled.

'I couldn't do it, Mam. I thought of you and Dad.' She swallowed the wrong way and began to cough. 'And I was missing Patsy more than I thought possible, and . . .'

'Eddie?'

'How is Eddie?'

'Coping. He's still bitter. It's not been easy for him, but the business is growing again, slowly.'

'I'm glad. Honest, I never thought – '

'No.' Agnes's voice was dry. 'Anyway, you'll maybe see for yourself tomorrow. He's to come for his Christmas dinner.'

'I can't!' Irene's voice quivered. 'He won't want . . . Oh, Mam, I've been such a fool!'

The front door slammed and Matty came in like a cheerful whirlwind – and stopped, open-mouthed, her smile dying. Then, she saw the misery in Irene's eyes, the painted face and too thin body in its skimpy blue dress, and her natural sisterly love surfaced above any lingering anger. She held out her arms.

'Irene. How lovely!'

And Irene burst into tears.

On Christmas morning, Aimée persuaded Oliver to go with her to Hightowers. 'Just for a few minutes.'

Thick frost crunched under their feet, and sounds of merriment were evident even before they reached the door. A huge Christmas tree stood in the hall, nestling in the sweeping curve of the staircase, where one had stood every year for the traditional family gathering in the days when Grandma Aimée was alive.

There were no members of the Howard family, barring herself, here now to appreciate its splendour; instead, the hall was filled with an excited, oddly assorted gaggle of people, men, women and children, who had never until now imagined that such beauty and luxury existed – people who, for a short time at least, could forget damp walls, and bread and scrape. The children were the most excited of all.

Aimée stood in the hall, leaning against Oliver, one arm closely linked with his, and suddenly, with an elusive whiff of Havana cigar, Grandpa Howard was very near. Her mind reached out to him with a sense of fulfilment, and in an instinctive gesture of protection, she drew her sable coat across her body. It's too soon to know for sure, Grandpa, she confided, but . . .

'Christmas is a time for families,' she murmured. 'Jane has her little girl, and Gerald and Megan's second is due any time now. And Nellie and Danny are thrilled with young Daniel . . .'

'Are you trying to tell me something, Dr Buchanan?' Oliver asked, giving her one of his penetrating looks.

'Goodness, what a question!' she teased him. 'I refuse to be interrogated on Christmas Day.' But the pink in her cheeks wasn't due entirely to the frost outside.

She heard squeals of joy coming from above and a moment later Dec came hurtling down the banisters, just as she and Gerald had done so many times.

'Come here while I belt you, you mannerless eedjut,' roared his father. 'That's no way to treat Dr Aimée's grandad's best stairs. There'll be no turkey for you, me lad, if you go on like that.'

'Turkey!' Dec sighed, his mouth salivating at the mere sound of the word. And, all around them, the voices stilled and heads turned.

'If Grandma and Grandpa are watching this,' Aimée whispered, her head against Oliver's shoulder, 'I think they'll be well pleased.'